continued...

TEMPTED AT MIDNIGHT

Jacquie D'Alessandro

BERKLEY SENSATION, NEW YORK

THE BERKLEY PUBLISHING GROUP
Published by the Penguin Group
Penguin Group (USA) Inc.
375 Hudson Street, New York, New York 10014, USA
Penguin Group (Canada), 90 Eglinton Avenue East, Suite 700, Toronto, Ontario M4P 2Y3, Canada
(a division of Pearson Penguin Canada Inc.)
Penguin Books Ltd., 80 Strand, London WC2R 0RL, England
Penguin Group Ireland, 25 St. Stephen's Green, Dublin 2, Ireland (a division of Penguin Books Ltd.)
Penguin Group (Australia), 250 Camberwell Road, Camberwell, Victoria 3124, Australia
(a division of Pearson Australia Group Pty. Ltd.)
Penguin Books India Pvt. Ltd., 11 Community Centre, Panchsheel Park, New Delhi—110 017, India
Penguin Group (NZ), 67 Apollo Drive, Rosedale, North Shore 0632, New Zealand
(a division of Pearson New Zealand Ltd.)
Penguin Books (South Africa) (Pty.) Ltd., 24 Sturdee Avenue, Rosebank, Johannesburg 2196,
South Africa

Penguin Books Ltd., Registered Offices: 80 Strand, London WC2R 0RL, England

This is a work of fiction. Names, characters, places, and incidents either are the product of the author's imagination or are used fictitiously, and any resemblance to actual persons, living or dead, business establishments, events, or locales is entirely coincidental. The publisher does not have any control over and does not assume any responsibility for author or third-party websites or their content.

TEMPTED AT MIDNIGHT

A Berkley Sensation Book / published by arrangement with the author

PRINTING HISTORY
Berkley Sensation mass-market edition / April 2009

Copyright © 2009 by Jacquie D'Alessandro.
Excerpt from *The Scot and I* by Elizabeth Thornton copyright © 2009 by Elizabeth Thornton.
Cover art by Jim Griffin.
Cover design by George Long.
Cover hand lettering by Ron Zinn.
Interior text design by Laura K. Corless.

ISBN: 978-0-425-22699-5

BERKLEY® SENSATION
Berkley Sensation Books are published by The Berkley Publishing Group,
a division of Penguin Group (USA) Inc.,
375 Hudson Street, New York, New York 10014.
BERKLEY® SENSATION and the "B" design are trademarks of Penguin Group (USA) Inc.

PRINTED IN THE UNITED STATES OF AMERICA

10 9 8 7 6 5 4 3 2 1

This book is dedicated to my son, Christopher. Honey, I know I mention you at the end of every dedication, but this book is for you—to celebrate the incredible, wonderful, honorable young man you've grown up to be. You make me proud every day and being your mom is my greatest joy. Just don't forget—no matter how grown-up you are I'm still your mother. So behave yourself! ☺

And as always, to my wonderful, encouraging husband, Joe. You are my other greatest joy. Thank you for all you do, and for the gift of our son—Greatest Joy, Junior.

Acknowledgments

I would like to thank the following people for their invaluable help and support:

All the wonderful people at Berkley for their kindness, for cheerleading, and for helping make my dreams come true, including Cindy Hwang, Leslie Gelbman, Susan Allison, Leis Pederson, George Long, Don Rieck, and Sharon Gamboa.

My agent, Damaris Rowland, for her faith and wisdom, as well as Steven Axelrod, Lori Antonson, and Elsie Turoci.

Jenni Grizzle and Wendy Etherington for being such supportive, fantastic buds.

Thanks also to the wonderful Sue Grimshaw of BGI for her generosity and support. If I could clone you, I would! And as always to Kay and Jim Johnson, Kathy and Dick Guse, and Lea and Art D'Alessandro.

A cyber hug to my Looney Loopies: Connie Brockway, Marsha Canham, Virginia Henley, Jill Gregory, Julia London, Kathleen Givens, Sherri Browning, and Julie Ortolon; and also to the Temptresses the Blaze Babes.

A very special thank you to the members of Georgia Romance Writers and Romance Writers of America.

My terrific book club buddies Susie Aspinwall, Sandy Izaguirre, Melanie Long, and Melissa Winsor for their kindness, friendship, and support.

And a very special thank you to all the men and women serving in our Armed Forces for the sacrifices you and your families make to keep our nation safe.

And finally, thank you to all the wonderful readers who have taken the time to write to me. I love hearing from you!

Prologue

He stood on the ship's deck, eyes closed, his face tilted toward the sun, and drew in a deep breath of tangy sea air as *The Wayfarer* cut through the white-capped Atlantic's waves. It had been ten long years since he'd smelled anything but stench. Since he'd had anything except filth beneath his feet. Seen anything other than darkness. Experienced anything other than agony.

But now that he'd escaped, justice would be served.

He opened his eyes and looked down at the ruined skin of his wrists where the manacles had held him. Those were only a few of the many scars that marked him. All were daily reminders of the horrors he'd suffered in that hellhole prison.

They're nothing compared to the horrors you're going to suffer.

The words that had kept him alive for a decade whispered through his mind, and he lifted his gaze. Dark blue water and puffy white clouds dotted the azure sky, stretching as far as he could see, but in a matter of days England would appear on the horizon.

Then he would have his revenge against the man who'd ruined his life.

Logan Jennsen.

Hatred seethed through him. Soon . . . soon everything that mattered would be taken away from that bastard. *Just as you took everything from me.*

The man's fingers clenched around the wooden railing. *Thought you'd fixed things nicely for yourself, didn't you, you bastard? Commit murder, then run off to England, with no one the wiser.*

A dark chuckle escaped the man. *But I know.* Oh, yes, he knew what Jennsen had done, and after an exhaustive search, he had finally discovered where Jennsen was.

"And I know something else you don't," the man whispered, the brisk sea breeze whisking away his soft words. "You killed the wrong man, Jennsen. *I'm* the one you wanted. And I can't wait to see the look on your face when you realize your mistake."

Ah, yes, that would be a sweet moment indeed, followed by even sweeter moments. *You're going to lose everything— just as I did. And then I'm going to kill you.*

And then his long-awaited revenge against Logan Jennsen would be complete.

Chapter 1

I wanted him the moment I saw him. The scent of his skin, of his blood, was a delicious, potent aphrodisiac that whipped me into a frenzy of need. He tempted me beyond all reason, and I couldn't resist him. I couldn't wait to sink my fangs into his throat.

The Vampire Lady's Kiss *by Anonymous*

"Do you see anything suspicious?"

Logan Jennsen paused beneath one of the soaring elms lining the gravel path in Hyde Park and slipped his watch from his waistcoat pocket, his casual actions in complete contrast to his tension-laced voice.

"Suspicious in what way?" Bow Street Runner Gideon Mayne asked in an undertone.

Logan made a pretext of checking the time. "No one appears to be paying the least bit of attention to me, but I can't dismiss the strong sensation that someone's watching me."

He noted how Gideon's sharp-eyed gaze immediately scanned the area as he, too, pretended to consult his own timepiece. Thanks to the bright afternoon sunshine after more than a week of gray, dismal January weather, the park was crowded with pedestrians, riders, and elegant equipages.

"From your tone I gather this isn't the first time it's happened," Gideon said, slipping his watch back into his pocket then bending down. He brushed a bit of dirt from the toe of his black boot, but Logan knew the Runner's gaze was further observing their surroundings.

"No. This is the third time in as many days. Which is why I asked you to meet me here. I hoped you'd see what I was missing."

"I don't see anything out of the ordinary," Gideon said, rising. "Yet. So let's keep walking."

That was one of the things Logan liked about Gideon and the reason why he'd asked the Runner to meet him—the man didn't waste time with unnecessary questions such as *Are you sure?* Or suggestions like *Maybe you're imagining it.* Over the past several months Logan had hired Gideon to perform investigative work relating to his business ventures and been extremely impressed with the results. So much so, he was considering hiring him on a full-time basis, provided he could tempt Gideon away from Bow Street. But Logan was confident he'd prevail. As he knew, every man had his price. And he had the money to pay it.

But there was more to it than that. Logan had come to like and respect Gideon not only for his investigative prowess but because, like Logan himself, Gideon had come from nothing and made something of himself. Unfortunately for Gideon, the financial rewards of his profession weren't very lucrative, and Logan wanted to help this man he'd come to regard as a friend. As he knew Gideon would turn down any offer he believed held a whiff of charity, Logan would need to tread carefully.

They stepped back onto the path and continued walking. "Anything else unusual going on?" Gideon asked, his tone as casual as if he were discussing the weather.

Logan considered for a few seconds, then said, "Two nights ago an intruder tried to board one of my ships. The first mate gave chase, but the man got away."

"Any description of the intruder?"

"Only that he could run like the wind and clearly knew his way around. Otherwise, it was too dark."

"You make any new enemies lately?"

A humorless sound escaped Logan. Based on the work Gideon had performed for him over the last few months, the Runner knew damn well that along with wealth such as Logan's came an influx of people who didn't necessarily wish him the best.

"Not in the last few days—that I know of. Or so I'd thought. Until my instincts began screaming that I'm being watched."

"Never ignore your instincts," Gideon said quietly.

Good advice, although Logan didn't need it. Listening to his instincts and acting upon them were how he'd escaped the poverty into which he'd been born. What had kept him alive through more harrowing experiences than he cared to recall. And he intended to listen to them now, even if Gideon couldn't confirm his suspicions.

"A man in your position . . . lots of people are going to be looking at you," Gideon said.

"They have been," Logan said dryly. He'd quickly grown accustomed to being the cynosure of all eyes after settling in London nearly a year ago. "The members of society regard me as if I'm some exotic, predatory bird who's landed uninvited in their cozy nest. The fact that I'm an American only serves to cast more rancor and suspicion my way. I'm well aware the only reason the ton tolerates me in their lofty ranks is because of my wealth."

"Does that bother you?" Gideon asked.

"It occasionally annoys me but mostly amuses me. As much as the esteemed peers would like to send me packing on the first ship back to America, they're even more anxious to seek my advice on financial matters and investment opportunities." A grim smile lifted one corner of his mouth. "Since there are numerous such opportunities in my own businesses, I take full advantage of their unwilling interest in me—which has proven very profitable all around."

Then he frowned. "But this recent feeling . . . it's different. A sense of menace." Indeed, it raised the hairs on the back of his neck and slithered eerie dread down his spine even on this bright, sunshine-filled day.

Gideon turned toward him. "You've felt this menace in the past?"

Too many times. "Yes, but not recently."

"Do you know what—or who—caused it in the past?"

Logan's jaw tightened. He'd never forget. "Yes."

"Perhaps this episode is from the same source."

He shook his head. "Impossible."

Gideon's eyes narrowed. "It would only be impossible if that source was . . . permanently extinguished."

Logan met the Runner's gaze. "As I said—impossible."

Gideon studied him for several seconds with an inscrutable expression, then gave a quick nod and returned his attention to their surroundings. Logan liked that Gideon accepted his word and didn't press him for details. Especially as it had saved him the trouble of lying. While he knew the lies he'd told countless times would slip from his lips once again without hesitation, he couldn't deny his relief in not needing to utter them now, particularly to this man he respected and had come to regard as a friend. He knew all too well the havoc lies could wreak on friendships. As a result, it had been a damn long time since he'd had a friend.

The path veered into two forks just ahead. When Logan struck out toward the right, Gideon asked, "Do you have a particular destination in mind, or are we just taking a turn around the park?"

"Park Lane," Logan said. "I've a meeting. With William Stapleford, the Earl of Fenstraw."

He felt the weight of Gideon's stare. "You don't seem pleased about it."

Damn. Was his discomfort so transparent that anyone could notice it? Or was Gideon's observation simply the result of him being extremely perceptive? He hoped the latter.

"I'm not pleased," he admitted. "There are financial matters the earl and I need to discuss, and I suspect it's not going to be pleasant."

Indeed, he knew damn well his discussion with the earl would be most *un*pleasant. Yet, just as unsettling, if not more so, was the possibility of seeing Fenstraw's daughter, Lady Emily.

Logan's jaw tightened. Was it possible his sense of dread was somehow connected to his imminent arrival at the earl's town house, courtesy of either the earl himself or his daughter? He hadn't seen her for the last three months as the entire Stapleford family had retired to their country estate. But they'd arrived back in London yesterday, and Logan knew it was only a matter of time before he and Lady Emily ran into each other at some function or another.

An image of the woman he'd been attempting—and irritatingly, failing—for months to forget flashed through his mind, and he bit back a growl of annoyance. Damn it, *why* couldn't he forget her? She was beautiful, yet beauty rarely captured his attention for more than a fleeting moment. He'd always preferred the unusual to utter perfection. And Lady Emily's gorgeous face and form were undeniably utter perfection.

Of course, her shiny dark brown hair *was* shot with those unusual deep red highlights that seemed to capture and reflect every bit of light in a room. She stood out among the pale blonds preferred by so many men of the ton like a glossy, ebony stone on a whitewashed, sandy beach.

And her eyes *were* an unusual shade of green. Rather like viewing an emerald through an aquamarine lens. Every time he looked into her eyes, he felt as if he were gazing into a fathomless ocean whose bottom was a verdant lawn. They reminded him of a painting he'd once seen of a goddess rising from the sea. He'd observed those clear, sparkling eyes twinkle with intriguing mischief and warmth while she was in the company of her friends, but they turned arctic whenever her gaze collided with his.

From the first time they'd met, soon after his arrival in London, she'd looked down her aristocratic nose at him, and he'd dismissed her as but yet another pampered, spoiled, supercilious society diamond, the exact sort of woman he had no liking nor use for. He'd take a fun-loving, bawdy, unspoiled barmaid any day over these stick-up-their-arse, blue-blooded society chits who, with their fancy gowns, glittering jewels, and haughty airs, clearly believed themselves superior to mere mortals.

Yet, as he'd become better acquainted with Lady Emily's circle, he found himself drawn against his will to that devilish gleam in her eyes and wondering what sort of mischief a proper earl's daughter could wreak.

Then he'd found out.

Three months ago. At Gideon's wedding to Lady Julianne Bradley—an event that had turned society on its ear. And prompted—at Lady Emily's suggestion—a brief, private interlude between her and Logan. An interlude that had led, at her initiation, to an unexpected kiss.

That damn kiss had turned him inside out and utterly shocked him as, until that point, she'd made it abundantly clear she regarded him with all the liking of something foul she'd scrape off the bottom of her dainty satin slipper. Instantly—or as soon as he'd recovered the wits she'd very effectively stolen—suspicion filled him as to her motives. He didn't for a minute believe her claim that she merely wanted to satisfy her curiosity. Why would she, when up until then she'd gone out of her way to avoid him, so much so, he wasn't certain if her avoidance more aggravated or amused him?

No, it seemed much more likely that she'd discovered her father owed him a fortune and had decided to play with Logan, attempted to lure him into forgiving the debt. As if a mere kiss—or anything else she might offer—could accomplish that goal. He *never* allowed personal feelings or pleasures to interfere with business.

Still, her sudden turnaround had thrown him completely off balance. If he'd been able to think clearly, hell, if he'd been able to form a coherent sentence, he would have demanded the truth from her regarding her motives. But speech had been beyond him, and she'd left the room before he'd gathered his incinerated wits. And that single kiss, which within seconds had burned out of control, had lit a fire in him he'd been unable to extinguish. And had rendered her frustratingly unforgettable.

The day after the wedding and that damn kiss, she and her family had departed for the country, and she'd been out of his sight ever since.

Unfortunately, she'd not been out of his thoughts.

"Does that meet with your approval?"

Gideon's voice yanked Logan from his reverie, and he turned toward the Runner. He found Gideon staring at him with an inquiring expression. "I beg your pardon?"

One of Gideon's dark brows hiked upward. "I said I'll accompany you the rest of the way to Lord Fenstraw's town house, then spy around outside for a bit. See if anyone's lurking about or if anything strikes me as odd."

"Thank you. I'll of course compensate you for your time."

Gideon's lips twitched. "Then I suppose I shouldn't tell you that the task is no hardship, as it gives me an excuse to wait around to accompany my wife home. She's visiting with Emily right now, along with Carolyn and Sarah. A book club meeting. The Ladies Literary Society."

Gideon's statement distracted Logan from his concerns of being watched, and his pulse jumped in the most ridiculous way at the knowledge that Lady Emily was indeed at home.

"I must admit I find myself very curious about what goes on at those book club gatherings," Gideon muttered.

Logan raised his brows. "At the *Ladies Literary Society*? What's there to be curious about regarding women chatting about Shakespeare and such?"

"They're not reading Shakespeare."

"Oh? What are they reading?"

"Stories that could make a courtesan blush. In fact, one of their previous selections was actually written by a courtesan. Very interesting information in that one. Some of it damn near made *me* blush."

Logan didn't believe anything could make a man like Gideon blush. He also found it difficult to imagine Gideon's very demure and proper wife reading such salacious material. And unsettlingly arousing to think of Lady Emily doing so.

A thought struck him, and his steps slowed. Was it possible that Lady Emily's claim of curiosity *had* been her true motive in kissing him? Had her scandalous readings left her wondering what it would be like to experience such intimacies? Hell, if that was the case, what else might she be curious about? Heat that had nothing to do with the bright sunshine sizzled through him.

But then his suspicions returned. Even if curiosity had played a part, clearly something more was afoot, and he had no doubt that that something had to do with the money her father owed him. Otherwise, why choose *him* to satisfy her curiosity—a man she obviously didn't like? Immediately on the heels of that question came a mental image of her . . . kissing a man who wasn't him. A lightning bolt of something that felt exactly like jealousy, but surely couldn't be, tore through him.

He blinked away the disturbing mental picture, then asked Gideon, "You don't object to Julianne reading such bawdy books?" he asked.

"Hell no. And if you had a wife, you wouldn't object to her reading them, either." Gideon slanted him a brief sideways glance. "Trust me on that."

Logan didn't doubt him, and much to his annoyance, he found himself imagining Lady Emily . . . reclined in his bed. Wearing nothing save a wicked grin. Peeking at him over the top of a salacious novel. "Quite the mischievous group, aren't they?" he murmured, pretending his skin didn't feel uncomfortably tight.

"Very much so," Gideon agreed. "Especially Emily. Got the devil in her eye, that one."

Hmmm. Yes, she did. And she also read bawdy books. How utterly unexpected. And disturbingly arousing.

"What was their latest selection?" he asked, merely to continue the conversation and make it appear to anyone who might be watching that they were simply two friends out for a walk. It wasn't as if he were really curious. Or would consider purchasing his own copy to read.

"*The Gentleman Vampire's Lover.*"

"Did you read it?" Logan asked.

"I did."

"And? Was it good?"

Gideon's lips twitched slightly. "Let's just say I found it very . . . stimulating. You might want to ask Emily about it."

Logan turned to stare at Gideon. "Why the hell would I want to do that?" The question came out much sharper than he'd intended.

Gideon shrugged. "Something happened between you two after my wedding ceremony. In the library. Based on what I observed, I thought maybe it was something . . . good."

Logan suddenly recalled that Lady Emily had literally bumped into Gideon when she'd fled the library following their kiss. He remembered how Gideon's amused voice asking, "*Is there a problem?*" had yanked him from the stunned trance he'd fallen into. And Logan had assured him it was nothing he couldn't handle.

Something good? *It wasn't good; it was great. Incredible.*

He cleared his throat. "You thought wrong."

Gideon said nothing, and Logan wondered what the other man was thinking. Like a damn sphinx, Gideon was—silent and inscrutable. Logan supposed that was useful for his

Bow Street job, but it sure as hell was frustrating otherwise. Couldn't read his thoughts worth a damn.

"I like her," Gideon finally said.

"Who?" Logan asked, although he knew damn well.

"Emily. She and Julianne have been close since childhood, and she's been a good friend to my wife."

"In what way?"

"Julianne's an only child, and her parents . . ." Gideon's words trailed off, and a muscle ticked in his jaw.

Logan nodded. "I've met the earl and countess. I'm no more fond of them than you. Very cold, overbearing people." They'd disinherited and banished their daughter when she'd gone against their demands to marry a titled gentleman and instead wed Gideon, a lowly commoner. As far as Logan was concerned, it was no loss to the newlywed couple, and he greatly respected Julianne for choosing the man she loved over everything else.

"Those are actually polite ways to describe Julianne's parents. Emily brought laughter and fun into what would have otherwise been a very lonely childhood for Julianne. I find myself fond of anyone who makes my wife smile."

Logan shook his head and chuckled. "Good God, that little bastard Cupid shot you with an entire quiver of arrows. I can practically see little hearts floating around your head, like a love-induced halo."

"No halos on me. But yes, that little bastard Cupid got me but good. And damned if it wasn't the best thing that ever happened to me." He shot Logan a sideways glance. "Why aren't *you* married? Hard to believe some matchmaking mother hasn't clubbed you over the head and forced you to the altar."

"The fact that I'm an uncouth colonial gives them pause, although I've no doubt my wealth would balance that out in the end. Plus, I seem to possess an unfortunate penchant for being attracted to women whose hearts are already involved elsewhere."

"That must be difficult."

"Indeed. Several lovely women have slipped through my fingers since my arrival in London."

"No, I meant about your wealth. Never knowing if your money is the attraction. It's a problem Julianne knew her entire

life. One I've never known. Nor would I care to." He flicked a
glance at Logan. "Can't say I'd want to be in your position."

A huff of surprise escaped Logan. "Well, that's not something I'm used to hearing. I've become accustomed to being
envied. In fact, I can't ever recall anyone *pitying* me because
of my wealth."

"Before Julianne, I would have said you're too bloody
rich to pity. But money never brought her true happiness. I've
never been wealthy, yet I didn't really know what happiness
was until I met her."

"So you're saying it's not money or things but people that
make the difference."

Gideon shrugged. "Seems that way to me."

Interesting. Logan knew damn well people sought his
acquaintance based solely on his money. God knows it was
the only reason with most of the British peers, and he couldn't
deny he'd grown more suspicious and cynical as his wealth
had multiplied. But having spent his formative years barely
one step above abject poverty, he was very adept at sidestep-
ping frauds and fortune hunters.

He also knew damn well that at this point there was no
chance he'd find a woman who wasn't attracted to his money.
The best he could hope for was a woman who was at least
honest about it and who found him equally as attractive as his
wealth. A woman he could respect and admire, who wasn't
haughty and supercilious and fond of staring down her aristocratic nose at him, and who set his blood on fire. It had so far
proven an impossible combination to find. While money made
most aspects of his life easier, there was no denying it complicated his personal relationships. And caused him to view
people and their motives through suspicious eyes, although
he'd done that long before he'd had two coins to rub together.
That wary mistrust had saved him more than once.

"We're nearing the earl's town house," said Gideon. "So
far I've observed nothing unusual."

Logan yanked himself from his brown study and realized
that Park Lane was indeed just ahead. His gaze scanned the
row of town houses across the thoroughfare and settled on the
aged brick facade of the one belonging to Lady Emily's father.
He now knew she was home, but would he see her?

Logan expelled an exasperated breath. Why the hell did he care?

Once again, the memory he'd been trying so hard to erase slammed into him with such force his footsteps faltered. Of soft, plush lips opening beneath his. Of lush, feminine curves pressed against him. Her taste and scent inundating his senses. The flood of unwanted, unexpected desire that had nearly drowned him.

He briefly squeezed his eyes shut and shook his head to dispel the unsettling mental picture that wouldn't let him go. Damn it, this simply wouldn't do. And it suddenly occurred to him that he hadn't kissed or touched another woman since his interlude with Lady Emily. Good God, no wonder he couldn't get her out of his head. He'd been more celibate than a monk.

What he needed was a woman. To put out this unwanted fire Lady Emily had started. To ease his body and fill his mind with someone other than her. Yes, that was a perfect plan, and he deserved a thump on the head for not thinking of it before now. There was a soiree this evening at Lord and Lady Teller's house. He'd make it a point to attend and find an attractive woman and seduce her. If he couldn't find one at the party who interested him, he'd damn well visit every pub in the city until he did. No woman at a pub would look down her nose at him.

"We'll separate here," Gideon said after they crossed Park Lane. "If I see anything suspicious, I'll report to you immediately. Remain on your guard, and let me know if you sense anything else. Until we determine if there's a threat to you, don't go out unescorted. Or unarmed."

Logan's gaze flicked down to his boot, where his knife was sheathed. "I'm always armed."

"Are you going out this evening?"

"I am. And I'll be careful, although as neither of us observed anything amiss. I'm wondering if I'm merely tired and preoccupied. If you'll come to Bow Street tomorrow, I'll see to your payment and I'll let you know if anything happens this evening."

Gideon nodded. "All right. Good luck with your meeting."

Logan drew a deep breath and nodded. There was business to attend to with the earl. Business that had nothing to do with Lady Emily. Her motives for kissing him were highly suspect; although, it didn't really matter what those motives had been. He was forewarned and had no intention of falling prey to whatever devilish plot she'd concocted. He had no desire to see her, no desire to speak to her regarding what had transpired between them, and certainly no desire to repeat it.

If he kept telling himself that enough, surely it would become fact.

He was about to turn to walk up the flagstone steps leading to the double oak doors of Lord Fenstraw's town house when the sense of menace he'd felt earlier hit him like a blow to the head. Senses on alert, his gaze scanned the entrance to the park across the street and riveted on a man standing in the shadow cast by a soaring elm. The man's gaze was fixed on Logan.

Everything inside Logan seemed to freeze. His breath. His blood. His heart. No . . . it couldn't be.

For several stunned seconds all he could do was stare. A carriage crossed his line of vision, and when it moved on an instant later, the man was gone. Logan's gaze darted about, but he couldn't find any sign of the man.

"Are you all right? You look like you've seen a ghost." Gideon's low voice infiltrated Logan's shock.

Damn it, it felt as if he had. "I thought I saw someone . . ." His words trailed off, and he shook his head, feeling foolish yet undeniably shaken.

"Who? Someone watching you?"

There were so many people in the park. Of course the man wasn't who Logan had thought. That was impossible. A slight resemblance combined with a trick of the shadows. "Just someone who looked like a man I once knew."

"Maybe it was him."

"No. That man . . . died. Years ago." He looked at Gideon. "I once heard that everyone has a double somewhere. Seems it might be true."

"Which man is it?" Gideon asked, looking toward the park.

"He's gone. It was nothing. And I'm due for my appointment." After one last look toward the now-deserted area around the elm tree, Logan forced back the unwanted memories the sight of the man had threatened to release and made his way up the walkway to the earl's town house.

Chapter 2

I held him in thrall, my lips hovering just above his. I could feel his heat, smell his desire, sense his pulse pounding at his throat. Need poured through me at the thought of my fangs puncturing his skin, his hot blood flooding into my mouth. And even though I afforded him the opportunity to push me away, to escape the impossible, dangerous situation in which he found himself, I knew he was exactly where he wanted to be . . .

The Vampire Lady's Kiss *by Anonymous*

Filled with an almost giddy sense of anticipation, Lady Emily Stapleford looked at her three closest friends. They were gathered in her drawing room for their first Ladies Literary Society of London meeting in three months, and she was about to pop with her news. Keeping a single secret was exceedingly difficult for her. Keeping two secrets bordered on impossible. Keeping three was completely out of the question. If she didn't tell at least one in the next few moments, she feared she'd explode like a pyrotechnic. While she was very good at keeping secrets others confided to her, she unfortunately was very bad at keeping her own under wraps for any extended period of time.

She opened her mouth to speak, but before she could announce that she had news, her childhood friend Lady Julianne Mayne said, "I have news."

Feeling somewhat deflated, she closed her mouth, simultaneously chafing at the delay to relate her own news and curious to hear what Julianne had to say. Before Julianne could speak, however, Sarah Devenport, Marchioness Langston, said, "Excellent, especially as I have nothing new to report other than the fact that I officially can no longer see my own feet." She rested her hands over her midsection, enormously rounded with the babe she wasn't due to deliver for another few weeks, although given her girth, to Emily it appeared as if the child could appear at any moment. She could only pray that wouldn't be the case.

"And I've ceased walking," Sarah continued, hints of uncharacteristic petulance and impatience lacing her normally matter-of-fact tone. "I can now only *waddle*. Every time Matthew claims he finds my ducklike stride adorable, I feel like coshing him with a skillet. Plus, he refuses to hear of me doing anything save lounge about on settees. Thank heavens I had our latest book selection to keep me entertained, or I'd have gone mad. It nearly required an act of Parliament for him to agree for me to come here this afternoon, even though Emily's house is a mere five minutes away, and even then he insisted upon escorting me."

"No doubt he's pacing the floors until you return home," Emily said, unable to hide a smile at the image of Sarah's normally urbane husband wearing a hole in the hearth rug.

"No doubt," Sarah grumbled.

"Just you wait, Julianne," said Sarah's sister, Carolyn, Countess Surbrooke, with a knowing smile. "I'm certain it won't be long before you're in a similar situation, and Gideon is a bundle of father-to-be nerves."

A scarlet blush rose on Julianne's cheeks. "Well, actually, that's my news. I found out last week, but I've been waiting for Emily to return to London so I could tell you all together." She pressed her hands against her flat midsection and smiled. "Gideon and I are going to have a baby. The doctor says in midsummer."

Squeals of delight chorused in the room, and hugs and kisses were exchanged. Emily had never seen Julianne look so happy and content. Three months ago her friend had given up her place in society and suffered ostracizing from the ton and disinheritance when she'd refused to marry in accordance with her parents' wishes and instead wed Bow Street Runner Gideon Mayne. Yet given Julianne's almost ethereal glow, she clearly didn't regret her decision in spite of the social and financial repercussions.

When they were all once again seated around the blazing fire, Emily found herself sitting back and observing her three friends. Sarah and Julianne chatted excitedly about their impending motherhood, while Carolyn looked on with a loving smile. Yet beneath that loving smile, Carolyn appeared somewhat subdued. Indeed, she looked drawn and pale, and her knuckles showed white where her hands lay clasped on her lap. Emily's heart went out to her friend. It was no secret in their little group that Carolyn wasn't able to have children. While Emily knew Carolyn was truly happy for Sarah and Julianne, she also realized that her friend must be feeling twinges of envy and sadness at her barren state.

Reaching out, she laid her hand over Carolyn's and gave it a light, commiserating squeeze, as Sarah and Julianne chatted on like a pair of magpies. Carolyn turned toward her and, to Emily's dismay, she noted a sheen of tears glittering in her friend's blue eyes. Before Emily could say a word, Carolyn whispered, "I . . . I'm happy for them."

"Of course you are." She searched her friend's face, and her concern heightened at her pallor. "Are you all right, Carolyn?

Carolyn blinked several times then smiled. "I'm fine."

Most people would have believed that serene smile and those calmly spoken words without question, but Emily knew her friend very well. Something was clearly troubling her. She vowed to ask her about it as soon as she could get Carolyn alone.

"And I'm very glad you've returned to London," Carolyn added. "You were missed. Very much." She withdrew her hand from beneath Emily's, took a deep breath, then with a smile, waded into Sarah and Julianne's conversation, which had shifted to their husbands.

Of course, Carolyn could easily join in any discussion regarding marriage, and with a start Emily realized that in spite of the fact that she loved her friends dearly, she couldn't deny that she felt . . . left out. After all, what could she contribute to conversations about marriage or impending motherhood? Nothing. She had no husband, and although she spent a great deal of time with her five younger siblings, that didn't qualify as motherhood. And in spite of the explicit, salacious, sensual reading selections of the Ladies Literary Society, reading was *not* the same as experiencing the passionate acts she knew her friends shared with their husbands. Indeed, she'd only just experienced her first kiss three months ago . . .

A wave of heat not at all related to her proximity to the fire roaring in the hearth engulfed Emily. The scene she'd spent the last three months unsuccessfully trying to forget invaded her mind's eye, replaying as if it had just occurred. Dark hair and intense ebony eyes. Strong arms pulling her closer. Hard, masculine body pressing into her. Firm lips settling on hers. Tongues tangling. Feeling . . . as she never had before. Sensations she'd never expected, at least not with him.

". . . Logan Jennsen." Julianne's voice, uttering the name that had haunted—and most certainly not in a good way—her every waking hour for months, jerked her from her musings.

"What about Logan Jennsen?" she asked, inwardly wincing at the unintentional sharpness in her voice.

Julianne turned toward her with a sheepish expression. "I know you don't like him, Emily, but—"

"That's correct. I don't."

Confusion clouded Julianne's eyes. "I've never known you to be to so ill disposed toward anyone. Especially someone you barely know."

Oh, she knew plenty about Mr. Logan Jennsen. More than she wanted to. Certainly more than she should.

"What it is about him that you so dislike?" Sarah asked.

"He's arrogant. And uncouth. Why, he's an *American*—a common *colonial*, for heaven's sake!" And he had a way of looking at her that made her feel uncharacteristically ruffled. And warm. And she didn't like it. Or him. Not one tiny bit. The fact that he'd aided in her father's financial downfall, a disaster that impacted her entire family, merely solidified her already poor opinion of him. She wasn't certain *how* her father came to owe Mr. Jennsen the enormous debt involved—her inadvertent eavesdropping on Father's conversation with his steward several months ago hadn't yielded enough details—but surely it was the result of some sort of chicanery on Mr. Jennsen's part as she'd never known her father to be fiscally irresponsible. Inept, yes. Irresponsible, no. That moment of madness that had passed between her and Mr. Jennsen at Julianne's wedding was just that: madness. An instant she'd initiated in a fit of pique and curiosity that she'd instantly realized would have been much better left unexplored. "You know he's only wormed his way into London society by virtue of his obscene wealth."

"Being rich is not a crime," Julianne pointed out mildly. "And I believe you've misjudged him. I've had the opportunity to spend some time with him while you've been away, and I quite like him."

"As do I," added Sarah.

"Me as well," said Carolyn.

Humph. Rusticate in the country for a few months, and a mutiny takes place. "What on earth would tempt you to spend time in that man's company?" Emily asked Julianne.

Julianne blinked. "Did you not hear the second bit of news I was just saying?"

No. Because I was thinking of that irksome man. And botheration, she still had her own news to impart. "Er, no. What news?"

"Mr. Jennsen has hired Gideon to do some investigative work for him. And I can attest that he is a very generous employer."

And a very generous kisser. However, of her three secrets, that was one she intended to keep to herself. Even if it killed her. Although she wasn't accustomed to keeping secrets from this trio of friends, how difficult could it be to keep this one? It wasn't as if she'd allow it to ever happen again. "Really?" Emily gave an elegant sniff. "I would have thought him extremely miserly."

"Why?" asked Sarah.

Because I don't want to think of him having any good qualities. She shrugged. "Isn't that how rich men stay that way—by not sharing their wealth?" If only her father had been wise enough to behave in such a frugal manner and not involve himself in any of Mr. Jennsen's financial schemes.

"Perhaps some men, but apparently not Mr. Jennsen," Julianne said. "I found him a bit intimidating at first, but I must admit he has grown on me."

"Hmmm. Like mold on cheese, I'd wager," Emily muttered.

Her friends laughed. "Actually, I think Mr. Jennsen is very attractive," Sarah said.

"Nonsense," Emily protested, ignoring her inner voice that instantly labeled her a liar. "Why, his nose has clearly been broken."

"So has Gideon's," Julianne pointed out, "and I don't think it detracts from his appearance in any way. In fact, I think it only enhances his rugged, masculine appearance."

"Whose?" Carolyn asked her. "Your husband's or Mr. Jennsen's?"

"Both, actually."

"Anyone can see Mr. Jennsen is not in the least bit classically handsome," Emily said stiffly. No, he wasn't. Why, without even thinking she could name a dozen men far more handsome. Yet Mr. Jennsen's looks were somehow . . . arresting. Compelling. Fascinating. And botheration, really quite spectacular.

Carolyn chose a biscuit from the silver tea tray on the table. "Discounting his looks—which, by the way, I find most pleasing—I believe that Mr. Jennsen is lonely."

An odd sensation tugged Emily's heart at the thought, one she ruthlessly shoved aside. "No doubt due to his uncouth manner and suspect business practices," she said tartly.

Carolyn's brows rose. "Suspect? From what Daniel says, the man is nothing short of a financial genius. Daniel's already invested in several of Mr. Jennsen's shipping companies and is most pleased with the results."

"As is Matthew," Sarah said. "He didn't care for Mr. Jennsen at first—"

"Most likely because he considered Mr. Jennsen a rival for your affections," Julianne interjected with a smile.

Sarah grinned. "Most likely. But Matthew's opinion has changed—enough so that he, too, has invested in a number of Logan's ventures. Matthew compares Logan to King Midas; whatever he touches turns to gold."

"Mr. Jennsen is perhaps a bit rough around the edges—" Julianne said,

"More than a bit," Emily cut in.

"But I agree with Carolyn about him being lonely," Julianne continued. "He lives in that enormous Berkeley Square mansion all alone—"

"He's hardly alone, what with a battalion of servants," Emily objected.

"Servants are not *friends*," Sarah stressed. "Or family. Or lovers."

"I imagine he doesn't want for female company," Carolyn mused, "although I've heard no on-dits about him being involved with anyone." A hint of mischief flashed in her eyes. She leaned forward and lowered her voice. "And as I told you, he's an excellent kisser."

Heat suffused Emily. Yes, he most certainly was. And she dearly wished Carolyn had never shared the tidbit of information that, before her marriage to Daniel, Logan had kissed her. It was that conversation of how masterful Logan had been that had sent her curiosity into orbit. And set her on the disastrous path that had led to her forget all the reasons she disliked the man and find out for herself if Carolyn was correct.

She was, most emphatically, correct.

And Emily had wished every day since that she didn't know it.

"An excellent kisser," Sarah mused, "just like Lord Damian in *The Gentleman Vampire's Lover.*"

"Oh, my, yes," Julianne agreed with a gushy sigh. "We've read some scandalous books together, but this latest selection"—she held aloft her copy of the slim, leather-bound book they'd all read—"was absolutely shocking."

Grateful to have the topic switched away from Logan Jennsen, Emily said, "And by absolutely shocking, she means . . ." She leaned forward and lowered her voice to finish, "Utterly, wickedly delicious. And so much more *detailed* than Polidori's story."

"I agree," said Carolyn. "I never would have believed that a vampire could be so . . . *sensual.*" She waved a hand in front of her face. "But that Damian . . . my goodness."

"Certainly made me yearn to have a handsome man nibble

and suck on my neck," agreed Sarah in her usual forthright manner.

"Me as well," chimed in Julianne.

Emily leaned forward and peered at what looked like a slight discoloration near the base of Julianne's throat. "Hmmm. Looks as if someone actually *has* been nibbling and sucking on your neck."

A crimson blush lit Julianne's cheeks, and her fingers fluttered over the spot Emily stared at. "I'm certain it's just a shadow."

Unable to resist teasing her, Emily feigned a skeptical look. "I think not. In fact, I'm certain it's due to your handsome, utterly besotted husband who, in spite of being married to you an entire three months, clearly shows no signs of becoming less enamored. Obviously you are keeping the man *very* busy. And happy. Nibbling and sucking on your neck."

She had to swallow a chuckle at Julianne's flustered expression. "'Tis merely the lighting in this room. Truly."

Emily turned to Carolyn and Sarah for their votes. "Love bite on her neck: the result of the lighting, or Gideon?"

"Gideon," they answered in laughing unison.

"You've been outvoted," Emily said, giving the official tabulation. "And you're blushing."

"I don't see how that's possible," Julianne muttered. "Thanks to Gideon, I no longer have anything left to blush about."

"And I've never seen anyone look happier about that," Carolyn said with a gentle smile, laying her hand over Julianne's.

Emily had to agree. A mere ten months ago, none of her friends had been married, and now all three were wed, and Sarah and Julianne were going to be mothers. Her gaze flicked to Carolyn, who continued to smile, yet in spite of her outward cheer, she still looked pale. And now that she was looking closely, Emily noticed her friend looked thinner than when she'd last seen her. Emily mentally renewed her vow to get Carolyn alone to discover what was amiss.

"Frankly, I'm jealous," Sarah grumbled, shifting in her seat and propping her feet on the nearest ottoman. "I'm so enormous, I have to turn sideways for Matthew to even hug me, let alone suck or nibble on my neck."

"From what I can see, the man can't keep his hands off you," Julianne objected. "Which is precisely how you ended up in your present condition."

"If anyone here has reason to be jealous, it's me," Emily grumbled. "All three of you are married to men you love, men who adore you and who clearly nibble and suck on your necks—at the very least—regularly. The happiness radiating off all of you makes it appear as if you've swallowed candelabras. And what do I have?" She heaved a sigh. "No man to love, no man who loves me." She didn't add that thanks to her fiscally inept father, financial ruin was about to crash down on her family's head. Although she had planned to tell her friends this afternoon, the secrets she'd been bursting to share not a quarter hour ago now seemed stuck in her throat. Stalling for time to find the right words, she said, "Thank goodness I read *The Gentleman Vampire's Lover* so I could live vicariously through the dark prince Damian and his beloved Melanie."

And live vicariously she had. The way the alluring vampire Damian had literally swooped in on Melanie and simply *taken* her . . . *Oh, my.*

"The ways he took her," she murmured. A heated shiver ran through her. Against the wall, on the floor, on the billiards table, bent over a chair, in the moonlit lake . . . The story had enflamed both her imagination and her body in ways she'd never before experienced. "Suffice it to say that Melanie wasn't the only one left breathless."

"Her sensual adventures were even more explicit than those in any of our previous book selections," Julianne said. Then her lips twitched. "Not that I'm complaining."

"Nor I," Sarah agreed. "I was very happy that Damian didn't turn out to be a complete villain. Like all of us, he was flawed, although I believe most of his actions were the result of loneliness and desperation rather than evil. In spite of his bloodlust, he was very . . . human."

"It was love that ultimately saved him," Carolyn said.

"Indeed," Emily said, helping herself to one of the excellent biscuits Cook had prepared. "And I agree about his loneliness. Being immortal, he'd outlived everyone he'd ever loved. He had no one . . . until he found Melanie."

"I adored how he referred to her as his *soul*," said Sarah.

"Oh, yes," Julianne agreed with a gushy sigh. "He hadn't had a soul for over six hundred years. Until he met her. It was wildly romantic. And his hunger for her, his need for her was so . . ."

"Romantic?" Carolyn suggested. "Profound?"

"Uninhibited? Carnal?" proposed Sarah.

"I'd call it *erotic*," Emily said. "The passages where he seduced her were so descriptive, they actually made me, um, perspire." And ache. And throb in the secret place between her legs.

That book isn't the only thing that's made you ache and throb recently, her inner voice whispered. To her profound irritation, another image of Logan Jennsen, his sensual lips, and the memory of their heated kiss slammed through her mind, suffusing her with heat and such intense want she gasped.

"Are you all right, Emily?" Julianne asked.

No. And it was all his fault. The man who'd awakened her senses and unsettled her in a way she didn't like one bit. A man she never wanted to see again.

A man you desperately want to see again, her inner voice scoffed.

"I'm fine," she lied, "just a bit of biscuit caught in my throat." She coughed twice for good measure then took a hasty sip of her tea.

"Those scenes made me perspire as well," Julianne said, her voice soft and shy. Another furious blush stained her cheeks.

"Me as well," Sarah added with an impish grin, pushing up her glasses. "Matthew was quite pleased with the results."

"As was Daniel," Carolyn said, although something in her tone and the way her gaze remained fixed on her lap made Emily wonder if the words were really true. Could whatever was troubling Carolyn have to do with Daniel?

Setting the question aside until it could be answered, she focused instead on the realization that it wasn't just her who'd been affected by the sensuality of Damian and Melanie's encounters. But at least her friends all had husbands to relieve whatever aches and throbs those explicit passages had inspired. Emily had only the memory of her encounter with Logan Jennsen—and that only served to make her aches and throbs *worse*. Which was thoroughly irritating, due to her extreme dislike of the man. If not for him, her father wouldn't be in the financial straits in which he found himself, or at least not as deeply in debt. And therefore he wouldn't have extracted Emily's promise to make a brilliant marriage—and quickly—before word of his financial downfall brought about the entire family's social ruin.

"Perhaps we should read more sedate books," Emily said with a frustrated sigh.

"No!" The word rang out in a trio of voices that sounded like a choir of dismay.

"Daniel is very pleased with our reading choices," Carolyn said.

Sarah sent her sister a smug smile. "Matthew is *extremely* pleased."

"Gideon is—"

"*Very, extremely* pleased," Emily broke in. "Yes, yes, I see where this is going. More talk of your wonderful husbands, talk I cannot participate in." She hadn't meant to sound ill-tempered but realized she had when her friends all exchanged a look. Then Sarah reached out and clasped her hand.

"Do you want to talk about it?" she asked Emily quietly.

"About what?"

Carolyn, her eyes filled with concern, scooted a bit closer. "About what is troubling you."

Her heart melted at Carolyn's obvious worry for her, especially since her friend was clearly troubled herself. Obviously the time had come to reveal her secrets. Knowing there was no point in prevaricating with the three people who knew her best in the world, she asked sheepishly, "Is it that obvious?"

"Yes," Sarah said. "At least to us, who love you. Your letters over the past three months while you were rusticating in the country were stilted. And unlike you."

At her father's insistence, Emily's entire family had departed London the day after Julianne's wedding for a stay at their country estate in Kent. In truth, at the time, Emily had been eager to escape the city and the memory of her encounter with Logan Jennsen. But after several days in the country, she'd realized the folly of longing for seclusion. For in spite of being surrounded by her rambunctious siblings, there had been little to occupy her time and less to engage her thoughts, except that which she desperately wanted to forget. Even on the several occasions when she'd attended an assembly and danced—with some very handsome and personable gentlemen—she'd found herself thinking of Mr. Jennsen and comparing her partners to him. And for reasons she could not fathom, her handsome and personable dancing partners invariably came up lacking.

But then she'd read *The Gentleman Vampire's Lover*, and the story had sparked an idea so outrageous, so impossible she hadn't dared share it with anyone. She embarked on her project and became completely immersed. Clearly her preoccupied mood had been obvious in her letters to her friends. She could have written to them about her undertaking but had decided to wait, hoping for good news, and frankly she'd been too embarrassed to admit she'd attempted something so far outside her realm of knowledge. She was doubly glad she'd refrained from confiding in anyone when, much to her dismay, she'd failed. Failure was something she was quite unfamiliar with and didn't quite know how to react to.

"You haven't been yourself at all this afternoon," Sarah said gently. "I miss that devilish spark in your eye. Won't you tell us what's wrong?"

To her chagrin, hot tears pushed behind Emily's eyes. Good heavens, what was wrong with her? She rarely cried, yet here she was on the verge of weeping. "No apology necessary. The fact is, I have two secrets." *Three secrets,* her brutally honest inner voice corrected.

Fine. Three secrets. But only two she was willing to share.

Three pairs of expectant eyes focused on her. She drew a deep breath then said in a rush, "I've alluded to some financial setbacks my family has suffered, but the truth of the matter is, the situation is now dire. My father has, through a series of very unwise investments and a dreadful spate of luck at the gaming tables, left us on the brink of financial ruin."

The words spewed from her like steam from a kettle. Pulling in a quick breath, she plowed on, "During our time in the country he conferred with his steward to try to work out some sort of arrangement with his creditors, but to no avail. Everything that isn't entailed is lost. Therefore, the only way to salvage the situation is for one of the children to make a brilliant marriage. As I am the eldest, he has asked me to do so. As quickly as possible."

For several long seconds the only sound that met the end of her recitation was the ticking of the mantel clock. Then Julianne cleared her throat. "I'm so sorry, Emily. I understand completely how it feels to have an unwanted marriage forced upon you."

Yes, Julianne would understand that perfectly, and she'd forever admire her friend for the courage it had required to take charge of her own happiness, incur the censure of society, disinheritance from her family, and marry the man she loved.

"Couldn't your father borrow money to pay the debts?" Carolyn asked.

Emily shook her head. "That would amount to nothing more than robbing Peter to pay Paul. He'd only be incurring a different debt, one that he wouldn't be able to repay." She blew out a sigh. "As you know, I've always hoped, planned, expected to marry—someday. That someday being after I fell madly, passionately in love, as you all have. Sadly, in spite of the plethora of eligible men I've met since my coming-out, that hasn't yet happened. So, since I've no desire to marry until I've found my perfect groom, I came up with an alternative. If I could earn enough money to get us out of debt, I wouldn't have to marry until I was ready. And I found the perfect way to do so." Her gaze took in her friends, who all looked at her with questioning gazes. "Inspired by our reading of *The Gentleman Vampire's Lover*, I decided to write my own vampire story and sell it."

Sarah blinked. "You wrote a book?"

"More of a short story. It's entitled *The Vampire Lady's Kiss.* I made my vampire a female. After all, men have all the fun in real life. Why should they in fictional stories as well?" Before her friends could answer what was a rhetorical question anyway, she hurried on, "Using the pseudonym Anonymous, I sent the story to several London publishers, and while they all praised the writing, unfortunately the story was still roundly rejected. They all claim that no one would be interested in a story featuring a vampire heroine.

Three sets of eyes blinked at her. Then Julianne shook her head. "Not interested? I've never heard such nonsense. *I'm* interested."

"As am I," Carolyn said, and Sarah nodded.

Emily smiled at her loyal friends. "Thank you."

"Why don't we make it our next book club selection?" Sarah suggested. "I'd love to read your story. Indeed, I think I'm a bit put out with you that you haven't let us read it already."

Warmth heated Emily's cheeks at the rebuke. "I'm sorry. I'd be honored for it to be one of our selections—after it is published. It's not that I didn't want you to read it, it's just . . ." She searched for the words to explain why she'd kept her writing private.

Carolyn shot her sister a frown. "You of all people should understand why she hasn't asked us to read it, Sarah. You don't like to show anyone your sketches until they're finished."

"But her story is finished," Sarah argued.

Julianne, her eyes soft with understanding, touched Emily's hand. "Yes, but I think for Emily, it's not truly finished until it is published."

Emily nodded gratefully. "Exactly. I wanted to surprise you, to present you with bound copies, proof of my success. Sadly, things haven't gone the way I anticipated. However, I sent it to another publisher just this morning, and I have no intention of being rejected again." A slow smile curved her lips. "I have a plan."

Her three friends exchanged uneasy glances. Then Julianne said, "Every time you say those four little words, a shiver runs down my spine. What follows them is usually something that could easily turn into a disaster. Remember when you had the plan to teach me to make a mud pie?" Julianne visibly shuddered. "I'm lucky I lived to tell the tale."

"You weren't supposed to *eat* it," Emily said.

"I was seven, and it was a *pie*," Julianne said with a sniff.

Emily waved her hand in a dismissive gesture. "That was nearly fifteen years ago. You can't deny I've come up with many fine plans since then."

"And many *un*fine ones as well," Julianne said darkly.

"Perhaps one or two. But this latest plan is sure to succeed." She paused for several seconds, making certain she had her friends' full attention. Then she leaned forward and whispered, "I'm going to become a vampire."

Chapter 3

The long, slow lick I laved against his neck drew a shudder of pleasure from him. The feel of his pulse pounding against my tongue was more than I could bear. I needed to feed. Now. And whereas for centuries I hadn't cared who met my needs and desires, now no one else but him would do. I opened my mouth and sank my fangs deep . . .

The Vampire Lady's Kiss *by Anonymous*

Three gazes, ranging from shock to concern, stared back at Emily. Sarah's brows and glasses both slid downward. "Become a vampire?" She turned to Carolyn and Julianne. "Dear God, poor Emily's suffered a blow to the head."

"I have not—" Emily began.

"Perhaps we should call a doctor," said Julianne, touching her fingertips to Emily's brow, clearly checking for signs of a fever.

Emily frowned and leaned back from Julianne's touch. "I'm not sick—"

"We simply must stop reading these salacious books that make our imaginations run amok," Carolyn said, gently patting Emily's hand. "I suggest *Hamlet* for our next selection."

"Yes, because surely a story littered with murder, poison-ings, stabbings, and all manner of mayhem won't cause our imaginations to run amok," said Emily in a dust-dry tone. "And you can all stop looking at me as if I should be trotted off to Bedlam or given a dose of laudanum. I didn't mean that I'm going to actually become a *real* vampire—"

"That's a relief," said Carolyn.

"I'm just going to *pretend* to be a vampire. To stir up interest. So female vampires become all the rage and the talk of the ton. In the hopes that the new publisher to whom I've submitted my story will then be anxious to publish it. And then, with all the interest in female vampires, people will run out and buy the story, and it will earn a healthy amount of money, thus enabling me to save my family from the financial ruin looming on the horizon, which in turn will allow me the time to make a love match."

"I think you really have been coshed on the head," Sarah muttered. "The only interest you traipsing about pretending to be a vampire will stir up is in how long it will take to have you committed to an asylum."

"No one will know it's me pretending to be the vampire," Emily said. "I intend to wear a disguise."

Julianne blinked. "You cannot be serious."

"I assure you I am. I've given this a great deal of thought and carefully planned every detail. If it's successful, I won't have to rush into marriage. And I tell you, my plan will work."

"Perhaps you'd better tell us exactly what this plan entails," Carolyn said, her voice dubious.

"Very well. Tonight I'll slip away from Lord and Lady Teller's soiree. I'll don my costume, which consists of a black cape, a mask, and fangs—"

"Where will this costume be?" Sarah interrupted.

"How do you intend to slip away?" Carolyn asked. "What about your chaperones?"

"Where on earth did you get fangs?" Julianne asked.

Emily ticked off answers on her fingers. "I'll hide the costume in the hedges outside Lord Teller's library before the party, which won't be difficult, since his town house is only six doors down from here. To slip away I'll claim the headache and excuse myself from the festivities for a short time.

Mother and Aunt Agatha won't question my story and will be so occupied catching up with their friends they'll never miss me. As for the fangs, I fashioned them myself from a piece of wood, which I then painted white. They fit directly over my own teeth and are very realistic. Quite frightening, in fact. Would you like to see them?" Without waiting for an answer, she opened her reticule. Leaning down, she slipped the pointed teeth she'd made over her own then raised her head. And smiled.

A trio of gasps echoed in the room. "Good heavens," whispered Julianne, resting her hand against her heart. "You really do look like a vampire."

"Yeth, I know," Emily lisped. Unfortunately, it was impossible not to do so with the false teeth in her mouth.

"What exactly do you intend to do?" Sarah asked, shoving up her glasses, which had again slid down her nose. "Dash through the party and flap your cape?"

"Of courth not," Emily said with a huff.

"Thank goodness. At least you haven't totally taken leave of your senses."

Emily removed the fake fangs from her mouth. "I'm going to dash across the terrace and flap my cape." She leaned forward and settled her gaze on Carolyn. "This is where I'll need your help, Carolyn."

"Me?" Carolyn's eyes widened, and she shook her head. "Oh, no. Please do not ask me to wear fangs and a cape—"

"Not at all," Emily cut her off. "At the agreed upon time, I'll enter the library, don my costume, then slip outdoors and appear at the terrace windows. All you need do is see the fanged vampire standing outside looking in. You'll act shocked and frightened and point me out to the gossipy ladies with whom you'll be standing—"

"What if she's not standing with anyone?" Julianne broke in.

"She'll make certain she is," Emily said patiently. "As soon as I've been seen, I'll dash back to the library, remove my costume, then rejoin the party."

"And if someone gives chase?" Sarah asked.

"I'm very fleet of foot, and I'll have a good head start. Before anyone can get close to me, I'll be back in the library, ready to steal back to the party. In all the commotion, no one will even notice I haven't been about. Of course I'll claim along with everyone else that I saw the vampire." She grinned. "And given the number of witnesses and the ton's love of gossip, news of a female vampire in Mayfair will quickly become the latest on-dit."

"I'm not a good actress," Carolyn said. "Why do *I* have to be the one to see you?"

"Because you're the only one I trust to do so. Sarah won't be attending the party due to her condition, and Julianne . . ." Her voice trailed off, and embarrassment filled her.

"And Julianne wasn't invited," Julianne finished for her. "You need not dance around the issue, Emily. We all know I haven't received any invitations since my wedding—except from you three. Nor do I expect to receive any in the future. My actions—and my parents—have seen to that. And lest you worry, let me assure you I have no regrets. Although I'm suddenly sorry to be missing tonight's soiree and the opportunity to try to talk you out of this madness."

"It's not madness," Emily insisted. "It's genius. Carolyn will make a very credible witness, as will the others."

"What if you're caught?" Sarah asked.

"I won't be," Emily assured her. "I can outrun each of my siblings, which is no small feat."

Sarah pursed her lips, and Emily could almost see the wheels turning in her friend's mind. Finally Sarah said, "I suggest you plant the seeds of such a sighting among the ladies before your little performance to whet their appetites. After all, we are hardly the only women who have read *The Gentleman Vampire's Lover.*"

"Yes, and you must make certain your fangs are seen, so people believe it is actually a vampire they are seeing—as opposed to merely an insane person skipping across the terrace while flapping their cape-clad arms," Julianne added, clearly getting into the spirit of things. "But how will the witnesses know the vampire is a female if all they can see is a mask and fangs?"

"I've attached long blond curls from an old wig of Mother's to the mask," Emily said.

Sarah winced and pressed a hand against the small of her back. "Oh, I wish I could be there," she grumbled.

"So you could talk her out of this, I hope," Carolyn said.

"No, so I could help," Sarah said. "Might as well, as it's clear she won't be talked out of it." She frowned, then brightened. "Our drawing room window has an excellent view of the park. Let me know the time of your performance, and I'll be sure to be glancing outdoors. Since I'm certain Matthew will be no more than three inches away from me, he'll see me doing so. I'll point outside and claim to see a cape-flapping apparition running through the park. We won't know what I saw was the vampire until the gossip reaches us, but that will give you one more witness."

"Excellent," said Emily, giving her friend a grateful smile. "The story will surely be reported in the *Times*. After several such sightings—"

"*Several?*" Carolyn asked, her eyes wide. "You plan to do this more than once?"

Emily nodded. "I think at least twice will be necessary. Perhaps three times. Surely not more than that. I'm certain that after the second sighting, there will be great interest in female vampires and thus my story. It will sell, I'll earn buckets of money, save my family from financial ruin—and myself from an expedient marriage to some rich man I'm not in love with." She leaned back and smiled. "Did I not tell you it was ingenious?"

Carolyn shook her head. "Clearly it hasn't occurred to you that it's dangerous for a woman to be flitting about alone in the dark. Or, no matter how fast you run, that you might be caught."

"Dangerous for a *woman*," Emily agreed, "but not for a vampire. Who in their right mind would accost a vampire? People run *away* from them lest they get bitten and sucked dry."

"She has a point," Julianne said.

Carolyn stared at Julianne. "I cannot believe you're condoning this."

"I admit there are risks," Julianne said softly, "but we've all heard the expression 'nothing ventured, nothing gained.' It's how I choose to live my life, and it's proven prophetic for me. The rewards of Emily's plan could be great. And save her from a loveless marriage." Her gaze touched on both Sarah and Carolyn. "Given that we've married men we love, men who love us, could we want anything less for Emily?"

"Well, no, but—" Carolyn began, but Julianne cut her off.

"No buts. Emily is in a desperate situation, and that calls for desperate measures." She took Emily's hands in hers. "Given my situation and the fact that I won't be attending any soirees, I don't know what I can do to help you, but you have my support. At the very least I can pray for your safety and success. And suggest that you bring a small vial of chicken blood to spill on the flagstones. Even if it's not discovered until the morning, it will lend credence to a vampire being on the premises."

Emily raised Julianne's hand to her lips and pressed a quick kiss against her loyal friend's fingers. "An excellent idea. Thank you."

"It's not that I don't want you to be happy," Carolyn said, looking troubled, "but I'm worried. Literally a thousand things could wrong."

"They could just as easily go right," Emily pointed out. "And they will. I have no intention of failing."

"But if you do?" Carolyn persisted.

Emily hiked up her chin. "Then I shall do what I have to, marry whom I must in order to save my family from ruin." And she would, as there would be no other alternative. At twenty-one, she was the only marriageable member of the family. Kenneth, William, and Percy were only sixteen, fourteen, and thirteen, Mary only eleven, and little Arthur—who'd come as quite a shock to the entire family—a mere seven. The thought of her beloved siblings, her parents, herself being shunned by society, of her siblings being denied proper educations, being forced to live in God knows what sort of poverty-like conditions simply wasn't to be borne. "However, I am hoping, praying, that it doesn't come to that."

Several long seconds of silence stretched between the group. Finally Carolyn said, "I'll do whatever I can to help you. Still, you must promise to be very, very careful."

"And run very fast," Sarah added.

"I will," Emily promised, relieved. "I know in my heart that this is the right thing to do and that everything will turn out all right. Besides, between my careful planning and the three of you helping me, what could possibly go wrong?"

❧

An hour later, after waving good-bye to her friends from the doorway, Emily turned to Rupert. "Where are Mother and Father?" she asked the butler. She needed to gather her costume and make her way to Lord Teller's town house to secret her props, and she needed to know her parents' whereabouts so as to best avoid them.

"Lady Fenstraw and the children departed a short time ago for Gunter's."

Excellent. Her brothers and sisters were gone as well, and Mother wouldn't be able to escape London's most popular confectioner's shop for at least an hour. "And Father?"

"His lordship is in his study. With that *American* gentleman."

Emily froze—an odd dichotomy to the heat that suddenly raced through her. "American gentleman?"

Rupert's long, thin nose twitched, and he raised it an inch. "Yes, that Mr. Jennsen."

"Oh, him," Emily said, proud of the dismissive tone in her voice. "Has he been here long?"

"About half an hour, Lady Emily."

Emily clenched her teeth. Good God, they'd returned to London less than twenty-four hours ago, and already Mr. Jennsen was harassing her poor father over the money owed him. Mrs. Waverly, the housekeeper, entered the foyer to consult with Rupert on some household matter, and Emily took the opportunity to escape. However, rather than heading toward her bedchamber to gather her costume, she instead made her way down the corridor and entered the library. Closing the door softly behind her, she tiptoed around the mahogany tables and overstuffed sofas and chairs, across the artfully placed Axminster rugs, and halted at the door set in the paneled wall, the door that led to the adjoining room.

Her father's study.

Dropping to her knees, she applied her eye to the keyhole and blew out a huff of annoyance. Father had placed his desk in a most unhelpful location. All she could see were the crystal decanters by the window. Rising, she pressed her ear to the crack in the door. The murmur of masculine voices reached her, but botheration, she couldn't make out what they were saying.

With a skill born of years of practice in the spying games she and her siblings had been fond of playing while growing up, she slowly turned the brass knob in painstaking increments, then silently opened the door the merest whisper of a crack.

And heard . . .

Nothing.

She pressed her ear closer and listened for nearly a minute, but when she heard nothing save continued silence, she swallowed a vexed sigh. Just her luck to open the door during a lull in the conversation. Why couldn't men keep up a steady exchange of dialogue like women? Good heavens, Father could stare into space and ponder for what felt like hours between sentences. Hopefully Mr. Jennsen hadn't just asked him the sort of question that required deep contemplation before he answered.

Or perhaps they'd paused for a drink. She dropped once again to her knees and applied her eye to the keyhole. And discovered that no one stood before the decanters. Which meant there was either a very extended lull in the conversation, or they'd concluded their meeting.

"Had I known you were so interested in what I had to say, I would have insisted your father invite you to join us, Lady Emily."

Emily gasped and whirled around at the sound of Logan Jennsen's familiar, deep voice. Her surprise and awkward position conspired to throw her off balance, and before she could catch herself, she tilted over. Her bottom landed on the wooden floor with a bone-jarring thud, and her back hit the door. The oak panel closed with a loud click that reverberated through the room.

Heart pounding with what was surely nothing more than extreme annoyance, she looked up at the man who had haunted both her waking and sleeping hours for the past three months. He stood directly behind her, regarding her through dark eyes that glittered with unmistakable amusement.

Obviously his meeting with her father was concluded.

His gaze raked over her in a thorough manner, taking in every aspect of her undignified position. Fire suffused her cheeks, and she bit back the very unladylike word that rushed into her throat. This was not *at all* the way she'd envisioned their next meeting.

No, in her imagination, which she'd been helpless to squelch, she'd looked spectacular, dressed in her finest ball gown, her features accented by golden candlelight, a half-dozen suitors surrounding her, hanging upon her every word. Not once had she imagined herself flat on her bottom, blotchy with embarrassment and guilt, garbed in a plain day gown.

He held out his hand. "May I assist you?"

Emily looked at his large, long-fingered hand and instantly recalled how it had felt cradling the back of her head while his kiss incinerated her where she'd stood. The sensation of that broad palm sliding slowly down her back. Cupping the curve of her buttocks. Pulling her tighter against his hard body. Inspiring an inferno that had melted her common sense and dissolved her better judgment.

A wave of heat flooded her now, inciting her anger at herself and her errant thoughts and at him for precipitating this awkward meeting. But she gave thanks for her anger, as it allowed her to gather the shreds of her dignity. Treating his proffered hand to a withering glare, she rose to her feet unassisted. Standing before him, she was forcibly reminded of how tall he was. Even after lifting her chin, the top of her head only reached his shoulders. His very broad shoulders. That were a mere arm's length away. Surely it was only her surprise and irritation—as opposed to his nearness—that rendered her breathless and uncharacteristically speechless.

He made a tsking sound. "Eye to the keyhole, ear to the door crack. Do you know what that makes you?"

Yes. Aggravated enough for steam to spew from her pores. Before she could reply, he said, "It makes you an eavesdropper."

She hiked her chin higher. "I'm nothing of the sort."

His lips twitched. "I see. Don't tell me, let me guess. You lost a hairpin?"

Vexing man! She was sorely tempted to rip a hairpin from

her coiffure and give him a good jab. Raising her chin another inch, she shot him a look meant to reduce him to ashes. "No, I did not lose a hairpin, and what I was doing in my own home is none of your concern. Indeed, the question here is what are *you* doing lurking about and sneaking up on me? Were you not escorted to the door?"

I assured your father I could show myself out."

"Yet you did not do so."

"For which you have only yourself and your clumsy eaves-dropping attempts to blame."

Rather than having the decency to look abashed, he continued to regard her with amusement. "Interesting that you'd mention sneaking, as it's precisely what you were doing, although not very well." He shook his head and made another tsking sound. "Indeed, your abilities at silently opening a door for the purposes of listening to other people's private conversations have all the subtlety of a cannon boom."

Good Lord, how had she, for even a single second, thought of him as anything other than a pest? A *gargantuan* pest. A gargantuan *ill-mannered* pest.

A gargantuan ill-mannered pest who kissed you until your toes curled, her inner voice whispered.

Her lips pressed together. Stupid inner voice. Actually, it was good that they'd met again in such an infuriating manner, as it erased all memory of their kiss from her mind. Erased every last bit of it. Absolutely.

"Why are you here?" she asked.

"Because I heard someone's poor attempt to eavesdrop, and I was determined to catch the culprit," he said very slowly, as if he were speaking to a dim-witted child. Then his lips curved into a slow smile. "And here you are."

That smile drew her unwilling attention to his mouth. To those perfectly formed male lips that looked both firm and soft. Those lips that had kissed her with a boldness and skill that had stolen her breath and left her filled with an ache that had yet to subside in spite of the passage of three months. Her fingers itched so badly to reach out and trace his mouth she had to grip her skirts to keep from doing so. Which only served to vex her further.

"I *meant*," she said in her most arctic tone, "why are you in my home? Couldn't you have waited a respectable amount of time before coming here to harass my father?"

His smile faded, and something she couldn't decipher flickered in his eyes, followed by unmistakable annoyance, which cheered her considerably. Excellent. The aggravating man *should* be annoyed. Certainly not amused. And at her expense, no less.

"And what do you consider a respectable amount of time, Lady Emily?"

"Actually, there is no respectable amount of time when it comes to harassing a gentleman. Of course, since you aren't one, you wouldn't know that."

"How fortunate for me that you're here to teach me such fundamentals. Why, if I hadn't caught you on your knees before the keyhole, I might never have been privy to that information. Do you have any other pearls of wisdom to cast before me?"

"As a matter of fact, yes. It is extremely impolite to skulk about in someone else's home. Do you know what that makes *you*?" she asked, throwing his question back at him. "It makes you a skulker."

"Says a woman caught with her ear pressed to the crack in a door and peering through a keyhole. Where I come from, eavesdropping is considered extremely impolite."

Since there was no point denying what she'd been doing, she merely gave an elegant sniff. "You need not make reference to where you come from. It is obvious in everything you say and do. As to door-opening techniques, I suppose you think yours is flawless."

"The fact that I was able to enter this room without you detecting my presence speaks for itself."

Fustian. He had a point. She narrowed her eyes. "Where is my father?"

"You're looking at me as if I absconded with him."

"Did you?"

"Of course not. He retired to the garden through his study."

"Was he . . . all right?"

"Yes. Why wouldn't he be?"

"I am concerned for him. I wondered if your meeting might have upset him."

He raised a brow. "It seems to me that if he has any reason to be upset, it would be over his daughter's unladylike penchant for listening at doors."

Her toe tapped against the carpet. "Do you plan to harp on that forever?"

"Not *forever*." He flashed a grin. "Probably."

Infuriating, uncouth man. And how horribly unfair that his grin was so attractive. Good thing she was completely immune to him, or she might well find herself charmed and disarmed. Instead, she shot a pointed look toward the door. "Please don't let me keep you from departing. Or did you intend to skulk about my house further?"

He took a step forward. "Do you plan to harp on *that* forever?" he asked softly.

Emily sucked in a quick breath and moved backward. Her back hit the door, halting her retreat, leaving her nowhere to go when he took another step toward her.

Dear God, he was so . . . close. Close enough that she could see the fine grain of his clean-shaven skin. Her gaze traveled over his firm, square jaw, imperfect nose, high cheekbones, and the dark slashes of his brows. His were not the fine-boned, delicate features of an aristocrat. No, his features were bold, the panes of his face stark, lending him a rough-edged air that hinted of a danger that should have repelled her. Instead, she found herself staring at him, unable to look away.

Like everyone else, she'd heard rumors about him, that he'd been born into poverty and had left America under mysterious circumstances. How much of it was true? How had he risen from such humble beginnings to such great wealth? He struck her as very determined, as the sort of man who wouldn't hesitate to do whatever was necessary to get what he wanted. A heated tingle rippled down her spine.

Her gaze settled on his. Heavens, his eyes were . . . fascinating. Dark and mysterious. They radiated keen intelligence and an intensity that seemed to pierce her skin, seeing directly into her soul and filling her with a heat and awareness she'd never before experienced.

She drew in a slow, deep breath and had to stifle a groan. Dear Lord, he smelled good. Exactly as she recalled. Like fresh linen mixed with a hint of shaving soap and sandalwood.

Her heart flipped over in her chest, and her tongue peeked out to moisten her dry lips.

His gaze dropped to her mouth, and she suddenly felt as if the room were bereft of air. Heat emanated from him, surrounding her, igniting an unwanted and humiliating flame inside her. Could he sense it? Good God, she prayed not. Before she could recover, he planted his hands on the door on either side of her head, caging her in.

"Do you?" he whispered.

She'd completely lost the thread of their conversation. And by the knowing look in his eyes, he realized it. She had to swallow twice to locate her voice. "Do I what?"

"Plan to harp on my skulking—as you call it—forever?"

"Not *forever*," she said, mimicking his earlier answer. "Probably."

"The way you were looking at me . . ." he murmured, his gaze raking her face, which she knew bore a scarlet blush, "made it seem as if . . ."

I wanted you to kiss me?

". . . you thought I might be making off with the Fenstraw family silver," he finished.

Surely the sensation racing through her was relief, not disappointment. "I wasn't thinking anything of the sort, Mr. Jennsen," she said, sounding distressingly breathless. "I'm well aware you can afford your own silver."

"Then what *were* you thinking?"

That in spite of my best efforts, I haven't been able to erase you from my mind. And that in spite of my better judgment screaming at me that it's unwise, I want to feel the magic of your kiss again. And again. So much so that it frightens me.
"You want the truth?"

"Absolutely."

"Very well. I was thinking that you're an ill-mannered pest." It was true, she insisted to her frowning conscience. She *had* thought that—several minutes ago.

Rather than looking angry, he nodded solemnly. "I see. And would you like to know what *I* was thinking?"

"Is there any point in me saying no?"

His lips twitched. "None whatsoever." He leaned a bit closer, and her pounding heart nearly stopped.

"I was thinking," he said softly, his warm breath caressing her cheek, "that this reminds me of our last meeting. Us . . . alone in a library."

Emily braced her rapidly weakening knees. What this man could do to her without even touching her was nothing short of alarming. *And thrilling,* her inner voice reminded her. *Don't forget thrilling.*

Summoning every bit of aristocratic upbringing that had been bred into her from the cradle, she favored him with her most scathing look. "I assure you *this* meeting will not end in a similar fashion."

"Oh, I'm aware of that. I've no intention of kissing you again. No matter how many times you may ask me to do so." As if his words weren't infuriating enough, the scoundrel then had the audacity to wink at her.

Emily's jaw dropped, then snapped shut so quickly her teeth clanked together. "You've no fear of that happening, Mr. Jennsen. I pride myself on not making the same mistake twice."

"As do I."

"Excellent. Then there is no problem."

"None at all." His gaze bored into hers for several more unnerving seconds. Then his eyes narrowed. "You're up to something."

In spite of her surprise, she kept her gaze steady on his. He might be able to unnerve her with his potent masculinity, but as the oldest of six children, she was most adept at acting the innocent when mischief was afoot.

"I beg your pardon?"

"You. Up to something. You have that gleam in your eye. I know trouble when I see it."

"I don't know what you're talking about."

"I also know a lie when I hear one." His dark eyes seemed to burrow right into her soul. "What are you planning?"

Of course he was merely guessing, trying to unsettle her. Unfortunately, he was succeeding. "Again, I have no idea what you're talking about. Nor do I care for being called a liar." Especially when she was lying.

His expression was inscrutable, and she cursed the fact that she couldn't read him as easily as he apparently could read her. He leaned closer. Mere inches separated his mouth from hers. "I allowed you to play with me once, Lady Emily," he murmured. "I won't allow it again. Whatever game you're attempting, you'll not succeed in drawing me into it."

She managed a very credible laugh. "Your conceit knows no bounds, Mr. Jennsen. While I admit I sought out your company at our last meeting—very foolishly, I might add—I did not today."

"No? You were clearly interested in what I had to say." His gaze flicked to her lips. "Makes me wonder what else you might be interested in."

"My actions were born out of concern for my father. Not from a desire to see you."

Liar, her stupid inner voice yelled.

"Yet here we are," he said, his voice so soft she had to press her shoulder blades against the door to keep from leaning closer to better hear his words. That thankfully served as a hard slap of reminder of who he was and all the reasons she didn't like him. Not that she could name them at the moment, but she knew there were reasons. Lots of them. And as soon as she was rid of him, she'd remind herself what they were. Better yet, she'd write them down, lest she find herself forgetting again.

Forcibly ignoring his alluring heat and intoxicating scent, she said, "The only reason *we* are here is because you've seen fit to trap me." She gave his arms a pointed look.

He slowly pushed away from the door and stepped back. "You could have easily escaped at any time. If you'd really wanted to. And you know it."

Yes, she did. And she didn't at all care for the fact that he knew it nor for his blunt manner. The gentlemen she was accustomed to speaking with never would talk to a lady in such a way. Polite gentlemen would never dare to throw such unvarnished truths, er, words at a lady.

She moved around him, giving him an exaggerated wide berth to demonstrate how much she didn't want to risk any part of her brushing against any part of him. As she headed toward the door, she said, "It's been . . . *interesting* seeing you again, Mr. Jennsen."

When she reached the door, she turned around and pulled

in a startled breath when she discovered him standing directly behind her. How annoying that a man of his size could move so silently.

"*Very* interesting, Lady Emily. Although perhaps not as interesting as last time. For your sake, I hope our next meeting finds you in a less undignified position."

Before she could fashion a reply, he offered her a formal bow—one that looked decidedly mocking—then opened the door, and without waiting for her to escort him quit the room. Speechless, she watched him stride down the corridor. How did such an annoying man manage to look as good exiting a room as entering one?

He stopped in the foyer, accepted his hat and coat from Rupert, then departed. It wasn't until the door closed after him that she realized she'd been holding her breath.

Our next meeting? Not if she could help it. Logan Jennsen was far too unsettling and perceptive to risk spending any time in his company. Although they were unfortunately bound to attend the same soirees, she intended to avoid him as best she could. Still, next time she would not only be completely dignified, she planned to be spectacular.

Chapter 4

I knew I should let him go, free him to be with someone more suited to him, someone mortal, but I simply couldn't. He attracted me, challenged me like no other. Even though I tried to engage my interest elsewhere, I desired no one other than him. I never should have allowed myself to taste him, because now I craved him all the time.

The Vampire Lady's Kiss *by Anonymous*

Logan paced the length of his private study, his mind reverberating with the same question that had plagued him since departing Lord Fenstraw's town house several hours earlier: *What is she up to?*

With a growl of frustration, he paused and raked his hands through his hair. Damn it, he couldn't recall the last time he'd felt so out of sorts and confused: two feelings he rarely experienced separately and almost never at the same time. But since that damn kiss three months ago, this confused, out-of-sorts phenomenon remained his daily companion.

And it was entirely *her* fault.

How was it possible for one small woman to be so damn maddening? Why couldn't he simply dismiss her from his thoughts, as he had so many others of her aristocratic ilk? Why was she proving such a puzzling problem for him? He was accustomed to both puzzles and problems, and normally he enjoyed both. It was a trait that had served him well in his business pursuits. He enjoyed the challenge of figuring out how to get around obstacles, finding solutions to perplexing difficulties.

But not in this case. No, the puzzle of Lady Emily was more like a toothache, one that continued to throb, no matter what course of action was applied. If only he were able to simply yank her out, as one would a troublesome bicuspid, and forget about her. But he knew well enough that that simply wasn't going to happen, although for the life of him he couldn't figure out why, or why he gave a damn. Therefore he needed to figure out what she was up to before the question drove him mad.

Three months ago, he'd wondered if she knew about the extensive debts her father owed him, if that had led, contrary to her claim of being merely curious, to her kissing him. Although he'd harbored his suspicions regarding her motives, he couldn't deny his masculine pride had secretly hoped her kiss had been the result of curiosity and desire. Based on their conversation earlier today, however, it was clear she knew about her father's debts to him. And as much as it annoyed him to admit to himself, he couldn't deny that disappointed him.

Yet it also greatly confused him. She knew her father owed him money; therefore, why wasn't she still attempting to charm him after having gone so far as to kiss him? Why wasn't she attempting to win his favor? Coax him with her feminine wiles? Instead, she was as prickly as a handful of pins. Which once again raised his suspicions and made him wonder, *What is she up to?*

He closed his eyes, and an image of her materialized in his mind . . . leaning against the door, looking up at him with those extraordinary eyes. He'd planted his hands on the oak panel to keep from giving in to the overwhelming desire to touch her. To see if her skin was still as soft. It would have been far wiser to have walked away. Being that close to her had proved an exercise in torture. Never in his life could he recall a woman smelling so good. Like an impossible combination of cake and flowers, as if she'd just eaten a delicious sweet while strolling through a blooming garden. The damn scent made him want to bury his nose against her velvety smooth neck and just breathe her in, then give her creamy skin a long, slow lick.

I've no intention of kissing you again. No matter how many times you may ask me to do so. His words to her echoed through his mind, and a humorless laugh escaped him. While it was true he'd had no intention of kissing her again, it had required all his will not to do so. And since he had learned long ago how pointless it was to lie to himself, he couldn't deny that if she'd asked—hell, even vaguely *suggested*—he kiss her again, he would have swooped in like a starving predator capturing its prey. What kind of fool did that make him?

He didn't know, but he knew he didn't like being *any* sort of fool. That meant he needed to stay away from Lady Emily Stapleford and whatever this damn spell was she'd cast upon him. It didn't matter what sort of scheme she'd concocted; he wouldn't allow her to draw him into it. He was more determined than ever to find another woman to put out this unwanted Lady Emily–induced fire. Tonight.

That settled, he moved toward his desk, where several pieces of correspondence awaited his attention. He'd just settled himself in his leather chair when a knock sounded.

"Come in," he called.

Adam Seaton, his factotum, opened the door and entered. Logan had hired the thirty-year-old four months ago and was so far pleased with his work. He was diligent, even tempered, organized, intelligent, and followed Logan's instructions without question. One look at Adam's drawn face told Logan something was seriously amiss.

"What's wrong?" he asked, rising.

Adam adjusted his spectacles then cleared his throat. "There's been a fire, sir. At the docks. I'm afraid *The Mariner*, as well as her entire cargo, was lost."

"And the crew?" Logan asked, his every muscle tense.

Adam's features tightened further. "Two deck hands were killed, sir. Five more, as well as the captain, were injured, although fortunately not seriously."

Logan felt as if he'd turned to stone. *The Mariner* had been fully loaded and scheduled to sail with this evening's high tide. The loss of the ship and cargo amounted to a hefty financial blow, although one he could weather. But the loss of those men . . . damn it.

"How did the fire start?"

"Several crew members who escaped reported that within seconds flames seemed to be everywhere, spreading very rapidly throughout the entire ship."

Logan's eyes narrowed. "Flames everywhere? The fire would have been contained to its source—at least for a short time—unless something flammable, such as lamp oil, had been used to accelerate the flames."

"Yes, sir."

"It was deliberately set." It was a statement rather than a question.

"It appears so, sir."

"Any other ships affected?"

"No, sir. Just *The Mariner*."

Logan allowed that to sink in for several seconds. His instincts were screaming that this was related to the sense of dread he'd been experiencing. And that this was no accident. And that he was the target.

"The men who died—what are their names?"

Adam pulled from his waistcoat pocket the small notebook he always carried. After flipping through several pages, he said, "Billy Palmer and Christian Whitaker."

"What about their families?"

Adam again consulted his book. "Palmer had no family. Whitaker leaves a wife and young daughter."

Logan's insides twisted at the thought of that child growing up without her father. He knew all too well what it was like to not have a parent. And that woman now alone . . . no one to take care of her. He knew what that was like as well. He didn't know what the hell was going on, but he was going to make damn sure no one else perished or was injured while he found out.

He sat down and reached for a piece of vellum and his quill. "Arrange for proper funerals for both men," he instructed Adam as he wrote. "See that the injured men receive the best medical care and are compensated for any wages they'll lose while convalescing. I'll need all of their directions so as to call upon them, and Mrs. Whitaker's as well."

Adam removed a folded piece of vellum from his notebook and handed it to Logan. "Right here, sir. Thought you'd be wanting them."

Logan nodded his thanks, impressed as he had been from the start with Adam's efficiency, although he almost found it disconcerting the uncanny way the man anticipated him. It was almost as if he'd known Logan for years rather than for only a few months.

"I can send letters or make the calls on your behalf, sir," Adam said.

"Thank you, no."

"I've already contacted Lloyd's," Adam continued. "There shouldn't be any problem with the insurance."

Logan nodded absently. He hadn't gathered his thoughts enough to consider that.

He quickly finished his note, then after sealing it, handed the missive to Adam. "I want you to personally deliver that to Gideon Mayne on Bow Street right away. He needs to be informed about this."

"Yes, sir." Adam tucked the letter and his notebook into his waistcoat then departed. Logan crossed the room and poured himself three fingers of brandy, which he tossed back in a single, bracing gulp. The liquor burned its way down to his knotted stomach. First someone following him, then an unauthorized person attempting to board one of his ships, and now this disaster. Things were going from bad to worse at an alarming rate. And it needed to stop. Now.

He grimly set down the empty glass then headed toward the door to make his calls. Mrs. Whitaker and her daughter were first on his list.

∞

When Emily arrived at Lord Teller's soiree that evening, the first person she sought out was Carolyn, who stood near a potted palm with Daniel. Carolyn wore a lovely blue gown that exactly matched her eyes . . . eyes that to Emily appeared tired. Indeed, as she drew closer, she noted that Carolyn looked pale and drawn, even more so than she had this afternoon. Still, she was smiling at whatever her husband had said and sipping from a glass of punch.

"Good to have you back in London," Daniel said when Emily joined them. "My wife has been missing your company and your Ladies Literary Society book club adventures." He shot Carolyn a smile, yet along with the obvious love shining in his eyes, Emily noticed the underlying concern. "I've been trying to discover what went on at today's meeting, but Carolyn's been very closemouthed."

"Oh, nothing that would interest you," Emily said with a dismissive wave of her hand. "Merely girly things."

"Hmmm. Perhaps Matthew, Gideon, and I shall start a gentlemen's literary society."

"Oh? And what would you read?" Emily asked.

"Nothing that would interest you," he teased with a dismissive wave that precisely matched hers. "Merely manly things."

Carolyn brushed her hand down Daniel's sleeve. "I wager I could persuade you to tell me all your literary society's secrets."

The heat that glowed in Daniel's eyes and the intimate look he bestowed upon his wife brought a sigh of pure envy to Emily's lips. *That* is how she wanted to be looked at. Every day of her life. By a man who adored her. Whom she adored in return. A fact that only served to reinforce the necessity of her plan, risks be damned. If she were forced to marry a man for purely financial reasons rather than love, she'd never know what Carolyn—as well as Julianne and Sarah—experienced when their husbands looked at them with such naked devotion and desire in their eyes.

"I wouldn't give up my secrets easily, my dear," Daniel said. "I predict it would require *hours* of effort on your part."

Carolyn gave a quick laugh, one that turned into a cough. After a quick sip of punch, she said, "Hours? I rather think you'd fold like a house of cards within thirty—"

"Minutes?" suggested Daniel.

"Seconds," Carolyn corrected.

He raised her hand to his lips. "I greatly look forward to seeing which of us is correct."

Carolyn smiled at him, although to Emily the smile seemed forced. "As do I." Carolyn's gaze wandered beyond Daniel's shoulder. "Lord Langston has just arrived. Didn't you say you wished to speak with him, Daniel?"

"Trying to get rid of me?"

"Of course not, but Emily and I can hardly discuss girly matters with a man about, now can we?"

It was clear to Emily that Daniel was reluctant to leave his wife's side, yet after a brief hesitation, he said, "I suppose not. I'll leave you ladies to your conversation." He pressed a kiss to Carolyn's fingers, made Emily a formal bow, then headed across the room.

The instant he left, Emily noted that Carolyn's shoulders sagged a bit, then she breathed what sounded like a sigh of relief. Without further hesitation, she took Carolyn's hand and drew her into a quiet, deserted corner, shielded from the rest of the room by a display of potted ferns set in enormous ceramic pots.

"Something is wrong," she said, her gaze searching Carolyn's face, alarmed by her friend's pallor and the violet smudges beneath her eyes.

Carolyn hesitated for several seconds, then gave a tight nod. "Yes, I'm afraid so." She squeezed Emily's hands. "I'm so glad you're back. I've wanted, needed someone to talk to."

"What about Sarah and Julianne? Or Daniel?"

Carolyn shook her head. "I don't want to tell Sarah anything that could upset her during these last weeks of her pregnancy. And Julianne has been so happy . . . I haven't had the heart to tell her. As for Daniel," she shook her head. "I simply haven't been able to bring myself to tell him yet."

"Tell him what?" Emily clutched at Carolyn's hand. "What on earth is wrong? You're scaring me."

To her dismay, tears glistened in Carolyn's eyes. "I'm afraid I'm . . . ill."

Emily's stomach tumbled to her feet. She didn't know what she'd expected—perhaps bad news regarding someone in Daniel's family or a friend, or maybe that Carolyn and Daniel had argued about something. But nothing like this.

"Ill?" she repeated, the word simply sounding wrong, as if someone else was saying it, from very far away. Her gaze raced over Carolyn. It was obvious her friend had lost weight. "Have you seen a physician?"

Carolyn nodded. I visited him six weeks ago—"

"*Six weeks* ago? How long has this been going on?"

"About two months."

Two months. Guilt and fear collided in Emily. While she'd been frittering away her time in the country, writing her story, Carolyn had been suffering. Alone.

"Why didn't you write me? I would have returned to London immediately."

"There was nothing you could do."

"I would have been here," Emily said quietly, her voice clogged with emotion. "I'm so very sorry I wasn't. But I'm here now. Tell me everything. What is ailing you?"

"I . . . I'm not sure what the problem is, and neither is the physician. But I fear the outcome is bleak."

The desolation in Carolyn's voice tore at Emily's heart. "Why? What are your symptoms? Surely it's just some dyspepsia or—"

Carolyn shook her head. "It's more than merely stomach upset. There are headaches. Terrible headaches. And a cough I cannot rid myself of. Alternating chills and fever. I've swooned half a dozen times in the past month."

Emily's stomach plummeted to her feet. That sounded . . . bad. "The physician offered you no explanation?"

"No. He said he'd never seen such an array of symptoms. He prescribed a tonic and laudanum for the headaches, but both rendered me so horribly nauseated, I stopped taking them."

"You said you haven't told Daniel, but obviously he knows something is amiss. How could you possibly hide the headaches and swooning? And you're noticeably thinner. 'Tis clear to me he's worried about you."

"He knows I've been sick and is very concerned. However, he is unaware of the severity of my symptoms. And he only knows about one of the swooning episodes." Carolyn drew a quick breath, then said, "Emily . . . the physician may never have seen such an array of symptoms before, but I have." At Emily's questioning look, Carolyn whispered, "Edward."

The name of Carolyn's first husband hung between them like a death knell. Before Emily could find her voice, Carolyn continued, "In the weeks before Edward died, he suffered terrible headaches and developed a cough. Nausea. He lost weight and fainted a number of times. Within a matter of weeks he was dead."

Dear God, Emily remembered only too well how quickly the formerly robust young man had faded. How his rapidly deteriorating condition had baffled his physician. How tragic his death at age twenty-eight had been. How utterly bereft it had left Carolyn.

"Last month I secretly wrote to Edward's former physician, who now lives in Surrey, and told him everything. I received a letter from him just this morning . . ."

Carolyn's voice trailed off, prompting Emily to ask, "And? What did he write?"

Carolyn expelled a short huff of breath. She tried to smile, but her lips merely trembled. "Although he gave me the name of another physician, a man on Harley Street he recommended I visit, the basic tone of his letter was apologetic. He agreed my symptoms matched Edward's, and his best advice was for me to make certain my affairs were all in order. To hope for the best but to anticipate the worst."

"No." Emily shook her head vigorously. "*No*," she repeated in a furious whisper. "You are young and healthy and shall overcome whatever this is. I *refuse* to believe otherwise. I refuse to believe it is the same malady that struck Edward. Have you contacted the Harley Street doctor?"

"Not yet."

"Then you must do so first thing in the morning." She squeezed Carolyn's hands. "And you need to tell Daniel."

"He'll be devastated. *I* am devastated." Carolyn's lips trembled. "We've only just begun our life together and now—"

"And now we shall concentrate on finding out precisely what is wrong and a way to fix it," Emily said fiercely, trying to infuse some of her passion and strength into Carolyn by sheer will. "You know Daniel will do everything in his power to help you. As will I. And Sarah and Julianne."

Carolyn shook her head. "I know I must tell Daniel, that I can't keep this from him much longer, but I refuse to give such news to Sarah before she gives birth."

"Surely she and Julianne suspect something's wrong."

"I told them what I've told Daniel: that I caught a chill that's stubbornly hanging on, combined with a bout of dyspepsia, which, according to the first physician I saw, is perfectly true."

"But you believe it is more than that?"

"I'm afraid so."

"You can't fool the people who love you, Carolyn, not indefinitely. The moment I saw you today I knew something was wrong, and I vowed to discover what it was even if I had to drag it out of you one syllable at a time. I realize you're trying to be noble and spare us heartache, but you need us. As we need you. We want to help. You must allow us to do so. Together we can conquer anything."

"If love alone could save someone, conquer illness, believe me, Edward would still be alive."

"You don't *know* you have the same illness Edward did," Emily insisted. "Why, my aunt Agatha has been swooning at least three times a week for the past two decades, and she's as healthy as a horse."

Carolyn managed a wobbly smile. "Your aunt Agatha's swooning consists of artfully arranging herself on chairs and settees."

"And it's fortunate we have so many, as she's constantly swooning. Carolyn, you mustn't give up hope."

"I haven't. It's just . . . I've felt so poorly and haven't wanted to worry anyone."

"Well, you need to simply forget about that," Emily said tartly. "It's the right of people who love you to worry about you." She shot Carolyn her sternest look, the one that always made her younger siblings' eyes widen with the knowledge that they'd overstepped their boundaries, and they were about to bear the consequences. "Don't make me run roughshod over you, young lady."

Carolyn gave a watery laugh, then Emily pulled her into a tight hug. They clung to each other for a full minute before easing back. With her arms still wrapped about Emily's waist, Carolyn said, "Thank you. I . . . needed that."

Emily's heart floundered in her chest. "You've been alone in this up until now, but no longer. You have me. And Daniel. Whom you must tell."

Carolyn nodded. "Yes. I shall. After the party tonight."

"Leave now," Emily urged. "Tell him now. You'll feel better after you do."

"Actually, I feel better now. Certainly better than when I first arrived. Talking with you has lifted my spirits."

"I still think you should go home."

Carolyn shook her head. "No. I really am feeling better, and I'm grateful to have something to do besides think. I want to play my role of vampire sighter."

Emily blinked. Good heavens, she'd completely forgotten about that. Her problems paled to insignificance compared to Carolyn's troubles. In spite of her brave words to Carolyn, she was gravely concerned for her friend, although she'd never let her know. No, she would remain the voice of cheerful optimism.

And pray as she never had before.

Carolyn pulled a lace handkerchief from her reticule and dabbed at her eyes. "Do I look weepy?"

"No. You look beautiful." Too pale, yet not as pale as earlier. And too thin. And heartbreakingly fragile. "Always beautiful. Am I a blotchy mess?"

Carolyn let out a chuckle. "You're spectacular. As always. The most vivid woman in any room."

"Says one of my dearest friends."

"That doesn't make it any less true. And speaking of spectacular, I've been thinking about your difficult situation."

A swell of pure love walloped Emily, and she had to blink back tears. Leave it to Carolyn to disregard her own problems to try and solve Emily's.

Forcing a smile and a quick laugh, Emily said, "I'm not certain *spectacular* is a word I'd use to describe my problem."

"I meant Logan Jennsen."

Emily went perfectly still. The name seemed to vibrate in the air between them. In an unsettling manner that left her ridiculously flustered. "I beg your pardon?"

"Logan Jennsen."

"You think he's *spectacular*?" Something that felt precisely like jealousy—but of course wasn't—rippled through Emily.

"Actually, I do. Indeed, I think he's the perfect solution to your problem."

Emily's lips puckered as if she'd just bitten into a lemon. "I believe Mr. Jennsen's area of expertise is in shipping rather than publishing. I don't think he'd have any interest in purchasing my story."

"I agree, although given his vast holdings, I wouldn't be shocked to learn he owned a publishing firm. I meant that he is rich. *Very* rich." Carolyn's steady gaze bored into Emily's. "And unmarried."

Emily felt her jaw drop. If she'd been capable of any other movement, she would have glanced down to see if the lower half of her face had actually fallen to the floor. She felt frozen to the spot—odd, considering the flare of heat racing through her. Much swallowing ensued to locate her voice. "You cannot mean what I think you mean."

"Well, at least you've stopped looking at me as if I'm made of glass and about to break."

"You're correct. I'm looking at you as if you're a lunatic."

"Which I assure you I'm not. Think about it, Emily. He's personable—"

"Uncouth."

"Handsome—"

"I've seen better."

"And most likely the wealthiest man in England."

That she couldn't argue with.

"*And* he's not opposed to getting married," Carolyn added.

"Well, *I* am opposed."

"If your plan fails, you'll have to marry. And soon."

"Which is why I'm determined not to fail." Marry Logan Jennsen. Good Lord, what a ridiculous idea. Ha! The mere thought made her want to laugh out loud. Double ha! That odd tingle skittering through her was surely just the vibrations of her inner laughter.

"In fact," Emily continued, "it's time to put my plan into motion." This was earlier than she'd wanted to start, but the sooner she did so, the sooner Carolyn could depart. "Let's go chat up the ladies, then I'll excuse myself. After about five minutes, look toward the terrace windows." She squeezed Carolyn's hands. "Are you sure you feel up to this?"

"Positive. Are you sure you still want to do this?"

"Absolutely." She smiled into Carolyn's eyes, refusing to dwell on the violet smudges beneath them. "Everything is going to be fine, Carolyn."

She prayed to God she was right.

Chapter 5

Raw need burned in his eyes, turning their smoky depths to ebony coals. He grabbed my shoulders and yanked me against his hard body. "You're mine," he said, his voice a hot, feral whisper against my lips. I couldn't deny it. I was his. But he was also mine. And I wasn't going to allow him to forget it.

The Vampire Lady's Kiss *by Anonymous*

Logan exited his carriage outside Lord Teller's Park Lane town house armed with his resolve to find a woman at the soiree to help him forget about his upsetting day and *she who he refused to think of anymore.* He was halfway up the stone walkway when a chill shivered through him, one that had nothing to do with the cold night air. He halted and quickly turned, his eyes scanning. Someone was watching him. He knew it. Could feel it.

His gaze took in the crowd of elegant carriages lined up along Park Lane, waiting to drop off party guests. Was the person watching him in one of them? Or were they across the thoroughfare, where the thick hedges and soaring trees of Hyde Park would offer a veritable plethora of hiding places for anyone who wished to remain unseen?

He peered through the darkness but could detect nothing amiss. Still, his every instinct remained on alert. After one final look about, he continued toward the town house, making a mental note to contact Gideon in the morning. To tell the Runner that Logan was certain he'd once again been watched. He'd also apprise Adam of his suspicions, so his keenly observant factotum could be watchful for anything amiss. A sick feeling was gathering in Logan's gut that the destruction of his ship, and thereby the deaths and injuries of his men, hadn't been an accident or a random act.

His mouth tightened into a grim line. Perhaps whoever was watching him would show themselves tonight. If so, he'd be ready. In the meantime, he intended to carry on as normal, as if he suspected nothing amiss. He'd enjoy the party. Find a warm and willing woman. And not think of *she who he refused to think of anymore*.

After surrendering his greatcoat, top hat, and walking stick to the butler, Logan entered Lord and Lady Teller's drawing room. And halted as if he'd walked into a wall. Damn it, what were the odds that, in a room overflowing with females, the first one he'd see was *her*?

Lady Emily stood near the terrace windows chatting with Carolyn and several other women. His gaze—which seemed to have developed a will of its own—traveled over her with an avidness that truly irked him. Her glossy curls were pulled back and threaded with sparkling gems that twinkled in the candlelight. Her emerald gown left an enticing expanse of creamy skin visible, skin he knew felt like satin. A hint of cleavage peeked above her bodice, and he bit back a groan as he vividly recalled the feel of her full breasts pressing against his chest.

Even from across the room he could see the hint of mischief glowing in her eyes, eyes he knew would be highlighted by the color of her gown.

Damn it, she looked spectacular. Vivid. She somehow made everything around her fade to boring shades of gray. He clenched his hands and pressed his lips together in a useless attempt to dismiss the overwhelming urge to plunge his fingers into her shiny hair and trail his mouth over her soft neck . . . silky skin he knew smelled and tasted delicious. His gaze settled on her bare throat, and his mind's eye instantly conjured up an image of an emerald necklace adorning that smooth, ivory skin. Yes, an emerald necklace . . . and nothing else. Except his hands. And mouth.

His gaze moved back to her plump lips, which were curved upward into a full smile. The sort she gave freely to others but had never deigned to give him. As if to prove his point, she glanced his way, and their gazes collided. And her smile collapsed.

Damn it, bad enough he was staring at her, but to be caught doing so was beyond irritating. All traces of mischief vanished from her eyes, leaving an expression of utter bleakness he'd never seen from her before. That desolate look stunned him and unexpectedly pulled at his heart. She was always so . . . lively. So animated. Even when she was staring daggers at him. Whatever had brought on that look must be of a very recent nature, as he'd detected no signs of unhappiness when he'd seen her earlier today. What had happened to elicit such sadness?

A surge of concern filled him, and before he could think better of it, he found himself taking a step toward her. Wanting, needing, for reasons he didn't understand, to offer some sort of comfort or help.

The instant he moved, however, she blinked, and her expression cleared. He halted, and for several long seconds they simply stared at each other. Then, before he could pull his attention away from her, she returned hers to her friends without so much as a flicker to acknowledge his presence.

An odd sensation he couldn't name rippled through him. Surely not hurt. He didn't care if she acknowledged him or not. Certainly not jealousy. What did it matter that she smiled at everyone save him? Clearly it was simply pure annoyance at being caught staring. And feeling foolish for imagining she'd welcome his assistance for whatever was troubling her. If indeed anything even was. No doubt her distress was due to some overblown "crisis" such as losing an ear bob or suffering a stain on her gown.

Well, he needn't worry about getting caught staring again, as he had no intention of even glancing her way for the remainder of the evening.

He accepted a glass of champagne he didn't particularly want from a passing footman and directed his attention toward the rest of the crowd and noted he wasn't the only man looking at Lady Emily. A young blond buck standing near the doors leading to the terrace was eyeing her as if trying to figure out which article of her clothing he wanted to remove first.

Logan's brows collapsed, and he searched his memory for the man's name . . . it reminded him of something unpleasant . . . something foul tasting . . . ah, yes, now he remembered. Castor oil. The ogling bastard's name was Lord Kaster. He had a sudden urge to introduce damn Lord Kaster's wandering eyeballs to his fist. And his perfectly coiffed blond head to the punch bowl. Just then another man claimed Kaster's attention, and the bastard managed, with an obvious effort, to pull his gaze from Lady Emily.

Feeling like a wet cat whose fur was being pet backward, Logan once again scanned the guests. It seemed as if everyone in London was in attendance. It never ceased to amaze him that so many people attended so many parties. For him they were a business necessity rather than a social enjoyment, and normally he wouldn't care for such a crowd. Indeed, he'd seriously considered remaining at home this evening. His visits to the men injured in *The Mariner* fire still weighed on him, and his meeting with Velma Whitaker and her daughter Lara . . . damn it, he'd never forget that woman's ravaged, tearstained face or that child's huge eyes staring up at him as she clung to her mother's skirt, her tiny chin quivering when she whispered, "Papa ain't comin' home no more."

He would see to it that they were taken care of financially, but as he knew all too well, money couldn't replace people or mend broken hearts. Nor would it erase the image of that fatherless child from his mind. That was ultimately why he'd decided to attend the party; if he'd remained at home, he would have sat and brooded, remembering things he had no desire to recall. And he would have been the one thing he was liking less and less.

Alone.

He'd been alone for years, and he was damn tired of it. He didn't want to be alone any longer. Especially not tonight.

This noisy, crowded party perfectly suited his purposes

this evening—the more guests, the larger his selection of women to choose from.

This time his gaze settled on a stunning blond standing near the punch bowl. Ah, Celeste Melton, Lady Hombly. The widow, whose much older husband had conveniently died two years ago after only a brief marriage, leaving her a countess and very wealthy, had, in the company of her solicitor, sought out Logan's advice on a financial matter several months ago. He'd advised her to eschew the investment she was considering and instead invest in one of his shipping ventures. She'd agreed and had made it plain she'd be interested in anything else besides advice he might want to offer. While there was no denying her outward attractiveness, like most flawless beauties, she failed to ignite a spark in him.

Tonight, however, he was primed to be lit on fire. The fact that Lady Hombly possessed pale blond hair and light blue eyes—the exact opposite of *she who he refused to think of anymore*—rendered her even more perfect.

He was about to make his way toward her when a voice beside him said, "Something, or should I say someone, seems to have thoroughly captured your attention, Jennsen."

Logan turned and met Daniel Sutton's speculative gaze. He couldn't deny he hadn't particularly cared for the earl when they'd first met at a house party at the estate of Daniel's best friend, and now brother-in-law, Matthew Devenport, Lord Langston. But over the last ten months Logan's opinion of Daniel had grown into one of liking and respect. He now considered him, as well as Matthew, a friend—surprising as he remained largely unimpressed with the British aristocracy. Titles meant nothing to him, nor did the estates tied to them. Aging relics and chains around a man's neck were all they were, enslaving him to marry and procreate so as to pass the title and aging relics on to the next poor, unsuspecting male who would then be burdened by it all, whether he wanted to be or not.

It suddenly occurred to Logan that between Daniel, Matthew, and Gideon, he had more friends now than he'd ever had. Of course, no one here in England knew about his past. They only knew what he was now: wealthy and successful. No one knew how he'd arrived at this point. The things he'd done. And hadn't done. And he intended to keep it that way.

Given all he had, envy was an emotion he rarely felt, but it was one all three of his friends inspired. Within the last year they all had married women they adored and who loved them in return. Although Logan had freakishly phenomenal good fortune with all things financial, his luck with finding a woman to share his life with was abysmal. While he was happy for his friends, the contentment and satisfaction he saw in them only served to remind him that in spite of all his wealth and material possessions, he didn't have anyone to share them with. He should be happy, but a vague feeling of discontent had been growing in him for a while, and lately it had become undeniable. He used to enjoy being alone, liked the solitude, but now being alone was just very . . . lonely.

"She looks lovely this evening," Daniel said, "but then, she always does."

"Who?" Logan asked.

"The object of your attention."

He tried to recall what Lady Hombly was wearing and utterly failed. He glanced toward where she'd been standing, but she was no longer there. "Er, yes. Lovely."

"I admit I'm a bit surprised, given your insistence you have no use for society diamonds, but I commend you on your good taste. She's as beautiful on the inside as she is on the outside, which is rare indeed."

Logan idly wondered if Lady Hombly and Daniel had been lovers before his marriage. "You know her well?"

Daniel looked at him with an expression that suggested he'd sprouted a second head. He glanced down at Logan's untouched champagne. "Are you foxed?"

"No." He glanced at the tumbler of amber liquid Daniel held. "Are you?"

"Of course not."

"Why the hell did you think I was?"

"Because you know I know her very well."

A peal of feminine laughter caught Logan's attention, and without meaning to, he found himself glancing toward the terrace windows. Lady Emily still stood among a group of women and several men, one of whom was Lord Kaster. And she still looked spectacular. Damn it.

"She's one of Carolyn's closest friends."

Daniel's voice yanked him back, and he forcibly focused his attention on his friend. "I wasn't aware your wife and Lady Hombly were so well acquainted."

Daniel's brow furrowed. "I don't believe they are."

"You just said she was one of Carolyn's closest friends."

"I was referring to Lady Emily, not Lady Hombly."

Logan nearly dropped his unwanted champagne. "Why were you referring to Lady Emily?"

"Because she is who you were staring at so intently."

Heat born of guilt infused Logan's entire body. "I most certainly was not."

Daniel's brows shot up. Then he blinked. "Good God, man, are you . . . *blushing*?"

"Of course not. It's merely very warm in here."

Daniel studied him for several seconds, then grinned. "You're lying."

Yes, I am. "No, I'm not."

"You were looking at Emily as if she were a treasure chest filled with gold bullion and you were a marauding pirate."

Precisely. "Ridiculous. What a lurid imagination you have."

"I know what I saw, Jennsen. I'm very observant."

"You're a pain in the arse."

"And you're still blushing." The damn man had the gall to keep grinning. "Bloody hell, I wish Matthew and Gideon were here to see this."

Logan could only thank God they weren't. "There's nothing to see."

"Clearly you require a mirror." Daniel leaned closer. "What is that? Why, it looks like steam wisping from your ears, Jennsen."

No doubt, because he felt like a volcano on the verge of eruption. "I have no idea what you're talking about." He made a great show of looking about. "Where is your wife? Surely she is missing you."

Something flickered in Daniel's eyes so swiftly Logan wondered if he'd imagined it. Before he could decide, Daniel said, "I'll join her in a moment."

"And what a fun moment that will be for me," Logan muttered.

Daniel took a sip of his drink and regarded Logan over the glass rim. "Would you like my opinion?"

"No."

"Except for you being an American," Daniel continued as if Logan hadn't spoken, "I believe you and Emily are actually quite well suited."

For several seconds Logan could only stare. An odd sensation that could only be utter disbelief rippled through him. "I believe you are a complete nincompoop."

"And you can't see the wood for the trees."

"You mean can't see the *forest* for the trees."

Daniel looked toward the ceiling. "The way you colonials speak is—well, never mind. What's important is that you agree—"

"Actually, I don't—"

"Because Emily is an exceptional young woman. Beautiful, accomplished, and hails from a distinguished family. As if that weren't enough, she's also intelligent, amusing, and kind."

Something that felt suspiciously like jealousy whispered through Logan at Daniel's extolment of Lady Emily's virtues. "*Kind?*" he repeated with an incredulous sneer. "The next time she's kind to me will be the first time. She's made no secret of the fact that she thinks I'm foul."

"Surely you've enough experience with women to know that they often say things and behave in ways that are in complete contrast to how they really feel."

Logan's hand holding his champagne halted halfway to his lips, and he frowned. Yes, he did know that about women. He just hadn't considered it could ever be the case with Lady Emily. Of course it wasn't.

After taking a sip of the bubbly wine, Logan said, "If she's so damn wonderful, why didn't *you* want her?"

"If fate had worked differently, perhaps I would have. As it turned out, I lost my heart to Carolyn the first time I saw her."

"I can assure you I did nothing of the sort with Lady Emily."

"Perhaps not at first, but I've seen the sparks between you. They were obvious at Gideon's wedding. And only moments ago in this very room."

Logan gave a quick laugh. "If there were sparks, I assure you they were born of nothing more than extreme annoyance."

"Doesn't matter. Any sort of spark can ignite a fire, my friend. Would you like to hear what else I think?"

"No. Would you like a black eye?" Logan asked in a falsely pleasant voice between gritted teeth. "Because that can be easily arranged."

Daniel threw back his head and laughed. "Ah, you colonials. So uncivilized with the fisticuffs."

"Yes, unlike you civilized aristocrats with your dueling pistols."

"Precisely. In addition to dueling, wc Brits also enjoy making wagers. I trust you recall the one you and I made several months ago?"

A smile pulled at Logan's lips. "Oh, yes. I very much enjoyed collecting that fifty pounds you lost because you fell in love with a society chit."

Daniel nodded. "That is true. However, I was referring to our *other* fifty-pound wager. The one that has yet to be settled. Regarding you, too, falling in love with a society chit." Daniel's grin turned smug, and he rubbed his hands together. "Based on the way you were staring at Emily, I'm guessing it won't be long before my fifty pounds is restored to me."

Logan shook his head. "You are, as you Brits say, daft. No, actually you are *doubly* daft. Fall in love? With that nose-in-the-air hothouse flower? By God, I'm going to laugh myself into a seizure."

"So I'm sure you'd like to believe. Does that mean you'd be willing to up our wager to one hundred pounds?"

"Absolutely." Logan shook his head. "How is it that you're attending this party rather than occupying a cell in some insane asylum?"

"They let me out for the evening," Daniel said lightly.

Logan knew his smile didn't reach his eyes. "Let's make it two hundred pounds."

"Done. It's going to be a pleasure relieving you of such a princely sum."

"It's going to be a pleasure relieving *you* of that sum."

Daniel shook his head. "Never going to happen. I saw how

you looked at her. And how she looked at you." He chuckled. "Oh, this is going to be interesting. Good luck, my friend. I'll leave you to your pleasure. As for me, I'm going to make a list of things I plan to purchase with my upcoming two-hundred-pound windfall."

After giving Logan a hearty slap on the back, Daniel moved off.

Damn annoying Brit. Had he just been thinking he liked the man? And what had Daniel meant when he said he'd seen how Lady Emily had looked at him? Even as he told himself not to, Logan turned toward the terrace windows, his gaze seeking her out, and saw that she was no longer with the group. He quickly scanned the room and noted her heading toward the archway leading to the corridor. He watched her pause and look about, as if making sure she wasn't observed. Then she continued on, walking with such an innocent air Logan could almost see a halo hovering over her head.

But he'd *definitely* seen that mischievous glint in her eye.

She slipped through the archway into the corridor, and Logan's eyes narrowed. And that same question came back to haunt him.

What the hell is she up to?

He didn't know, but he intended to find out.

❦

Dressed in her cape, mask, and fangs, her fake blond curls falling to her collarbone, Emily stood in the shadows outside the terrace window and pulled in a calming breath. A burst of frosty wind cut through the voluminous folds of her black, hooded cape, and a few snow flurries blew by. She wasn't certain if her shiver was more from the cold or anticipation or apprehension. Even given her normally intrepid spirit, now that the moment was upon her, she couldn't help but worry. She simply could not fail. Too much was at stake—her entire family's reputation and financial future, as well as her own future happiness. Although there were risks involved, this was the right thing to do. The only thing to do.

She mentally ran through her plan once more then nodded. It would work. It had to. She would not fail. And by not failing, by this time next week, all her problems would be solved.

She reached into the pocket of her cape and withdrew a small glass vial filled with chicken blood she'd pinched from the kitchen that afternoon. However, when she tried to remove the cork stopper, it broke right at the rim of the vial. Fustian! She had no time for delays.

She tried to dig out the cork, and when that failed, tried to push it into the small bottle, but neither worked. She glanced up and noted Carolyn casting anxious glances toward the window. Realizing she had no more time to waste, she shoved the vial back in her pocket.

Time for her performance to begin. *Everything is going to go perfectly.*

With that mantra echoing through her mind, she moved closer to the terrace windows. Carolyn stood in the group of half a dozen chattering women Emily had brought together. She spied Lady Redmond, Lady Calvert, and Mrs. Norris, three of the ton's most notorious gossips, and inwardly nodded. As an added bonus, Lord Kaster stood with the group. Having a gentleman witness could only aid her. Excellent. All was in place.

When Carolyn's gaze wandered toward the windows, Emily stepped out of the shadows and into the pool of candlelight spilling onto the terrace from the drawing room.

As soon as she locked gazes with Carolyn, Emily pushed her hood farther back to reveal her blond curls and masked face, raised her arms, and bared her teeth. Through the glass she heard Carolyn's startled cry. Saw her eyes widen with shock and fright as she pointed toward the terrace.

The group with Carolyn turned, and in an instant pandemonium reigned. Emily heard screams and the unmistakable shout of *"Vampire!"* Ladies Redmond and Calvert's gazes were fastened on Emily's fangs, and their lips were moving so fast they appeared as blurs. Mrs. Norris's open mouth resembled a carp, as did Lord Kaster's. Two ladies standing nearby went down like tenpins, and a rush of people headed toward the windows.

Heart pounding with elation at her success, Emily drew her hood forward and swiftly retreated into the shadows. The instant she was clear of the pool of candlelight, she lifted her skirts and took off at a dead run back toward the library.

I did it! I did it! The words pounded through her brain as she ran. *I did—*

Oof. Something jerked her back, and she went down in a heap. Stunned, she shook her head and rose and tried to resume running, but she couldn't move forward. She looked back, and frustration rippled through her. Damnation! Her cape was caught in the prickly hedges. Gathering up handfuls of material, she gave a mighty yank, but that only served to dig the thorns in deeper.

Heart pounding so hard she could hear it in her ears, Emily yanked several more times, hoping the material would simply rip, but no such luck. She'd fashioned the cape of out heavy gabardine to ward off the cold, never thinking it would prove to be her nemesis. She gave one last desperate tug, but the material failed to yield. She could hear male voices shouting, and panic assailed her. They would be upon her any second.

Fear shook her fingers as she hastily unfastened the cape and shrugged out of the garment. It had no sooner fallen to the ground than she heard the terrace doors burst open and angry male voices spill into the night.

"—do you suppose it really was a vampire—"

". . . if so, it was a *female* vampire—"

"—we should give chase . . ."

"—better to call the authorities . . ."

". . . don't want to risk being bitten."

"—I say we get the fiend—"

Dear God. She continued her mad dash to the French windows leading to the library. Praying she wasn't observed, she entered the dimly lit room and closed the glass-paned panels behind her.

She'd no sooner moved in front of the heavy velvet draperies than she heard a male voice yelling, "A cloak! I've found the fiend's cloak." Several seconds passed, then the same male voice said, "There's something in the pocket . . . it's a glass vial of . . . my God, it looks like *blood*."

"She must have gone to the park," came another male voice. "Let's go!" Seconds later, she heard the pounding of feet, which then faded.

Holding her hand to her chest, she pulled in ragged breaths and closed her eyes. Good God, that was close. Too close. Terrifyingly close. All her perfectly thought-out plans had nearly gone awry. And her cloak was gone.

Filled with frustration and still shaking, she untied her mask and removed her fangs. Still, beneath her frustration, a bubble of elation brewed. While things hadn't gone precisely according to plan, at least she'd been seen. And seemingly believed to be a female vampire. Hopefully, the story would gather steam and spread like wildfire. And save her and her family.

Right now, however, she had to return to the party. She looked down at the wad of black silk, blond curls, and white fangs she held. Where to put them? She didn't dare open the window to dump them in the bushes lest she be caught or they found. Her gown had no pockets nor had she brought a reticule.

That left only one place. With a sigh, she wrapped the fangs in the mask then carefully tucked the small bundle into her bodice, nestling it between her breasts. She was peering down into the gap between her skin and her satin gown, making a minute adjustment so the pointy tooth didn't puncture her, when a deep, familiar voice sounded directly behind her.

"An interesting predicament you appear to be having, Lady Emily. May I offer my assistance?"

Chapter 6

We flew through the night together, above the trees, sur-rounded by stars and moonlight, and I'd never felt so free, not since before I'd entered this hellish, lonely exis-tence where everyone I loved eventually died, leaving me alone. I realized in that moment I would have to make him immortal. For in spite of all the things I could do, I couldn't live without him.

The Vampire Lady's Kiss *by Anonymous*

Emily gasped and pulled her fingers from her bodice as if her cleavage had burned her. She whirled around and met Logan Jennsen's glittering ebony regard. The whiff of sadness she fancied she'd seen when their gazes had met earlier in the drawing room was gone, replaced by a probing intensity that nailed her in place. Dressed in formal black attire and backlit only by the low-burning fire in the grate, he appeared dark and dangerous. He positively stole her breath—and not sim-ply because he'd startled her half to death.

Good God, how had he managed to sneak up on her like this again?

"Wh . . . what are you doing here?" she asked, instinctively stepping back, hoping he wouldn't notice the guilty flush she felt creeping up her neck. Her fingers brushed against the velvet drapes, and she clutched at the soft material.

"The same as you, I would guess."

I sincerely doubt it.

"You didn't answer my question," he said in a low, silky voice. His gaze dipped to her bodice, above which her chest rose and fell with her rapid breaths. She forced herself to slow her breathing so he wouldn't see how much he'd unnerved her. "Do you require some assistance?"

The thought of his fingers dipping into her bodice made her feel as if she stood in a ring of fire. In the next heartbeat, the thought of him discovering her mask and fangs effectively doused the fire.

She gathered her scattered wits and raised her chin. "Thank you, but no. I merely wished to find a quiet spot." She shot him a pointed look. "A quiet, *unoccupied* spot."

"As did I. Yet here you are." His gaze wandered upward, pausing on her mouth. When his eyes finally met hers, his seemed to breathe smoke. "And we once again find ourselves alone in a library."

Yes. And she knew where *that* could lead. To . . . *the most incredible moment of my life* . . . pure temptation. Which could lead directly to . . . *the most incredible moment of my life* . . . trouble.

"A mere coincidence," she said with a disdainful sniff. "I was suffering from the headache."

"Then it is fortunate you escaped the drawing room. Only moments ago pandemonium broke loose."

"Indeed? Nothing's amiss, I hope."

"Apparently several ladies saw an intruder of some sort outside on the terrace. They're claiming it was a vampire. A female vampire."

Emily widened her eyes. "Never say so! How fascinating."

His brows rose. "You're not frightened at the thought of a blood-sucking creature wandering about peering in windows?"

She hiked up her chin. "I'm not the coward you seem to think I am."

"I've never thought you were a coward. A nose-in-the-air hothouse flower, a great amount of trouble, and a pest, yes. A coward, no." Before she could inform him that *he* was the hugest amount of trouble and the biggest pest who'd ever breathed air, his gaze shifted to the French windows behind her. "They say this female vampire ran toward the park, which would mean she'd have had to pass by these windows. Did you see anyone?"

She inwardly smiled. Here was her perfect opportunity to provide more fodder for the vampire story. She assumed a thoughtful frown. "Actually, I did see a shadow, but dismissed it as nothing more than a guest wandering outdoors for a bit of air."

"Rather *frosty* outside for that, don't you think?"

"Some people enjoy the cold weather. Find it bracing." She offered him a sweet smile. "Clearly you're of a more delicate constitution."

There was nothing in the least bit delicate about the way he towered over her and the way his eyes narrowed. They swept over her in a manner that had her locking her knees to keep from squirming. When his gaze once again met hers, she had the uncomfortable feeling that he somehow knew exactly what she'd been doing. She felt as if the word *guilty* glowed from her skin.

"Did you see what this 'shadow' was wearing?" he asked.

She deepened her frown and pursed her lips. "A dark cloak, I think. Yes, now that I think upon it, I'm certain of it. I didn't give it any thought at the time . . ." She arranged her features in a look of stunned amazement. "Oh! Do you suppose it could have been . . . her? The female vampire?"

His gaze seemed to lance through her. "I suppose it's possible. Assuming there is such a thing as a vampire, female or otherwise."

"You don't think there is?"

"I've never given it any thought."

"Perhaps you should. Especially as there appears to be one flitting about." Her gaze dropped to the slice of skin showing above his collar, and she had to clutch the drapes tighter to keep from giving in to the overwhelming urge to touch him. "You wouldn't want to risk getting bitten."

He stepped closer, cutting off her breath. "I think that depends on who is doing the biting." He reached out and clasped her upper arms. His warm fingers pressed into her bare skin below her gown's cap sleeve, racing heat through her and sending her heart crashing against her ribs.

He went perfectly still. "You're cold."

She cocked a single brow. "Indeed? Well, you're uncouth and overbearing. And really very impolite. Tell me, are all Americans that way, or is it just you?"

"I meant temperature cold." His fingers flexed, and he studied her as if she were a specimen under a microscope. "Were you outside?"

Botheration. How he could possibly detect any trace of cold when her skin where he was touching her felt as if it were on fire she'd never know. Still, he was too clever and observant by half. Which meant she needed to be very careful. And distract him as quickly as possible.

She raised her chin to the regal tilt employed by generations of Stapleford women who were about to utter falsehoods. "Certainly not. I did, however, open the window briefly so as to get some fresh air."

"To relieve your headache."

"Exactly."

She was about to pull herself from his grasp, truly she was, but she found herself rooted to the spot when his gaze skimmed over her with a leisurely thoroughness she surely would have considered insulting if she didn't find it so irritatingly arousing.

When his eyes finally settled once again on hers, he said in a husky voice, "You appear quite cured."

Actually, she felt a bit unsteady. The way he was looking at her . . . so intently, wasn't helping the wobbly state of her knees in the least. She gave herself a mental slap. "Er, yes. The bracing air worked wonders."

"With the window open . . . you were fortunate not to have met up with the hideous vampire."

She blinked, then frowned. "*Hideous?* What makes you say hideous?" Humph. In spite of her plan going a bit awry with the vial of blood not opening and losing her cape, she'd made a rather dashing vampire, if she said so herself.

His brows hiked upward, no doubt at her umbrage-filled tone. "A long-fanged bloodsucker? How else would one describe such a creature?"

"I'll have you know I recently read a vampire story, and the creature was most attractive."

"Based on the screams from the ladies this evening, I fear tonight's vampire was of the hideous, rather than the attractive, sort." He released one of her arms and brushed a single fingertip down the side of her neck. "'Tis fortunate that you closed the window before the vampire caught sight of you. It would have been a dreadful shame for this perfect skin to be marred by a bite."

That featherlight caress stole the air from her lungs. Good Lord, his touch just felt so incredibly *good*. Even though she commanded herself to remain perfectly still, to her horror, she leaned into his hand.

His eyes seemed to catch fire at the slight movement, and she pulled in a quick breath. There was no mistaking the desire burning in those dark depths.

"Something wrong, Lady Emily?"

Emily licked her dust-dry lips, a gesture that shifted his attention to her mouth and kindled a deeper smoldering in his eyes. "Wrong?" Heavens, was that squeak her voice?

"Yes. You know, amiss." He took a step closer. Less than a foot separated their bodies, a space that was simultaneously much too little and far too much. "You seem . . . flustered."

Dear God, no doubt because she was. To the point where she could barely think. A situation made all the worse by the fact that he appeared so completely *un*flustered. Indeed, the aggravating man sounded *amused*.

"I'm fine. Perfectly fine."

He nodded solemnly. "Yes. You are. Perfectly fine." She might have accepted the huskily spoken words as a compliment, but he didn't look or sound particularly happy about saying them. Indeed, she thought he meant to release her, but instead he slowly lowered his head until his lips hovered next to her ear.

"Clearly the vampire didn't sense that you stood just beyond these windows, because this bit of skin"—he brushed his lips against her neck—"is simply too delicious to resist."

Oh, my. Emily's eyes slid closed. His warm breath coasting over her skin elicited a barrage of heated tingles that skittered outward, igniting her every nerve ending. He nuzzled her throat with his lips—those beautiful male lips—and instead of shoving him away as she should have, she tilted her head to give him better access.

A shudder of delight ran through her at the light scrape of his teeth against her skin, skin she hadn't known was so sensitive until his mouth had proven it to be so three months ago.

She shouldn't want this again, shouldn't allow herself to make the same mistake twice. But, God help her, she *did* want it again. With a desperation that simultaneously frightened her in its intensity and confused her, for she couldn't fathom why *this* man elicited such a passionate reaction in her. But regardless of any fright or confusion, she wanted this, if only to prove the pleasure she'd experienced at his hands three months ago had been real and not imagined.

Logan drew a deep breath, squeezed his eyes shut, and fought against the desire raging through him. Never in his life had he been near any woman who smelled this damn good. Sugar and flowers . . . it was a ridiculous combination, yet one that tempted him beyond anything he'd ever known. One that made him want to lay her down in a bed of rose petals then run his tongue over every inch of her.

Still, he might have been able resist her, except at that moment she wrapped her arms around his neck and stepped forward, erasing the few inches separating them. With that single touch it was as if a dam burst inside him, releasing a torrent of pent-up wants and needs that had been suppressed for far too long. Anything resembling sanity was swept away, and with a low growl, his arms went around her, crushing her to him.

Any thoughts he might have entertained over the past three months that he'd imagined how good she'd felt pressed against him vanished in a heartbeat. She fit against him as if a master sculptor had carved her just for him. Every lush curve molded against him, all that voluptuous female softness melting into his hardness.

He urged her closer, and through the fog of lust engulfing him, he heard her sigh of pleasure. With a growl he couldn't contain, he trailed his lips over the pale column of her throat, lingering over the spot where her pulse throbbed. By God, she felt so good. Tasted so good. He lightly sucked on her fragrant skin, the delicate floral sweetness filling him with a fierce craving for more. He dragged his mouth upward, nibbling and kissing the delicious skin beneath her jaw.

His lips finally met hers, and a low groan reached his ears.

Whether the noise rose from his throat or hers he couldn't tell and frankly didn't care. All that mattered was tasting more. Touching more. Breathing in more.

His tongue explored the velvety warmth of her mouth with a desperation he couldn't seem to control. She tasted exactly as she had three months ago. Like sweet, silken heat. Some small part of his brain attempted to tell him to slow down, show some finesse, but his body was beyond obeying. He felt as if he'd come home after a long, lonely, arduous journey.

He deepened the kiss, rediscovering all the delicious, seductive warmth he'd found three months ago, sinking farther into the bewitching spell she'd somehow weaved around him. His usual calm, clearheadedness gave way to a demanding reckless impatience he couldn't recall ever feeling before . . . except for the last time he'd kissed this woman.

Want more . . . need more . . .

The words pounded through him, a pulsing mantra he couldn't ignore. While his tongue continued to explore her mouth, he skimmed one hand down her back to cup the rounded curve of her buttocks and hauled her tighter against him. His erection nestled against her softness and, unable to stop himself, he slowly rubbed his arousal against her. Need jolted through him, crumbling to dust whatever small bit of his good intentions may have remained.

His other hand came forward to brush over her delicate collarbone and explore the shallow hollow of her throat where her pulse beat hard and fast. His fingers dipped lower, feathering over the satiny skin just above her bodice. He cupped her breast, and she arched her back, pressing her hard nipple into his palm.

Want more . . . need more . . . His fingers slipped beneath her bodice. Touched warm, soft skin and . . . something hard?

He pressed his fingers deeper. Yes, something hard.

What the hell?

Before he could think, she gasped, broke off their torrid kiss, planted her hands on his chest, and gave him a mighty shove that in his surprise pushed him back several feet.

"Wh . . . what in God's name are you doing?" she asked, pressing her hands to her chest.

Damned if he knew. One moment he'd been sane and in

complete control of his faculties. The next minute he'd looked into those sea goddess eyes, gotten a whiff of her skin, and taken leave of his senses.

Breathing hard, his gaze raked over her. Her breaths came out in short, shallow pants through her moist, parted lips. Her eyes were wide and fixed on him, and when he gazed into them, he felt as if he were drowning. She looked well kissed and slightly shocked, and he wanted nothing more than to yank her into his arms again.

She performed some sort of readjustment maneuver on her bodice, and his gaze narrowed on the smooth skin rising from the neckline of her gown. She had something nestled between her breasts. He knew women often tucked handkerchiefs there, but that wasn't a handkerchief he'd felt. And whatever it was, she hadn't wanted him to discover it. Once again that familiar Lady Emily–induced question flickered through his mind.

What the hell is she up to?

The way she was clutching her hands against her bodice would lead one to believe she harbored the crown jewels in her cleavage. He found himself curious and frustrated and suspicious. And aroused to the point of pain. And fiercely annoyed—mostly at himself for losing control in such an uncharacteristic manner.

What would have happened if she hadn't pushed him away? Oh, he could lie to himself, pretend he absolutely could have stopped kissing her, touching her, could have stepped away before things went any further, but in truth, he wasn't certain he could have.

An image flashed in his mind of her skirts pushed up to her waist and his head buried between her soft thighs . . . discovering if she tasted like sugar and flowers everywhere. His erection jerked, and he muttered a soft curse and raked his hands, which damn it, weren't quite steady, through his hair.

The way this woman affected him, tempted him beyond his control, unsettled him in a way that utterly confounded him. In a way he didn't like.

Just to make certain he didn't touch her again, he backed up several more paces and forced himself to focus on something other than her gorgeous eyes and kiss-swollen lips. Such as the fact that she was hiding something. He wanted nothing more than to confront her with the knowledge that there was more than her breasts—her lush, soft breasts that fit so perfectly in his hand—

Focus, man, focus. Right. Focus. More than her, um, womanly mounds of flesh hidden beneath her bodice, but he decided it was wiser to keep that information to himself. For now. Instead, he said, "I was kissing you."

She pushed a stray tendril of hair from her cheek and stared at him as if he were speaking a foreign language. "I beg your pardon?"

"You asked what I was doing. I was kissing you. And in case you didn't realize it, you were kissing me back."

Her mutinous expression made it patently obvious she wanted to deny it, but that would have been along the lines of denying grass was green. "I meant with your hand. It was . . ." She made a vague gesture toward her chest.

"Inside your bodice," he supplied helpfully when she seemed at a loss. "Touching your breast." *And whatever the hell else you have hidden in there.*

"Precisely. Do you know what that makes you?" she asked.

Damn lucky. "What does that make me?"

"A . . . a groper. And that is not *kissing.*"

"No, but I'm afraid that kissing leads to touching. And vice versa. Something you'd do well to remember."

She lowered her hands and planted them on her hips. "You say that as if the debacle that just happened between us was my fault."

Debacle? The word slapped him like a cold, wet rag, forcibly reminding him that she was precisely the sort of false society diamond he couldn't tolerate: all flash with no substance. "Not at all. I accept full blame for what happened between us. I shouldn't have touched you. In any manner." No, he shouldn't have. And he'd make damn certain he didn't again. As soon as he left this room. But for now, he stepped forward and lightly grasped her chin between his fingers.

"But if you won't be honest with me, at least don't lie to yourself, Lady Emily. You didn't think our kiss was a debacle when your body was pressed against mine, and your tongue was in my mouth."

She gasped, and he could see a scathing response brewing in her eyes. Before she could utter it, he released her then stepped back. "I suggest you return to the party. Now. Before anyone misses you, or you're discovered here with me."

For several seconds they simply stared at each other. She looked confused and bemused and irate and, to his profound annoyance, more appealing than any woman he'd ever seen. Arousal still lingered in her eyes, and to his further irritation, he had to clench his hands to keep from touching her. He really did need for her to leave now.

It appeared as if she wanted to say something, but instead she merely offered him a quick nod then headed swiftly for the door. Logan forced himself to keep looking toward the window and not turn around. Seconds later the door softly clicked closed, and he pulled in a long breath, one that unfortunately held the subtle remnants of flowers and sugar.

He squeezed his eyes shut and dragged his hands down his face. As much as he wanted to know what she was up to, he really needed to stay away from her. That was the smart thing to do. The intelligent thing to do. He was a smart, intelligent man. Not the sort of man to allow his suddenly unruly passions to govern him.

But then he recalled the bleak desolation he'd seen in her eyes earlier and realized he wanted to know more than simply what mischief she was up to. For reasons he was at a loss to explain, she inspired a protective instinct in him that he'd successfully buried years ago. One he had no desire to resurrect.

Yes, he needed to stay away from her. *Far* away.

How the hell difficult could that be? He could do that. Easily. Absolutely. No problem at all. Starting right now. He would rejoin the party and seek out that lovely woman he'd been about to approach.

Yes, that's precisely what he'd do.

As soon as he recalled that other woman's name.

❧

"There you are," Carolyn whispered. "I was getting worried." She pulled Emily toward the nearest corner of the drawing room. Feeling more than a little dazed, Emily merely followed.

"Your plan worked perfectly," Carolyn said in an undertone once they were situated behind a group of potted palms.

"The vampire sighting is on everyone's lips. Lord Teller sent for the authorities and said he plans to contact Bow Street as well. Several ladies swooned and . . ." Her voice trailed off, and she frowned. "Emily, are you all right?"

Honestly, she didn't know. Her encounter with Logan Jennsen had left her reeling to the point that she'd quite forgotten about her vampire masquerade. She swallowed and gave Carolyn what she hoped was an encouraging smile.

"I'm fine, and delighted everyone is talking about the vampiress. You gave a marvelous performance."

"It wasn't difficult. You looked very frightening."

"Unfortunately, I fear all didn't go as planned." She quickly related the problems with the vial of blood and her cape. "I barely made it through the library windows without being discovered."

"Thank goodness you weren't caught. I think that's proof enough that this is a dangerous enterprise. You need to give thanks that it went as well as it did and abandon any thoughts of doing it again."

Emily shook her head. "I must do it once more. This sighting just whetted the appetite. The next one will make everyone ravenous. And except for that tiny glitch with the cape and the blood vial, everything went perfectly according to plan." Well, except for that and Logan's nearly discovering her—and what she'd hidden in her bodice.

Carolyn shook her head. "I really don't think—" Her words chopped off and she leaned closer to Emily, her gaze fixed on her neck. "What is that?"

Emily feathered her fingers over her throat. "What?"

"There's a mark on your neck." Carolyn reached out and rubbed Emily's skin with her gloved finger. "I thought it might be a smudge of dirt from your escapade, but it's not coming off."

Emily froze. A memory of warm, marauding lips exploring her neck slammed into her, engulfing her in a wave of heat. She gave a laugh that sounded far more nervous than she would have liked then covered her neck with her hand. "Must be stubborn dirt. I'll make certain to wash thoroughly before I retire."

Carolyn's expression mirrored the one Emily's mother favored her with when she'd caught her eldest child in a Banbury tale. "That isn't dirt," Carolyn said in a hissing whisper.

She grabbed Emily's arm and dragged her farther into the shadowed corner. "I know a kiss mark when I see one, and it wasn't there when we spoke earlier."

Emily winced at the thought of her mother or Aunt Agatha seeing the mark. "Is it very noticeable?"

"No. It's faint and will be gone by morning. The question is, how did you get it? And who gave it to you?"

"That's two questions." Emily ran her fingers over her neck and forced away the arousing memory of Mr. Jennsen's sensual mouth lightly sucking on her skin. "Would you believe it's a vampire bite?"

The look on Carolyn's face made it patently clear she would not nor that she'd allow the subject to drop. Trying her best not to blush, Emily finally said, "While I was in the library, well, I wasn't alone the entire time. No sooner had I hidden my mask and fangs in my bodice than . . ." She cleared her throat. "Mr. Jennsen entered the room." At least she prayed that was the series of events. Was it possible he'd seen her tucking the items into her bodice? Suspicion filled her. He hadn't wasted much time trying to insinuate his hand down there. His large, warm hand with those long, clever fingers—

She broke off the errant thought when Carolyn's eyes goggled. "Are you telling me that *he's* the one who kissed you?"

"Yes."

"Logan Jennsen."

"Correct."

"With your permission?"

Emily chewed on her bottom lip. "He didn't ask for permission."

"Did you try to stop him?"

"Um, no."

Understanding, along with a hint of amusement dawned in Carolyn's eyes. "Nor, I take it, did you want him to stop."

"Um, no." At least not until she stood in danger of him discovering the mask and fangs in her bodice. And even then it taken all her will to push him away. But she couldn't bring herself to share that information with Carolyn. It was too . . . private. Too intimate. Too mortifying.

"Well, this is an unexpected turn of events."

"I agree. The man is odious and uncouth."

Carolyn raised her brows. "So you've always said—an assessment I disagree with, by the way. But that mark on your neck indicates you've changed your mind."

"No. It merely means that I think he's a passable kisser."

Carolyn folded her arms. "*Passable?*"

"Oh, all right, excellent," she said, unable to hide her irritation, although precisely what she was irritated at, she didn't know. No doubt Logan Jennsen. Yes, he was why she felt so unsettled and ruffled. When Carolyn seemed to be waiting for more, she added in a hiss, "*Extremely* excellent. As you well know."

Carolyn studied her for several seconds. "Does that upset you?"

Yes. The word rushed into Emily's throat, and she clamped her lips shut to contain it. Since she didn't want to lie to her friend, she told her the absolute truth. "I don't know. I'm very confused. I don't understand *why* I allowed him to kiss me. Or why he'd want to. We don't like each other. He thinks I'm a troublesome, useless hothouse flower, and I think he's the most dreadful pest."

"I think you must like each other more than you realize. Clearly there's a physical attraction between you." Carolyn's expression turned to one of concern, and she reached out to clasp Emily's hands. "But you must be careful. If you'd been discovered together, the scandal would have ruined you."

"I know," Emily said in a miserable voice. "But I'm afraid I wasn't thinking of that at the time. Good Lord, here I am, masquerading as a vampire to save myself and my family from financial ruin, yet I placed myself in a position to suffer an even worse social fate. And with a man I don't even *like.* What is *wrong* with me?"

"Perhaps you like him more than you believe."

"But I don't like him *at all*," Emily wailed in an undertone.

To her astonishment, Carolyn laughed, and in spite of her misery, Emily was deeply grateful for whatever she'd done to make her smile. She almost looked like her usual self. "Darling, clearly *at all* is no longer true."

"But it is. I find him irritating and insufferable. It's inexplicable that he's such a good kisser."

"No doubt he's had a great deal of practice."

No doubt. And that knotted Emily's stomach in a manner she refused to examine too closely.

Carolyn's gaze shifted over Emily's shoulder. "Well, so long as you're certain you think he's foul—"

"Oh, I definitely do—"

"Then you won't mind that he seems quite taken with Lady Hombly."

Emily blinked. Then frowned. Then turned to see what Carolyn was looking at. And froze. At the sight of the gorgeous Lady Hombly staring up at Mr. Jennsen as if he were the most fascinating man on earth. He in turn was listening to whatever the gorgeous widow was saying with the rapt attention a jewel thief would bestow upon a cache of diamonds. He leaned closer, and gorgeous Lady Hombly whispered something to him that made him laugh. Mr. Jennsen did indeed seem very taken with her, a fact that twisted Emily's insides with a most unpleasant sensation and filled her with a sudden urge to slap Lady Hombly's gorgeous face.

"Of course I don't mind," she said, returning her attention to Carolyn, proud of how breezy her voice sounded. "She is welcome to him."

And she was. Emily certainly had more important things to worry about than who Mr. Jennsen might be kissing next. Why, she had a cape to make and another vial of blood to gather and a vampire sighting to plan—all before her next masquerade two nights from now. Because her next vampire adventure would go off without any mistakes.

And without any further interaction with the uncouth, irritating, and *fickle* Mr. Logan Jennsen.

Chapter 7

❦

I could only be with him in darkness. It was with great reluctance that I left him as the dawn approached, hating that we would be apart until the day gave way to night. Hating that a mere mortal woman could touch him in the sunlight, walk with him in the park, be a part of his everyday existence—a daytime life that would never, could never include me.

The Vampire Lady's Kiss *by Anonymous*

Logan walked along the winding gravel path in Hyde Park and wondered for what had to be the dozenth time in the past hour what the devil was wrong with him. He had every reason in the world to be to happy. The weather was exceptionally fine, the early afternoon sun bright in a deep blue sky, the winter air invigorating and crisp rather than biting. He had a gorgeous woman in the form of Lady Hombly accompanying him on this walk through the park, her slender arm linked through his. Given the way Celeste kept brushing her ample bosom against his biceps and the heated glances she'd been tossing his way, her interest in sharing more than a walk with him was unmistakable. She was flirtatious, complimentary, attentive, and clearly experienced in lighthearted affairs. Indeed, he didn't doubt that given a private setting, he could seduce her in a thrice. Yes, he had every reason to be happy.

So why the hell wasn't he?

The sense of menace, of being watched, that he'd recently felt was absent at the moment, although his instincts cautioned him to remain alert, that this lull might merely be the calm before the storm. Still, all was quiet now. So why, instead of enjoying himself and Celeste's company, was he plagued by this irritating feeling of discontent? Why, rather than being flattered by the stunning Celeste's attentions—as any man with a pulse would be, especially a man who hadn't had a woman in months—was he finding her so . . . uninteresting? So . . . unappealing?

Damn it, she was perfect, exactly what he needed: a beautiful, warm, willing woman with whom to engage in a short-term liaison to slake his urges. Unlike many women of her class, she was even capable of discussing topics other than fashion and the weather. And here she was, looking at him with an expression that suggested he was a strawberry ice, and she harbored a craving for sweets.

Without a doubt he could have had her last night, yet something had stopped him. Something he was at a loss to explain. His body craved release, but rather than seek it with her, he'd gone home alone. Desperate to clear his mind and relax, he'd ordered a hot bath, but as soon as he submerged his body in the water and closed his eyes, the images he'd fought to hold at bay had inundated him.

Of *her*. The woman he desperately wanted to forget. Was *determined* to forget.

His fevered imagination, further fired by the passionate kiss they'd shared in Lord Teller's library, had envisioned her extraordinary eyes gleaming with mischief and arousal, her lush lips that felt so damn delicious beneath his.

And in a heartbeat, rather than soothe him, reclining in the heated water had only inspired fantasies. He'd imagined her joining him in the tub. Touching him. Straddling him. Her breasts filling his palms, his tongue laving her nipples. Her wet body sliding over his . . . taking him into his silky, tight heat . . .

With his arousal bordering on pain, he'd been unable to

stop himself from stroking his hard length, imagining it was her soapy hands bringing him pleasure, her fingers gliding over him. His climax had thundered through him, ripping her name from his throat in a harsh rasp.

His release had temporarily satisfied him physically, but ultimately it left him feeling empty. Unfulfilled. And more lonely than ever. He'd tossed and turned in his bed for the rest of the night, unable to erase her or his erotic fantasies of her from his mind, disturbed that in spite of his best efforts to envision someone—*anyone*—other than her, she filled every corner of his mind.

Damn it all to hell and back.

He drew in a sharp breath, and would have sworn that even now he could smell her alluring scent. God knows, her taste still lingered on his tongue.

"Was it something I said?"

The throaty feminine voice jerked him from his unsettling thoughts, and he turned toward Celeste. She was gazing up at him with a combination of amusement, exasperation, and curiosity. She clearly expected some sort of reply from him. Damn it, he actually felt a flush heat his face. He cleared his throat then said, "I beg your pardon?"

"I was wondering if it was something I said that resulted in that ferocious frown you're sporting."

Inwardly cursing himself, Logan instantly smoothed out his features. He'd called upon her an hour ago, determined to take her up on the invitation her eyes and demeanor had issued last night. Yet, once inside her home, he found himself incomprehensibly unwilling to seduce her. No, instead he found himself suggesting they take a walk in the park. And now here he was, once again thinking about *her*. And apparently frowning.

"It's nothing you said," he assured her. Especially since he had no idea what she'd said. "Forgive me. I'm afraid I was preoccupied. What were you saying?"

He forced himself to focus his attention on her, and they passed the next several minutes discussing a play they'd both attended several weeks earlier. Yet, in spite of her engaging, amusing conversation and the admiring warmth glowing from her eyes, he wasn't engaged or amused, and once again his mind drifted to *her.* To her lips . . . that soft, plush mouth that had opened so willingly beneath his. Her lips that curved so readily into that impish, alluring smile—for everyone save him. Lips he was inexplicably determined to have smile at him like that.

And then, as if his thoughts had somehow conjured her up, they rounded a corner in the path, and there she was. His footsteps stuttered, and he blinked to make certain she wasn't merely a figment of his overwrought imagination. But no, it was definitely Lady Emily, standing about twenty yards away among a group of people. And her lips were curved in that impish, alluring smile. But it wasn't directed at him. No, instead it was aimed at the tall young man standing beside her. A young man Logan didn't recognize, who laughed at whatever she said, then reached out his hand to lightly chuck her under the chin.

Logan's jaw clenched at the familiarity of the gesture. Clearly Lady Emily and her escort were well acquainted, a fact that was made even clearer when she reached up and teasingly tugged the brim of his hat down, lowering it over his eyes. The young man shouted a protest and made a playful grab for her, but with a merry laugh she adroitly sidestepped out of his reach.

"Ah, Lord and Lady Fenstraw and their brood," Celeste murmured, slowing their progress and nodding toward the group. "You're acquainted with them, are you not?"

Brood? Logan studied the group for several seconds, and the tension that had gripped him suddenly relaxed. Based on the resemblance, there was no doubt the young man Lady Emily had been smiling at was one of her brothers. There were also four other children of various ages—obviously Lady Emily's other siblings—as well as her parents and a handsome elderly woman Logan recognized as her aunt Agatha, whom he'd met on several occasions and who often served as her chaperone. The group was rounded out by an enormous dog and a trio of puppies' whose leads appeared hopelessly tangled.

He'd known Lady Emily was the oldest of a number of children, but he'd never met the younger members of the family. He performed a quick head count and inwardly shook his head. Six children. And four dogs. Good God, how did they keep track of them all?

"I've met Lady Emily, her parents, and her aunt," he replied, "but none of the other children."

"As it appears we can't avoid them, it seems you're about to."

Her tone had him glancing down at her. "It sounds as if you'd prefer to avoid them."

She gave a small shrug. "In truth, I would."

"You don't like them?"

"It's not that, it's just that there are rumors flying about that the family is facing some dire financial problems."

"You think they mean to rob us of our money?" he suggested in an undertone with a perfectly straight face.

She gave a quick laugh and pressed her breast against his arm, a gesture he dearly wished ignited some spark in him, but one that unfortunately left him cold. "Of course not. It's just . . ." her voice trailed off, and again she shrugged. "Well, you know how it is."

His jaw tightened. Yes. He did. Very well. He knew how the upper class liked to consort only with their own kind. And how easily they would cast aside anyone who fell from their lofty ranks, either financially or socially or both. He knew damn well that if it weren't for the fact that he was obscenely wealthy, this titled woman clinging to his arm wouldn't toss water on his untitled self, even if he were on fire.

"Of course, I don't know if the rumors are true," Celeste continued in an undertone, "and even if they are, Lady Emily will most certainly come to the rescue by making a brilliant marriage to a wealthy man who will refill the family coffers. 'Tis high time she married anyway. I've heard whispers that the earl is entertaining a number of offers for her."

Logan's insides seemed to curdle, and his gaze fastened on Lady Emily. She wore a dark blue velvet pelisse and matching bonnet, garments he suspected would highlight her extraordinary eyes. Dark curls shot with red framed her face, and even at a distance he could see her cheeks bore a becoming splash of color courtesy of the invigorating air. At the moment she was crouching down to talk on eye level with a boy Logan guessed was the youngest of the family, who held the lead of the tremendous brown dog, a beast that was nearly the same size as the boy. He watched her smile at the lad, then tweak his nose and give his chestnut locks that matched her own an affectionate ruffle. It was easy to imagine that based on her looks alone men would be lined up outside the earl's town house to seek her hand.

She straightened and, as if feeling the weight of his regard, turned toward him. Their gazes met, and she stilled. For the space of a single heartbeat her smile remained, and for Logan, everything—the crowd of chattering people and rambunctious animals surrounding her, the woman holding his arm—faded away. Except her.

Then her smile disappeared like a snuffed-out candle, and another layer of color washed over her cheeks. Her gaze shifted to Celeste, who still clung to his arm in a manner that was beginning to make him feel as if he were a brick wall and she an acre of ivy. Her eyes widened slightly, and she lifted her chin in that haughty way that simultaneously annoyed and amused him.

"Good afternoon," Logan said, approaching the group. He greeted Lord Fenstraw by touching the brim of his hat, then made a formal bow to the ladies. "Lady Fenstraw, Lady Agatha, Lady Emily."

Logan nearly laughed at the varied reactions the sight of him caused. Lord Fenstraw's countenance paled several shades, as if he feared Logan planned to demand payment for the funds owed him right here in the park. After an initial few seconds of consternation, Lady Fenstraw's expression turned speculative, as if she was calculating how much he was worth. Lady Agatha offered him a dimpled smile and, as was her habit whenever they met, she leaned toward him and spoke in an overly loud voice.

"Good afternoon, Mr. Jennsen," Lady Agatha shouted. Logan couldn't decide if she spoke to him in such a manner because she herself was hard of hearing, or if because she thought he was. Or perhaps she believed, as he was a colonial, that he didn't speak English.

And last but not least, Lady Emily looked as if she'd bitten into a lemon.

"I believe you're all acquainted with Lady Hombly?" he said.

Celeste exchanged greetings with Lady Emily and her family, and Logan noted that the look Lady Fenstraw bestowed upon Celeste indicated she was damn near bursting with curiosity about the nature of the widow's relationship with Logan. As if to prove it, she said, "Yes, of course we know Lady Hombly, but I wasn't aware that *you* knew her, Mr. Jennsen. Imagine, meeting up with you while we're taking a family constitutional and enjoying this unusual but glorious weather. Allow me to introduce my younger children."

Logan found himself shaking hands with Kenneth, Viscount Exeter, the tall young man whose hat Emily had lowered. Logan judged him to be about sixteen, and he greeted Logan with a friendly smile. He was followed by William and Percy, both of whom were lanky and possessed the somewhat awkward air of boys hovering on the cusp of manhood. Both boys had the same eyes as Emily, complete with mischievous glint. Next came Mary, whose hair bow was askew, no doubt from her none-too-successful efforts to control the trio of prancing, yipping puppies and untangle the leads she held.

Finally was Arthur who, after offering Celeste a bow and shaking Logan's proffered hand, pushed up his spectacles then nodded toward his enormous dog. "This is Tiny."

Logan couldn't help but laugh. "I believe she's bigger than you."

Arthur grinned, revealing a gap where he'd lost a front tooth. "She is *now*, but when Emily gave her to me, she was tiny. I've taught her how to shake hands. I'll show you." He turned to the dog and said, "Shake, Tiny."

Tiny instantly raised a dinner plate–sized paw and slapped it on the front of Celeste's dove gray pelisse. She gave a startled cry and stepped back. Tiny's paw slid down the length of the garment, leaving a long streak of black dirt in its wake.

"I'm awfully sorry," said Arthur, flushing to the roots of his hair. "I guess she hasn't quite gotten the hang of it yet. Would you like my handkerchief?" He produced a square of linen from his pocket that looked as if it had already been used to wipe off several Tiny paw prints. Tiny gave a single loud, deep woof, then planted her bottom on the ground and licked her chops.

"That means she's sorry," Arthur said, still holding out his handkerchief.

Celeste's horrified gaze moved from her stained pelisse to Tiny. The look she sizzled on the dog was surely meant to relegate her directly to the doggie afterlife. The look she cast at Arthur's handkerchief, then at the lad himself wasn't much warmer. Logan didn't think he'd ever seen any woman look quite so seriously displeased as Celeste. Or any young boy look quite so abashed. Emily moved to stand next to him and settled her hand on his shoulder. Logan noticed her give the lad a comforting squeeze.

"Oh, dear," said Lady Fenstraw, moving toward Celeste. She shot her son a frown. "Clearly Tiny requires more lessons, Arthur."

Arthur looked at the ground and scuffed the toe of his boot against the gravel. Even Tiny looked mournful. "Yes, Mother."

Lady Fenstraw turned back to Celeste, who looked as if she were chewing on glass. "Your lovely pelisse is a *disaster*. It will need to be cleaned immediately lest the stain set. And of course you cannot be seen about with your garment in such a deplorable condition. What a shame! Where is your carriage?"

"We came in my carriage," Logan said. "It's on the far side of the park." He turned to Celeste. "I'll escort you back—"

"Nonsense," Lady Fenstraw interrupted. "Our town house is much closer, barely a five-minute walk." She commandeered Celeste's arm. "My abigail Liza is a veritable wizard with stains. We can enjoy a nice cup of tea while we wait, then our carriage can take you home."

"I can escort Lady Hombly—" Logan began, as he felt obligated to see her safely home, but his offer was cut off by Lady Fenstraw.

"On the contrary, I'm certain Lady Hombly wouldn't want to deprive you of your walk and the enjoyment of this unseasonably lovely weather," Lady Fenstraw insisted. "We'll suffer through months of dreary rain and biting cold before we see another day like this."

Celeste turned to him and said, "Lady Fenstraw is right. No need for *your* outing to be ruined as well." She shot Arthur and Tiny another killing glance. "Although I hate to cut our afternoon short, I can't bear for this pelisse to be ruined. Do you mind terribly if I leave?"

"Of course not," he said. Surely it was disappointment he felt rather than relief.

She offered him a smile, then leaned closer and said in an undertone only he could hear, "I'll be home this evening."

Lady Fenstaw adjusted her bonnet then said, "Fenstraw, please accompany us home. Agatha, you stay with Emily, the children, and Mr. Jennsen." She smiled at Logan, then deftly propelled Celeste down the path, with the earl following in their wake.

Several seconds of silence followed their departure, and Logan couldn't shake the feeling that somehow they were all pawns in a chess game in which Lady Fenstraw had just maneuvered the pieces to her advantage. As for the outcome, while he harbored no regrets that Celeste had departed, he certainly wasn't pleased to find himself in Lady Emily's company. Damn it, how could he hope to forget her when he kept running into her? And based on her puckered expression, she wasn't any happier at the prospect of spending time with him.

Kenneth broke the silence by offering his aunt Agatha his arm and suggesting they resume their stroll. William and Percy began to playfully push and swat at each other as they made their way down the path behind their brother and aunt. Logan watched Emily, who without heed to the rough gravel, knelt down in front of Arthur and framed his bespectacled face between her hands. There was no missing the love and compassion in her eyes. Logan saw the lad blinking back tears, and his heart went out to him. He recalled all too well being that age and determined not to cry. He quickly looked away, knowing the boy would be even more embarrassed if he suspected his tears were noticed.

His gaze fell upon Mary, who was still attempting to untangle her energetic puppies' leads. Feeling the need to do something besides stand about, he walked toward her. "May I offer some assistance?"

Mary laughed and smiled up at him, and Logan found himself charmed by this sprite who looked like a younger version of her older sister. "Actually, yes," she said. "If you could hold Romeo, I'll try to free Juliet and Ophelia."

In the blink of an eye Logan found himself holding a wriggling, tail-wagging pup who was clearly determined to lick something. Anything. Pulling the squirming ball of fluff to his chest, he crouched down, hoping to help, but instead was instantly set upon by the other two small dogs who were even more determined than Romeo to find something to lick.

"Perfect," Mary said, crouching beside him as Romeo tried his best to wet Logan's chin while the other two tried to climb onto his knees. "If you'll just keep them occupied like that for a moment, Mr. Jennsen, I'll be able to untangle the leads."

Logan leaned back and looked down at Romeo, who promptly gave his chin a swipe of pink tongue. "Romeo, are you?" He cleared his throat then quoted, " 'But soft! What light through yonder window breaks?' "

Mary glanced up from her task. "You enjoy Shakespeare, Mr. Jennsen?"

"I do. And I'm guessing by your dogs' names that you do, too."

"Very much." She lowered her voice to a conspiratorial whisper. "Of course, I haven't told them the tragic ends suffered by those they're named after."

"Good idea," Logan whispered back. "Best to just inform them they're named for literary masterpieces."

Like her sister, she smiled readily. Unlike her sister, she smiled readily at him. "My thought precisely. And even though those characters met tragic ends, those names are better than the ones Mother suggested."

"Oh? What did she suggest?"

"Barker, Whiner, and . . ." She leaned a bit closer. "Piddler."

Logan had to struggle to keep a straight face. "I believe you made the right choice with Romeo, Juliet, and Ophelia."

"Of course I did. Especially since they can't help it if they bark, whine, and piddle. That's what puppies are *supposed* to do." She made a triumphant sound. "Finally untangled." She scooped up a pup under each arm then rose. Logan, with Romeo tucked in the crook of his elbow, did the same.

"You're very naughty," Mary scolded the dogs. "And very fortunate you're so cute." She nodded toward Tiny. "She's their mama, you know."

Logan scratched Romeo behind the ears and smiled when the panting dog gazed up at him with adoring eyes. "I can see the resemblance."

"Mother says they'll have to be sent to the country soon. She said she can't possibly tolerate four dogs the size of Tiny in London, although Kenneth insists the puppies won't grow as large as Tiny because their father is a small dog." She looked up at Logan with a puzzled frown. "I don't see how that makes a difference, do you?"

All of Logan's instincts warned him that this was a topic he should avoid as one would a bad rash. "Er, I couldn't say. I suppose only time will tell."

"All untangled?" came Lady Emily's voice from behind him.

Filled with relief at the interruption, Logan turned. Lady Emily and Arthur, led by Tiny, approached. One look at the boy's face made it clear he hadn't been entirely successful in holding back his tears. Something seemed to shift inside Logan's chest for this young boy who'd tried so valiantly not to cry, and he offered them a smile.

"Here you are, Emily," Mary said, handing her a puppy. "You look left out, being the only one without a dog."

Emily snuggled the ball of fluff to her face and laughed when she received a doggie kiss on her nose. "You are a wet kisser, Ophelia," she murmured.

"That's *Juliet*," Mary said. She set Ophelia down, and the puppy immediately began pulling on the lead. Mary set off at a brisk trot, quickly catching up to her leisurely strolling aunt and brothers.

Logan reached out his free hand and patted Tiny's enormous head. "I've met your babies," he said to the dog, "and very high-spirited, fine children they are, madam."

Tiny clearly agreed. Tail wagging, she gave Romeo a loving sniff then gifted Logan's glove with a couple of licks. His glance flicked to Arthur. Noting that the boy still appeared somewhat forlorn, Logan looked into Tiny's soulful brown eyes and said, "Shake, Tiny."

Tiny instantly offered a massive paw to him, one that Logan easily caught and to which he gave two quick pumps. After releasing the paw he scratched behind the dog's ears, much to her obvious delight.

"Good girl," he murmured. "Clearly it is Lady Hombly who doesn't know how to shake properly." He turned to Arthur and offered the boy a conspiratorial wink. He felt the weight of a stare and turned toward Lady Emily. She was regarding him with an odd expression he couldn't decipher.

Arthur sniffled, recalling his attention. The boy jerked his head in a nod. "You need to put out your hand to catch her paw for it to work, like you did," he said to Logan. "*Everybody* knows that."

Logan nodded. "Yes, but . . ." He leaned down to whisper in the lad's ear, "You know how *girls* can sometimes be." He straightened and made an exaggerated eye roll.

Arthur sniffled again then laughed. After performing an exaggerated eye roll of his own, he whispered back, "Oh, yes, sir, believe me, I know."

"I heard that," Lady Emily said in an arid tone.

"Oh, except for you," Arthur said, giving her arm a brotherly pat. "You're not like other girls."

Emily pursed her lips, tapped her chin, and narrowed her eyes at her brother. "Hmmm. I'm not certain whether I've just been complimented or insulted."

"Aw, I meant it in a good way, Emmie. You know that."

Her bright smile rivaled the sun. "Excellent." She set Juliet on the ground. "I suggest we walk before we lose sight of the others."

Logan set down Romeo, and the three of them struck out on the gravel path, with Arthur in the middle, all being tugged along by their respective canines.

"Do you have any sisters, Mr. Jennsen?" Arthur asked.

"No. No brothers, either." He smiled down at the boy. "There are no more at home like me."

Lady Emily muttered something that sounded suspiciously like, *For which we can all be grateful.*

Romeo paused to sniff at a tuft of grass, and Tiny followed suit. Juliet, however, was clearly in the mood for a run and continued to pull Lady Emily along. After Logan deemed her out of earshot, curiosity compelled him to ask Arthur, "How is your sister not like other girls?"

Arthur scrunched up his face for several seconds, clearly giving the question deep thought. "Well, most ladies, like Lady Hombly, my mum, and my aunt Agatha, don't like dirt. Always complaining about it, they are, even Mary sometimes if she's wearing a favorite dress. But dirt doesn't bother Emmie. She likes to make mud pies and crawl around in the dusty eaves at our country house and paint with her fingers."

He pondered another couple of seconds then added, "She doesn't mind bugs, either. She always helps me catch fireflies in the summer. She can bait a hook even better than Percy, capture more frogs than Will, *almost* catch more fish than Kenneth, and net more butterflies than Mary. Emmie's good at *everything*."

They started walking again, and Logan digested this surprising information. Mud pies? Catching frogs? Fireflies? Baiting a hook? That didn't sound like a haughty, nose-in-the-air hothouse flower. Perhaps he'd misunderstood.

"Your sister really does all those things?"

"Yes."

"Your sister *Emily*."

"Yes. You sound surprised, sir."

"I suppose because I am." Thunderstruck, actually.

Arthur nodded. "It's because she's beautiful. Mother says beautiful women aren't supposed to get dirty—ever. I guess that's why Emmie likes to walk in the rain and swim in the lake—to wash off the dirt she gets doing all those other things."

An image of Lady Emily, rising from the lake after a swim, water sluicing down her form, rose unbidden in his mind, and he quickly shoved it aside. Damn it, the last thing he wanted to do was think of her being all wet.

"Emmie's lots of fun," Arthur continued. "And she doesn't get angry the way some girls do. Like when I teat squirted her."

Logan blinked, then frowned. "I beg your pardon?"

"Teat squirt. You know, with a cow's teat. We have four jerseys at our country house. Got Emmie right in the eye just last week." Arthur gave a guffaw and slapped his knee. "You should have seen her face! Milk hanging on her eyelashes and dripping right off her nose."

Logan's gaze fastened on Lady Emily's back ahead of them and tried to reconcile the perfectly dressed woman with the perfect posture with this hoyden Arthur was describing. "How did she respond to this, er, teat squirt?"

Arthur grinned, displaying the empty space where another

tooth would soon grow. "Teat squirted me right back. Never seen a girl with such aim. Mary can't hit the side of the stable with a handful of rocks."

"What about your brothers?"

"They have good aim, but Will and Percy are mostly away at school now, and all Kenneth wants to talk about is going on his grand tour."

Logan looked ahead at the tall young man walking beside his aunt, and the two younger boisterous boys dashing around them. Grand tours and schooling were expensive. Given Lord Fenstraw's massive debts, he didn't see how a grand tour could be financed. Or more years of schooling, not only for Percy and William, but for Arthur as well. And Mary would require a governess. Plus all the other expenses involved with keeping a household filled with six children. An unexpected sense of guilt pricked Logan, followed instantly by a whisper of *That is neither your problem nor your responsibility.*

Precisely. Fenstraw should have thought about providing for his family before he made reckless investments and gambled away his fortune.

A feminine laugh pulled his attention away from the boys. Up ahead Lady Emily and Mary were giggling at the puppies' antics. He watched Lady Emily give her sister a quick hug, and his heart seemed to roll over. Such open, loving affection was foreign to him. God knows he'd never experienced it. From a distance he'd observed Lady Emily lavish such affection upon her friends Sarah, Carolyn, and Julianne, but something about seeing her with her family, watching her interact with them, the protective, loving kindness she'd bestowed on Arthur, was showing him a side of her he hadn't considered or suspected existed.

And based on what Arthur had told him, he now knew some of the things that that mischievous glint in her eye hinted at. What other mischief besides catching frogs and lake swimming and teat squirting—and kissing men in libraries—was the surprising Lady Emily capable of?

He didn't know, but he suddenly found himself wanting to know more. Much more. Right now.

He turned to Arthur and smiled. "Let's catch up with your sisters."

Chapter 8

I approached him slowly, fangs bared, my hunger for him so intense it bordered on pain, my need beyond anything I'd ever before felt. Never in all the centuries I'd wandered the earth had I ever wanted anything more than I wanted him.

The Vampire Lady's Kiss *by Anonymous*

"I understand from Arthur that you're something of a champion frog catcher."

Emily forced herself to keep looking straight ahead and not turn toward Mr. Jennsen. From the corner of her eye she'd noted him and Romeo fall in step beside her and Juliet. Her heart had jumped in the most ridiculous and annoying fashion, and she'd determined to ignore him, if for no other reason than to prove to herself that she was capable of doing so.

Of course, even when she hadn't been able to see him from the corner of her eye she'd been painfully aware of him and had been horrified to realize she'd put a bit of extra sway in her step, knowing he walked behind her.

Botheration. *Why* was it so difficult to remember she didn't like this man? That because of the enormous debt her father owed him he could swiftly and single-handedly bring about her family's financial ruination, regardless of whatever other debts were outstanding? That he was nothing more than a coldhearted businessman who only cared about increasing his own wealth, without consideration of who was hurt in the process? That he was an uncouth colonial?

She knew all that, yet somehow, whenever she was near him, something happened to her, something that made her forget all those things and simply made her want . . . things no proper young woman should want. And certainly not with *him*.

She flicked her gaze around and noted that Mary and Arthur, pulled along at a brisk pace by Tiny and Ophelia, were far enough ahead to give her and Mr. Jennsen a modicum of privacy. Which she didn't want. Not at all. Why, on top of everything else, the man was nothing more than a rake, what with showing up at the park with Lady Hombly on his arm. Humph. Clearly they'd hit it off famously last night, and not moments after he'd kissed *her* in the library, the fickle swine.

Yet, he'd surprised her with the kindness he'd shown Arthur. Stunned her, actually. She couldn't deny that him asking Tiny to shake and his male commiseration had lifted Arthur's spirits from the doldrums into which they'd fallen, a feat she'd been unable to completely accomplish. She hadn't expected him to act so . . . decently. Especially toward a boy whose dog's actions had brought an abrupt end to his outing with Lady Hombly.

Lady Hombly . . . it had been a jolt seeing them together, although why it should have been she wasn't sure. Even a blind person could have seen last night the way the stunning widow looked at him—as if he were a mutton chop and she were a salivating mongrel. Not that Emily cared, of course. No, not a bit.

Still, she'd found herself studying Lady Hombly, trying to determine if the widow looked . . . kissed. She'd been unable to tell, which had filled her with an idiotic hope that Mr. Jennsen hadn't kissed her. Because surely if he had, given his skill, Lady Hombly would have looked very well kissed indeed.

And now he stood beside her, his steps shortened to match hers, and her pulse was misbehaving in the most aggravating way. She would have preferred to simply ignore him, but doing so might make him think she was perturbed by his being with Lady Hombly. Which of course she wasn't. No, not a bit.

Then it suddenly occurred to her that it wouldn't be a *terrible* idea to act civilly toward the man to whom her father was so deeply in debt. If doing so could buy her family a bit more time, then she'd make the sacrifice and endure his company. She instantly brightened. Heavens, why hadn't she thought of that before now? She barely refrained from smacking herself on the forehead. Yes, she'd speak with him, engage him in polite conversation—for her family's sake.

She cleared her throat then informed him, "I am not *somewhat* of a champion frog catcher. I am *the undefeated champion.*"

When he didn't respond, she turned and looked at him. A mistake, as she found herself unable to look away. His profile was marred by his less-than-perfect nose, yet that flaw only served to lend his face a boldness, a rough ruggedness that hinted at danger, something that shouldn't have been attractive yet somehow was. And really, that imperfection was a blessing, for without it he would have been far too handsome. Ridiculously so.

"You don't believe I'm the undefeated champion?" she asked.

He turned to took at her, and her heart skipped at the penetrating regard in his dark eyes. "I believe you." A frown etched a line between his brows, and his gaze roamed her face, as if she were a puzzle he was trying to solve. "It's just a title that I never, in a million years, would have thought to ascribe to you." His frown disappeared, and amusement lit his eyes. "But then, I never would have thought to call you a teat squirter, either."

Emily drew in a quick breath and snapped her attention back to the path in front of her. An embarrassed flush crept up her neck. "Clearly you and Arthur had an interesting discussion."

"*Very* interesting."

"Obviously I need to remind him of what are and aren't proper topics of conversation."

"Please don't do so on my behalf. It was one of the most

refreshingly honest conversations I've had in ages. And far more entertaining than the usual topic of the weather." He shook his head. "Never in my life have I heard more discussion of the climate since arriving on your shores. Personally, I find talk of catching frogs, lake swimming, baiting fishhooks, making mud pies, and teat squirting far more fascinating."

He chuckled, and she turned toward him, favoring him with her most fulminating look. Instead, the annoying man had the nerve to grin at her. "I hear your aim is impeccable."

Emily gave him a patently false smile. "It is. I only wish a cow were nearby so I could give you a demonstration."

His smile grew broader. Fustian. The man really had the most attractive smile, one that showcased even, white teeth and creased a pair of shallow dimples in his cheeks, which framed those beautiful, masculine lips. "I assure you I'd return the favor. And like yours, my aim is excellent."

She raised her brows and looked down her nose at him, or at least as much as was possible with someone so much taller than she. "You would shoot milk at a lady?"

"If she shot me first, yes. I live by the motto: one teat squirt deserves another."

He sounded perfectly serious, yet there was no missing the laughter lurking in his eyes, and Emily had to press her lips together to keep from chuckling. "You realize that motto amounts to 'an eye for an eye.'"

A whisper of something she couldn't decipher passed over his features, diluting the amusement. "Yes, I suppose it does. I've found those are words to live by."

"Well, they're certainly more appropriate party chatter than 'one teat squirt deserves another.' I've never heard of such a silly motto."

"Oh? And what is yours?"

Emily considered, then, thinking of her vampire masquerade, she quoted, "'Swift and resolute action leads to success'—"

"—'self-doubt is a prelude to disaster,'" he said, finishing the quote in unison with her. His brows shot upward. "You're familiar with Addison's *Cato*?"

"Obviously. You sound surprised."

"I suppose I am." He murmured something that sounded

like "And not for the first time today." Then he said, "Clearly you're well read."

"Again, you sound surprised."

"Yes, but only because I thought the Ladies Literary Society partook solely of scandalous fare."

Emily stumbled in her surprise and no doubt would have landed on the gravel with an ignominious splat if he hadn't caught her arm to steady her. For several seconds they stood on the path, Emily stunned into silence by his mention of her book club and his use of the word *scandalous* to describe what they read. Surely he couldn't possibly know . . . Could he? A heated blush suffused her entire body.

Yet it wasn't just his unexpected comment that rooted her in place and made her skin tingle. It was his touch. The warmth of his hand seeped through the layers of her gown and pelisse, shooting a tingling awareness all the way down to her feet, one made all the more powerful by the backs of his fingers pressing against the outer curve of her breast.

"Are you all right?" he asked, his gaze scanning her from head to toe.

"I . . . I'm fine."

Or she would be as soon as he released her. His gaze returned to hers. His dark eyes were unreadable, and she dearly wished she knew what he was thinking. Were his thoughts anything like hers? Was he as aware of her as she was of him? Did he feel this same palpable tension in the air between them? Did he want to touch her again—as much as she wanted him to?

Or . . . was he thinking about the scandalous fare of the Ladies Literary Society and judging her? The mere idea of him doing so stiffened her spine and raised her chin. There was no reason for her to be ashamed or embarrassed, especially with him. She didn't care what he thought of her. Not a bit.

His hand slipped from her arm, and she had to fight the urge to press her palm to the spot where he'd held her, to retain the delicious warmth of his touch. The puppies yanked against their leads, jerking her attention away from him and that darkly penetrating gaze.

"It's a shame you need to hide what you read," he said as they resumed walking.

"What do you mean? What do you know of the Ladies Literary Society?" she demanded.

"Only that the name of your book club is misleading. But I applaud your cleverness. Why open yourself to censure from people who believe women should only read Shakespeare and the like?"

She didn't even try to hide her surprise. "You don't believe that's all women should read?"

"No. I think people should read whatever gives them enjoyment." He slanted her a sideways look. "Although I must admit your choices of a mistress's memoirs and, most recently, *The Gentleman Vampire's Lover* caught me unawares."

Emily blinked. "How do you know what our reading selections are?"

"Gideon Mayne told me."

"And people think *women* like to gossip," she murmured, shaking her head.

"We weren't *gossiping*. Merely talking."

"About personal matters that are none of your concern. I'm not certain what they call that in America, but here in England, that is gossip." In spite of the unsettling realization that he knew so much about her book club's sensational reading fare, her lips twitched. "An interesting title for you to bear, Mr. Jennsen: Champion Gossiper."

"It's certainly better than Champion Teat Squirter."

She couldn't help but laugh at his bone-dry tone. "Touché."

He halted as if he'd walked into a wall. Emily paused and turned to face him and found him staring at her. "Is something amiss?" she asked.

"I . . . I think you just *smiled* at me." He leaned forward and peered intently at her mouth. "Yes, by God, you did. The telltale upward curve of your lips still lingers."

She instantly flattened her mouth into a straight line. "You're mistaken. That was merely an aberrant facial tic."

His gaze jumped up. "Then how do you explain that hint of amusement I see in your eyes?"

"Simply the result of the bright sun." She squinted to prove her point.

"My dear Lady Emily, while I may not know all the oddities and intricacies of Brit speak, I know what a Banbury tale is. And I definitely know when I'm hearing one." His lips curved slowly upward until his entire face was creased with a wide grin. "You smiled at me. Admit it."

Botheration, why was she charmed? Why wasn't she instead annoyed? And why on earth was it necessary to force herself not to smile again?

She raised her chin and resumed walking. "I don't know what you're talking about."

He fell into step beside her and chuckled. "Fine. Be that way. But I know what I saw. And as such, I feel compelled to repeat what I told you last night: if you won't be honest with me, at least don't lie to yourself."

Heat whooshed through her. She remembered that unnerving statement all too well, spoken after she'd named their passionate kiss a debacle. And his words that had immediately followed: "You didn't think our kiss was a debacle when your body was pressed against mine, and your tongue was in my mouth."

God, no, she hadn't, much to her dismay. The memory of their passionate exchange slammed into her, so vivid that she had to press her lips together to contain the gasp of pleasure that rose in her throat. She turned toward him, and to her annoyance, he appeared completely unperturbed by his reference to their steamy kiss. Very irritating, as she felt so . . . steamy. Clearly he wasn't thinking of their kiss at all.

But then he turned to her, and she nearly stumbled again at the look in his eyes. Those fathomless, dark orbs burned with the same fiery intensity and unmistakable desire as they had last night just before he'd kissed her. Her heart stuttered, and she knew, *knew* that if they were somewhere private, he would kiss her again. And that she would let him.

Before she could gather her thoughts and fashion an appropriate reply—something other than the grossly *in*appropriate *I want you to kiss me again more than I want my next breath*—he shifted his gaze from hers and drew several long, slow breaths. He then nodded toward the path ahead. "A very entertaining young boy."

With an effort she redirected her attention to where he was looking and saw Arthur, kicking up gravel as he ran behind Tiny. A wave of love for her brother swamped Emily, along with a swell of relief at the subject change.

"Indeed he is. I enjoy every minute I spend with him. And the others as well." She hesitated. "Thank you for the kindness you showed him earlier. And Mary as well. That was very . . . considerate."

He slanted a glance her way. "I'm sure you don't mean to sound so flabbergasted that I'd do something considerate."

"In truth, I am."

A huff of laughter escaped him. "Well, that at least was honest."

She shook her head. "I didn't mean that I thought you incapable of behaving in a decent or kind manner . . ." *At least not* completely *incapable.* "But the fact that your kindness was extended toward a young boy whose dog had disrupted your afternoon, and well, toward a child in general—many adults wouldn't have even noticed he was upset or have taken the time to make him feel better. Or have noticed that Mary needed assistance."

"In that case, you're welcome, although there's no need to thank me. I like children. There is no artifice about them, and their needs and demands are few." His lips curved upward. "And they say the most *interesting* things."

As she had no desire to hear of any other potentially embarrassing things Arthur might have shared with him, she said quickly, "You mentioned you have no brothers or sisters. I cannot imagine such a thing."

"Just as I can't imagine five younger siblings. How do you keep track of them all?"

A quick laugh escaped her. "It's not always easy, yet there's always at least one of them close by. Loneliness hasn't been a problem."

"I imagine not. There is quite an age difference between you and Arthur."

She nodded. "Fourteen years. I was an only child for five years, and that was the only time in my life I was ever lonely. My parents were convinced they'd never have another child, which crushed me, as I longed for a sibling, and my parents as well, as they wanted a male heir. Finally, to everyone's joy, Kenneth came along, followed quickly by Will, Percy, and Mary. Arthur was quite a surprise. A truly delightful one."

They paused for a moment while Romeo and Juliet sniffed at a tuft of grass. "Julianne has no siblings, and as a child she felt very alone—except for the times she spent with me. Was your childhood lonely?"

He stared off into the distance. Silence swelled between them, and she wished she could read his thoughts. Finally, after they resumed their walk, he said quietly, "Yes, my childhood was very lonely."

Those soft words seemed pulled from somewhere deep inside him, and although she would have wished it otherwise, they tugged on her heart.

"You're very fortunate," he continued. "You've led a charmed life."

"Yes . . ." Or at least she had until a few months ago, when she'd learned of her family's impending financial doom. "From what I can see, you lead a charmed life as well."

"Perhaps now. But not always. And I've never had . . ." He waved his hand before them. "This."

She looked around. "A huge park?"

He turned toward her, and she was struck by the desolate look in his eyes. "A family. People who loved me." He looked down at the gamboling, tongue-lolling dogs. "Pets. Growing up I had . . . nothing."

His words startled her. She'd heard rumors regarding his humble beginnings—that he hadn't been born into his wealth and had earned it through his uncanny business acumen. But she hadn't considered he'd been *unloved*.

"While I can imagine making do with less luxurious creature comforts," she said, "I can't conceive of an existence without my family's love and loving them in return."

"As I said, you are very fortunate."

Before she could stop herself, her curiosity compelled her to ask, "What of your parents?"

A muscle ticked in his jaw. "My mother died shortly after I was born, my father when I was nine."

Another surprise. And another tug on her heart. "I'm sorry

you suffered such losses. With both your parents gone, who raised you?"

A humorless laugh pushed past his lips. "I did. *I* raised me. At least until I was thirteen. Then I was fortunate enough to meet a man who took me under his wing. He put a roof over my head, offered me honest employment, and taught me everything I know about business. Meeting Martin Becknell changed my life. Enabled me to become who I am today. I owe him . . . everything."

"But what did you do between the ages of nine and thirteen?"

"I . . . survived. One day at a time. One hour at a time. Sometimes one minute at a time."

Shock rendered Emily mute. How could a boy that age possibly survive all alone in the world? She tried to imagine one of her brothers reduced to such dire circumstances and simply couldn't. The mere thought made her hurt all over. She found it equally impossible to envision this robust, successful man as an orphaned child who survived one hour at a time. A wave of sympathy and compassion for that lonely boy washed over her. "Were you . . . frightened?"

He drew in a deep breath and briefly squeezed his eyes shut. When he looked at her, his eyes resembled flat, black stones. "Every minute. Of every day."

Those words, spoken in that soft rasp that seemed dragged from his soul reached deep inside her and grabbed her heart. Dear God, he'd been barely older than Arthur. Envisioning her sweet, carefree brother being unloved and alone and afraid filled her with an ache she couldn't describe.

Without thinking, she reached out and touched his arm. "I'm so sorry. I cannot imagine how difficult that must have been. You must take great pride in all you've accomplished against such daunting odds."

He stopped walking the instant she touched him, and she halted as well. His gaze dropped to her hand resting against his sleeve, and with a jolt she realized how forward the action must seem to him. She pulled her hand away, and for several seconds he frowned at the spot where her glove had rested, and she wondered if perhaps, as when he'd touched her to keep her from falling, he could feel the warmth of her hand through the layers of his clothing.

Finally he raised his gaze to hers. "I do take pride in my success. I've been both very poor and very rich, and I have to tell you, very rich is much better."

They resumed their leisurely stroll, and she searched for something to say, but her mind was reeling with this startling information about him . . . information she wasn't at all happy to know. Because it made him . . . human. And touched her heart. In a way she didn't want this man to touch it.

She didn't *want* to know anything likable or admirable about him. Anything that would garner her respect. Yet she couldn't ignore the fact that what he'd done—the way he'd risen above such difficult circumstances to where he was today—was remarkable. Extraordinary. Surely any man who could accomplish that must be . . .

Remarkable. Extraordinary.

Oh, dear. She absolutely did not want to think of Logan Jennsen in those terms. For if she did, then she stood in real danger of . . . *liking* him. And she absolutely did not want to like Logan Jennsen.

But she greatly feared it might be too late.

Chapter 9

I wanted to know everything about him and kept hoping he'd reveal something, anything that would make me less enamored of him. But every conversation, every touch only made me want him more. I despaired of ever getting enough of him.

The Vampire Lady's Kiss *by Anonymous*

Now why in God's name had he told her all that?

Logan walked beside Lady Emily and mentally slapped himself on the forehead. Good God, he'd spouted out information like a boiling teakettle spewing steam, telling her things about himself, his childhood, that he hadn't spoken of nor allowed himself to think about in years.

But even more confounding than the fact that he'd told her so much was that he couldn't figure out *why* he'd told her. For some inexplicable reason he'd confided personal aspects of his past to her that he'd never even been tempted to divulge to another woman. Damn it, something about her made him say things and act in ways that utterly baffled him.

Of course there were things he'd never tell her . . . that he'd never tell anyone.

He stole a peek at her from the corner of his eye and noted she appeared lost in thought. It was a damn good thing he wasn't normally drawn to flawlessly beautiful women, because if he were, well, he'd be hard-pressed to name one more perfectly stunning than Lady Emily.

Nor one who'd ever surprised him as much. Until today he'd considered her nothing more than a hothouse flower, yet she clearly enjoyed the brisk weather and lengthy walks. And, like so many people of her class he'd encountered, he'd thought her self-centered, but seeing her with her family . . . it was obvious she loved them a great deal. He'd always believed her haughty and rather cold and aloof, but clearly there was a warm, loving side to her nature. The compassion and protectiveness she'd shown Arthur had touched something inside him, something that had been sorely lacking in his own boyhood. What he would have given at that age to have someone lay a comforting hand on his shoulder, to commiserate with his hurts and try to make them better. And her loyalty: she'd looked like she wanted to flay Lady Hombly alive, and would have if the widow had made the mistake of casting one more hateful look toward Arthur.

Then there was the concern and sympathy she'd shown when Logan had spoken of his childhood. Some of her class would have expressed disgust at his upbringing, or lack of it. But instead she'd offered him the same compassion she'd shown Arthur, and it had affected him in a most unsettling way. In a way he couldn't fully describe, as it was something he'd never before felt.

Yes, it appeared there was more to Lady Emily Stapleford than he'd suspected. The qualities he'd glimpsed in her today were among those he most admired, and not ones he'd ever have thought to credit her with, and he found that discovery very disconcerting. He did not want to like this woman. Bad enough that he should desire her. *Desire her fiercely,* his annoying inner voice interjected.

Fine. *Fiercely.* His *fierce* desire for her was unwanted and complicated enough. If he were to *like* her on top of that . . . he shook his head. That would just further confuse an already unwelcome situation.

As he no longer wished to dwell on his desire—fine, his *fierce* desire—he decided he'd best resume their conversation, but on a much less personal and serious subject.

After clearing his throat he said, "You know, even my vast wealth has never afforded me a title of such distinction as you bear."

She turned toward him, and damn it, he found himself all but drowning in those eyes, which looked more blue than green today, thanks to the deep azure of her pelisse. They twinkled with that whiff of mischief he unwillingly found so alluring.

One dark brow hiked upward. "Oh? You'd aspire to be *Lady* Logan Jennsen?"

"Hmmm. While that does have a certain flair, I meant Undefeated Champion Frog Catcher."

"Ah." She heaved an exaggerated sigh. "I'm afraid there can be only one Undefeated Champion Frog Catcher. You shall therefore have to aspire to a lesser title."

He shook his head. "I refuse to settle for second best. Tell me, what do you do with all the frogs you catch?"

"We usually conduct either races or a jumping competition. The winner is named Frog King. Then we release them."

"Frog King . . . named after the fairy tale?"

"I suppose, although of course our frogs don't turn into handsome princes."

"Not that it did the prince in the story much good."

"Why do you say that? The evil spell was broken, and he was no longer a frog. As the handsome prince, he was able to marry the beautiful princess."

"Yes, but what sort of woman was she? She had nothing but her beauty to recommend her. She was spoiled and self-ish and only kept her word to the frog that so kindly helped her when forced to do so by her father. She then treated the frog badly and didn't like him at all—until he turned into the rich and handsome prince. *Then* she loved him." He shook his head. "I always felt sorry for that poor bastard, being leg-shackled to that shallow piece of goods. The story just proves something I've always believed."

"And what is that?"

"That what constitutes beauty is nothing more than one man's opinion. The prince thought the princess stunning, yet I wouldn't have found her the least bit attractive. I'd prefer a woman who looked like a frog but who possessed integrity and a kind and honest heart."

A disbelieving sound escaped her. "Says a man escorting one of the most beautiful women in the ton."

Relief rippled through him that the pride and vanity he'd suspected she possessed—traits he couldn't abide—had shown themselves. Thank God. He couldn't possibly like a woman who was so boastful of her own beauty. "That's rather conceited of you," he couldn't help but point out, even though he was relieved.

She blinked. Then her eyes widened, and she laughed. "Heavens, I didn't mean *me*. I was referring to Lady Hombly."

Logan's relief evaporated like a puddle in the desert, and a frown tugged down his brows. Lady Hombly. Damn. He'd forgotten all about her.

"I wasn't aware you and Lady Hombly were so well acquainted," she continued.

"We're not."

"Indeed? She seemed quite devastated that your outing today was cut short."

"I believe the source of her devastation was the dirt on her pelisse."

"There's no need for false modesty, Mr. Jennsen. I'm sure she was equally devastated at being deprived of your company."

"I assure you, I have no false modesty. Nor any misconceptions as to why many people seek me out."

"Your sparkling wit and impeccable manners?" she guessed in a tart tone.

"Naturally. Of course my financial expertise and fortune have *nothing* to do it."

She shook her head and made a tsking sound. "How cynical you are."

"I prefer to call it realistic."

"You claim people only seek you out for your financial expertise, yet it seems you spend all your time and energies on your business ventures."

"Most of it, yes."

"What else do you enjoy doing?"

He considered for several seconds then said, "Negotiating deals, investment ventures, increasing my business's holdings—that is what I enjoy, and at the risk of sounding full of myself, I'm very good at it."

"Yes, but what do you do for *fun*?"

He frowned. "Fun?"

To his annoyance she laughed. "Yes—*fun*. Surely it's a word used in America."

When he continued to frown, she said, "Good heavens, you're in a bad way. Surely there's something else you enjoy doing. Discounting all things business related, when is the last time you truly enjoyed yourself?"

He turned toward her and allowed his gaze to rest on her lips for several seconds. Then he asked softly, "Do you really want to know?"

"I . . . Yes." She moistened her lips, drawing his attention again to her mouth. That plump, gorgeous mouth that had felt so damn good crushed beneath his. "Of course."

He raised his gaze back to hers. "Last night. When I was kissing you."

Fiery color rushed into her cheeks, and he had to fist his hands to keep from reaching out to touch the wash of color his words had provoked. "A . . . and before that?" she said in a breathless-sounding voice.

"Are you sure you want to know?" he asked again.

This time she merely nodded.

"Three months ago. When I was kissing you."

He could hear her shallow, rapid breaths. "And before that?"

After several seconds' pondering, he realized he couldn't recall anything not related to his work. Which both surprised and unsettled him. He debated whether to tell her the truth, then decided there was no point in lying. Indeed, he found himself oddly reluctant to be less than truthful with her.

"I don't know," he admitted. His gaze raked her face. "You're blushing, Lady Emily."

Her color bloomed even deeper, captivating him further, damn it. "Because discussing"—she lowered her voice to a hiss—"*kissing* is . . . improper."

"As opposed to actually engaging in the kissing?"

"That is improper, too, as you very well know."

"Well, you *did* ask."

"Yes, but I expected your answer to be more along the lines of a horseback riding outing. Or a fox hunt. Or a soiree."

"And miss the opportunity to see your face turn such an enchanting color? My dear Lady Emily, I'm many things, but I'm certainly not a fool."

Or perhaps he was. He'd wanted to discuss a safer, less personal topic, and here they were talking about kissing. That was hardly less dangerous, as it made him want nothing more than to kiss her again. Right here. Right now. Convention and their audience be damned.

Best to change the subject once again, this time to something completely safe. "Tell me, have you heard any further reports about last night's so-called vampire sighting?"

She raised her brows. "So-called?"

He raised his own brows at the umbrage in her tone. "I'll believe it when I see it for myself."

Something flickered in her gaze, something that brought the *What the hell is she up to?* question roaring back into his mind. "The sighting was all Mother and Aunt Agatha could talk about this morning," she said. "Even my abigail had heard the news and could speak of nothing else."

"It certainly added an interesting element to last night's festivities," he said. "Speaking of last night, when I arrived at the party, I saw you across the room and you appeared . . . upset. As if you'd lost your best friend. I hope I'm mistaken, and nothing was amiss?"

Lost your best friend. His words reverberated through Emily's mind, shooting a shiver of dread down her spine. How odd he would choose that phrase, when it's precisely how she'd felt after speaking to Carolyn. While part of her refused to believe, accept that anything was wrong with her friend, another part of her was terrified that Carolyn's fears would prove correct.

The fact that her distress had been so obvious that he would detect it disturbed her. Even more disturbing was the sudden urge to unburden herself to Mr. Jennsen, to confide her fears to him. Of course she couldn't, wouldn't, but this strong desire to do so confused and disquieted her. Surely it was merely born of the need to discuss her worries with someone, anyone. Normally she would have Sarah or Julianne, but in this case she didn't, as Carolyn didn't want them to know.

Still, her conscience balked at telling him an outright lie. Therefore she hedged, "I had heard some news that distressed me, but all is well now." And it would be. It *had* to be. Carolyn simply could *not* be ill.

"I'm glad to hear it."

"Actually, when I first saw you last evening, I thought the same thing: that you appeared upset." She hesitated but couldn't help but ask, "Were you?"

She'd fully expected him to shrug off her inquiry, but after a brief pause, he nodded. "I'm afraid so. I'd found out earlier in the day that one of my cargo ships was destroyed. A fire at the docks. She was set to sail at sunset."

"Oh, dear. That means the ship was fully loaded?"

"Yes."

"So you lost a great deal. I'm sorry."

"Thank you. But material things can be replaced. Unfortunately, the captain and five deckhands were injured." A muscle ticked in his jaw. "And two men lost their lives."

Emily pressed her hand to her chest, above the spot where her heart had just turned over. "How tragic."

"Yes. I visited the injured men and am happy to report they will all make full recoveries."

"You must be very relieved."

"I am. But the men who died . . ." His voice trailed off, and then he let out a long, tired-sounding sigh. "One of the men who died, Billy Palmer, had no family. But the other man, Christian Whitaker, left behind a wife and young child. Facing Velma Whitaker and her daughter Lara yesterday was the most difficult thing I've ever done. The looks in their eyes . . ." He shook his head, then turned to her. There was no missing the tight misery etched into his features. "I needed to say something to them, but what words are adequate to comfort a woman whose husband is gone? To tell a child she'll never see her father again?" He briefly squeezed his eyes shut. "I know what it is like to grow up without a father. It isn't a fate I would wish on any child."

"I'm sure they don't blame you," she said, her heart hurting for the widow and her daughter, and also feeling the need to console him. "It was an accident, not your fault."

Something undecipherable ghosted across his features— something that spoke of past hurts—then he turned his attention back to the path. "They have every right to blame me," he said quietly. "Anything that happens with regards to one of my ships or businesses is ultimately my responsibility."

"I'm sorry," she said. Then a humorless sound escaped her. "Suddenly I know precisely how you felt about inadequate words."

He nodded. "Sometimes the right words just don't exist. But I thank you. Both for the consoling sentiments and for listening." After a brief pause he said, "The others have reached the end of the path and are starting back this way. Shall we turn around?"

"All right." Romeo and Juliet were only too happy to fall in with the plan, as was Emily. For reasons she didn't care to examine closely, she hoped her family didn't catch up to her and Mr. Jennsen too quickly. For she inexplicably didn't want their opportunity for private conversation to end. Even more inexplicably, she felt as if could talk to him all day long. As if she *wanted* to talk to him all day long.

Oh, dear.

"Um, Lady Emily, I hate to be the one to tell you this, but your puppy is chewing on my puppy's ear."

Emily looked down at the pair of rambunctious dogs straining on their leads, and laughter bubbled up in her throat. "So I see. Well, *your* puppy just nipped at *my* puppy's tail."

"Which is no less than your puppy deserved for chewing on my puppy's ear."

Just then, Romeo's active pink tongue swiped several times over Juliet's nose. Juliet responded with a series of licks to Romeo's nose. Face once again flaming hot, Emily raised her chin and kept walking, steadfast in her determination to not look his way.

"I would point out that my puppy just kissed yours—and was kissed in return, very thoroughly I might add," he said, his voice serious, "but I've already been warned that talking about kissing is improper."

"Precisely," she said in her most prim voice. "I'm delighted you learned your lesson."

She risked a quick peek at him and found him studying her with a look she couldn't translate. "Actually, I learned a great deal today, Lady Emily."

Yes, as had she. Unfortunately, rather than confirming her poor opinion of Mr. Jennsen and rendering her able to dismiss the bothersome man from her thoughts, she instead found herself perhaps, maybe, just a bit on the brink of actually *liking* him. Which meant that ridding him from her mind would prove even more difficult.

Which was very vexing indeed.

They walked on for several minutes, silence swelling between them, and she again found herself wondering what he was thinking. Was he, as she was, remembering last night's kiss? Or their first kiss, three months ago? She pressed her lips together to stifle a groan of dismay. Why, oh *why*, had she allowed her curiosity to get the better of her and initiate that first encounter? That single unwise decision had led to her present dilemma of having her mind filled with the one man she least wanted occupying it.

They rounded a curve, and she saw the end of the pathway. Although her heart unwisely yearned to remain in his company, her common sense knew the sooner she ended this encounter, the better. In only another moment they would reach Park Lane, where they would naturally part company. Which was good. She'd spent far too much time in his unsettling and distracting company this afternoon. She needed to return home and sequester herself in her bedchamber in order to finish hemming her hastily sewn together cape for tomorrow night's vampire sighting. She needed to firmly keep her focus on rescuing her family from financial ruin with her wits rather than by having to marry a man with a fortune—instead of concentrating on the very man to whom her father owed so much money. What satisfaction it would bring her to be able to satisfy that debt! *Then* she'd stop thinking about him. Absolutely.

As they neared the end of the path, Emily glanced over her shoulder. The rest of her family hadn't yet rounded the corner and were nowhere in sight. No doubt they'd stopped at a bench with Aunt Agatha to allow her to rest, and guilt slapped Emily for walking so far ahead. Of course, Aunt Agatha was in good hands—Kenneth, William, and Percy were always very solicitous of her—but she'd been so preoccupied with Mr. Jennsen, she'd completely forgotten the others were in the park.

Humph. Just another reason to get away from Mr. Jennsen

as quickly as possible. Clearly he was detrimental to her thought processes. And with everything she needed to prepare for her upcoming vampire masquerade, she needed all her wits about her.

Since she had no idea how far behind the rest of her group was or how long it would be until they caught up, it was best she escaped him now. With Park Lane just ahead and her family's town house only across the street, she said, "I bid you good day, Mr. Jennsen. I hope you enjoy the remainder of your afternoon."

Instead of replying, he halted in such an abrupt manner, Emily found herself stopping as well. She turned toward him, noting his frown. There was no missing the sudden tension in his stance as his dark eyes scanned the area.

"Is something amiss?" she asked.

He didn't answer for several seconds, and she followed his gaze, noting nothing other than the normal assortment of people walking about in the park and along Park Lane and the usual collection of equipages making their way down the thoroughfare. The only thing of note was perhaps that the area was more populated than usual, no doubt due to the fine weather.

Finally he said, "I just thought . . ." His eyes scanned around again, then he shook his head. "It's nothing." He looked at her, and she could tell that something had unsettled him. "I'm afraid I must go," he said abruptly.

Unreasonable pique assailed Emily at his brusque statement. Well, of course he must go. It wasn't as if she were going to prolong their afternoon and ask him to tea. It was way past time they parted company. She was anxious they do so. But at least she hadn't made it sound as if she couldn't get away from him fast enough. Uncouth man. What a relief to recall one of the reasons she didn't like him. One of the *many* reasons.

She inclined her head in her most regal manner. "I wouldn't dream of keeping you from the rest of your day. I bid you good afternoon, Mr. Jennsen." She turned to walk away, but he stayed her with a hand to her arm. Refusing to acknowledge the heat that ran through her at his touch, she raised her gaze to his. "Is there something else?" she asked, proud of how cool she sounded.

"Yes. I'll escort you home."

She nodded toward the town house directly across the road. "I *am* home."

"I'll escort you all the way home. To your door."

"You said you needed to leave."

"I do. As soon as I've escorted you—and Romeo and Juliet—to your door."

To her chagrin, she'd forgotten he held Romeo's lead. "I've no wish to delay your departure." And she really needed to get away from him. His touch. Now.

One corner of his lips twitched. "I'm certain you're anxious to be rid of me, but I've no intention of reinforcing your view that I'm an ill-mannered, uncouth colonial by not depositing you on your doorstep."

"Depositing? You make me sound like an ungainly sack of potatoes."

His gaze flicked over her, and her heart skipped at the heat that flared in his dark eyes. "'Ungainly sack of potatoes' isn't quite how I'd describe you." When she didn't respond, he raised his brows. "You're not going to ask how I *would* describe you?"

"Certainly not."

"Curiosity demands I ask why not."

"Such a question would be nothing more than an impolite fishing expedition for compliments." True, yet she suddenly found herself very much wanting to hear something flattering from him.

"How do you know my description would be complimentary?"

Embarrassment warmed her skin. Botheration, she *didn't* know. And that sorely irked her. Yet she couldn't decide if she was more annoyed at him for failing to spout flowery words as any gentleman of the ton would have immediately done, or at herself for the assumption that he'd harbor any good opinion of her.

She hiked up her chin. "I don't know that your description would be complimentary. Indeed, now that I think upon it, I suspect it wouldn't be."

"You might be surprised."

"I don't care for surprises."

"I suppose you find them impolite as well."

"As a matter of fact, I do."

"And you're never impolite."

In spite of his serious expression, she had the distinct

impression he was laughing at her. "I strive to steer clear of impoliteness, yes."

He nodded solemnly. "Always impeccably polite . . . yet not always completely proper. You present quite the interesting puzzle, my lady."

By God, she wished she could inform him in the coldest of tones that her behavior was always completely proper, but to make such a claim to a man she'd passionately kissed—twice—would only serve to brand her a liar. Of gargantuan proportions. Which was extremely vexing, as she *was* proper—*most* of the time. Except for the harmless silliness she engaged in with her siblings. And, well, her Literary Society readings. And, well, she supposed her vampire masquerade wasn't *exactly* proper. And then there were those two kisses—

Oh, very well, fine. So she was only proper *almost* most of the time.

The puppies strained impatiently on their leads, and they all stepped into the road. "I appear to have left you speechless," he said. "I'm guessing that's a first."

"I'm not speechless. And I'm nearly always proper," she stated in her most prim tone.

"I agree. But it's that 'nearly' that makes you so—" His words cut off when a loud shout sounded to their right. Emily paused and turned.

A well-dressed gentleman pointed toward a rapidly fleeing youth. "Stop, thief! He's stolen my watch!"

Several people nearby began yelling. A young man just exiting the park attempted to give chase, but it was instantly obvious he was no match for the fleet-footed pickpocket.

So engrossed was she in the scene, it took Emily several seconds to realize someone was shouting her name. She turned around. And froze.

A carriage barreled toward her at breakneck speed, the horses' flashing hooves churning up dirt and dust. Juliet's lead dropped from her nerveless fingers. The dog dashed to safety, but Emily couldn't move. Shock and terror and disbelief all conspired to turn her into an icy cold statue whose feet were nailed to the road.

And it clicked in her mind that those several seconds would cost her her life.

Chapter 10

I led him to my bedchamber, intent upon seducing him. Yet the moment the door closed behind us, he took my hand. Whispered my name. And with that single touch, that one word, I found myself seduced.

The Vampire Lady's Kiss *by Anonymous*

"Emily!"

Her name burst from Logan's throat, that single shouted word ringing with only a fraction of the terror gripping him. He dropped Romeo's lead and rushed forward, knowing only seconds separated her from a certain death under the churning hooves and spinning wheels bearing down on her.

He snatched her around her waist then used all his strength to dive for safety, praying it was enough to get them both out of the way. In spite of his best effort to cushion her fall with his body, they landed with a skidding, bone-jarring thud that shot pain through his entire body a heartbeat before the carriage thundered past. Chunks of dirt and rock rained down on them, and he curled his body around hers in an attempt to shield her from the worst of the debris.

The carriage rolled past, and the screaming of its wheels

faded, replaced by shouts and the sound of running feet. With his heart beating hard enough to break free of his chest, Logan pushed himself up to look down at Lady Emily, whom he still held wrapped in his arms. And his pounding heart seemed to stop.

Her eyes were closed, and a streak of dirt marred one creamy cheek. Her bonnet was askew, and a single dark curl fell across her forehead from her disarrayed hair, a slash of bright color against her ghostly pale skin. She lay limp and still, and for several seconds he couldn't breathe. Couldn't think. Could only stare in wordless, terrified horror while a single word screamed through his mind: *No!*

Just then her eyelids fluttered open, and he found himself looking into those fathomless sea-colored depths. The intensity of his relief damn near left him shaking.

She stared up at him, searching his face, then moistened her lips. "You've lost your hat," she whispered.

Holy God, he'd almost lost much more than that. From the corner of his eye, he noticed his crushed and ruined hat. A shudder ran through him that she could have—they both could have—met with that same fate. He had to swallow twice to find his voice. "I have others."

"D . . . did you save me? Or are we both dead?"

"Not dead," he assured her, his voice less than steady. "But I'm not yet certain you're unscathed. Does anything hurt?"

Before she could answer, people pressed in on them from every direction.

"Are you all right?" asked a man.

"Either of you hurt?" asked another, leaning down to offer his handkerchief.

Logan's gaze didn't waver from her wide eyes that continued to stare into his. "That's what I'm trying to determine. Can you move your arms and legs, Lady Emily?"

He continued to gently hold her while she gave each of her limbs a gentle, experimental shake. "Everything appears to be in working order." Her gaze ran over him. "What about you? You bore the brunt of our fall."

"I'm fine." Which was an utter lie. He couldn't recall ever being so sickly frightened, so deathly terrified. The image of that carriage bearing down on her was forever burned into his brain. Damn it, his insides were still shaking.

Just then Kenneth, Will, Percy, and Arthur, along with Tiny, followed closely by Mary, who held Ophelia's lead, and Lady Agatha, pushed through the dozen or so people who had gathered around them.

"Emmie!" Arthur cried, dropping to his knees beside her. "Are you hurt?"

"I'm fine," she said quickly, offering what was clearly meant to be a reassuring smile to her siblings. Logan and Kenneth helped her sit up then stand, Logan's jaw tightening when she winced and rubbed her hip.

"What happened?" Percy asked, offering her his arm while Will took her other side.

"A man was robbed. I stopped when he shouted, not realizing there was a carriage coming. I would have been run down if not for Mr. Jennsen's quick thinking. Thanks to him, I'm unhurt, and a terrible accident was avoided." She looked at Logan, and he saw something in her eyes that he'd never expected to see there: Admiration. And gratitude. They seemed to knock the remaining air from his lungs.

"You're very much the hero, sir," she said softly, "and I thank you. And I am relieved that you weren't injured in the process."

"You're welcome." He wanted to say more, but those were the only two words he could push past his tight throat and his mounting fury. Because he didn't believe for a moment that what just happened was an accident. The driver had made no attempt to pull up his horses or turn them to avoid a collision and instead had run them directly at Emily. There was no possible way he couldn't have seen her.

Pulling his gaze away from her, he looked at the bystanders. "Did anyone recognize the driver of the carriage?" he asked them.

"Was too busy looking at the footpad who stole my watch," said the man who'd been robbed.

Several others murmured they'd also been too occupied with the thief to notice the oncoming carriage until it had already passed. Much as Logan himself. Damn it, he hadn't noticed Lady Emily had stopped walking. He'd kept moving, distracted by the sense of menace, of being watched, that he'd so strongly felt only moments earlier as they'd approached the end of the park's path. He'd halted and looked about but hadn't seen anyone or anything suspicious. Although the feeling lingered, he'd momentarily pushed it aside, determined to see Lady Emily safely home. He'd then planned to walk back through the park to see if he could discern anything. And then call upon Gideon Mayne.

Well, he very nearly hadn't seen her safely home. Nor did he believe that the speeding carriage had been an accident. Indeed, he wouldn't be surprised if the theft had been set up as a diversion. He hadn't seen the driver, had only caught a glimpse of a hooded black cloak.

Sir Samuel Wright, a prominent banker Logan often did business with, approached him. "Glad to see neither you nor Lady Emily were hurt, Jennsen," Sir Samuel said. "The carriage driver was wearing a black hooded cloak. I didn't recognize the vehicle."

Neither had anyone else, apparently. A gentleman whose name Logan didn't know but whom he recalled seeing at last night's soiree offered, "I couldn't see the driver's face as he wore a dark hooded cloak, as Sir Samuel said."

"And your name, sir?" Logan asked.

"Lord Calvert."

After Logan had introduced himself, Lord Calvert turned to the rotund woman, clearly his wife, clutching his arm. "Did you see anything?"

"Just the hooded cloak," replied Lady Calvert, whose excited agitation had her turban feathers twittering, making Logan certain she was torn between the desire to swoon and the determination to stay alert so as not to miss anything.

"Heavens, another mysterious person in a hooded cloak, just like at Lord Teller's party last night," continued Lady Calvert in a breathless voice. Her eyes widened, and her feathers bobbed even faster. "Oh, my, do you suppose the carriage driver was another *vampire*?"

While several of the bystanders gasped at the suggestion, Logan was more inclined to look skyward. He glanced at Lady Emily to see her reaction and was surprised to see she looked . . . smug? Surely not, yet unless he was mistaken, and he didn't think he was, that was a self-satisfied gleam in her eyes. Now what the devil was that all about?

Before he could think on the matter, Lord Calvert said, "Don't be ridiculous, my dear. Everyone knows vampires only flit about at *night*. The sun would melt the diabolical creature."

"Which would explain the hooded cloak," Lady Calvert insisted. "Why else would the driver wear such a garment on such a fine day?"

A murmur went up in the crowd, and Logan again had to fight the urge to look skyward. He didn't bother to suggest the reason was that the driver didn't want to be recognized— because the speeding carriage had been no accident.

"Lady Emily needs to return home," he said firmly, hopefully ending any further vampire speculations. After he again assured the crowd that he and Lady Emily were unhurt, the bystanders dispersed, leaving Logan with the Stapleford clan.

"Can't thank you enough for saving our girl," Kenneth said, extending his hand. "You have our deepest gratitude."

Logan shook the young man's hand, then William's and Percy's as well. Mary, who held all three puppies' leads, offered him a smile and her thanks. Aunt Agatha grasped his hand between both of hers and said very loudly, "Well done, Mr. Jennsen. Such bravery! Can't thank you enough."

Arthur approached him, but instead of extending his hand as his brothers had, the lad wrapped his arms around Logan's waist and hugged him tight. "Thank you, Mr. Jennsen. Thank you for saving Emmie."

Logan's heart seemed to shift on its moorings, touched by their gratitude, and Arthur's demonstration touched him most of all. He couldn't recall the last time anyone had hugged him in such a spontaneous way. Indeed, he didn't believe anyone ever had. He rested his hands on Arthur's shoulders and looked at Lady Emily over the boy's head. Their eyes met, and he experienced a sensation that felt like a direct blow to his heart. Her face was still pale and marred with a streak of dirt, and it was all he could do not to push everyone out of the way, sweep her into his arms, and carry her the rest of the way home. Damn it, if something had happened to her—

He cut off the thought. She was unhurt. As was he. But only by the grace of God. It wasn't an accident, of that he was convinced. And he was determined to find who was responsible and why. And then stop him.

Logan walked with them up the flagstone walkway to the door. As the others filed into the foyer, he touched Lady Emily's arm. "You're certain you're all right?" he asked quietly.

Her eyes softened, and her bottom lip trembled in a way that again made him want to snatch her into his arms, only this time to kiss that lovely plush mouth. To feel her pressed against him. To breathe in her sweet, flowery scent. To touch her soft skin.

"Yes, thanks to you," she replied. "Are you certain *you're* all right?"

He wasn't. And wouldn't be until he found out what the hell was going on and who was responsible. But he said, "I'm fine."

Her gaze skimmed over him. "I fear your greatcoat cannot make the same claim."

He glanced down at the tears and dirt marring the navy blue wool. "I have others." He then lowered his hand from her arm, unsettled by how reluctant he was to stop touching her. "Take care. Be careful."

She offered him a rueful smile. "Rest assured I won't ever step out into the road again until after I make certain there isn't a moving carriage anywhere near me."

"Good. Then I shall bid you farewell."

"Would . . . would you like to come in for some tea or perhaps something stronger after your ordeal?"

Damn it, he wanted to. Very much. Too much. But there were things he needed to do, things that couldn't wait. And besides, he didn't want to prolong their time together. Did he? God help him, only a few hours ago he would have answered with an emphatic no. But now . . . now he wasn't certain.

"Thank you, but I must go."

Was that disappointment that flashed in her eyes? "Oh. Of course. Well, thank you again."

He offered her a formal bow, then made his way down the walkway, fighting the overwhelming desire to look back, to capture one last glimpse of the woman who had so thoroughly surprised him today. Who'd almost lost her life today.

He managed to win the battle until he closed the town house's wrought-iron gate behind him. Then he could no longer resist, and he paused to glance back toward the house. She stood framed in one of the narrow-paned windows flanking the double oak doors. He watched as she dropped to her knees in front of Arthur so she was on eye level with the boy and pulled him into her arms. Arthur hugged her as if he'd never let her go. He didn't release her until they were set upon by Romeo, Juliet, and Ophelia. She smiled . . . that enchanting smile that engaged her entire face and lit up her eyes.

And then she turned her head, and their gazes met. Even through the glass he could see her surprise that he was still there. A wave of embarrassed heat rushed through him at being caught gawking at her like a green schoolboy in the throes of his first infatuation. She slowly inclined her head in a nod, and he responded with a quick nod of his own then swiftly departed toward the park before he made an even bigger ass of himself.

∞

An hour later, after a fruitless walk through Hyde Park during which he didn't sense anyone watching him, Logan entered the foyer of his Berkeley Square mansion and was greeted by a stone-faced, unflappable Eversham, who didn't so much as bat an eyelash at the torn and dirty state of Logan's greatcoat or remark about his missing hat.

"I'll see to it this is brought to the tailor, sir," the butler droned in his arid monotone, holding the ruined garment as far away from his impeccable self as possible.

Logan often wondered what it would take to elicit a reaction from the man. He knew the haughty butler didn't wholly approve of his American employer, but Logan also suspected that somewhere, underneath all that British stiffness, Eversham secretly enjoyed working for the wealthiest man in the city. It had become something of a quest for Logan to ruffle his feathers. He had thus far failed.

"Don't you want to know what caused this disaster to my outerwear?"

"Only if you insist upon telling me, sir."

"I was nearly run down by a carriage."

Eversham's inscrutable expression didn't change. "As you're standing here, 'tis clear that 'nearly' is the operative word."

"Yes. I'm certain you're delighted no harm came to me."

"Naturally, sir. Your continued good health is a constant source of joy to me."

Damn, that plank-down-his-breeches demeanor never failed to amuse Logan, although he'd rather be hanged at dawn than admit it. "As yours is to me, Eversham. Of course, your joy would be much more convincing if you actually smiled, you know."

"I am smiling, sir," replied the stone-faced Eversham.

"Of course you are. Although next time perhaps you'd stomp your foot. Just to make your joy a bit more obvious."

"If that is what you wish, sir."

Obviously today wasn't the day Logan would complete his quest.

"I'll need another coat and hat," Logan said.

"In general, sir, or immediately?"

"Immediately." He knew damn well that Eversham knew exactly what he'd meant, yet the butler took delight—or as close to delight as the granite-faced servant could—in occasionally pretending not to understand Logan's meaning because Logan spoke *American*, as opposed to English. Logan supposed it was a point of pride with the stuffy man. In truth, Logan enjoyed occasionally tossing out words or phrases he knew would annoy Eversham. He was well aware it wasn't an employer-servant relationship that would work for everyone, but he found it amusing, and as far as he could tell, in spite of him never so much as cracking a grin, so did Eversham.

"Please tell Mr. Seaton that my plans have changed, and I won't be available to go over the accounts with him until later today," he said as Eversham helped him into a new coat.

"I'll be delighted to tell him the moment he arrives, sir."

Logan frowned. "Arrives? Adam isn't here?"

"No, sir. Mr. Seaton departed the house shortly after you and has yet to return."

"Did he say where he was going?"

"No, sir."

Clearly something unexpected had come up, as Adam was supposed to be readying the accounts for Logan's review. Damn. Hopefully there wasn't another problem at the docks.

He accepted a new hat from Eversham, then climbed into

his carriage. "Covent Garden, number four. Bow Street," he instructed Paul, his coachman.

A quarter hour later, Logan entered the brick building that housed the offices of the Bow Street Runners. A few minutes after that, he found himself seated across from Gideon, who looked uncharacteristically undone.

"Is something amiss?" Logan asked.

Gideon shook his head. "No. Did you see Julianne? She just left."

Ah. A visit from his wife. No wonder he looked so rumpled. "I didn't see her. Is she well?"

"She's perfect." He ran his hands through his already mussed hair. "And pregnant."

Envy wormed through Logan. A beautiful wife, a child on the way . . . That sounded damn good. And so . . . not lonely. "That explains your half-deliriously-happy, half-terrified expression. Congratulations."

"Thank you." Gideon studied him for several seconds then narrowed his eyes. "Something has happened."

"Yes." Logan explained the afternoon's events, concluding with, "I'm convinced it wasn't an accident. In fact, I think the robbery was a ruse to divert attention away from the carriage until it was too late."

"Which means it was a premeditated act, rather than spur of the moment."

"Exactly. Have you discovered anything about who might be watching me?"

"Not yet, but I'm working on it. As is one of my most trusted and tenacious investigators. Who knew you would be walking in the park today?"

Logan considered. "Lady Hombly, of course. Her butler Thurman—she mentioned our plans to him when we departed her house. My butler and coachman. And my man of affairs, Adam Seaton. I've no idea if any of them mentioned it to anyone else."

"You're certain Emily wasn't expecting to see you?"

"Yes. Our encounter was completely by chance."

"And you didn't sense you were being watched until near the end of your walk?"

"Correct." Although he had to wonder if that was because

he wasn't being observed until then, or because his attention had been so intently focused on Lady Emily.

Unable to remain seated, he rose and paced the length of the room. Then he halted in front of Gideon's desk. "Given everything else that has occurred—the attempted break-in at the docks, the destroying of my ship, my repeated sense of being followed—it's too coincidental to think the carriage incident wasn't deliberate."

"I'm inclined to agree with you. If the carriage was merely out of control, the driver would have shouted a warning and wouldn't have hidden his identity beneath a hooded cloak."

"Exactly." His gaze bored into Gideon's. "But *I* wasn't the person nearly run down. Lady Emily was."

Gideon studied him over steepled fingers. "You believe someone was trying to hurt *her* rather than you?"

Logan raked his hands through his hair. "I don't know. It seems much more likely that I was the intended victim and she was simply in the wrong place at the wrong time. Yet while it's true I was nearby, that carriage was aimed directly at her, not me. Still, I cannot fathom why anyone would wish to harm her."

"Whereas you could have any number of enemies."

"Yes."

"Maybe the driver gambled you would leap to her rescue and hoped to make you a victim that way."

"Perhaps, although that seems a roundabout way to go about it. If he wanted me dead, or at the very least grievously injured, why not simply shoot me or stab me and be done with it?"

"It's much easier to escape in an already speeding carriage—which can be blamed as an accident—than it is to get away from a shooting or stabbing."

"True." Logan commenced pacing again. "I've been giving this a great deal of thought. Maybe this person is trying to exact revenge on me not by physically harming me, but rather by trying to hurt me in other ways. By sabotaging my ship, hurting my business, thus damaging me financially."

Gideon slowly nodded. "That is certainly possible. But again, why try to hurt Emily? Unless the culprit also wishes to hurt you by harming anyone you care for. Perhaps whoever is watching you believes Emily is important to you." Gideon paused then asked, "Is she?"

Logan halted his pacing. An emphatic *no* instantly rose in his throat, but he found he couldn't utter it. He even coughed — twice — in an effort to dislodge the denial, but couldn't. Which was ridiculous. She wasn't *important* to him. It wasn't as if he *cared* for her, at least not more than one acquaintance would care for another. Certainly not more than he cared for anyone else.

Then why have her kisses turned you inside out? His annoying inner voice asked. *And why did your heart nearly stop when you believed her hurt today?*

His brows bunched into a frown. Both questions were easily answered. He'd been so long without a woman, any female's kiss would have affected him. And naturally he wouldn't want to see her—or anyone—hurt.

He noted Gideon watching him closely. Finally he said, "We were simply walking in the park. Her entire family was present."

"That's not what I asked you."

Right. He'd asked if she was important to him. Logan cleared his throat. "There's nothing between us." Right. Except those kisses and a desire he could neither talk himself out of, it seemed, control. "At least not in the way you're implying."

Gideon's brows raised. "I wasn't implying anything. I merely asked a simple question."

"Then the answer is . . ." *Yes. No. Damn it, I don't know.* "She means no more than anyone else. We are . . . friends." He nearly choked on the bland word. Friends? He'd never before had a *friend* he wanted to kiss until neither of them could breathe. Whose clothes he wanted to rip off—with his teeth. Who he wanted to spend a fortnight with—naked. For starters.

"Maybe the driver believes you are more than friends. Or maybe that is enough for him—to hurt your friend."

Pure rage washed through Logan at the suggestion. "Well, then we need to find out who this bastard is and stop him. Now. Before Lady Emily or anyone else is hurt." An image of Velma and Lara Whitaker flashed in his mind. "Or killed." A muscle ticked in his jaw. "When I find out who his responsible for this—"

He bit off the rest of his words. Best not to say them to a man committed to upholding the law. "Until I do, I want to hire someone to watch her during the day. Starting immediately. Whoever you think is best. To make certain she's safe."

Gideon didn't say anything for several seconds. Then he cleared his throat. "Because she's not important to you."

"Because she almost was killed today," Logan said evenly. "I neither want nor need more deaths on my conscience."

Gideon nodded. "I know of someone, but he won't come cheap."

"I doesn't matter how much it costs."

"Two men will probably be necess—"

"Just one," Logan said. "To watch her during the day."

"What about at night?"

"I'll watch her at night."

Gideon's brows shot upward. "Oh?"

He leveled a cool look on the Runner. "We attend the same soirees. It will be easier and call less attention than if a stranger is watching her."

"And what about when these soirees are over? Do you intend to skulk about in the hedges beneath her bedchamber window?"

"If that's what it takes, yes."

Logan saw the speculation that flickered in Gideon's eyes, but he frankly didn't care what the other man might think. He'd learned long ago that if he wanted something done correctly, it was best to do it himself. It had absolutely nothing to do with the unpleasant way his stomach tightened at the thought of another man remaining close to her during a soiree.

A long silence stretched between them, then finally Gideon nodded solemnly. "I understand."

Logan had the feeling that Gideon put a wealth of meaning behind those two little words, certainly much more than they warranted, but as he had no desire to prolong the conversation, he merely said, "Good."

"What about you?" Gideon asked. "Don't you want protection for yourself?"

"I can handle myself, and I've already instructed my factotum to hire extra security for my ships and warehouses. I intend to keep myself as visible as possible, hopefully to draw this bastard out."

"Make certain you're armed," Gideon said, "lest you be sorry if you do draw him out."

Logan shot a grim glance at his boot, where his knife was sheathed. "Rest assured, he'll be the sorry one. And now I'll let you return to your work."

After they shook hands, Gideon said quietly, "We'll find whoever is responsible, Logan."

Of that Logan was sure, for he wouldn't rest until he'd done so.

He just hoped it would happen before anyone else was hurt.

Chapter 11

❧

It had been centuries since I'd experienced anything even remotely resembling vulnerability, yet as he slowly undressed me, he stripped away more than my clothing, leaving my heart, my feelings, completely exposed. I was supposedly the powerful one—immortal, invincible—but his touch, the desire in his eyes, rendered me utterly defenseless.

The Vampire Lady's Kiss *by Anonymous*

After indulging in a warm bath to wash away the remnants of her ordeal and soothe the myriad aches she'd sustained from her jarring landing, Emily's abigail Noreen helped her change into a fresh gown, clucking over her like a mother duck. Emily then dismissed the young woman and crossed her bedchamber to the delicate cherrywood escritoire in the corner, where she quickly penned and sealed a note, which she brought to Rupert in the foyer.

"I'd like that delivered immediately please, to Mr. Gideon Mayne at number four Bow Street. And please have the messenger wait for a reply."

"Yes, Lady Emily."

"Are there any letters or messages for me?" she asked,

hoping Carolyn might have penned a missive to tell her how her conversation with Daniel had gone. She hesitated to call on Carolyn, afraid she might interrupt an important discussion between them.

"No letters or messages," Rupert reported.

Emily nodded. Well, she'd see Carolyn, along with Sarah and Julianne, at Sarah's house this evening for a Ladies Literary Society meeting. She'd find out then how her friend was faring.

"I'll be resting in my bedchamber. Please advise me when you have an answer to my letter."

She returned to her bedchamber, but rather than resting she settled herself on the settee near the fireplace and set to work on the cloak she'd need for tomorrow evening's masquerade. She'd cut the simple garment from a length of black bombazine she'd found in a trunk in the attic that morning so all she needed to do now was sew the hem. Luckily it was a simple stitch that required little concentration, for her mind kept wandering from the task at hand to the man she'd tried so unsuccessfully to forget.

The man who had saved her life.

A tremor ran through her as she recalled her utter terror, watching that carriage race toward her, certain she was about to draw her last breath. Then the shocking sensation of his arms wrapping around her, shielding her with his body. The skidding, bone-thudding fall. Then opening her eyes to find him looking down at her, his ebony gaze filled with so much worry and fear, for several seconds she thought she must be dead. But then she'd realized that she was enveloped in his strong arms, the lower half of her body pressed against him, and decided that if she'd died, she'd surely gone to heaven.

There was no doubt he'd saved her life and at great peril to his own. In addition to all the other unexpected things she'd discovered about him during their walk, she now knew he was brave. Chivalrous. And heroic. And—

Oh, dear God, it appeared she actually did *like* him.

Botheration. Perhaps she'd clunked her head on the ground when she'd fallen—that would explain these unwanted warm and *liking* feelings swirling through her. Yes, surely that was all this was—a bump on the head. After a good night's sleep, she'd be right back where she'd been before seeing him in Hyde Park: convinced he was nothing more than an ill-bred American with a money pouch where his heart belonged.

So she'd discovered he possessed some good qualities. Didn't *everyone*, no matter how odious, possess at least a few? Of course. This . . . whatever it was she was feeling for him was obviously a combination of sympathy for his difficult childhood, gratitude for him saving her, and some odd infatuation, no doubt the result of him being so completely unlike the sort of British gentlemen she was accustomed to.

Yes, that's all this was—a bit of liking mixed in with a temporary infatuation that would quickly pass. For he wasn't at all the sort of man she wanted to like or desire. She wanted what Sarah, Carolyn, and Julianne had. A man who adored her. A man she adored in return. Why, look at the lengths she was going through with her vampire scheme just so she wouldn't be forced into a loveless marriage with a wealthy man in order to save her family. The last thing she needed was to be tempted by Logan Jennsen, a man whose first, second, and third loves were his business. A man whose idea of fun was—

Kissing you.

Her needle faltered, and she stuck herself in the thumb. Uttering a word her mother would have considered most unladylike, she pressed her lips together and forced herself to concentrate on the task at hand. She'd just completed the bottom hem when a knock sounded on her door. After hastily secreting the cloak behind a velvet pillow on the settee, she scooted to her bed and arranged herself on top of her pale blue counterpane. "Come in," she called.

Noreen entered bearing a note on a silver salver. "This just arrived for you, Lady Emily," her abigail said, her eyes filled with concern. "Can I bring ye somethin'? A spot of tea or a bite to eat?"

"Thank you, no. I'd like to continue resting."

Noreen bobbed a curtsy then quit the room. The instant the maid closed the door behind her, Emily broke the seal on the note and scanned the contents.

Dear Emily,

As I am previously engaged tomorrow afternoon, I am unable to accompany you on your errand. However, I have arranged for another Runner, Mr. Simon Atwater, to escort you. He is completely trustworthy and will have the information you require. As you requested, Mr. Atwater will call for you at three o'clock tomorrow afternoon.

Yours truly,
Gideon

Emily breathed a satisfied sigh Excellent. But that meant she now had even more to accomplish between now and tomorrow afternoon.

"Which means no more time to daydream about Logan Jennsen," she muttered.

Unfortunately, she suspected that was easier said than done.

⚮

At eight o'clock that evening, Emily entered Sarah's private sitting room. Her heavily pregnant friend attempted to arise, but after flailing her arms for several seconds, collapsed back in her cushioned chair before either Emily or Julianne, who stood near the fireplace, could assist her.

"Don't get up," Emily said, hurrying forward to greet first Sarah then Julianne with a hug and kiss.

"Damnation, I'm like a fat beetle trapped on its back," Sarah grumbled, shoving a loose curl off her forehead. "I want you to know it nearly required a military coup to convince Matthew I was fit enough to entertain the Ladies Literary Society this evening. He acts as if I can't pour a few cups of tea and chat. Maddening man."

"He's concerned you'll tire yourself," Julianne said, clearly trying not to laugh at Sarah's disgruntled expression. "Gideon is already behaving in a similar manner."

"I'm not tired. I'm—"

"Irritable?" Emily supplied helpfully. "Cranky? Cantankerous?"

"Grouchy, cross, ill-tempered, and petulant?" Julianne suggested.

Sarah shot them both a glare that could curdle milk. "I'm *exhausted*—from being treated as if I'm a fragile piece of glass on the verge of breaking."

"Where is this brute of a husband who worships you and loves you to distraction and only wants what is best for you and your babe?" Emily asked.

"Yes, where is the beast?" Julianne seconded.

A bit of the annoyance drained from Sarah's expression. "He's currently taking a brandy in the library—and no doubt pacing furiously, worrying that his offspring will arrive any minute. You cannot imagine the wear he's inflicted upon the poor hearth rug."

She winced, and with a mighty heave, lifted herself several inches, shifted, then plopped back into the seat. Then gave a satisfied smile. "Ah. That's better, although how I will ever get out of this chair remains a mystery. I swear I feel as if I've been expecting this child *forever*."

"Where is Carolyn?" Emily asked as Julianne poured tea from the teapot that Sarah clearly couldn't reach.

"She isn't coming. She sent a note that she's feeling a bit unwell and won't be joining us."

Emily's hand shook, sloshing some tea over the edge of her cup onto the saucer. "Unwell?"

Sarah nodded, sending her spectacles sliding down her nose. "Nothing serious, just a slight headache. She thought it best to rest this evening so she'll be fully recuperated for Lord Farmington's soiree tomorrow evening. She doesn't want to miss your vampire masquerade."

Emily quickly bent her head over her teacup to hide her concern and the moisture that pooled behind her eyes. Dear God, Carolyn must feel poorly indeed. She never missed a gathering such as this. Last night she'd said she would tell Daniel what was going on and her concerns, and had promised to contact the Harley Street physician Edward's former doctor had recommended. Had she done so? Guilt suffused Emily for not sending Carolyn a note today, but she'd fully expected to see her this evening.

She wanted so badly to discuss the situation with her friends, yet she couldn't betray Carolyn's confidence. But the knowledge weighed heavily upon her, as did knowing her dear friend felt ill. She made a mental vow to call upon Carolyn tomorrow morning.

"Speaking of the vampire masquerade," Julianne's voice broke into her thoughts, "Sarah and I are all but perishing to know the details of your first outing. There was no mention of it in today's *Times*, but surely there will be tomorrow."

"I certainly hope so," Emily said.

"Details," Sarah commanded. "We who were not involved in last night's scheme demand details."

She related the story of her masquerade, pausing for dramatic effect before saying, "After showing myself on the terrace—which I'm delighted to report caused quite a stir—my cape became entangled in the bushes."

"Oh, dear," Julianne said, her eyes wide. "What did you do?"

"In order to avoid being discovered, I had to discard it. I then ducked into the library through the same window I'd used to exit the house. I removed my mask and fangs and hid them inside my gown. Then I returned to the party." She didn't add that she'd only returned to the party after Mr. Jennsen kissed her senseless. Again.

"So your outing was very nearly a disaster," Sarah said.

"On the contrary, except for the cape and the vial of blood, it went perfectly."

"Thank goodness it turned out well, and you accomplished your goal." Julianne reached out and laid her hand over Emily's, her eyes filled with concern. "But it was a close escape. Surely there's no need for you to risk another masquerade tomorrow night."

"Oh, but I must. Because I don't *know* if I accomplished my goal, although people seem to be talking about the vampire." She quickly told them what Lady Calvert had said in the park earlier that afternoon. "That gives me hope, but another sighting is imperative to fan the flames. And besides, I'm determined to do it properly tomorrow night. No more tangled cape in the bushes. Just a smooth, perfect performance."

"Or you could be caught and bring down upon your head a scandal the likes of which would ruin you and be reported in the *Times* for months," Sarah said. The instant the words left her mouth, she heaved a sigh. "I'm sorry. I don't mean to be the voice of gloom and doom. I'm just so . . . oh, dear. I guess I *am* cranky and cantankerous."

"You're expecting," Emily said, squeezing her hand. "And acting just as my mother did when she was expecting my sister and brothers. But very soon you'll have a beautiful baby to show for it."

Sarah's eyes glistened with tears behind her glasses. "I know. I'm just worried. About you and this vampire scheme. About the unknown of giving birth. About Matthew surviving the ordeal without ripping out his hair. About Carolyn, who I think is acting strangely, even though she insists everything is fine. I'm just worried about everything—and that's so unlike me." She gave a mighty sniffle and looked at Julianne. "Just you wait. In a few months you'll be a waddling, worried mess just like me."

Julianne's lips curved into a tremulous smile. "I'm looking forward to it. Gideon is going to be an incredible father, and I cannot wait to bestow on our child all the love my parents never showed me." She turned to Emily. "By the time my baby arrives, your story will be published and your family's financial woes long behind you."

"Yes," Emily agreed, praying it would happen just that way. "That will certainly silence the doubters."

"Doubters?" Sarah repeated. "Did someone claim the creature they saw last night wasn't a vampire? From what you told us, Lady Calvert certainly believes she saw one."

"Mr. Jennsen is highly skeptical," Emily said with a sniff.

Sarah and Julianne exchanged a quick look. "Oh? He attended last night's party?" Julianne asked.

"He saw you masquerading as the creature?" Sarah added.

"Yes, he attended, no, he didn't see the vampire. Which is why he's skeptical."

"So you spoke to him last night after your masquerade," said Sarah, her voice ripe with . . . something. "What else did he say?"

We once again find ourselves alone in a library . . . this bit of skin is simply too delicious to resist . . . you didn't think our kiss was a debacle when your body was pressed against mine, and your tongue was in my mouth.

Heat raced through Emily as she recalled snippets of his words, words she could never repeat to her friends, and she took a quick sip of hot tea in the hopes of blaming the fire burning her cheeks on the steamy beverage. After clearing her throat, she said, "We didn't talk very much." *We were too busy kissing.* "But we had a chat earlier today."

That last unwise statement was clearly the result of her jangled nerves, and she instantly wished she could snatch it back. Both her friends raised their brows in speculative fashion.

"You saw Mr. Jennsen today?" Julianne asked. "When? Where?"

Botheration. Instead of hemming her cloak, she should have sewn her lips closed. "We met by chance in the park."

When she didn't elaborate, Sarah prompted, "And you chatted . . ."

"Yes."

"About what?" Julianne asked.

"Um, Romeo and Juliet, mostly."

Sarah frowned. "You discussed Shakespeare?"

"No, Tiny's puppies." To assuage her conscience, which pricked her for being less than forthcoming about Mr. Jennsen, and also because it was more than likely that someone, such as the gossipy Lady Calvert, would repeat the tale, she said, "At least we chatted until the near accident." After she related what happened with the carriage, both Sarah and Julianne stared at her with wide, horrified eyes.

"Dear God, you could have been killed," Sarah said in a shaky voice.

Julianne reached out and clasped her hand. "You would have been if not for Mr. Jennsen. Emily, he saved your life."

It was all she could do to suppress the gushy sigh that rose in her throat. "Yes. I know."

Julianne and Sarah exchanged another look. Then Julianne said gently, "You realize what that means."

"Well, yes, of course. I told him how grateful I was. So did my family."

Sarah gave her head an impatient shake. "No, not that. It means he must *care* for you."

For several seconds Emily's blood seemed to still, and her

heart lurched in her chest. Then she said, "Don't be ridiculous. He would have done the same for anyone."

"Risked his own life in such a way? I don't think so," Julianne said softly.

"Well, I do," Emily insisted. "Only a complete cad would have stood by and done nothing."

"Which only serves to prove what I've been saying all along," Sarah said. "Logan Jennsen is not, in any way, a cad. Perhaps now you won't think so ill of him."

"I . . . I don't think ill of him." And she didn't, although she wished she did. The myriad emotions and feelings he now inspired were so much more complicated than when she simply disliked him.

Anxious to change the subject, she attempted a smile. "It all ended well, so now I must concentrate on making tomorrow night's vampire sighting a complete success. For surely after another sighting, the *Times* will report on the matter, and the story will take on a life of its own. Then I'll be certain to sell my story and earn a princely sum."

"And then we can concentrate on finding you a man you can fall in love with," Sarah said.

An image of Logan Jennsen popped into Emily's mind, and she very firmly pushed it aside. For while she might reluctantly like the man, unwisely and inexplicably desire him, there was absolutely no possibility of her falling in love with him.

Absolutely none.

Chapter 12

❧❧

I lay back upon my pillows and opened my arms to him. He came willingly, eagerly, either not realizing or not caring about the danger that awaited him. My fangs throbbed, and I knew the bloodlust raging through me would have to be satisfied tonight.

The Vampire Lady's Kiss *by Anonymous*

Logan stood in the shadows of the lone elm tree rising from the frozen ground in the small garden behind Lady Emily's town house. The moon cast the area with a silvery glow that flitted in and out with the clouds blown about by the brisk, frigid wind. His every breath fogged the air in front of him, and although he blew into his gloved hands, the bitter cold seeped into his skin.

Yet he barely felt the discomfort as he looked up at the window of Lady Emily's bedchamber. A dim light flickered, a lone candle, he guessed, and he wondered if she were reading. Or preparing for bed. The thought of her behind those French windows, removing her clothes, then sliding between soft sheets, her silky hair spread over her pillow, filled him with a heat that belied the frosty January night.

And he'd been thinking of her constantly.

All day. All evening. And most especially since relieving Simon Atwater, the Bow Street Runner Gideon had sent to guard her, and taking up his post after she returned from her visit to Sarah's town house. He'd thus far seen no one lurking about, detected nothing suspicious, which he prayed meant she wasn't in any danger. He pulled out his pocket watch and slanted the gold piece up to a sliver of moonlight. Just after midnight. It was going to be a long, cold night.

Unless . . . he allowed his imagination to wander and promptly envisioned her lying in her bed. Naked. Her beautiful eyes glazed with arousal. Her tongue peeking out to slowly wet her full lips. Nipples cherry red and erect. He saw himself kneeling between her splayed thighs, urging them wider apart. A groan rose in his throat at the vivid mental picture filling his mind of her glistening folds, swollen and wet with need. For him. He reached out to touch her—

"What in God's name are you doing here?"

That whispered hiss coming from directly behind him startled him so he nearly yelped. He simultaneously whipped around and fell into a crouch, his fingers wrapping around the hilt of the knife in his boot. And found himself staring at a fur-trimmed pelisse. He jerked his head up. Lady Emily stared down at him.

"Are you going to answer me, or do you intend to simply squat there all night?"

Muttering an obscenity, he slipped his knife back into its sheath then rose. "What in God's name are you doing here?" he demanded in a hoarse whisper.

She cocked a brow. "I believe that is what I asked *you*."

"And what the hell do you mean by sneaking up on me like that?" Damn it, the woman had shaved a decade off his life.

"Considering that you've sneaked up on me more than once, it seems only fair that I return the favor."

"I could have slit your throat."

Her other brow rose. "With what? Your rapier reflexes?"

Annoyance—at both himself and her—flooded him. He treated her to his fiercest narrow-eyed glare, which, damn it, didn't appear to intimidate her in the least. "With the knife in my boot," he replied in an icy tone.

A frosted puff of air blew from her lips. "I could have coshed you half a dozen times before you reached for that knife."

He gritted his teeth. Damn it, she was right, which only served to aggravate him further. Again he asked, "What are you doing out here?"

"I saw you. From my window. Skulking about, which seems to be a habit of yours. So I came outside to find out what you are doing out here. Other than waiting to slit my throat." She crossed her arms over her chest. He heard a faint tapping sound and realized it was her shoe rapping against the hard ground. "Well?"

By God, he felt like an idiot. And it was all her fault. If he hadn't been distracted by thoughts of her, naked and aroused, and glistening and naked . . . he shook his head to dispel the erotic image lingering in his mind. If he hadn't been distracted by those thoughts, she wouldn't have been able to sneak up on him. He considered lying about why he was here, but really, there was no plausible explanation other than the truth for why he'd be in her garden at midnight.

"After today's incident with the carriage, I was . . . worried. So I decided to check around a bit. Make sure no one suspicious was lurking about."

The irritation faded from her eyes, and she blinked several times. "You were worried? About . . . *me*?"

A muscle ticked in his jaw. "Yes. Do you know what that makes me?"

"A . . . *worried* skulker?"

He narrowed his eyes. "Just worried."

"H . . . how long have you been out here?"

Damn. Again he wanted to lie, to say five minutes, but his conscience balked at telling her less than the truth. "A few hours."

"A few *hours*?" she repeated in a stunned whisper. "How long did you intend to stay?"

Hell, no point in prevaricating now. "Until dawn."

"Because you were worried about me." She said the words slowly, as if she were having trouble comprehending them.

He pressed his lips together and jerked his head in a tight nod. Clearly the only way to make her understand was to admit the entire truth. "The carriage today . . . I don't think it was an accident." He quickly told her about the recent spate of incidents against him, concluding with, "I believe someone is trying to hurt me. He may be attempting to do so by hurting anyone close to me. If he saw us together at the park, he might have thought we were . . ."

"Close," she finished when he hesitated.

"Yes. I wanted to make certain you were safe, so . . . here I am."

"And you've been out here for hours," she murmured, still sounding and looking stunned. "And intended to stay out here for many more hours."

"Yes."

Her mouth opened and closed several times with no words coming forth. He'd be hard-pressed to name anyone he'd ever witnessed appear more confounded than she did.

Finally she cleared her throat. "That's very . . . nice of you."

"It has nothing do to with nice. I simply feel responsible. Although I must say it's rather insulting that you continually appear so amazed that I might do something nice—if indeed this was an act of niceness. Which it is not."

She appeared not to hear him. Indeed, she was looking at him as if she'd never seen him before. "Well, as you can see, I'm fine."

"Yes." She was. Exceedingly fine. She stood in a swatch of moonlight that painted her skin with an ethereal silver glow and made her eyes appear radiant. He had to fist his hands to keep from reaching out to touch her.

"You must be cold," she said. "I've only been out here for a few moments, and I'm chilled to the bone."

He *had* been cold. Until he'd thought of her naked and aroused, and glistening and naked and . . . damn it, there went his errant thoughts again. He shoved them aside, but the damage was done. He felt as if his skin were on fire.

"I'm quite all right. You, however, need to return to the house." Now. Before he gave in to the temptation to yank her into his arms and put out this damn inferno she'd ignited inside him.

She nodded. "I do need to go back inside." She brought her gloved hand to her nose and rubbed. "I think I'm frozen. I can't feel my face." Then she reached out and touched his arm. "Please come inside with me. Father has some excellent brandy. It will help rid you of the chill."

He stilled, from both her touch and her offer. And was appalled at how much he wanted to accept. "Your family would hardly approve of that, any more than they would of you being out here."

"My parents retired over an hour ago and are notoriously sound sleepers. They'd never know you were about."

"What of the rest of your family?"

"All very sound sleepers."

"Except for you, it seems."

Her gaze shifted to the ground. He had the distinct impression she was blushing, and he cursed the darkness that prevented him from knowing.

"I . . . I wasn't tired. But once I fall asleep, I'm just like the rest of my family. It's as if we were hit on the head with an anvil."

A huff of laughter escaped him, frosting the air between them. "That's one way to get a good night's sleep."

A slow smile curved her lips, and damned if he didn't feel as if the sun had just risen over the horizon. "Yes, if you can stand the horrid headache." Her hand slipped from his sleeve, and she wrapped her arms around herself. "Please come inside and warm yourself before the fire. After all you've done for me today, it is the least I can offer you."

A small voice inside him warned he was playing with fire, but her beautiful eyes gleamed like moonbeams, beseeching him, and his resistance crumbled. "Very well. But just for a quick warmer. Then I'm resuming my watch."

"It clearly hasn't occurred to you that you could watch me much better if we're in the same room together."

Oh, it had occurred to him. In vivid detail. And that room had been her bedchamber. Where she'd been naked and aroused, and glistening and naked and . . . good God, he wasn't going to allow his thoughts to travel down *that* path again. Absolutely not.

"Come." She strode toward the house, and he fell into step behind her. A moment later she opened a set of French windows. Clearly this was how she'd exited the house. He shook his head. Damn. He must have been sorely distracted with his erotic thoughts to have missed her slipping outdoors from windows that were clearly visible from where he'd stood.

He followed her inside then watched her close and lock the

paned glass panel. He turned to survey the room and stilled at the sight of the enormous globe and floor-to-ceiling bookshelves filled with leather-bound volumes. Bloody hell, as the Brits were so fond of saying.

The library.

Images of the passionate interludes he'd shared with this woman the last two times they'd found themselves alone in a library flashed through his mind, leaving a trail of heat in their wake.

"Would you like a brandy?" she asked, heading toward a set of crystal decanters set on a table near the brick fireplace where a low-burning fire glowed, casting the room in flickering gilded shadows.

"In a minute." He snagged her arm and gently redirected her toward the hearth. "Let's get you warmed up first."

When they stood before the fire, he turned toward her. And his heart performed some sort of acrobatic maneuver at the sight of her red nose, trembling lips, and chattering teeth. She looked chilled to the bone and achingly beautiful and more appealing than any woman he'd ever seen. And he realized that he never should have set foot inside with her. The next quarter hour or so until he could escape back into the cold where he belonged was going to be nothing more than an exercise in torture. Well, so long as he kept his hands—and lips—to himself, he'd get away without further complicating matters between them.

He crouched down and after removing his gloves he stoked the banked fire with the brass poker. A stream of bright sparks twirled upward, dancing toward the flue. He then used the bellows to fan the flames. A bright fire quickly caught, emanating heat.

Rising, he set his hands on her shoulders and vigorously rubbed his palms up and down her arms. "You'll thaw out quickly," he said, keeping his movements brisk and businesslike, refusing to think about the fact that he was touching her. About how small and delicate she felt beneath his hands.

"What about you?" she asked, her gaze locked on his, her chin still quivering with cold.

Thanks to you, I feel as if my skin is aflame. "I'm used to the cold. It doesn't bother me very much."

A mighty shiver ran through her, and he had to fight the

overwhelming urge to draw her into his arms and warm her up
with something more interesting than a rubdown. "How does
one get used to the cold?" she asked through chattering teeth.

He hesitated then shrugged. "Spend enough nights sleeping outdoors, and you eventually become inured to the discomfort." He didn't add that eventually you become inured to
everything except the will to survive one more day.

Sympathy filled her eyes, and he shook his head. "No need
to feel sorry for me. I don't regret any of those hardships. They
made me what I am today." His lips turned up in a half smile.
"You know, an uncouth colonial."

The sympathy in her eyes gave way to a sheepish expression.
She was clearly about to say something, but instead went perfectly still when he pressed her hands between his, then lifted
them to his mouth. With his gaze steady on hers, he expelled
a long, slow breath against her fingers. "Feeling warmer?" he
asked, the words brushing his lips against her gloves.

Her gaze shifted from his eyes to his lips, and he had to
stifle a groan. Damn it, he felt that look as deeply as if she'd
actually kissed him. Her attention lifted back to his eyes.
"Yes, warmer," she whispered.

He exhaled another long, slow breath then reached out to
brush a single fingertip over her cold cheek. "Can you feel
your face yet?"

"Y . . . yes."

God, he wanted to keep touching her, but given this woman's detrimental effect on his control, he knew he shouldn't.
Yet he couldn't seem to stop. He would—just not yet. In spite
of the temptation she represented, as in all other aspects of his
life, he could control himself. He *would* control himself.

He released her hands and reached for the front closure of
her pelisse. "The fire's hot now. You'll feel the warmth better
without this on."

She stood wordlessly as he unfastened the garment then
slid it slowly from her shoulders and down her arms to reveal
a gown in a shade of blue that reminded him of a warm, sunlit
sea. He instantly wished the room were more brightly lit so he
could better distinguish the amazing things he knew the color
would do to her sea goddess eyes, how it would bring out the
aquamarine beneath the emerald.

A subtle whiff of flowers and sugar reached him, and he found himself pulling in a deep breath to capture the elusive scent. Damn, every time he smelled her he just wanted to bury his face in the sweet curve where her neck and shoulder met and simply breathe her in until he figured out how she managed to smell so delicious.

Without taking his gaze from her, he set her pelisse over the nearby wing chair then reached for her hand. And slowly pulled off her glove. Set it on top of her pelisse. Then he pressed her smooth palm between his and gently massaged.

She drew in a quick breath, which she released on a long sigh. "Oh, my," she whispered. "That feels marvelous."

It did indeed. If he'd ever touched softer skin, he couldn't recall the circumstances. He slipped off her other glove, then treated that hand to the same gentle massage, caressing each slim finger with long, slow strokes. "Feel better?"

She moistened her lips with the tip of her tongue, a flick of pink that rushed blood to his groin and peeled a thick layer off the control he prided himself upon. "Yes," she whispered.

Gritting his teeth, he forced himself to release her, step back, and turn to face the fire. "Good. In that case I'll . . ." *Leave. While I still can.* God knows that was the smart thing to say and do. Instead, he found himself saying, "Take that brandy now."

He listened to the rustle of her gown as she walked to the decanters, but he deliberately didn't look at her, just to prove to himself that he could keep from doing so. He removed his greatcoat, laying it on the seat of the wing chair.

"Here you are," she said softly.

As he couldn't avoid doing so, he turned toward her. And stifled a groan. She was so damn lovely. Whereas the moon had bathed her in silver, the light from the fire washed her with an array of reds and golds, bringing out the highlights in her glossy hair. With his gaze locked on hers, he reached for the snifter. Their fingers brushed, and he gritted his teeth against the sizzle that shot up his arm. Damn it all, it was ridiculous as well as unnerving that he should be so affected by such an innocent, inconsequential touch.

Forcing himself to turn back toward the fire, he took a hefty swallow of the brandy, savoring the burn down his throat and the resulting heat in his belly. Which wasn't at all welcome, since the last thing he needed was more heat anywhere near his belly. He quickly set the snifter on the mantel.

"You were right," he said, staring into the flames, "it is excellent brandy."

"I'm glad you like it, although I don't know how you can stomach the stuff. I tried it once." From the corner of his eye he saw her shudder. "Blech. Its flavor is what I imagine poison tastes like. It was even worse than the infamous grass cakes."

Before he could stop himself, he turned his head toward her. She was looking into the fire, holding out her hands to absorb the warmth of the flames, although how in God's name she could still be cold he couldn't imagine. Between the heat emanating from the hearth and that inspired by her nearness, he felt as if he were about to combust.

"Grass cakes?" he repeated.

She turned to face him, and their gazes met. He instantly felt the pull of those eyes, drawing him into their sea-colored depths.

She nodded. "A cake made out of grass. Thus the name."

"Where on earth did you come by such a culinary disaster, and what could have possibly induced you to eat it?"

"The cakes were my very own recipe, prepared in the garden at our country estate in Kent. I was all of seven years old. I made them because I'm very fond of spinach and, well, the grass looked like spinach. However, I found out that grass, especially when mixed with garden soil, tastes nothing like spinach." A smile lifted the corner of her lips. "I tried to entice Kenneth to taste my creation, but he ran away."

"Smart man. I would have done the same." A shudder ran through Logan. "I don't care for green food."

"Not even asparagus?"

"No."

"Broccoli?"

"Especially not broccoli."

"Peas?"

"They're tolerable. Barely. But not in the mushy style you Brits fancy."

"Oh? You prefer your peas crunchy?"

"Actually, I prefer them absent."

"Hmmm. Do you know what that makes you?"

"Very smart?"

"A green food hater."

He considered, then nodded. "A title I accept, although it isn't anywhere near as grand as Campion Frog Catcher."

"Do you like nuts?"

"They're not green, so yes. Besides, doesn't everyone like nuts?"

"I certainly do. And fortunately for us, so does my father."

"How is that lucky for us?"

For an answer, she crossed the room to the enormous mahogany desk in front of the bookcases flanking the French windows. He watched her open a drawer and slip out a square metal box.

"It is lucky for us," she said as she returned to the fireplace, "because Father keeps a secret supply of our cook's special recipe nuts hidden in this room."

"Obviously your father needs a new hiding place."

She laughed, and he found himself enchanted and unable to look away. "Oh, he finds new ones all the time. But I'm quite expert at discovering them. This time he went for the desk, a very obvious place, no doubt deducing I wouldn't think to look in such a likely location." She lifted the lid off the box and held it out to him. "I promise you've never tasted anything like this before."

He picked out a nut and held it in front of the fire to better see. "What's on it?" He tilted his head and gave the coated morsel a suspicious look. "It's not encrusted with grass and garden soil, is it?"

"Hardly. That's *my* secret recipe, not Cook's. Just taste it."

He shot her a sidelong glance. "You're not having one?"

"Of course I am. Indeed, once I get started, I find it nearly impossible to stop. It's merely polite for the hostess to offer treats to her guest before she indulges."

He flicked an askance look at the odd-looking nut coated with God knows what, then nodded toward the box. "You first."

She laughed. "Are you always this suspicious?"

"Actually, yes."

She made a tsking sound. "That's no way to go through life."

"I must disagree, as it's served me well so far. Doesn't your father notice the depletion in his cache?"

"Oh, yes. But he thinks Mother is the culprit, and since he'd never deny her anything, he simply pretends he doesn't notice."

"I see. But in fact it is *you* who makes off with the nutty treats."

"Guilty as charged, I'm afraid."

"Why does your father believe your mother is the nut thief?"

Her eyes gleamed with mischief, and her lips twitched. "I may have told him she was."

Laughter rumbled in his throat, but he swallowed it and shot her a severely disapproving look. "Do you know what that makes you?"

"Ingenious?"

"A teller of false tales and a thief. I must say, Lady Emily, I'm stunned."

"No you're not. What you are is afraid. Of that tiny little nut you're holding. I must say, Mr. Jennsen, I'm stunned."

Damn. Hoist on his own petard. He hated it when that happened. He heaved an exaggerated sigh and looked at the nut he held between his fingers. "Clearly there's only one way to redeem myself."

"Correct. But if it's any consolation, I promise you'll like it."

He turned so that he fully faced her. The warmth of the fire rose between them, and he had only to reach out his hand to touch her, to feel that silky skin that beckoned him like a siren's call. "And if I don't? What will you give me instead?" he asked softly.

She pulled in a quick breath, and her eyes seemed to darken. And suddenly it seemed to him as if the air surrounding them turned steamy and thick with tension. And awareness. God knows he was painfully aware of how alone they were. How close they stood. How beautiful she was. And how much he wanted to kiss her. Touch her. Feel her pressed against him. Hear that deep-throated moan that escaped her when she melted in his arms.

"I . . . I don't think it will be a consideration. You're going to like it."

"Perhaps. But I'm a man who likes to be prepared for all possible outcomes."

"I see. However, if you don't like the nut, I'm afraid I have nothing else to offer."

Without even giving the matter any thought, he could name several dozen things she could offer. Unable to resist any longer, he reached out his free hand and brushed a single fingertip along her soft cheek. Her skin felt like warm velvet. "A pity. In that case, I'll accept a forfeit. Of my choice. To be named later."

She leaned away from his touch, and her eyes narrowed. "Why, that's outrageous. You could ask for anything!"

One corner of his mouth pulled upward. "Yes, I could. But given your certainty that I'll enjoy this treat . . ." He held the nut aloft. "I see no reason for you to refuse."

She pursed her lips. "You obviously think me a fool, Mr. Jennsen. However, given my vast experience with five devilish younger siblings, I'm not so gullible as to be lured into such a potentially disastrous wager."

"Very well. The forfeit must be within reason."

"Better, but still not acceptable."

He considered for several seconds then said, "The forfeit I choose must be agreeable to you."

"And if it isn't?"

"Then I'll have to choose something else that you deem satisfactory."

"And if I don't like your second choice?"

"Then I'll have to continue suggesting until I hit upon something you *do* like. Does that meet with your approval?"

She pondered a bit then nodded. "Yes, that is acceptable."

"Then we are agreed." He held out his hand, and after a brief hesitation, she slipped her hand into his. Their palms met, and heat rushed up his arm. He looked down. His large brown hand seemed to swallow her small pale one. Damn if he didn't like the way her slender fingers looked wrapped around his, the way her warm, soft palm felt nestled against his.

Instead of releasing her hand after their brief shake, he raised it to his lips and lightly kissed the backs of her fingers. Her skin was satiny smooth and bore the faint scent of sugar and flowers. "You're quite a formidable negotiator," he said.

She made a breathy sound that rushed blood straight to his groin. "As I've told you, I've had much experience." She slipped her hand from his then gave the treat he still held a pointed look. "The next move is yours, Mr. Jennsen."

"Logan. In the spirit of our amiable discourse and agreeable wager after such intense negotiations, I think it only fitting we be on a first name basis. Don't you?"

"What I think, *Mr. Jennsen*, is that you are once again procrastinating and showing your fear of a tiny little nut."

With his gaze steady on hers, he slipped the nut into his mouth. A buttery sweet flavor exploded on his tongue. He bit down, surprised by the unusual consistency, which was somehow soft and crunchy at the same time. The taste filled his mouth, so delicious he nearly groaned out loud. Watching her all the while, he slowly chewed then swallowed.

"Well?" she asked, a smug smile playing around the corners of her mouth.

"I didn't like it." Which was the truth. He'd absolutely *loved* it. And would make certain he gained the recipe so his own cook could prepare it.

Her face sank like a cannonball tossed in the Thames. "I beg your pardon?"

"I. Didn't. Like. It."

Her eyes narrowed, and she planted her hands on her hips. "You're lying. You enjoyed it. I can tell."

Damn but he liked, admired, the way she stood up to him, didn't kowtow to him or ply him with insincere compliments or say what she thought he wanted to hear, all of which had become a wearying part of his existence since gaining his wealth. And on top of that, she was just so damn lovely. And he was so damn lonely. And the temptation to touch her was just too overwhelming.

"Very well, I'm lying. But I intend to collect my forfeit just the same."

She shook her head. "That's not the way it works."

"I know. But playing by the rules didn't get me where I am." He erased the distance between them in a single step and drew her into his arms. "I'll be collecting my forfeit. Right now. In the form of a kiss."

Chapter 13

My desire for him was so strong it frightened me. Because I knew I couldn't control it. It made me act recklessly, say things, do things, want and need things I otherwise never would have.

The Vampire Lady's Kiss *by Anonymous*

Emily knew she should protest. Push him away. Refuse him if for no other reason than that he wasn't playing fairly. One didn't get to collect a forfeit unless the wager was won—and he'd lost. He'd *admitted* he lost. How arrogant and maddening that he shoved aside all the acceptable rules of wagers simply because he wanted to!

She absolutely should listen to her inner voice, which frantically tried to remind her that kissing him the first time had been a mistake. The second time a *huge* mistake. That doing it a third time would be tantamount to insanity. Her mind knew it, yet her heart—her rapidly fluttering, sometimes foolish, but never lying heart—whispered that *this* was what she'd wanted from the instant she'd seen him tonight from her bedchamber window.

Another taste of his thrilling touch. To know one more

time the magic of his kiss. If she were completely honest, she'd have to admit she'd wanted more from the instant their first kiss had ended.

So before anything like better judgment could intrude, she rose up on her toes, wrapped her arms around his neck, and parted her lips.

"Yes," she whispered. "Kiss me."

His mouth covered hers in a searing kiss that stole her breath. Yes . . . *this* is what she'd longed for. *Craved.* This excitement, this passion. Her Ladies Literary Society's sensual readings had ignited her curiosity, her desire to know what all the heroines of her books had experienced, most recently Melanie in *The Gentleman Vampire's Lover.* The passion of a man's kiss, the wonder of his touch.

She'd never considered that she might experience it with this particular man, but there was no denying the way he made her feel. So . . . alive. As if part of her had lain dormant until he awakened it with his kiss. And . . . hot. As if fire pumped through her veins. And desperate. As if no matter what he did to put out the inferno he'd lit within her, it wouldn't be enough.

His tongue explored her mouth, a favor she returned with equal fervor, savoring his delicious taste she recalled so well. The hints of brandy, sugar, and cinnamon only rendered him more appealing to her senses. Dear God, she felt as if could drown in him.

He deepened the kiss, and with a groan she leaned into him, reveling in the sensation of his strong arms pulling her tighter, his hard body touching her from chest to knee, so close that a sheet of vellum couldn't have fit between them. His arousal pressed against her midsection, and she squirmed against the fascinating, enticing ridge, aching to feel that hardness at the juncture of her thighs where a throbbing, needy pulse beat.

She heard him moan harshly, his breathing ragged, and in the next heartbeat it seemed as if his hands were everywhere. Sifting through her hair, scattering pins, combing through her loosened curls. Trailing down her throat, over her chest. Palming her breasts. Her nipples hardened, and she arched her back, wanting more, desperate for more.

He broke off their kiss, and she moaned in protest, a sound that melted into a sigh of pleasure when he dragged his mouth down her neck. "Your scent . . ." he said in a rough rasp. "God, you smell so delicious." He touched his tongue to her throat. "Taste so delicious. What is that fragrance?"

Good Lord, she could barely think, and he expected her to speak? "Peony," she managed to say. "My favorite flower."

Her head fell limply back, and a shiver of delight racked her as his wicked mouth blazed a trail over her chest. His fingers slipped beneath the short capped sleeves of her gown and impatiently tugged. She lowered her arms, her limbs shaking with the desperation of wanting to feel his hands, his mouth, on her breasts.

Before she could even draw a breath, he'd yanked her bodice and chemise down to her waist with a single, hard jerk. A tiny part of her brain tried to interject that she had to end this madness. Now, while she still could. But the inferno within her incinerated the protest, which stood no chance against the need consuming her.

His magical fingers played with one nipple, while his warm tongue circled the other, then drew the tight, aching bud into the heat of his mouth. Emily's gasp of pleasure turned into a long moan, and she arched her back, offering more of herself. The feel of his mouth and hands on her was heaven and torture at the same time. Too much, yet not enough. Not nearly enough.

Feeling the sort of wicked abandon she'd known existed but until this moment had only read about, she lifted her arms and tunneled her fingers through his thick, silky hair then ran her curious, eager hands over the breadth of his wide shoulders. He drew her nipple deeper into his mouth, swirling his tongue around the peak, lightly grazing her with his teeth. Dark pleasure rippled through her, and she clutched his shoulders lest she slither to the floor.

He kissed his way back to her mouth, and she eagerly parted her lips. His tongue danced with hers, and she slipped one hand inside his jacket, resting her palm above his heart, which beat as fast and hard as her own. But just like everything else since the instant he'd touched her, it wasn't enough. She leaned back, breaking off their kiss just enough to whisper against his mouth, "Touch you. Want to touch you."

With a low growl, he released her. She braced her knees

to keep from melting into a puddle at his feet, and while his mouth continued to circle hers, his tongue teasing her bottom lip, he yanked off his jacket. It fell at his feet, and his waistcoat and cravat quickly followed. He then jerked his linen shirt from his buckskin breeches and hauled it upward, over his head.

"Touch me," he commanded in a raw voice filled with the same intense need careening through her. His eyes burned into hers like twin coals. He took her hands and pressed them against his chest. "Damn it, touch me."

Emily gasped at the feel of his skin beneath her palms. He leaned down to kiss her again, but she stepped back and ran her eager gaze over him.

Oh, my. What a sight he was. Smooth, warm skin stretched over hard muscle sprinkled with dark hair. She splayed her fingers, marveling at the combination of textures, then dragged her hands slowly downward. She wasn't certain what fascinated her more: the satiny ribbon of ebony hair that bisected his abdomen then disappeared into his breeches or the rippling muscles that contracted beneath her palms.

Logan pulled in a ragged breath, then released it in a shudder of pleasure that tightened his grip on her waist. The feel of her hands on him, her fingers tracing over his abdomen, was driving him mad. The sight of her, bodice pulled down, her full breasts topped with tight coral nipples still wet from his mouth, hair falling over her shoulders and down her back in loose disarray from his impatient fingers, wasn't helping him retain whatever small vestige of his sanity remained.

Stop this . . . he knew he should stop this, but God help him, he simply couldn't. Not yet. Not when her lips were moist and parted and arousal gleamed in her eyes. Not while her touch felt . . . ahhhh . . .

"So good," he murmured, leaning down to lightly nip her neck. "That feels so good. Don't stop." *Don't ever stop.*

He skimmed his hands up the curve of her waist and cupped her breasts, rolling her taut nipples between his fingers. She responded with a low moan and leaned forward to press a kiss to the center of his chest. She dragged her open mouth to his nipple and slowly circled it with her tongue, damn near stopping his heart.

His groan of pleasure turned into a growl of pure need

when her hand drifted lower. Coasted over his hip, then halted just short of touching him where he most wanted her to.

"Don't stop now," he whispered hoarsely against her lips. He grasped her wrist and pressed her hand against his erection. His eyes slid closed, and he gritted his teeth against the intense pleasure, fighting for control—a battle that was well and truly lost when she caressed him through his breeches. Damn it, it had been so long since he'd been touched. And her touch felt so incredibly *good*. And he wanted her so badly.

Helpless to remain still, he rolled his hips and thrust into her hand. With a groan that felt dragged from his soul, he fisted his hands in her silky hair and covered her mouth with his. His tongue danced with hers, exploring the delicious, velvety softness. Her fingers curled around his erection and squeezed, and he swore he was going to lose his mind. And realized he stood in grave danger of spilling against her hand.

Yet he couldn't stop. His tongue thrust deeper, a blatant imitation of the act his body desperately screamed to share with hers. He might possibly have been capable of retaining his last ounce of control had she given any indication she wanted to stop, but instead she pressed her breasts tighter against his chest, and something inside him seemed to snap.

The demands of his body overruled everything else, and whatever was left of his restraint and good intentions burned to ash. Without breaking their kiss, he scooped her into his arms and lowered her to the hearth rug, following her down with his body, insinuating one leg between hers, urging her thighs apart. He kissed his way along her jaw, then lower, over her chest, one hand playing with her breasts, while his other hand glided down her body to the hem of her gown.

He swirled his tongue around her nipple then drew the puckered bud into his mouth as his hand slipped beneath the layers of material then glided upward. His palm skimmed over the curve of her stockinged calf, along the length of her slender thigh, then unerringly found the slit in her drawers.

He raised his head and looked down at her. By God, she was gorgeous. Disheveled and flushed, her breaths coming hard and fast through her moist, parted lips.

"Look at me." His words were a harsh whisper in the quiet room.

She opened her eyes, and his entire body tightened at the glazed arousal fogging their normally clear depths. "Spread your legs," he demanded.

Her gaze locked on his, she splayed her thighs. His first touch to her feminine folds dragged a groan from both of them. She was so wet. And hot. He teased her with a lazy fingertip while his other hand continued to play with her breasts. She squirmed, spreading her legs wider, and her hip slid against his erection. Swallowing an obscenity, he clenched his jaw against the insistent ache and pressed his hard flesh against her.

He slipped a finger inside her and closed his eyes briefly. She was so damn tight. And soft. And he was so damn hard. He eased another finger inside her and gently pumped. Pressing his palm against her tender nub, he slowly rotated. Her eyes slid closed. A gasp pushed past her parted lips, and she arched into his hand, seeking more. He was only too happy to provide it.

"I feel so . . . so . . ." Her voice evaporated into a long sigh.

"Wet," he whispered. "Hot. Tight."

"Y . . . yes. And aching. And . . ." she lifted herself into his hand. "Desperate."

God, he knew all about desperate. He wanted her so badly he was damn near shaking.

He began a relentless, ruthless assault on her senses and body, wanting to feel her come apart in his arms, his lips and tongue circling hers, the fingers of one hand teasing her nipples, while his other hand stroked her feminine folds, pushing her ever closer to the release he was determined she have.

But she distracted his plans when she insinuated her hand between them and cupped his erection straining against the confines of his tight breeches. He sucked in a sharp breath, and his exploring hands stilled.

"I want to touch you," she said in a breathless whisper. "As you're touching me. Please . . ."

Gone was the wise voice in his head that should have warned him against giving in to her plea, that would have reminded him he was little more than a touch away from exploding. Instead, he slipped his fingers from her body and sat up. Rose to his knees between her splayed thighs. And opened his breeches.

Her gaze riveted on his straining erection, and he clenched his hands, his every muscle rigid with anticipation. Her eyes widened, and she licked her lips, a gesture that coaxed a pearl of fluid to leak from the tip of his arousal.

She sat up then slowly reached out. Brushed a single fingertip over the engorged head. "You're wet, too," she whispered.

He would have answered, but words were simply beyond him. The only sound in the room was the crackling of the fire and his harsh breathing.

"And hot," she murmured, wrapping her fingers around him. "And so hard."

Damn it, she had no idea. Indeed, if he'd ever in his entire life been harder, he couldn't recall the circumstances. Hell, he couldn't recall his own name. Only one word pounded through his mind, growing in intensity with each passing second.

Emily.

Emily, Emily, Emily.

She ran her fingers down his length, and a guttural groan he couldn't suppress escaped him. Her fingers stilled. "Did I hurt you?"

"No. God, no. Don't stop." *Don't ever stop. Just keep touching me. Because nothing has ever felt so good.*

Her soft hands continued to stroke him, driving him closer to a release he was no longer certain he could contain. When he was a single stroke away from spilling, he grasped her wrists.

"Enough." The single word was all he could manage. Wild, raw need clawed at him like talons with an intensity he'd never before known, shoving aside everything except the desperation to satisfy it. Had to have her. *Had to.* Now.

He urged her onto her back then shoved her skirts to her waist. *Have to have her. Feel her. See her. Have to.* The impatience with which he jerked down her drawers should have appalled him. Instead, it fueled this dark, vicious hunger consuming him. He tossed aside the delicate cotton, hooked his hands beneath her knees to raise them, then spread her legs.

Nestled in a thatch of dark curls, her sex glistened in the gilded firelight, swollen folds that beckoned him like a thief to treasure. The scent of feminine musk mixed with flowers and sugar filled his head. With a growl vibrating in his throat, he settled her calves over his shoulders, cupped his hands beneath her bottom, and lowered his head.

He teased her without mercy, his mouth and tongue and fingers relentless, sliding, gliding, delving, licking, sucking. Her breathing grew harsher, her movements against him more frantic. When he sensed she hovered on the edge, he plunged two fingers inside her and suckled her aroused nub of sensitive flesh.

A startled cry burst from her lips, and her hands clutched his shoulders as she pulsed around his fingers. He lifted his head, and he knew he'd never seen a more beautiful or erotic or arousing sight as Emily in the throes of passion.

When her spasms subsided, the ruthless demands of his body overwhelmed him. He withdrew his fingers from her sheath, and before he could think of the countless reasons why he shouldn't, he slid on top of her and settled his erection in the warm cradle of her thighs.

Breathing heavily, he supported his weight on his forearms and looked down. His shaft rose between them, the base nestled tightly against her mons. Need—naked, raw, unstoppable, and unlike anything he'd ever experienced—pounded through him, ripping away every last shred of coherent thought. He had to end this torture. Had to sink into her tight heat. Feel that snug, velvety softness surrounding him. End the profound loneliness, this aching need that had haunted him for the past three months.

He squeezed his eyes closed and rubbed himself against her. Shards of dark pleasure shot through him, and with his heart thundering in his chest, he prepared to enter her. Then he stilled at the incredible sensation of her fingers wrapping around him. He opened his eyes and looked down. Saw her pale fingers stroking him. His gaze shifted to her face. Her beautiful eyes still bore the glazed expression of a well-pleasured woman, and he found himself drowning in that look.

She stroked him again, and he was helpless not to thrust into her hand. It had been too long, and he'd been on the edge of release for what felt like forever, and he couldn't hold back another instant. He thrust again, and his climax shuddered through him, racking his body with convulsive waves.

When they ended, he lowered his forehead to hers and fought to get his ragged breathing under control. Himself under control. For several long seconds he breathed in her scent, absorbed her trembling beneath him.

Then reality—and sanity—returned with the force of a blow to the head. And he froze.

Damn it, what the hell sort of madness had come over him? If she hadn't touched him, if he hadn't spilled as a result, he would have taken her virginity. Without a doubt he would have completely compromised her.

He wasn't a reckless man, yet something about her made him feel that way. Act that way. Made him say and do things he normally never would. He wasn't by any means perfect, but he tried to live honorably, and he certainly wasn't in the habit of lifting the skirts of innocent young women.

With a groan, he raised himself off her, inwardly wincing at the evidence of his release gleaming on her stomach. He hadn't suffered such a loss of mastery over himself since he was a green lad. Yet he could only thank God her touch had caused him to do so, otherwise, she'd no longer be a virgin. And while he supposed one could argue that she still was one, she'd certainly lost a great deal of her innocence at his hands. And mouth. Yet as far as he was concerned, whether or not he'd actually completed the act inside her body was irrelevant. His intent had been to do so, and he'd been a mere breath away from thrusting into her.

Self-loathing filled him. What the hell was wrong with him? Yet even as he asked himself the question, he knew the answer. *She* was what was wrong with him, this woman who he desired with a passion he neither understood nor had ever felt before. But even though she was what was wrong with him, the blame and responsibility for his actions was his alone. It wasn't her fault that she rendered him all but paralyzed with lust. She was a gently bred aristocrat, and he'd just pawed and groped her with an utter lack of finesse, treating her as if she were a common doxie.

A muscle flexed in his jaw, and without ceremony he reached for his jacket and pulled his handkerchief from the pocket. She rose up on her elbows and watched in silence as he wiped away the evidence of his spent passion. When he finished, he gently pulled up her bodice to cover her breasts and lowered the hem of her gown to her ankles. He then handed her the rumpled mess that was her drawers. Grabbing his shirt, he stood, then turned his back to her to offer her a modicum of privacy to set herself back to rights.

After slipping his shirt over his head, he tucked the linen ends into his breeches then fastened them. He'd just finished tugging his jacket into place when he heard a rustle of material behind him. He drew a bracing breath then turned.

The sight of her, her hair disheveled, her lips kiss-swollen, and her eyes huge, tugged at his heart. And made him feel even more of a bastard than he already felt.

"Mr. Jennsen . . . are you . . . all right?"

A humorless sound escaped him. "After what just happened between us, do you think you can bring yourself to call me Logan? Because I sure as hell intend to call you Emily."

She moistened her lips then nodded. "Very well, Logan. Are you . . . all right?"

Her question ignited his temper, and anger coursed through him—not at her, but at himself. For allowing the situation to go as far as it did. For allowing himself to lose control. For forgetting about everything except her and the fiery passion and profound need she inspired. He'd been wrong to enter the house, wrong to come into this room. Wrong to touch her. He'd known it, yet he'd done it anyway. And now he had to pay the price for his actions.

And a hefty price it was.

"Actually, no, I'm not all right."

"Yes. I can see that. You seem . . . angry?"

He gave a tight nod. "I am, but not at you. Just at myself."

"Because you regret what happened between us."

It wasn't a question, and he couldn't deny it. Yet he somehow couldn't bring himself to say he regretted touching her. Kissing her. Feeling her melt in his arms. He dragged his hands down his face. Good God, he was truly losing his mind.

Because he wasn't quite ready to say what needed to be said, he instead asked, "Where did you learn to kiss like that?"

"I'm very well read."

"Well read? Good God, do you Brits have instruction manuals on such things?"

"No, but kissing and things of . . . *that* nature frequently occur in my Ladies Literary Society's readings." Before he could think of a reply, she added softly, "And I learned from you."

"Given how good you are at it, surely there have been others."

"No." She lifted her chin as if daring him to doubt her. "Only you."

Something that felt precisely like relief swept through him. *Only you.* But her words merely served to reinforce what he needed to do. Something he'd never thought he'd have to do for such a reason and wouldn't have to do if only he'd stayed the hell outside. But, no. Instead, he'd entered the library, or as he should simply rename it, the Damn Temple of Temptation.

"I see." He cleared his throat, drew a fortifying breath, then stepped toward her. Reaching out, he took her hands in his, and for reasons he couldn't explain, he felt better now that he was touching her. Regarding her steadily, he said, "I didn't mean for things to go as far as they did."

Her gaze lowered to the floor, and she nodded. "Nor did I." She looked up again, and when their eyes met, his heart seemed to roll over. "But when you kissed me, touched me . . ." She lifted her shoulders in a helpless gesture. "I'm not quite sure what happened."

The sense of elation, of thank God it wasn't just me, that rippled through him utterly aggravated him. Shoving it aside, he said tersely, "What happened is I lost control. I take complete responsibility for what passed between us. It shouldn't have happened."

"No, I suppose not."

"*Definitely* not. But it did. And as it was my fault, I'm prepared to do what is necessary."

A small frown furrowed her brow. "What do you mean?"

Sucking in a bracing breath, he pushed from his throat—through his gritted teeth—the words that would change his life.

"Emily, will you marry me?"

Chapter 14

He stood before me naked, his body hard with desire, his eyes dark with need. I shrugged my robe from my shoulders and walked slowly toward him and ran my tongue lightly over my fangs. It was time to make him completely mine.

The Vampire Lady's Kiss *by Anonymous*

Emily stared at Logan in mute stupefaction. Surely she hadn't heard him correctly. It took her a good ten seconds to find her voice, and even then she had to clear her throat twice in order to speak.

"I beg your pardon?"

He frowned, and his lips flattened into a grim line. "Will you marry me?"

Good God, she *had* heard him correctly. Yet his question so flabbergasted her, she couldn't think of a word to say.

His frown deepened. "Is there something wrong with your hearing? Have you lost your ability to talk?"

Annoyance rippled through her and thankfully loosened her knotted tongue. She pulled her hands from his and stepped back. "My hearing is fine, as is my ability to speak, although I must admit your question leaves me at a loss for words."

"I believe there are only two possible answers," he said in a clipped voice, "both of them very simple: yes or no."

"True. However, I cannot fathom why you would ask me such a question." Her gaze shifted to the brandy snifter on the mantel. "Are you foxed?"

"Certainly not," he said, sounding both annoyed and offended. "One sip of brandy does not render one intoxicated."

"Were you drinking before you arrived here?"

"No. But I suddenly wish I had been."

"Well, if you aren't foxed, then I can only guess that you somehow damaged your ability to reason when you . . ." Her voice trailed off, and she waved her hand at his groin then around her stomach. "Clearly some of your brain leaked out in the process."

His expression turned thunderous. "Clearly some of my brain leaked out at some time prior to that, or I wouldn't find myself in this situation." He drew himself up and clasped his hands behind his back. "I'll have your answer to my proposal, please."

Emily could only stare at him in amazement. "You weren't jesting?"

"Damn it, no, of course not. What man in his right mind would ask such a question in jest?"

"Precisely why I'm questioning your mental acuity. Other than being completely insane, why would you ask me such a thing?"

A muscle ticked in his jaw. "I compromised you."

Heat suffused her as the memory of his hot seed spilling against her skin flashed through her mind. She shoved the recollection aside and raised her brows. "I agree that things went much farther than either of us had anticipated or was wise, facts I'm certain I'll regret once I've had the opportunity to think upon the matter, but we didn't do . . . *that*. We're the only two people who know what passed between us, and I've no desire to extract a proposal from you for something that, in spite of your protestations to the contrary, is as much my fault as yours."

His frown collapsed into in a scowl, then his expression turned to one of disbelief. "Did you . . . did you just turn me down?"

Clearly he was stunned, and it occurred to her that given his vast wealth, it was indeed nearly impossible to conceive that any woman would refuse his offer. "Yes. While I appreciate the noble and chivalrous gesture, it is completely unnecessary."

"I disagree." He dragged a hand through his hair. "Clearly you don't understand. I would have made love to you. I was going to—"

"But you didn't. Therefore your conscience is clear. I absolve you of all guilt and responsibility. I remain . . . intact and have no worries about a dubious outcome on my wedding night, which will someday occur—with a man I am madly, passionately in love with. For I have no intention of marrying for any reason other than love. Certainly not because I was kissed."

"We did a hell of a lot more than kiss, Emily."

Another wave of heat shivered through her. Indeed they had. And as soon as she was alone, she intended to relive every magical moment.

"Yes, but nothing that warrants us marrying. And by the way, as much as I appreciate the gesture, that had to be the worst proposal in the history of proposals."

Irritation flickered in his eyes. "Oh? And why is that?"

"For starters, you looked like a convicted man being led to the gallows. And the words sounded as if they were being dragged from the depths of hell, while you were chewing on shards of glass. I'm surprised your teeth didn't shatter from being clenched so hard."

"A proposal wasn't exactly how I'd intended to end the evening."

"Clearly. Nor did you lower yourself to one knee."

"How remiss of me," he said in a tight voice dripping with sarcasm.

"Have you ever proposed to anyone before?"

"No."

"I thought not. At least not to an Englishwoman. Perhaps an American might be enchanted with such an informal offer of marriage, but I can assure you that on this side of the world it will not get you far. I would advise you to practice—perhaps in front of a mirror while keeping in mind that women like a bit romance—before you try it again."

Good heavens, he looked as if the top of his head were about to blow off. 'Twas clear he was trying to keep hold of his temper, although she couldn't fathom why he would be angry. Indeed, the vexing man should be *relieved* she'd turned him down.

"Thank you so much for that bit of unsolicited advice. And forgive me for insulting your tender sensibilities with my dreadfully informal offer. I hearby accept your refusal and bid you good night." He offered her a stiff, formal bow then strode to the wing chair to gather his greatcoat.

Emily watched him, a sense of loss she couldn't explain filling her. Her heart ached with the surety that he was saying more than good night.

He was saying good-bye.

She should be glad. No, thrilled. Ecstatic. Instead, she felt completely churlish and foolish. A sinking sensation swamped her insides, one that dragged her stomach down to her toes.

Before she could think to stop herself, she moved to the wing chair, where he'd just donned his coat, and reached for his hand. He stilled at her touch. Glanced down at her fingers entwined with his, then back at her face with an indecipherable expression.

"Logan . . . I . . ." she wet her suddenly dry lips. "I'm sorry. Your offer—it was very kind. And noble. Honorable and chivalrous." She squeezed his hand. "But ultimately unnecessary. Even so, I thank you."

A bit of the tension drained from his tight features. "You're welcome. Although obviously you're once again shocked that I'd do something kind. Or noble. Or honorable. Or chivalrous."

She offered him a tentative smile. "Since you seem to be making a habit of it, perhaps someday I won't be."

"I hope I live to such a ripe old age." He glanced down at their clasped hands then looked into her eyes. Her breath caught. Heavens, she'd never seen such dark intensity in any man's gaze. "I'm truly sorry for my lack of control, Emily. My only excuse is . . ." He frowned and shook his head. "There is no excuse."

She had the distinct impression he'd been about to say something else then changed his mind, and she wondered what that something was.

Surely she should be experiencing remorse or guilt over what had occurred between them, but instead she felt so compellingly, incredibly *alive*. Exhilarated. So much so she found herself admitting, "I . . . I never felt like that before, Logan."

His expression softened, and she found herself ridiculously wishing that he'd repeat the sentiment—that he'd never felt that way before, either. Or that what had happened between them was something he'd never forget, because she was certain she never would.

He raised her hand and brushed his lips over the backs of her fingers, a gesture that rippled a barrage of tingles up her arm. "So where does this leave us?" he asked. "Are we . . . friends? Or merely two people who meet in various libraries and kiss?"

A breathless sound escaped her. "I think we are perhaps . . . friends." Although how that had happened she wasn't quite certain. Somehow he'd managed to worm his way beneath her guard. For surely only a short time ago she'd detested this man.

"Even though I am an uncouth colonial?"

"I suppose. Although, that *will* prevent us from being *very good* friends."

"I see. Although given what transpired in this room tonight, I think we're already better friends than most."

Heat flamed her face, and she marveled at the gamut of emotions this man could make her feel in such a short span of time. Desire to ecstasy to shock to annoyance to despair to guilt to laughter to heated awareness. Good heavens, no wonder she was confused.

"Better friends than most," she agreed.

His eyes seemed to darken, and he slowly brushed a single fingertip over her cheekbone. "You are so incredibly lovely."

She'd received more eloquent, flowery compliments in the past, but none of them had ever elicited the rush of pleasure that Logan's words evoked.

"Thank you. So are you. In a very manly way, of course."

His lips twitched. He lowered her hand, and she immediately missed the warmth of his calloused palm pressing against hers. "You mentioned earlier that you've no intention of marrying for any reason other than love," he said, fastening his coat.

"Yes." He'd be shocked speechless if he knew the lengths she was going to in order to insure she was able to do just that.

"I thought love was the last reason you British aristocrats married."

"In many cases it is. But for me, well, I want nothing more. My parents were a love match, and I've been fortunate enough to be surrounded by love every day of my life. It's something I couldn't imagine living without. Indeed, the thought of a cold, businesslike marriage terrifies me." Her gaze searched his. "I want the sort of marriage that Sarah, Carolyn, and Julianne have."

"Julianne gave up a great deal for love."

She shook her head. "No. She gained everything because of love. It's worth the risk. And any sacrifice."

He shrugged. "I'm afraid I wouldn't know. I envy you that you've known such love your entire life."

"And I'm so sorry that you haven't. I hope someday you find it."

"Thank you. And I hope your dream of marrying for it someday comes true. And on that note, I must go."

She walked with him across the room to the French windows. "You're going home?"

He hesitated then shook his head. "I'll be in the garden until dawn. At that time a Runner will relieve me."

"Surely that's not necessary."

"I think it is."

"I hate to think of you out there all night. In the cold."

One corner of his mouth turned up. "Then don't think of me."

She barely swallowed the *Ha!* that rose to her lips. "Would you like a blanket? Or—"

His fingertips against her lips cut off her words. "Thank you, but no. I'll be fine. I'm used to the cold, remember?"

Before she could argue further, he asked, "What are your plans tomorrow?"

Her guard instantly went up. As she didn't want to tell him about one of her errands, she told him about the other. "I'll be calling upon Carolyn in the afternoon." She'd planned to do so in the morning, but when she'd returned from Sarah's, she'd had a brief note from Carolyn. "Please don't be worried. Come tomorrow afternoon for tea. Daniel and I will be out in the morning." She dearly hoped the reason they'd be out would be to visit the doctor on Harley Street.

"Are you attending the Farmingtons' party tomorrow evening?" Logan asked.

His question hit her like a slap, a stinging reminder of the vampire masquerade she would undertake tomorrow. The results of which would determine her future. "Why do you ask?"

Something that looked like suspicion flickered in his eyes, and she feared her question hadn't sounded as casual as she'd intended. "I simply wondered, as I'm planning to attend. If you are, perhaps you'll save a waltz for me."

His invitation caught her completely off guard. He'd never approached her for a dance before. Indeed, she'd never seen him dance with anyone. "I . . . I didn't think you danced."

"I'm unfamiliar with most of your English dances, but I can perform a passable waltz."

She dared not deny she planned to attend, but good heavens, the last thing she needed was for the very observant Logan to be watching her, waiting for a waltz to play. "I'll be there but, ah, I'm not certain what time I'll be arriving or leaving," she said, inwardly wincing at how unconvincing she sounded, even to her own ears.

His gaze bored into hers for several seconds, and although his expression remained impassive, she could almost hear him thinking, *What is she up to?* Most likely because that's precisely what she would have been thinking if she were him. Indeed, she felt as if the words *I'm up to something* were painted on her face.

"Well, perhaps if you don't arrive too late or depart too early, we'll see each other there," he said softly.

She forced a smile. "Yes, perhaps."

He gave her another long look, and she managed, with a great effort, to hold his gaze. After murmuring, "Lock the windows after me," he slipped outside and disappeared into the darkness.

Emily secured the glass panels then leaned her forehead against the cold pane and closed her eyes. A series of images flashed through her mind, leaving a fiery trail in their wake. Logan's hands and mouth on her. Her hands on him. The delicious weight of his body pressing into hers. The magic he'd made her feel. The sort of magic she'd previously only read about. The sort that Sarah, Carolyn, and Julianne knew so well. The sort Emily had never expected to experience until she was wed.

Yet something happened to her every time Logan touched her. Something that made her forget everything save him.

He was out there in the garden. Watching over her. After he'd given her more pleasure than she'd ever imagined could actually exist, in spite of all her scandalous readings. After he'd offered her marriage.

His earlier words drifted through her mind. *Then don't think of me.*

She heaved a heavy sigh. If only that were possible. But she knew the chances of expunging him from her mind for so much as an instant were slim.

Very slim indeed.

~

The instant Logan stepped outside, he sensed he wasn't alone. He immediately crouched down to slip his knife from his boot, then remained perfectly still, his back pressed against the brick of the town house. Covering his mouth with his gloved hand so the frosty puffs of his breaths wouldn't be visible, he scanned the area. He saw nothing amiss, but his every instinct warned that someone lurked nearby.

His suspicions were confirmed less than a minute later when he heard a slight scratching sound coming from the other side of the terrace. He slowly rose and craned his neck, but he couldn't see over the tall hedges that separated the area where he stood from the other part of the small garden. He looked up and grimly realized that Emily's bedchamber was directly above where he'd heard the noise.

Knife in hand, he moved cautiously forward, taking care not to step on any dry twigs or dead leaves that would give him away. He'd only taken two steps when a whiff of something reached him on the frigid air.

He halted and sniffed. And recognized the unmistakable

scent of a spent match. His eyes narrowed. Excellent. If the bastard was smoking, he'd be momentarily distracted.

Logan continued moving forward, making his way around the terrace. He rounded the corner and halted again, this time at the sight of a dim orange glow just visible from around the next corner. A glow that was far too big to come from a mere cheroot. The scent of smoke reached him, and his heart stuttered as realization hit him: *fire*.

He took off at a dead run and seconds later rounded the corner of the terrace. A figure wearing a hooded cape was dashing away from hungry flames licking upward from a fire set directly below Emily's balcony.

Logan sprinted forward, yanking off his greatcoat. Clearly the fire had just been lit, but given how quickly it was catching, the bastard must have doused the logs and sticks and surrounding area with something flammable, lamp oil by the smell of it. He tossed his greatcoat over the fire then stamped out the flaming bits of dormant grass that the voluminous garment hadn't covered. While stomping on his coat to make certain the fire was completely smothered, he looked up and caught sight of the hooded figure rounding the corner at the end of the row of town houses.

Mouth flattened into a grim line, Logan quickly ascertained the fire was indeed snuffed, then sprinted after the arsonist. When he rounded the corner, he skidded to a halt, looked left and right, but saw no sign of the bastard. Damn! Then he looked across the street into the park and caught sight of a flapping cape.

He sped across Park Lane and entered the park, legs churning up the ground. He could see the bastard up ahead, and he pumped his arms and legs faster, satisfaction filling him when he realized he was gaining ground. His hopes of catching up doubled when the bastard lost his footing and fell to the ground, skidding on the rough gravel.

He was up in a heartbeat, however. Damn it, he ran like the wind, and Logan pushed himself not to lose the few seconds he'd gained when his quarry had fallen. In spite of his best effort, he lost sight of him at a bend in the heavily tree-lined path, and when Logan rounded the corner, the arsonist was nowhere in sight. Muttering an obscenity, he continued a bit farther, but when there was no sign of the bastard, he slowed then halted.

The instant he stopped moving, the report of a pistol rent the air. A hot sting sizzled through Logan's system, and with a grunt he dropped to the ground and slapped his right hand over his upper left arm where white-hot pain throbbed. The warm wetness seeping onto his palm left no doubt he'd been shot.

Before he could determine the extent of his injury, the faint sound of rapidly fading footfalls had him jumping to his feet. Up ahead, he saw the billowing cape of the man he sought. He started running, but seconds later, the man mounted a waiting horse. He disappeared into the darkness, and Logan knew it was fruitless to give further chase.

Frustrated and angry enough to chew glass, he moved into the shadows of the soaring elms and shrugged off his jacket to probe the aching wound on his arm. After a quick examination, he breathed a sigh of relief. He'd merely been grazed. But it still stung like the fires of hell. Damn it, he'd forgotten how much such a wound hurt. Indeed, he'd hoped to never again have the misfortune of remembering.

He gave his ruined shirtsleeve a mighty yank, tearing the material from the shoulder. He fashioned a snug bandage from the linen, then shrugged back into his jacket. The cold bit into his skin, but he barely noticed the discomfort as he broke into a brisk run back toward Emily's town house.

When he arrived, he immediately went to the site of the fire. The scent of smoke rose from his ruined greatcoat. Crouching down, he carefully pulled back one corner of the garment. A wisp of trapped smoke drifted upward, but no glowing embers remained of the smothered flames.

Evidence of arson, however, was plentiful. Stacked sticks and kindling, oil lamp residue, several spent matches. He looked up at Emily's balcony directly above him and pulled in an unsteady breath filled with both relief and self-recriminations. Thank God he'd stopped the bastard before the fire spread to the house. But damn it, had he remained outside where he belonged rather than engaging in a tryst with the woman he was trying to protect, this near disaster wouldn't have occurred. He would have caught the bastard, and this series of dangerous events would be over. Instead, Emily's house had nearly caught fire, the bastard had gotten away, and Logan's arm throbbed like a son of a bitch.

He didn't doubt that tonight's arsonist was the same man who'd burned his ship, injured his men, and caused the deaths of Billy Palmer and Christian Whitaker.

He looked down at the remnants of the smothered fire, and a rage he'd only ever felt once before in his life swamped him. That last time he'd done what he'd had to, and he would this time as well.

"You won't get away again," he vowed softly. "I'm going to find you and make you rue the day you were born. And then make you rue the day you ever tried to hurt her." Yes. And then he'd make sure the bastard never hurt anyone ever again.

Chapter 15

His skin slid over mine until the weight of his body pressed me into the mattress. I splayed my thighs and groaned in pleasure when he sank inside me, finally filling me. I'd waited for him for so long . . . waited for him forever. And now he'd be mine for eternity.

The Vampire Lady's Kiss *by Anonymous*

Logan arrived at his Berkeley Square mansion shortly after dawn. He'd had to force himself to leave his post outside Emily's town house, even though he'd been confident that the burly and very capable Simon Atwater, who'd returned to relieve him, could handle any difficulties that might arise.

He'd just stepped into the foyer and closed the door when Eversham appeared at his elbow, startling several years off his life. Damn it, the man moved like a ghost.

"Good morning, sir."

"Good morning," Logan replied. He shrugged out of his scorched, odorous greatcoat, which he'd been forced to don due to the frigid weather, and handed the ruined garment to the butler. "I think the only recourse is to burn that."

Eversham's long nose wrinkled at the charred material and smoky scent clinging to the blackened navy blue wool. "It appears that's already occurred, sir."

"Yes. There was a bit of a fire."

"Which you appear to have put out with your coat."

"That's precisely what happened. Why, it's almost as if you were there, Eversham."

Something flashed in the butler's eyes, gone so fast Logan wondered if he'd imagined it. "This is the second greatcoat you've destroyed in as many days. You've quite a penchant for it."

Logan shrugged modestly. "It's a gift."

Eversham's impassive gaze flicked over Logan's blood-stained, torn jacket sleeve. "I take it that is blood?"

"Yes. I was shot."

Eversham's expression didn't so much as flicker. Good God, could *anything* elicit a reaction from the man? Clearly he wouldn't satisfy his quest to ruffle the butler's feathers this morning.

"I see. It must have been quite a party. Will an amputation be required?"

Logan suppressed a chuckle at the almost hopeful tone in the man's voice. "Not this time. I'll try to be more accommodating next time."

"As you wish, sir. A doctor?"

"No. It's merely a flesh wound."

The stoic butler gave a disdainful sniff. "Clearly your jacket and shirt are ruined as well."

"I'm afraid so."

"Harrison will be most distraught," he said referring to Logan's valet. "He is not accustomed to his *gentlemen* coming home in bloodstained tatters."

"Yes, but I'm afraid it couldn't be helped. I'll need some bandages and hot water sent to my bedchamber."

"Yes, sir."

"And a bath."

Eversham's nose twitched. "A request for which we can all be grateful."

Logan hiked up one brow. "Why Eversham, are you insinuating I smell bad?"

"*Bad* is rather an optimistic description, sir."

"Oh? And how would you describe my smell?"

"Hideous comes immediately to mind. As do repulsive and repugnant. You are most certainly fragrant in a way I'd suggest you don't want to be."

"Yes, well that's what fire and blood can do to a man," Logan said lightly, heading for the stairs.

An hour later, freshly bathed and dressed, his wound cleaned and bandaged, Logan entered the dining room and headed for the sideboard. He was halfway through a plate laden with eggs and thinly sliced ham and had just accepted a second cup of steaming coffee from a footman when Eversham appeared in the doorway carrying a precisely folded *Times* on a silver salver.

"Mr. Seaton has arrived, sir," he said, bringing the newspaper to Logan. "I've shown him to your study."

Logan glanced at the mantel clock and noted that Adam was nearly a quarter hour late—very unusual for his normally inhumanly prompt factotum. Even more so as he'd been late returning to the house yesterday afternoon after being delayed, as he'd explained to Logan, by a meeting with Lloyd's of London regarding their insurance claim for the burned ship.

"Thank you, Eversham. I'll join him shortly."

Eversham withdrew, and Logan unfolded the newspaper. His attention was immediately caught by a headline on the first page: "Is a Vampiress Wreaking Mayhem in Mayfair?" Forking in another bite of egg, he read the accompanying article.

> *More than a dozen witnesses claim to have seen a blond-haired, long-fanged creature lurking on the terrace during Lord and Lady Teller's annual soiree. When the creature realized it had been seen, it ran, vanishing into the night but leaving behind its hooded cape, in the pocket of which was a vial of blood—from its latest victim perhaps? That same night a young man identified as Harry Snow was found dead in St. Giles in an alley near the alehouse where he worked. The magistrate reports Snow had clearly struggled with his assailant and that among other injuries there were two puncture marks on his neck. Coincidence? Or the work of a vampire? Now all of London is wondering: Was*

the creature truly a vampire as the witnesses claim? Surely
so many esteemed members of society couldn't be wrong
about what they saw. Assuming they're not, what can be
done to rid London of her bloodsucking presence?

Logan reread the brief article, his gaze lingering on the
words *hooded cape*. Last night's arsonist had worn that exact
sort of garment, as had the carriage driver who'd nearly run
down Emily. He very much doubted it was a coincidence.
The fact that a hooded intruder had been lurking outside the
party both he and Emily had attended sent a chill through him.
Female vampire? A humorless sound escaped him. He didn't
believe that for a minute. Nor that any of these strange hap-
penings were caused by a woman. Certainly the person he'd
chased last night had been a man. In fact, he strongly suspected
that this supposed fanged creature was the murdering arsonist
he sought. As for the blond hair, anyone could don a wig.

Would the bastard show himself at Farmington's party this
evening? "I sure as hell hope so," Logan muttered. "Because
believe me, I'll be ready."

After finishing his breakfast, he made his way down the
corridor to his private study, where Adam awaited him. They
had much work to do today, some of which Adam would have
to complete on his own, as Logan needed to take time this
morning to pay a previously unplanned visit to Gideon at his
Bow Street office to inform him of last night's fire at Emily's
town house.

He turned the brass handle to the study door, and the oak
panel silently swung open. Adam stood bent over Logan's
desk, sifting through the contents of his top drawer.

"Looking for something?" Logan asked, crossing the
threshold.

Adam started then straightened. Logan thought the young
man looked flushed. Hopefully he wasn't coming down with
some sort of fever.

"A pen nib," Adam said, holding one up. "Mine broke."

Logan glanced at the silver nib, then frowned at the bandage wrapped around Adam's palm. "What happened to your
hand?"

Adam lowered his hand and shrugged. "'Tis nothing. Just

a slight burn." He flashed a smile. "Damn teakettle." He slid
Logan's drawer closed and walked quickly to his desk, which
sat perpendicular to Logan's. Picking up a fat folder, he said, "I
have the invoices for the hospital project. They need to be—"

"You were late this morning."

A wash of red suffused the young man's face. "Yes, sir. I'm
sorry. I'll stay late this evening to make up the time."

"That's not necessary, nor why I mentioned your tardiness.
But you were also late returning here yesterday afternoon—"

"Again, I apologize. As I explained, I was unavoidably
detained at Lloyd's."

Logan nodded, although he wondered if something not
related to his job was bothering Adam. He seemed preoccupied. Of course, Adam might be thinking the same thing
about Logan, and rightfully so. Perhaps Adam was being
driven to distraction by a woman as Logan was. In which
case, the young man had his full sympathy.

They sat down to work, and for a full hour Logan managed
to push Emily entirely from his mind. Almost. They were only
partway through the stack of invoices when Eversham entered
the study bearing their usual midmorning repast of coffee for
Logan, tea for Adam, and a platter of biscuits. After drinking
half a cup, Logan consulted his pocket watch then rose.

"I've an appointment," he said, taking one last swallow of
coffee. "I'll be going directly to the warehouse from there,
then onto my other engagements for the day."

Adam frowned and consulted his schedule. "I've nothing
written down for you this morning."

"It's a personal matter. I'll see you at the warehouse at
eleven."

"Yes, sir."

Logan strode into the foyer, where Eversham helped him
into but yet another greatcoat. "I didn't know I had so many
of these damn things," he muttered, wincing at the pull in his
bandaged arm.

"This is your last one," Eversham replied. "However, Harrison has placed an order at Schweitzer and Davidson for
another half dozen."

"Excellent. That should last me until the end of the month."

He climbed into his carriage, instructing Paul, "Number

four Bow Street." As they wended their way toward Covent Garden, Logan noted the slate gray cast to the sky. Leaden clouds hung low in the frigid air, a complete contrast to yesterday's bright, sunny weather, when he'd walked through the park with Emily.

Emily . . . her name reverberated through his mind, along with the heart-stopping image of her climaxing that felt branded behind his eyes. The memory of her kiss-swollen lips moist and parted, porcelain skin flushed, nipples erect and wet from his mouth, her gasp of pleasure melting into a long moan, her taste lingering in his mouth . . . it all inundated him, and he shifted in his seat. She'd been so damn beautiful. So damn desirable.

And she'd flatly turned down his proposal.

He shook his head, bemused and confused in spite of the fact that he was, of course, delighted she'd refused him. Thrilled. And naturally relieved. Since the moment he'd become acquainted with the British aristocracy, he'd declared that the last thing he wanted was some hothouse society diamond for a wife. Unlike many men, he harbored no aversion to marriage, but he did harbor a profound distaste for marrying one of the supercilious, nose-in-the-air, cares-for-nothing-save-jewels-and-parties, upper-crust chits he'd found himself surrounded by. He'd lost count of how many times he'd said he'd rather marry a barmaid than be leg-shackled to a haughty aristocrat.

Yet, there he'd been, forced by honor and his own code of integrity to offer marriage to the exact sort of woman he'd sworn he didn't want.

Except . . . he could no longer describe Emily in such unflattering terms. Oh, he was certain there were still elements of the supercilious hothouse flower about her, and there was no doubt she was trouble, but as he'd so unexpectedly discovered, there were also other aspects as well. Surprising, likable, admirable aspects.

And she'd flatly turned down his proposal.

His very poorly executed, unromantic proposal.

A quick laugh escaped him, one aimed at his own conceit. Given his wealth, he'd simply assumed that when he finally chose a woman to marry, she'd gladly agree to do so. He might not bear a centuries-old title, but there wasn't a duke or earl or lordship in the whole damn country he couldn't buy several times over. His was the sort of wealth that could render even the most reluctant woman suddenly willing.

Except, it seemed, Emily.

A woman whose family faced certain and imminent financial ruin, the sort that could only be saved by either a huge inheritance—of which there was none in the offing—or a brilliant marriage by one of the Stapleford children. As Emily was the only one of marriageable age, the responsibility fell to her. She obviously adored her family, yet she'd turned down the opportunity to marry a man who possessed the means to rescue them from debt and assure their financial future.

Because she wanted to marry for love.

Or was it simply that she couldn't bear the thought of marrying *him*? Damn it, that rankled, particularly since he'd believed she was coming to like him. At least a little. As he'd come to like her, at least a little. Surely her love for her family would take precedence over any aversion she felt toward him. And as for any aversion, she sure as hell hadn't shown any toward him last night.

That meant there was only one conclusion to be drawn: she was up to something. But what? Of course, that was the same question he'd been asking himself about her for a while. And he was now more determined than ever to find out.

The carriage stopped, and Paul's double tap indicated they'd arrived at Bow Street. A few minutes later he accepted a seat opposite Gideon in the Runner's office. He detailed the events of last evening—except those involving his tryst with Emily—concluding with, "Things are escalating, Gideon. In order to insure Emily's safety, someone must guard her at all times, someone I trust to do the job properly. I want to hire you."

Gideon watched him through unreadable eyes. "Having someone watch her twenty-four hours a day will require more than just one man."

"Then I'll pay however many other men you deem necessary to get the job done. The cost is irrelevant." He named an amount he felt certain was equal to a half year's salary for a

Runner. When Gideon simply remained silent, Logan impatiently doubled the offer.

Then Gideon reacted, but not in a way Logan would have expected. Instead of jumping at the offer, unmistakable anger glittered in Gideon's eyes.

"I don't want or need your charity, Logan."

Logan's own anger sparked. "I'm not offering you charity, damn it. It's a job."

"For a ridiculous amount of money."

"It's my money to spend as I see fit, and I happen to think you're worth that amount. Why don't you?"

Gideon frowned. "It's not that—"

Logan leaned forward. "Then what is it? You're married now. With a child on the way. There's more to consider than just yourself. Believe me, I'll expect results. And if I don't get them, you'll answer to me."

Gideon pondered for a bit, and Logan cursed that the man was so unreadable. Finally he said, "I'll accept the job, but first I want you to answer two questions."

"Fine. What are they?"

"You've already nearly been run down by a carriage, spent the night outside her town house in the bitter cold, and been shot, and now you're parting with a veritable fortune to insure her safety. Have you given any thought as to why you're willing to go to such lengths to protect this woman?"

An uncomfortable sensation seized Logan, tightening his insides. Actually, he hadn't given it any thought—purposely. At least not beyond the obvious answer. Because it simply wasn't a question he wanted to examine too closely for fear of the answer.

"I believe it's my fault she's in danger," he said quietly. "Therefore it's my responsibility to make sure she's not hurt. Or worse."

"That's all there is to it?"

Yes. No. Damn it, I don't know. I hope so, but I just don't know anymore. "Yes."

Gideon nodded slowly, then said, "Even with the arsonist acting quickly, the garden behind the town house is small. How did you happen to miss him being directly under Emily's window?"

Logan kept his features impassive, a contrast to the tight knot twisting his insides. "You said two questions; that's three."

"I'm asking it anyway."

He considered not answering but figured that would just lead to further speculation. Since there was no way in hell he'd tell Gideon or anyone else what had occurred between him and Emily, he simply said, "I was distracted."

Gideon's gaze seemed to bore into him for what felt like an eternity but was surely no more than twenty seconds. Finally he said, "I understand."

Logan frowned. "Understand what?"

"Precisely what you're going through."

"Oh? You had a crazed arsonist who, for reasons you don't comprehend, set fire to your ship, killing and injuring your employees, and attempted to harm your friends?"

"No. I meant I understand what you're going through with regards to Emily, how you could have been so distracted while guarding her, as I suffered through the exact same thing with Julianne. Believe me, I know how distracting a beautiful woman can be. How she can tie you up in knots." Gideon's eyes narrowed. "And you know bloody well that's what I meant."

Yes, damn it, he had. That didn't mean he had to admit it. Still, he found himself asking, "So what did you do about it?"

"You sure you want to know?"

Logan's instincts told him to say no and change the subject. Instead, he found himself saying, "Yes."

"I fought my feelings for her until I simply couldn't any longer. Then I made love to her. And then I married her. And I've been the happiest bloody man in the kingdom ever since."

Well, he'd almost made love to Emily and had asked her to marry him and been refused. And he'd pretty much been miserable ever since. Not exactly the same heartwarming scenario Gideon had ended up with.

Gideon leaned forward. "You're fighting a losing battle, Logan. It's obvious to me you care for Emily. Deeply. You may not *want* to care for her and may not be ready to admit it, but you do. It's written all over you. Trust me; I recognize the signs. I look at you and see myself three months ago. God knows I didn't want to fall in love with Julianne. I fought it every step of the way, but in the end I was helpless against it. Be warned: no matter how fast you try to run from those sorts of feelings, they'll catch up with you. Just as they did with me. And they'll bite you right on the arse."

"What a lovely, vivid description," Logan said dryly. "But I can assure you nothing's bitten me, on the arse or elsewhere." Good God, he'd only just realized he liked the woman—a little bit. Just because he'd been distracted one time by her didn't mean it would ever happen again. His situation with Emily was nothing like Gideon's and Julianne's. Gideon didn't know what the hell he was talking about.

Gideon shrugged. "Don't say I didn't warn you. When you least expect it, the realization is going to hit you like a brick to the head."

"Well, that's certainly preferable to being bitten on the arse."

"Maybe, but I think it really depends on who's doing the biting." Gideon stood, and Logan did as well. "I'll see to hiring men to watch her," Gideon said. "Atwater will keep watch for the remainder of the day. I'll personally relieve him. Do you know her plans for this evening?"

"She's supposed to attend Lord Farmington's soiree. I'll be there as well. I'll contact Farmington and arrange for an invitation to be delivered to you." Logan considered for several seconds then added, "Matthew won't be there, as Sarah is due any day, but Daniel and Carolyn were no doubt invited. If they attend, I believe I'll take Daniel into my confidence. Couldn't hurt to have another set of eyes looking out for Emily."

"Good. But don't worry if he's not there. Between the two of us, she'll be safe."

They shook hands, and Logan took his leave. As he climbed into his carriage, Gideon's words echoed through his mind. *Between the two of us, she'll be safe.* Logan intended to see to it that those words were true.

Chapter 16

He was buried deep inside me, and my pleasure was nearly upon me, when I sank my fangs into his neck. I barely heard his gasp as I flew over the edge into ecstasy, overwhelmed by the erotic combination of his hard body thrusting into mine and the delicious, hot tang of his blood filling my mouth.

The Vampire Lady's Kiss *by Anonymous*

Emily exited the grimy brick building and pulled in an unsteady breath. Gray clouds hung low in the sky, making the already dreary surroundings in this run-down area of Whitechapel even more gloomy. A fetid mixture of garbage and unwashed bodies and God only knows what else clung to frigid air punctuated with the sounds of people yelling, dogs barking, and children crying.

"The hack is waiting just around the corner," said Mr. Atwater, pointing ahead. Emily nodded, still feeling too overwhelmed by what she'd just experienced to speak. She held tightly to the massive arm of the burly Runner, knowing the dangers that lurked in these rough parts of London, and she offered up a prayer of thanks for his comforting and intimidating presence. She never would have ventured into this area of London alone, and on the occasions when she did come to the more run-down sections of the city, she made certain she was well-protected. He made her feel safe in a place that was without question highly unsafe.

Still, today's outing had left her unsettled in a way she'd never experienced before. They turned the corner, and relief filled her at the sight of their hired hack. As they approached the vehicle, she noticed that another carriage had stopped behind it. A beautiful, pristine ebony-lacquer equipage with intricate gold scrollwork painted on the trim that was completely out of place in this area. She frowned. A carriage that looked familiar—

She halted as the door opened and Logan stepped from the interior. He was reaching up to put on his top hat when he caught sight of her. He froze, arm raised, and for several seconds they simply stared at each other. Then Logan's gaze shifted to Mr. Atwater. His mouth pressed into a thin line, and he settled his hat on his head—with a bit more force than seemed necessary. His long, rapid strides quickly erased the distance between them. He didn't stop until a mere arm's length separated them.

"What in God's name are you doing here?" he asked through clenched teeth. "Do you have any idea how dangerous this area is?"

Annoyance at his high-handedness shot through Emily. Before she had an opportunity to answer, he turned to Mr. Atwater. "You'd best have an excellent explanation as to why Lady Emily is in Whitechapel, Atwater, although I cannot imagine what that explanation possibly could be."

Emily prevented Mr. Atwater from speaking by squeezing his arm. "Mr. Atwater accompanied me in order to assure my safety while I paid a visit."

Logan's brows collapsed into a dark frown. "A visit? Who could you possibly be visiting in this part of London?"

With her gaze steady on his, she said, "The same people I gather you're here to see: Velma Whitaker and her daughter Lara."

His frown turned into a look of confusion. "But how . . . why . . . ?" He shook his head, then turned to Mr. Atwater. "I need a moment with Lady Emily."

Mr. Atwater's gaze cut to Logan's carriage. "I'll keep watch outside."

After giving the Runner a terse nod, Logan took her arm and escorted her to his carriage, helping her inside. He closed the door, enclosing them in a private cocoon of luxury at complete odds with the poverty surrounding them.

He sat opposite her on the plush brown velvet squabs and fixed her with a steady stare. Then he said quietly, "Please explain how and why you're here."

Emily moistened her lips, a gesture that drew his gaze to her mouth. His eyes darkened, and a wave of heat engulfed her. Determined not to let him know how much his nearness affected her, she raised her chin and cleared her throat.

"After our conversation in the park yesterday, I couldn't stop thinking about Mrs. Whitaker and her daughter, the hardships they'll face without Mr. Whitaker to provide for them and protect them. So yesterday afternoon I sent a note to Gideon asking if he could find out where Mrs. Whitaker lived and accompany me to her home. He wrote back that he was previously engaged and couldn't come with me, but he'd send Mr. Atwater, who has been watching over me since this morning, along with Mrs. Whitaker's direction."

"So you came to visit them," Logan said softly.

Emily nodded. "I gathered together some things for Mrs. Whitaker and Lara—"

"What sorts of things?"

"Clothes mostly. Some household goods: candles, linens, soap. Some books and a doll that were stored in the attic. Several hampers of food Cook put together. I also sent notes round to Sarah and Carolyn, who donated items as well. As did Julianne, in spite of her greatly reduced circumstances."

For the space of several heartbeats he said nothing. Then he reached out and clasped her hand. His fingers wrapped around hers, and even through the layers of their gloves she felt his warmth.

"That was very kind of you."

To her mortification, hot tears pushed behind her eyes. To hide them she turned from him and looked out the window. And all she saw was the dingy, chipped bricks and dirty windows of the building where Mrs. Whitaker and Lara lived. It wasn't as if she hadn't seen people in similar circumstances, yet something about the pair had touched her deeply.

"I don't feel kind. I feel . . ." She expelled a long breath. "I feel so many things. Sympathy, pity, and profound compassion. Just as I do every time I venture from the rarefied air of Park Lane and come to areas such as this."

She felt him go still. "Every time?" he repeated softly. "Are you saying this isn't the first time you've been to Whitechapel?"

She cursed her runaway tongue. Blinking back the moisture in her eyes, she turned to him and nodded. "Over the past three years I've been numerous times. And to other poverty-stricken areas of London as well." A humorless sound escaped her. "They aren't difficult to find."

"But why would you . . ." His words drifted off, and unmistakable realization dawned in his eyes. "You bring donated household items to people in need."

She nodded, feeling suddenly embarrassed for not keeping quiet. "It's nothing, really. Just clothes Mary and the boys have outgrown or things I won't wear again."

"You do this often?"

"Usually once a month. Three years ago, I discovered one of our maids crying. I asked her what was wrong, and at first she didn't want to tell me, but finally she confided how she'd had a letter from her sister telling her that the sister's husband had died, leaving her to provide for three small children and another on the way. I felt so bad for the young woman, I decided to do what I could to help. So I collected some funds and household items and . . . that's how it began."

"A very worthwhile cause."

"Yes, but there is much poverty and suffering. I always feel as if I've merely wrapped a small bandage around a gushing wound. But mostly I feel guilt. By virtue of a mere accident of birth, my life is filled with comforts that Mrs. Whitaker and Lara and others like them have never known. It all seems somehow so unfair—that one person can have so much and another so little."

She turned to look out the window again. "Yet Mrs. Whitaker shared everything she had with me. Something about her and Lara just . . . touched me. Deeply. She brewed tea and served biscuits and treated me as if royalty were visiting. They live in a single room . . . just one room. It was spotless but so worn. She was so worn. And tired. Yet so brave. I don't think I've ever met a braver person. And Lara, dear God, that child simply broke my heart. She looked at me with those huge brown eyes and—" Her voice broke, and another wave of tears flooded her eyes.

She felt his fingers under her chin, urging her to look at him, and she turned her head.

"And what?" he prompted.

"And even though I was trying to help, I felt unworthy to be there. In that small room kept so scrupulously clean. Do you know I've never had to clean anything in my entire life? Not a single dish or pan or teacup. I felt selfish and overdressed and pampered and useless and undeserving."

A tear dribbled down her cheek, and he reached out to capture it on the tip of his glove. "I felt exactly the same way the first time I came here," Logan said quietly. "I wanted to bundle them both up and bring them home with me, but I knew that would have insulted her. Your method of donating much-needed goods is an excellent one."

"Thank you, but as I said, it's not nearly enough. I want to do more." She bit back the humorless laugh that rose in her throat. Given her family's looming financial ruination, there would be nothing left to give away. Indeed, she might soon find herself in the same sort of straits as Mrs. Whitaker. A shudder ran through her at the mere thought.

"I may have a way to help them," Logan said. "I came here today with an offer for Mrs. Whitaker, one I hope she'll accept."

"What is that?"

"I've recently purchased a country estate in Kent, about two and a half hours outside London. The housekeeper has chosen to remain with the previous owner; therefore, I'll need to fill the position."

Understanding dawned. "And you're going to offer the job to Mrs. Whitaker."

"Yes. She and Lara would live in the country, and she'd be doing me a great service. I need someone competent I can trust to run the household."

Emily's heart turned over, and shame washed through her for all the times she'd thought badly of this man. "That's very kind of you. And you'll note that I don't sound the least bit surprised."

But he shook his head. "It's not kindness but responsibility. What *you* did, and have done for others like her, that is pure kindness. And even though I had no idea you were involved in such an enterprise, you'll note that I don't sound the least bit surprised. Although for your own safety I wish you wouldn't venture into unsafe parts of the city."

"I would never come without adequate protection. You can't deny Mr. Atwater could frighten off any would-be criminals with a mere look."

"True. But you could send someone else to deliver the donations."

"You mean such as a man with a pistol? While I remain in the warmth and comfort of my family's Mayfair town house?"

"Exactly. In fact, I think that's an excellent idea."

She shook her head. "No. Lest you think my reasons are completely unselfish, let me assure you they're not. I *need* to do this. It makes me feel . . . necessary."

"That isn't selfish. It's human nature to want to feel needed. Please think of me the next time you're soliciting donations. And if you ever decide you'd like to expand your charity, let me know. Perhaps I'd be able to help." One corner of his mouth lifted. "Rumor has it I know a bit about business ventures."

Botheration, the combination of his touch, the warm intensity in his gaze, and that self-deprecating half smile simply dazzled her. "Yes, I've heard that rumor."

He lifted her hand to his lips and pressed a kiss against her fingers, a gesture that effectively melted her spine. "I don't know what to say other than thank you."

"There's no reason to thank me, Logan. I did so little."

"I disagree. You did a great deal. For a woman you didn't even know."

"That's not true. I knew her through you."

"I'd merely mentioned her. You took the initiative to find her, and it is a kindness I won't forget." He pressed another kiss against her fingers, and she caught her breath at the unmistakable heat in his eyes. She knew that look. It was the same one that had kindled in those dark depths each time just before he'd kissed her senseless.

"Do you know what I want to do right now?" he asked.

Her heart skipped a frantic beat. She certainly knew what she wanted him to do right now. Kiss her senseless again. Which of course, he couldn't. In spite of the gray clouds, it was broad daylight. Mr. Atwater stood not a yard away. And hadn't she decided at some point that kissing him again was a bad idea?

"Deliver me back to Mr. Atwater?" she guessed.

His gaze dropped briefly to her lips. "Actually, that is the very last thing I want to do. But unfortunately, it is what I must do."

Emily forced herself to swallow her ridiculous disappointment and nod. "Yes, of course."

Logan released her hand and opened the door. When she moved forward to exit the carriage, he shook his head. "I want you and Atwater to take my coach. I'll take your hack."

"That isn't necessary. I'm perfectly safe with Mr. Atwater."

"If I weren't certain of that, I would escort you home myself. However, I'd feel much better if I knew you were with my driver Paul, who I trust implicitly." His serious gaze rested on hers. He reached out and traced her cheekbone with his fingertip. "Please, Emily. I need to know that you're safe."

Something in his quiet, fervent tone, in the probing intensity of his regard, melted her insides. "Very well."

He nodded, then without another word exited the carriage. He spoke briefly to Mr. Atwater then to his driver. Mr. Atwater climbed inside, taking the seat Logan had vacated. His sheer size swallowed the spacious interior.

"Until tonight," Logan said. Before she could reply, he closed the door, then nodded to his coachman. The carriage pulled away, and Emily turned around and watched through the rear window until they rounded the corner, and Logan disappeared from view.

Five minutes later, as they were slowly making their way through the labyrinth of narrow streets, the carriage jerked to a sudden halt, nearly tossing Emily to the floor.

The horses loudly whinnied, and the driver called out,

"Whoa!" Then he yelled, "You there! Out of the way!" The words were followed by a grunt then a loud thump.

Emily's gaze flew to Mr. Atwater, but before she could even blink, he'd pulled a knife from his boot. In his other hand he held a pistol. "Stay here," he whispered tersely.

Heart pounding, Emily nodded. In the next instant, Mr. Atwater leapt from the coach. Emily shrank back in her seat, every muscle tense, wishing she had a weapon of some sort. With no other options, she reached up to pull several pins from her hair. It wasn't much, but it was better than nothing.

No sooner had she yanked out a pin than the glass window behind her head shattered. She opened her mouth to scream, but the sound was cut off when large hands reached into the opening and wrapped around her neck.

Black dots danced before her eyes as impossibly strong fingers pressed against her throat, cutting off her air. She reached up to claw at the hands but to no avail. She stabbed at them with her hairpin, desperately trying to wound him, but his grip only tightened. She tried to pull in a breath, but it was impossible. Her eyes rolled back in her head, and then the world went black.

Chapter 17

❧

*He raised his head and stared down at me through glazed
eyes. Breathing heavily, he brushed his fingers over the two
small punctures on his neck. "What have you done to me?"
he whispered. "I've made you mine," I answered. Silence
swelled between us. Finally he said, "I always have been."*

The Vampire Lady's Kiss *by Anonymous*

Logan sat on a hard wooden chair before Velma Whitaker's
fireplace and accepted the cup of tea she'd insisted upon making
him. His gaze shifted to Lara, who slept on a small bed in
the corner, her arms wrapped around what had to be the doll
Emily brought her.

Mrs. Whitaker must have seen the direction of his gaze,
because she said, "I've never seen the child so delighted as
Lara were with that doll. Yer lady is very kind, Mr. Jennsen.
Beautiful, too. Like an angel of mercy."

He supposed he should have corrected her assumption that
Emily was his lady, but instead he merely said, "Yes, she is."

"It's very kind of ye to visit as well."

He took a sip of the tea then cleared his throat. "Actually,
this is more than just a social call." He repeated to her what

he'd told Emily about needing a housekeeper for the country estate he'd recently purchased, concluding with, "I'd like to offer you the job." He then named a salary that was double what he paid his housekeeper in Berkeley Square, but damn it, he owed this woman. He would have just given her the money, but he knew her pride wouldn't allow her to accept it.

Her eyes widened, and she pressed a hand to her chest. "I . . . I don't know what to say." Then her eyes narrowed. "That seems an awful lot o' money fer a housekeeper."

"The house will require extensive renovations, so there's a great deal of work involved. And you should know that I'd want you to start as soon as you can settle your affairs here in London. Are you interested?"

She drew an unsteady breath then said softly, "Don't think I don't know what yer doin', Mr. Jennsen."

"I'm offering you a job. One that will require a great deal of hard work."

"It's more than that, and we both know it." She glanced over at her sleeping daughter then met Logan's eyes. "And I thank ye for it. For givin' me the chance to make a decent life for myself and Lara. I accept the job."

Logan's throat tightened. Damn it, he didn't deserve her thanks. If it weren't for him, her husband wouldn't be dead. He set his teacup on the small table next to his chair and stood. "Excellent. My man of affairs, Adam Seaton, will be in touch with you in the next several days. If you need anything in the meantime—"

His words were cut off by a loud banging on the door, punctuated by a frantic shout of, "Mr. Jennsen, 'tis me, Paul. You must come at once!"

For several stalled heartbeats Logan couldn't move. Then he jumped to his feet so quickly his chair tipped backward and crashed to the floor. He ran across the room and yanked open the door. Paul leaned on the jamb, breathing heavily, a trail of blood staining his cheek from a gash on his temple.

Logan forced out the only word he could manage around the lump of dread clogging his throat. "Emily—?"

Paul sucked in a gasping breath. "Attacked. Must come, sir. I'll tell you on the way."

Everything within him seemed to simultaneously freeze

and turn into a tight ball of fire. Without a backward glance, he raced after Paul, who led him through a labyrinth of narrow streets. In halting words, the driver related what had happened.

"A man stepped in front of the carriage. I pulled up sharp to avoid runnin' him down. In the blink of an eye the bastard swung a club. Stunned me good, he did. Next thing I knew, Mr. Atwater were callin' for me. Apparently the bastard had broken the back window of the carriage and were stranglin' Lady Emily."

Logan swore his heart stopped. "Is she . . ." Damn it, he couldn't even bring himself to think it, let alone say it.

"I don't know, sir. Mr. Atwater, he shot the attacker deader than a brick and was seeing to Lady Emily. Told me to get you from Mrs. Whitaker's place."

"How serious is your injury?"

"Got me a headache that'll hurt like the devil for a day or two, but I'm fine. Been hit harder in me pugilist days."

They turned a corner, and Logan's footsteps faltered at the sight of his carriage, the back window broken. A body lay on the cobblestones in a pool of blood among shards of broken glass. Logan glanced at the man's face, but there wasn't much left of it. Atwater's shot had apparently been at very close range. The carriage door hung open, and with his heart in his throat, Logan sprinted forward.

He skidded to a halt outside the door and looked into the interior. And his lungs ceased to function. Emily lay across one of the brown velvet cushions, eyes closed, skin completely colorless, except for the glimpse of an angry red mark on her neck. Simon Atwater knelt on the carriage floor chafing her delicate wrists with his huge hands, murmuring in a rough voice, "Wake up now, Lady Emily. You hear me? Wake up."

Logan grasped the doorframe. This couldn't be happening. She couldn't be . . . He shook his head. No, she couldn't be. He reached out an unsteady hand and clasped Atwater's shoulder. The Runner looked over his shoulder, his expression grim.

"Her breathing's returned to normal," he said. "She woke once briefly but then fainted."

The relief swamping Logan damn near rendered him light-headed. "I'll watch over her," he said tersely. "You see to Paul and the body."

Atwater departed the carriage, and Logan moved inside, pulling the door closed behind him. He knelt on the floor and picked up her soft hand. He pressed it against his chest, then reached out with his other hand to caress her cold, waxy cheek.

"Emily . . . wake up. It's me, Logan. Can you hear me?"

His anxious gaze skimmed over her. Her bonnet was untied, and the top two buttons of her burgundy pelisse unfastened. Atwater must have done both so nothing constricted her breathing. From this angle he could see the extent of the red marks encircling her neck. A combination of fear, sympathy, and feral rage raced through him. He wanted to scream, rail at the heavens, break something—like the neck of the bastard who'd done this to her, if he weren't already dead.

He brushed his fingertips over her slightly parted lips, his skin absorbing the warmth of her shallow breaths. "Please wake up," he urged, forcing himself not to look at the frightening marks marring her porcelain skin so he wouldn't sound as frantic as he felt. Unable to stop himself, he leaned forward and touched his lips to her forehead. "Emily . . . please, please wake up." He lightly kissed each of her eyelids, repeating his plea, clutching her hand, pressing it against his thudding heart.

His lips cruised lightly over her pale cheek to the tip of her nose, then across her other cheek, punctuating each kiss with another plea, each one growing more desperate with every second that ticked by and she remained motionless.

Finally his lips brushed against hers, once, twice, as he fought to hold back the panic threatening to consume him. "Please wake up, Emily," he whispered against her mouth. "My beautiful Emily. Please, sweetheart, please . . ."

She moaned, and he quickly straightened, anxiously scanning her face. Her eyelids fluttered open. Confusion clouded her beautiful eyes as they settled on him.

"Emily." Her name whispered from him like a prayer. He briefly squeezed his eyes shut, absorbing the profound relief racing through him. "You're awake." Thank God.

A tiny frown furrowed her brow. "I fell asleep?" she asked in a hoarse voice.

He shook his head and reached out to brush a loose curl from her forehead. "Do you remember what happened?"

She tried to swallow and grimaced. Then her eyes widened and filled with fear. Her free hand flew to her neck, and she struggled to rise. "A man . . . he tried to—"

He cut off her words by touching his fingers to her lips and gently pressed her back into the cushion. "I know. There's no need to worry. He'll never hurt you or anyone else ever again. Mr. Atwater saw to that." Keeping the graphic details to a minimum, he briefly told her what had transpired.

When he finished she whispered, "So Mr. Atwater saved my life."

Barely. Not trusting his voice, he nodded.

Her gaze shifted to where he tightly held her hand clasped to his chest before meeting his eyes once again. "I was dreaming that you were kissing me, and when I woke up, you were."

"Yes," he agreed, although he'd been so swamped with panic he'd barely been aware of what he was doing. He just knew that he had to be close to her. Had to touch her. Had to keep talking to her. Had to make her wake up.

"Do you know what that makes you?" she asked.

An aching tenderness filled him at the question. "Extremely fortunate?"

"A prince," she murmured. "Like the fairy tale. The one where the handsome prince's kiss awakens the princess."

"The story of the sleeping beauty."

"Yes. Except I am not a princess."

"No, but are you are a beauty. And besides, I am not a handsome prince." He managed a slight smile. "As you are so fond of reminding me, I am merely an uncouth American."

She didn't return his smile. Instead, she regarded him through very serious eyes. "You may not be a prince, but you are handsome. Extremely so."

Unable to stop touching her, he brushed his fingers over her smooth cheek. "I'm going to remind you that you said so when you're feeling better and want to take those words back, wondering what came over you."

"I won't change my mind. And except for a sore throat, I feel fine." As if to belie her statement, however, her eyes pooled with tears. "It happened so fast, Logan. And I . . . I was so frightened."

His heart seemed to break free of its moorings and plunge

in his chest. "I know, sweetheart," he said, pressing her hand to his lips. "I'm so sorry."

"I tried to get away, but he was too strong. I used a hairpin for a weapon and jabbed at his hands, but I couldn't breathe." She sucked in several quick breaths, as if she suddenly couldn't get enough air. "I couldn't breathe, and then everything went black."

A red haze settled over Logan's vision, and he was only sorry the son of a bitch who'd hurt her and frightened her was already dead, thus denying him the pleasure of ending his miserable life.

He moved onto the seat and gathered her up in his arms, settling her across his lap to cradle her against him. Her arm curled around his neck, and with a sigh she nestled her head against his shoulder.

He closed his eyes and pressed his lips against her temple, overwhelmed with the emotions swirling through him. The scent of flowers and sugar filled his head, and for a long moment he simply breathed her in, absorbing the feel of her in his arms and offering up a fervent prayer of thanks that he was able to do so. Indeed, he felt as if he could have stayed in that very spot, just holding her, feeling her snuggled against him, forever. It was an unsettling notion, one he'd never before experienced with any other woman.

When he finally felt as if he could trust his voice to be steady, he said quietly, "The good news is that it's over now. The man responsible is dead. There's nothing to fear any longer."

"But who was he?"

"I'm not yet certain. But it doesn't really matter. All that's important is that it's over. And that you're safe."

She lifted her head, and he looked down into her eyes. And as always, he felt as if he were drowning. A tremor racked him at how close he'd come—again—to losing her, this woman who was a constant source of frustration, confusion, and wonder. Who he kept discovering unexpected things about, things that surprised and unsettled him as they kept showing her to be very different than the haughty hothouse flower and useless society diamond he'd thought.

Instead, she was kind, loving, generous, and compassionate. Witty and amusing. She inspired a storm of feelings in him, a depth of passion and raw need he'd never before experienced. Suddenly Gideon's words that Logan had dismissed only a short time ago echoed through his mind: "You're fighting a losing battle . . . no matter how fast you try to run from those sorts of feelings, they'll catch up with you . . . and bite you right on the arse."

He drew a deep breath, and the question hit him like a blow to the heart, stunning him.

Was it possible he'd been bitten right on the arse?

Good God, was it possible he . . . *loved* her?

Is *that* what this whirlwind of torment and desire, need and longing was? Damn it, he didn't know. How could he when he had nothing to compare it to? Somehow he'd always imagined that love was something calm. Reasonable. Rational and logical. Like smooth sailing on tranquil waters.

What he felt for Emily defied that description, indeed was its complete antithesis. The emotions she evoked ran the gamut from ecstasy to anguish, anger to euphoria, pleasure to pain. There was nothing calm, reasonable, rational, or logical about the way she made him feel. Made him lose control. Made him forget everything except her. Tranquil waters? Ha! More like being cast adrift on stormy seas in a leaky rowboat without any oars.

No, this disturbing internal tumult couldn't be love. It was merely a potent combination of lust, infatuation, and desire, all compounded by a severe drought of physical intimacy.

He immediately brightened. Of course he didn't love her. He was simply confusing his hunger for her and concern for her welfare with something deeper. He'd been without a woman for so long, he'd naturally desire one—*any* one. And of course he'd feel concern for *anyone* who'd nearly been run down by a carriage and almost strangled.

Yes, but you don't want any other woman, his heart pointed out. *And while you'd feel concern for anyone who'd nearly been run down by a carriage and almost strangled, you most likely wouldn't want to kill the person responsible with your bare hands. Or have experienced that heart-stopping moment of indescribable pain when you'd thought she was gone.*

Hmmm. It appeared his mind didn't have a ready answer

for that. Which while unsettling, wasn't surprising, given all that had transpired. He was an intelligent man. He wouldn't be so foolish as to fall for a woman who'd professed she would only marry for love; and she clearly didn't love him, as she'd already refused to marry him.

"Are you all right, Logan?"

Her question snapped him from his thoughts. He blinked and found himself staring into those utterly distracting eyes. "Er, yes, I'm fine."

"Are you certain? You've the oddest look on your face."

He instantly wiped his face clean of all expression, wondering what he'd looked like. "I'm just relieved that you're safe." Which was true, although not precisely the truth.

"You were staring at me as if you'd never seen me before."

He was spared the need for a reply when a knock sounded on the carriage door. He gently set her away from him then said, "Come in."

Simon Atwater opened the door, and relief filled his sharp gaze when he saw Emily. "You're awake," he said.

She nodded and reached out to clasp his hand. "You saved my life, Mr. Atwater. You have my deepest gratitude."

A rush of color suffused Atwater's face. Good God, the man was *blushing*. The Runner was staring at Emily with a dazed expression, one that irked Logan, yet one he could begrudgingly sympathize with. She and those eyes were nothing short of dazzling.

"Only wish he'd never gotten his hands on you, my lady," Atwater muttered. He stared into Emily's eyes for several more seconds as if in a trance, then cleared his throat and turned to Logan.

"I paid a lad to deliver a message to the magistrate. I expect he'll arrive shortly. I'd like to see if you recognize the attacker. Then I suggest you take Lady Emily home."

Logan nodded. "I'll be back in a moment," he said to Emily then exited the carriage. Atwater had covered the body with a plain wool blanket taken from Paul's seat. Logan crouched down and lifted one corner.

"Do you recognize him?" Atwater asked.

"A good part of his face is gone."

"Keeping him pretty wasn't my main concern."

"Thank God for that." Logan examined what was left of the man's features. "I can't be positive, given his condition, but I don't think I recognize him. Was he carrying anything that might give a clue to his identity?"

"Nothing. But you'll note what he's wearing."

Logan pulled the blanket back farther. "A black hooded cape."

Atwater nodded. "Just like the bloke who set the fire last night."

A muscle ticked in Logan's jaw, and he flicked the blanket back into place. "I want to know everything you can find out about this bastard. I want to know his name, why he was after me, and why he tried to hurt Lady Emily. I don't care how much it costs or how many men you need to hire to see the job done. I want no stone left unturned."

"I'll see to it. In the meantime, you can be content that he's been stopped."

"Yes," Logan agreed. He held out his hand to Atwater. "You have my thanks. And gratitude."

"Glad it's over and that Lady Emily is all right. As you won't be requiring my services any longer, I'll return to Bow Street after I'm done with the magistrate."

Logan nodded then looked toward Paul, who was comforting the horses. "You all right?"

"Yes, Mr. Jennsen." He climbed onto his perch. "Ready when you are."

Logan opened the door to the carriage. Emily sat exactly where he'd left her. To his relief, her color had improved. He was about to climb in when she said, "Before you take me home, I must see Carolyn."

Logan shook his head. "You can see her tomorrow. You're going home, taking a hot bath, then going to bed to await a visit from the doctor."

She raised a brow. "I fear you're mistaken. I've no need of a doctor. Carolyn is expecting me, and I need to see her. And I must do it now. If I go home first, I'll have to answer dozens of questions, and I won't be able to escape the house again for hours. Certainly not before Lord and Lady Farmington's party."

Logan's entire face tightened into a scowl, and he sent up

a prayer of thanks that he *hadn't* fallen in love with such a maddening woman. "Surely you don't think you're going to a party this evening."

Her other brow rose. "Surely you don't think you can stop me."

He narrowed his eyes. "You need rest, Emily." His gaze dipped to the terrifying bruises blooming on her neck. "You suffered a terrible ordeal."

"I *survived* a terrible ordeal. I'd much prefer to be out among friends than lying in bed and brooding about it."

"You need rest."

"First I need to see Carolyn. She's expecting me."

Before he could argue further, she slid closer to the door and rested her hand against his arm. Her touch stilled him. Even through the layers of his clothing, a ripple of heat shot straight to his core.

"Please, Logan. I really must see her. Today. I wouldn't insist if it weren't terribly important."

"What could possibly be so important that it cannot wait until tomorrow?"

Her eyes turned troubled and imploring. "I . . . I'm afraid I cannot tell you. I wish I could, truly I do, but it would mean breaking a confidence, and I cannot."

He wanted to say no, that he was taking her directly home, and that was the end of it. But apparently he could deny her nothing, because he found himself saying, "A *brief* stop. No more than a quarter hour. Then you're going home and taking that bath. You may not be sore now, but you will be within a few hours. A hot soak will help soothe the aches."

She nodded solemnly. "I agree. And thank you."

He called out Carolyn's direction to Paul then settled in the seat next to Emily and took her hand in his, entwining their fingers. To offer her comfort after her harrowing experience he told himself, but the truth was he simply couldn't stand not to touch her. Cold air blew in through the broken back window, but Logan didn't feel it. All the fright and terror he'd felt earlier twisted inside him, turning into an inferno of heat and need and desire he couldn't control.

With his gaze steady on hers, he reached out and flicked the velvet curtains closed on the two side windows. Her eyes widened, but the way her pupils dilated told him all he needed to know and wiped away any thought he might have entertained that he'd be able to stay away from her for the duration of the ride. Shadows engulfed them, and without a word he reached for her. He framed her beautiful face between his hands and lowered his mouth to hers.

He'd intended the kiss to be gentle, sweet, and tender, but the moment his lips touched hers, all coherent thought ceased to exist. With a deep groan, he gathered her into his arms and pulled her onto his lap, cradling her as close as he could. Yet it wasn't close enough. He sank deeper into the kiss, yet it wasn't deep enough. One hand slipped inside her pelisse to cup her breast, but it still wasn't enough.

He ran his hand down her torso to the curve of her bottom to hold her tighter against him. Her hip pressed against his erection, and he was helpless to contain the low growl that vibrated in his throat. More, damn it, he wanted more. She was like a thirst he couldn't quench, a hunger he couldn't satisfy. He wanted her so badly he was shaking.

Her tongue danced with his, and her fingers sifted through his hair, shuddering pleasure through him. Her slightest touch set him on fire. He wanted nothing more than to strip them both bare then put out this inferno she'd lit in him. Which was precisely why he had to stop. Now. While he still could.

With an effort that cost him, he gentled the kiss then raised his head. Her rapid breaths pelted against his face.

"How do you do that?" she whispered.

"Do what?"

Her eyes opened halfway, and his grip on her tightened at the arousal glowing in their depths. "Make me forget everything. Except you. Make me want . . . things I shouldn't. How can you make me feel so quivery and hot all over with something so simple as a kiss?"

He didn't know, but he was damn glad he did, because hot and quivery were exactly how she made him feel by virtue of a mere touch. A single look. And as far as he was concerned, there was nothing *simple* about kissing her. No, the problem was that it was too damn complicated.

"You have the same effect on me," he whispered against her mouth.

"I do?"

A huff of incredulous laughter passed his lips. He gave a slow thrust upward, pressing his erection against her hip. "Yes, you do. Obviously."

"I suppose I shouldn't be glad, but I am. I'd hate to think it was just me."

He rested his forehead against hers. "Not just you," he assured her, and wondered if she had any idea the will he was exerting to keep from touching her in the way he wanted to.

Just then the carriage rocked to a halt. Logan flicked back a corner of the curtain. "We've arrived at Carolyn's town house," he said softly.

Emily blinked several times, as if coming out of a trance, then gasped. "Good heavens." She scrambled off his lap and quickly fastened her pelisse and retied her bonnet. "Do I look . . . undone?"

His gaze skimmed over her flushed face and reddened, moist lips. She looked aroused and thoroughly kissed and more desirable than any woman he'd ever known. "You look perfect."

She reached out and grabbed his hand. "Logan, I don't want Carolyn to know what happened today."

He raised his brows. "It's going to be difficult to keep it a secret once she sees your neck."

"I'll adjust my fichu so she won't see it."

"Why the secrecy?"

She hesitated, then said, "Carolyn already has enough on her mind, and I don't want to add to her worries."

He wanted to ask what Carolyn had to be worried about but decided not to press her. "I won't mention what happened."

He helped her alight from the carriage and escorted her up the short walkway to the town house where Carolyn and Daniel lived. They surrendered their outerwear to Barkley, after which Emily surreptitiously rearranged her lace fichu around her neck.

"Lady Surbrooke is expecting you," the butler said to Emily.

"I take it you want to speak to her alone?" Logan said under his breath.

When Emily nodded, he handed Barkley one of his calling cards. "If Lord Surbrooke is available, I'd like to see him."

"I'll see if he's in, sir," Barkley said, placing the card on a sliver salver.

He watched Emily follow the butler down the corridor. After they disappeared from view, he paced the length of the foyer, too restless to sit. Barkley returned a few minutes later and announced, "Lord Surbrooke will see you, sir."

He followed the butler down the same corridor. Logan's gaze lingered on the closed door to the drawing room as they walked past, and he couldn't help but wonder what Emily and Carolyn were discussing. Emily had seemed so serious; not a whiff of mischief in her eyes. Clearly something was amiss. Whatever it was, he hoped their conversation resolved the matter. In the meanwhile, he'd toss back a bracing swallow of Daniel's no doubt excellent brandy.

Because after the last few hours, he sure as hell needed one.

Chapter 18

It hadn't occurred to me that once he became part of my world that other female vampires would find him as irresistible and appealing as I did. I quickly discovered my oversight. It had been a very long time since I'd experienced jealousy. I didn't like it one bit.

The Vampire Lady's Kiss *by Anonymous*

After Barkley departed, closing the door after him, Emily crossed the threshold and walked toward the fireplace where Carolyn stood. One look at her friend's face told Emily all was not well. Concern flooded her, and she reached for Carolyn's hands, alarmed at how cold they were in spite of her proximity to the fire.

"Something's happened." Emily stated the obvious, trying her best to sound calm despite the fear, dread, and alarm knotting her stomach at her friend's ashen pallor and the dark circles under her eyes. She looked exhausted and drawn. "You and Daniel went to the doctor this morning?"

Carolyn shook her head. "We went to Gunter's for an ice. It's one of our favorite places."

Confusion filled Emily. "When you wrote that you and

Daniel had plans for this morning, I assumed it was to see the doctor. Especially after you weren't feeling well last night."

Guilt flashed in Carolyn's eyes, and she turned to look into the fire. A sense of disbelief came over Emily. *Surely* Carolyn had told Daniel. However, Carolyn's continued silence fueled her suspicions and prompted her to ask, "What was his reaction when you told him about your concerns for your health?"

When Carolyn didn't respond, Emily's fears were confirmed.

"You didn't tell him." It was a statement rather than a question.

Carolyn pressed her lips together and shook her head. She turned to look at Emily. Her blue eyes swam with tears. "I couldn't. I'd planned to yesterday, but the weather was so fine Daniel drove the phaeton to Regent Street. We strolled along and shopped, and it was such a beautiful, enjoyable day, I couldn't bear to ruin it with bad news."

"You were feeling well?" Emily asked hopefully.

"Yes, in the morning. But as the afternoon wore on, that changed. By the time we arrived home, I was exhausted, and it seemed every part of me ached. I barely had enough energy to make it to my bed to lie down. I was so sorry not to be able to attend our meeting."

"We missed you." She gently squeezed Carolyn's cold hands. "And I've been so worried. Have you made plans to see the Harley Street doctor Edward's physician recommended?"

Carolyn hesitated, then whispered, "No."

Dismay filled Emily. "But why? If it's because you don't want Daniel to go with you, I'll accompany you. We can go right now. Right this minute."

Carolyn's gaze rested on Emily's, and the utterly calm, impassive expression in her eyes shivered cold dread down her spine. She wasn't sure what was coming next, but she was certain she wasn't going to like it.

"Emily . . . I'm not going to go to the doctor."

The bottom dropped out of Emily's stomach, not only at the words but at the quiet determination and finality in Carolyn's voice when she spoke them. "But you must—"

"No. Please try to understand. After much soul searching

I've accepted that I'm facing the same fate Edward suffered, which means that my time is limited."

Despair gripped Emily, and she shook her head. "You cannot be sure—"

"Yes. I can. As much as I may wish it otherwise, I lived through this with Edward, and I *know.* I know what is coming in the weeks ahead. If I see the doctor, he's going to insist upon the same thing Edward's doctor did for him: that I remain in bed, bundled in blankets, dosed with laudanum, and hope for a cure. Well, that cure never came for Edward, and he spent the last weeks of his life confined to his bed, drifting in and out of consciousness as he wasted away. It was a horrible fate for him and a devastating heartbreak for me to witness."

Her eyes begged Emily for understanding. "If I tell Daniel, he will have me to the doctor in a thrice, a doctor who will confine me to bed, and Daniel will insist on carrying out his orders in the hopes of me being cured. And my life will end like that, instead of enjoying whatever time I have left, and my husband will be forced to spend weeks watching me fade away. I cannot do that. I *refuse* to do that to either of us. Which is why I went with my husband to Gunter's this morning instead of to the doctor's office. And why I'm not going to tell him until it's absolutely necessary."

It felt as if a jagged hole had been ripped in Emily's chest. "But Edward died almost four years ago! Advances have been made, cures found. You cannot give up hope this way."

"There's a difference between giving up hope and accepting your fate."

"But surely Daniel has noticed your pallor."

Carolyn averted her gaze to once again look into the fire. "He knows of my previous visit to the doctor. I've convinced him it's nothing more than dyspepsia and a lingering chill."

"So Daniel believes that all you have is a common stomach ailment and a case of the sniffles."

"Yes, that recur frequently." She turned back to Emily. "And that's what I want him to believe. For as long as possible." Her gaze searched Emily's. "It may not be the decision you would make for yourself, but it's what I must do. Please say you forgive me and that you'll try to understand."

Emily lifted their joined hands then lowered her head to press her lips to the back of Carolyn's fingers. Tears flooded her eyes. *Dear God, this cannot be happening. I cannot be losing her.* The pressure in her chest hurt so badly she could barely breathe. Her heart broke not only for Carolyn but for Daniel, who loved her so deeply. What would she do if faced with a similar situation? Dear God, she didn't know. But surely living each day to the fullest was a better alternative than wasting away in a sickbed.

Finally she raised her head and pulled in a shaky breath. "I will do anything you ask."

Carolyn's bottom lip trembled. "Thank you."

"But I have one request."

"What's that?"

"Please, please, *please* let me arrange for you see another doctor. Someone obscure, who has no connection to you or Edward or his previous physician. I'll go with you. We'll give a false name for you; that way, if you decide not to follow the doctor's advice, he'll never know. Daniel won't know. No one will know except you and me. The worst that will happen is you'll find out for certain you're correct, and as you're already convinced, what can be the harm?"

"As I'm already convinced, what can be the point?"

She could barely speak around the lump clogging her throat. "Because I love you," she whispered. "And I need you to do this. After you do, I swear I won't mention it again."

Carolyn heaved out a weary sigh and slipped her hands away. Emily had to force herself to let her go, to not tighten her grip. She watched Carolyn move slowly toward the settee. "Very well. If you make the arrangements under a false name, I'll go."

Emily's relief was tempered by the sudden unsteadiness of Carolyn's movements. She seemed to sway on her feet. Alarmed, Emily reached for her, but before she could grab her, Carolyn's eyes rolled back, and she collapsed onto the floor with a sickening thud.

"Carolyn!" Heart in her throat, Emily dashed forward and dropped to her knees beside her fallen friend. She tapped Carolyn's pale cheek and shook her shoulder. "Carolyn, can you hear me?"

There was no response, and Emily feared that in addition to whatever had caused her to faint, Carolyn had struck her head on the floor. Her only comfort was the shallow rise and fall of her chest.

Terrified, Emily jumped up and dashed to the door. She yelled for Barkley as she flew down the corridor toward the foyer. Before she reached the marble entryway, Daniel, followed by Logan and Barkley, met her.

"What's wrong?" Daniel asked, clasping her shoulders.

"Carolyn. She fainted. I couldn't catch her. I think she hit her head." The words came out in a rush.

Daniel immediately released her and started down the corridor at a dead run. "Send for Dr. Waverly, Barkley," he shouted over his shoulder. "And I want hartshorn and cold compresses immediately."

Emily followed him, with Logan on her heels. When she entered the drawing room, Daniel was kneeling beside Carolyn, gently tapping her cheek and shaking her shoulder, his face pale and tight with concern.

"She has a lump on the back of her head," he said tersely, his gaze not straying from Carolyn's waxy face.

Emily grabbed a pillow from the settee, dropped to her knees, and gently slipped it beneath Carolyn's head. She then picked up her friend's cold hand and patted it urgently, praying for Carolyn to regain consciousness.

"Carolyn, darling, please open your eyes," Daniel urged, his fervent words lancing pain through Emily. An image of him assaulted her: mere weeks from now, begging his dead wife to open her eyes.

She squeezed her eyes shut, consigning the horrible mental picture to the fires of hell. She couldn't think like that. Couldn't. Wouldn't. Yet one look at Carolyn's sunken, pale face made it impossible not to.

Barkley, his countenance puckered with concern, dashed into the room, followed by a grim-faced footman bearing a large bowl and a stack of folded linen strips. Emily jumped to her feet to prepare a compress.

"Dr. Waverly has been sent for," Barkley reported, handing Daniel the hartshorn.

Daniel nodded. He waved the reviver beneath Carolyn's

nose. On the third pass, she finally groaned, and her eyelids flickered open.

"There's my beautiful bride," Daniel murmured, setting aside the hartshorn. Without taking his eyes off Carolyn, he reached out for a compress, which Emily set in his hand.

Carolyn's eyes shifted from him to Emily, then to Barkley and Logan, before resettling on Daniel, who brushed back her hair and laid the compress on her forehead. "What happened?" she whispered.

"You fainted," Daniel said in a calm voice, but Emily could hear the tension beneath his outward composure. She prepared another compress and was about to cross to the crystal pitcher on the desk to pour a glass of water, but saw that Logan had already done so.

Carolyn frowned and raised a hand to touch her hair. "My head hurts."

"That's because you whacked it on the floor when you went down like a tenpin." Daniel lifted her hand to his lips and pressed a kiss against her fingers. Emily saw the slight tremor that racked his broad shoulders, and a piece of her heart simply broke off. "We're either going to have to cover all the floors with goose down so you don't bump your head, or you're simply going to have to cease this swooning," he said with a half smile Emily knew was for Carolyn's benefit. "I know which choice I prefer."

"I'm sorry. I . . . don't know what came over me." She attempted to sit up, but Daniel shook his head and gently urged her back down.

"Oh, no. You're staying right there until Dr. Waverly arrives."

Carolyn's eyes widened, and her gaze flicked to Emily. "I don't need a doctor. I merely need a drink of water."

Logan stepped forward and handed Daniel the glass he'd poured. Daniel nodded his thanks then helped Carolyn take a few sips. When she finished, she offered him a weak smile. "See? I feel much better. Now if you'll just help me up—"

"I'll do no such thing, and you're not moving," Daniel said kindly but firmly.

"But—"

"No buts, Carolyn." Daniel turned over the compress. "Dr. Waverly will be here soon. We're going to get to the bottom of these fainting spells. Today."

"It's merely the dyspepsia. My stomach felt off, therefore I didn't eat enough, which left me light-headed."

"And now you have an egg-sized bump on your head. Which the doctor is going to examine. After *he* tells me you're all right, then I'll let you stand up."

Her gaze shifted to Emily, and Emily could clearly read her thoughts: that the doctor wasn't going to tell Daniel she was all right. She could see Carolyn was distressed, but it was obvious Daniel wasn't going to hear of Dr. Waverly not being summoned. Her breaking heart absorbed another blow when a look of utter defeat clouded Carolyn's eyes.

"We'll give you some privacy," Emily murmured, "but I'd like to stay in the house, to hear the doctor's report, if that's all right."

"Of course," Daniel said. "Why don't you wait in the library? I'll let you know what Waverly says."

"Thank you." Emily looked at Carolyn and tried to form her lips into an encouraging smile but suspected she failed.

She and Logan quit the room, and he followed her down the corridor to the library. As soon as she crossed the threshold, she headed for the tall windows, touched her hands to the cold glass, and strove to gather herself. She heard Logan close the door, then silence filled the room. She stared at the small garden with unseeing eyes until she sensed him standing directly behind her.

"I don't suppose there's any point in suggesting you go home and rest." His quiet words brushed across her nape, sending a heated shiver down her spine.

Not trusting her voice, she shook her head.

"I would ask if you're all right, but I can see that you're not," he said in a voice so tender it filled her eyes with the tears she was trying so hard not to shed. "Do you want to tell me what's troubling you? I give you my word that anything you say will remain in this room."

She managed to hold on to her composure for nearly ten seconds before a sob broke free from her throat. Before she could so much as draw in breath, he'd turned her around and pulled her into his arms. To her utter mortification, another sob, then another broke from her, and then the dam burst.

Unable to do anything else, she wrapped her arms around his waist and buried her face against the hard wall of his chest. The tears she could no longer contain spilled from her eyes, wetting his shirt, but he didn't seem to notice or care. As he had in the carriage earlier, he simply held her and let her cry. One large hand slowly rubbed her back while he peppered gentle kisses against her hair and listened to her halting words as she unburdened herself of the heartbreak of Carolyn's situation she could no longer keep inside her.

When she finished, she raised her head to find him looking down at her with solemn eyes. "I'm more sorry than I can say to hear that," he murmured, cradling her face between his palms and gently brushing away her tears with the pads of his thumbs. "I think you were very wise to insist she see another doctor. You're a loyal and true friend."

"I don't feel like one at the moment. I shouldn't have told you."

"I disagree. Keeping all that inside you isn't healthy. Don't you feel better now that you've let it all out?"

Since she couldn't deny it, she nodded.

"Good. Now, about a doctor: I know of one I can recommend, if you'd like. He's very discreet and quite innovative in his treatments. I can arrange it so he'll see Carolyn tomorrow."

"Thank you." She didn't feel even the slightest twinge of surprise that he'd be so kind.

"You're welcome." He pressed something into her hand, and she realized it was his handkerchief. She wiped her eyes then gave her nose an unladylike blow.

"Feel better?" he asked.

She nodded. "I'll have this laundered before returning it."

"Keep it. I have others."

She looked down and ran her finger over his initials embroidered in maroon on the corner of the snowy linen square before meeting his gaze once more. "Thank you for listening. And comforting me—again. I'm sorry I cried all over you— again." Embarrassment swept through her. Good Lord, how many times could she cry on this man in a single day? She just prayed that she wouldn't have cause to do so again.

She'd expected a teasing reply from him, but instead, he gently brushed his fingertips over her still damp cheek and regarded her through very serious eyes. "I'm glad I was here. That you aren't going through something so distressing and painful alone. Alone is so very . . . isolating. Feel free to cry on me anytime you want."

Her bottom lip trembled, and to her horror another flood of tears pooled behind her eyes. Damnation, if he was going to insist on being so kind, she'd find herself taking him up on his offer immediately. "This is the second time today you've come to my rescue. I had no idea you were such a knight in shining armor."

One corner of his mouth lifted, drawing her attention to his beautiful lips. "I had no idea you were such a damsel in distress."

She pulled her gaze back up to his eyes. "I'm usually not. Indeed, I'm usually no trouble at all."

There was no mistaking the heat that kindled in his eyes. "Now I'll have to disagree with you on that." His gaze dropped to her mouth. "You, my dear, are the very epitome of trouble."

She objected to his words and would most certainly voice that objection as soon as her pulse stopped misbehaving at the potent intensity of his gaze. Before she could, however, he leaned forward and brushed his lips over hers in a feather-light kiss that was over much too quickly and left her wanting more. After dropping another quick peck on her forehead, he released her and stepped back. She had to lock her knees to keep from swaying on her feet.

"What was that for?" she asked—a far more prudent question than *Why in God's name did you stop?*

"We're in a library," he said, his expression grave. "I thought it best we keep with tradition."

"I see," she murmured, which was far more prudent than pointing out that if they kept with tradition, tongues and extensive groping would have ensued.

"Of course, if we truly kept with tradition," he continued, a devilish gleam filling his gaze, "tongues would have been involved and extensive groping would have ensued."

Emily could only stare. Egad, could the man read her mind? She cleared her throat and hoped he wouldn't notice the furious blush she felt creeping into her cheeks. "That would hardly be appropriate," she said in her most repressive tone.

"I agree." He shot her a wink. "Next time."

She opened her mouth to tell him . . . something . . . certainly to give him some sort of set down, then she realized what he was doing. He was trying to distract her, take her mind off Carolyn. And for at least a couple of minutes, he'd succeeded. A combination of confusion and gratitude spread through her like warm honey. Good Lord, if she wasn't careful, she might come to like this man very much. Far too much.

A knock sounded on the door. "Come in," she said quickly, taking a step away from Logan to put a proper amount of distance between them.

Daniel entered and closed the door behind him. Emily's heart broke at how worried he looked. "Dr. Waverly is with her," he said, his voice sounding hoarse. He moved to the fireplace, where he sat down heavily on the long sofa in front of the hearth. He pulled in a ragged breath and dragged unsteady hands down his face. Then he looked up at Emily with such a bleak expression, she knew Carolyn had finally told him.

"This isn't simply dyspepsia," he said quietly. "But you already knew that."

"Yes," she whispered. "At least I know that's what she believes."

A humorless sound escaped him. "As ridiculous as this sounds, I'm glad she fainted and hit her head today, as it forced her to finally tell me the truth." He stared at Emily through devastated and confused eyes. "How could she not tell me?"

Aching for him, Emily sat beside him and took his hand. He squeezed her fingers so hard she nearly flinched. "She loves you so much, Daniel. She couldn't stand to see you worry. Couldn't stand to taint your time together with illness."

"As if I weren't already worried, what with her looking so pale and not eating and everything else. Dyspepsia . . . how could I have been such an idiot to have simply accepted that? To not have forced her to see another doctor?"

"She didn't want to—" Emily began.

"The *hell* with that," Daniel shouted, the anger and fear in his voice echoing through the room. Then he squeezed his eyes shut and drew a shuddering breath. When he finally turned to Emily, gone was the imperturbable, suave nobleman. In his place was a man with haunted, terrified eyes, who was unraveling like a pulled thread. "She cannot die, Emily, she simply can't. *Can't.* She is . . . everything." He looked at the floor, closed his eyes, and whispered, "Everything."

"I know," Emily murmured around the hard lump clogging her throat. "I know." She looked up at Logan, who stood behind the sofa then cut her gaze to the decanters. He nodded and crossed the room, returning a moment later with generous brandies for himself and Daniel and a sherry for her.

He sat next to Emily, and three of them remained on the sofa, sipping their drinks, the silence broken only by the unrelenting ticking of the mantel clock. After a quarter hour, Daniel rose and wordlessly paced. Logan took her hand, entwining their fingers, and she was grateful for the show of support and the warmth of his palm pressing against her cold skin.

Another quarter hour passed. Then another. Daniel paced like a caged animal. Just when she didn't think any of them could stand it any longer, a knock sounded. Daniel sprinted across the room, while Emily and Logan jumped to their feet. Daniel grabbed the brass handle and yanked open the door to reveal a grim-faced Dr. Waverly.

"I need to speak with you, my lord," the doctor said. His gaze flicked to Emily and Logan. "Privately."

"Of course." Daniel turned toward them, his manner composed, but Emily saw the profound fear in his eyes. "I'll return as soon as I can." With that, he quit the room, closing the door behind him.

Emily couldn't speak. Dear God, the doctor's face . . . he'd looked so . . . grave. She felt as if her insides were collapsing. She turned to Logan, and without a word he opened his arms. And without a word she walked into them. Wrapped her arms around his waist. Buried her face against his chest. Clung to him. Tried to remember how to breathe. And did the only other thing she could: she prayed.

She wasn't certain how much time passed as she listened to the comforting sound of Logan's steady breathing and strong heartbeat beneath her ear and prayed as she never had before. Finally a knock sounded at the door. She lifted her head, but before she could move from Logan's embrace, Daniel entered the room. And her heart dropped to her feet at the sight of his red-rimmed eyes and pale face.

As if in a trance, he crossed the room. She would have met him halfway, but she didn't trust her unsteady legs to carry her. Instead, she stood next to Logan, clutching his arm, and waited.

Daniel stopped an arm's length away from them. His gaze bounced between them, then he raked hands that were visibly shaking through his hair. Unable to look into his disbelieving eyes, Emily turned her head to press her face into Logan's sleeve.

She heard Daniel swallow, then say in a raw voice, "She's . . . expecting."

"Expecting what?" Emily whispered against Logan's sleeve. *To die? Please, God, no. To recover? Please, God, yes.*

"A child," came Daniel's dazed-sounding reply. "She's expecting a child."

For several seconds, silence swelled in the room. Then Emily jerked her head up and stared at Daniel. "*What?*"

A noise that sounded like a half laugh, half sob broke from Daniel's chest. "Carolyn is pregnant. We're going to have a child."

Emily's eyes felt as if they were going to pop from their sockets. "But . . . but she always said she wasn't able to have children."

"That's what she thought. What her doctor during her marriage to Edward had told her." A bemused, dazed smile touched the corners of Daniel's lips. "Obviously he was wrong."

Relief was turning her knees to porridge. "She's not ill?"

"Not a bit."

"There's no doubt?"

"None. The doctor says she's nearly four months along. Her symptoms are common for expectant mothers, and those symptoms that aren't are merely the result of a lingering chill worsened, he believes, by Carolyn's worrying. Dr. Waverly is convinced that one's mental state can profoundly affect one's physical state. The bump she sustained on her head is nothing to worry about. He wants her to rest as much as possible to regain her strength and said the nausea and light-headedness should pass within the next few weeks. The headaches will pass once she starts eating regularly again."

A delighted laugh burst from Emily, and she reached out to grasp Daniel's hands. "I can't believe it! Not only is she not ill, she's going to be a mother!"

Daniel's entire face lit up with a huge smile. "Yes, she is."

"And you're going to be a father," Logan added, clapping him on the shoulder. "Congratulations."

"And I'm going to be a father," Daniel agreed. His smile instantly changed into a look of utter panic. "Bloody hell, I need to sit down."

With a laugh, Emily and Logan helped him to the nearest chair. "May I see her?" Emily asked once he was seated and Logan was pouring him a brandy.

"Yes, of course. She's resting on the sofa in the drawing room. In fact, she refused to be moved until she sees you."

"Then if you'll excuse me," she said and hurried off to the drawing room. Ten seconds later, she was hugging Carolyn, and they were both laughing and crying at the same time.

"You should be ashamed of yourself for scaring us like that," Emily said, shooting her a frown that was completely ruined by her happy laugh.

"I'm so sorry. I still cannot believe it." She laid her hand on her midsection, and her eyes glowed with wonder. "It never once crossed my mind that I could be pregnant."

"I'm so happy for you," Emily said, squeezing her hand. "Good heavens, the Ladies Literary Society is going to have to be renamed the Ladies with Babies Literary Society."

Carolyn laughed. "So it would seem. Now all we need to do is get you married and with child."

"As soon as I fall in love, I'll be delighted to oblige you. And I'll have all the time I need to find someone to love as soon as my vampire scheme is successful and I sell my story for a fortune. Did you see the article in the *Times*?"

"I did." A frown puckered Carolyn's brow. "But I worry about you perpetrating another masquerade tonight, especially since I won't be attending the party to help you. The doctor insists I rest. Surely you've done enough."

Emily shook her head. "Another sighting is needed to really push the story forward."

"But don't you think . . . ?"

Her words trailed off, and Emily waited. "Don't I think what?" she prompted.

"Well, that you could fall in love with a rich man? That would solve all your financial problems. And you wouldn't have to dress up like a vampire."

Emily had a strong suspicion as to where this was leading, and to her chagrin, her heart skipped a beat. "Hmmm, yes falling in love with a rich man would be helpful. I don't suppose you have any particular rich man in mind?"

Carolyn pretended to deliberate, and Emily couldn't help but chuckle.

"What?" Carolyn asked, her eyes wide with innocence.

"Don't give me that look. I know what you're up to. And by the way, you are *the* most horrid actress."

Carolyn dropped all pretense. "He's a good man, Emily. And I truly believe he cares for you."

There was no point pretending she didn't know who "he" was. "He tolerates me. Barely. And perhaps likes me. Just a little." She shook her head. "It's not enough. I want what you, Sarah, and Julianne have. I want love. Passion. And I'm willing to do whatever is necessary to get it."

Carolyn's gaze probed hers. "How do *you* feel about *him*?"

Emily's pulse stuttered at the question. "I tolerate him. Barely. And perhaps like him. Just a little."

"Do you desire him?"

Her face flushed hot, a sign that wasn't lost on Carolyn. "No need to answer," Carolyn said, her voice tinged with smugness. "That blush gave you away."

"I won't deny he is . . . mildly attractive." Her conscience coughed to life at the gross understatement and smacked her in the head.

"Indeed he is. Lady Hombly certainly thinks so. Actually, it was very apparent at Lord Teller's soiree that she thinks him *extremely* attractive."

Not for the first time Emily experienced an urge to slap Lady Hombly's gorgeous face. She raised her chin and gave an elegant sniff. "She is welcome to him."

"So you said at Lord Teller's party. Because you're not in the least bit interested."

"That is," *completely wrong*, "absolutely correct."

Carolyn shook her head. "And you think *I'm* a horrid actress? Darling, if you ever walked the boards, they would throw rotten tomatoes at you."

"I'm a good enough actress to play a vampire tonight—a performance that is going to save my family and set my future."

Yes, a future that included love and marriage and children. One that didn't include Logan Jennsen. That was for certain. For, after all, while he might find her desirable, in the end he believed her nothing but trouble.

And that, sadly, wasn't enough.

Chapter 19

❦

When I saw the beautiful, seductive vampire approaching
my mate, I bared my fangs and let out a warning growl.
"He's mine," I warned her. Her slow smile was filled with
challenge. "We'll see about that," she answered.

The Vampire Lady's Kiss *by Anonymous*

Champagne glass in hand, Logan stood in a quiet corner of
Lord Farmington's drawing room, shielded from the crowded
party by the potted palms rising from enormous cloisonné
planters. He scanned the formally attired crowd while listening with half an ear to snatches of the conversations floating
around him, most of them revolving around the recent vampire sighting and subsequent *Times* article.
"... *never heard of a female vampire* ..."
"... *must have killed that man in St. Giles—*"
"*I actually saw the creature's terrifying fangs* ..."
"*—wonder when she'll strike again.*"
"*Do you think it could be tonight?*"
"... *best not to roam outside at night until she's caught.*"
While he knew damn well dangers lurked in the dark,
he didn't put any credence in the vampire report and had no

desire to partake in any speculations. Dozens of people he recognized filled the room, but for reasons he didn't quite understand, he felt disinclined to mingle or converse with any of them.

You liar, his inner voice sneered. *You know damn well why you don't feel like it. It's because there's only one person you want to mingle or converse with, and she isn't here.*

His lips flattened in annoyance. Damn irritating inner voice. Why couldn't it just for once shut the hell up?

Fine. The only person he wanted to see, longed to talk to, yearned to look at was Emily. He'd known she wouldn't be here, as before departing her town house, he'd extracted her promise to spend the evening resting. He'd also known that neither Matthew nor Daniel would be in attendance, and although he'd secured an invitation for Gideon, now that his enemy was dead, there was no reason for the Runner to be here.

Yet still he'd come, although he wasn't quite sure why.

You liar, his inner voice sneered again. *You know damn well why. It's because you couldn't stand another night alone in that big, empty house.*

He mentally consigned the aggravating voice to the bowels of hell but couldn't deny the truth. Fine. He was sick to death of being alone. The prospect of another solitary night had filled him with an aching emptiness so profound it had compelled him to attend this foolish party just so he wouldn't have to suffer another evening in his own company. He'd even considered asking Adam to stay for dinner, perhaps join him in a game of chess, but his factotum had been anxious to depart once his duties for the day were complete, claiming some pressing prior plans. Given his odd behavior of late, Logan again wondered if Adam had a woman. God knows that would be cause enough for acting in an uncharacteristic manner.

Yet in spite of the temporary diversion this soiree provided, it was clear that coming had been a mistake. For even though he was surrounded by dozens of partygoers, he still felt utterly alone.

Through the palm fronds he caught sight of Celeste. He hadn't given the beautiful Lady Hombly so much as a passing thought since she'd hurried off yesterday to save her pelisse from Tiny's dirty paw prints. Dressed in a daringly low-cut pale green gown that highlighted her bountiful breasts, her blond hair upswept.to show off her long, slender neck, her stunning features arranged in a perfect smile, she conversed with a dark-haired man who hung on her every word and whose appreciative gaze made it clear he very much liked what he saw. Not that Logan could blame him. She was undeniably gorgeous. And.she undeniably left him cold. The man so clearly enamored of her, whoever he was, was welcome to her.

He briefly considered going home but decided against it. At least here there was noise. Laughter. Conversation. Music. At home there was nothing save a hollow, echoing quiet that would leave him undisturbed with his thoughts. Thoughts that all revolved around *her*, which is precisely what he was trying to avoid. Heaving a sigh, he lifted his hand to toss back the rest of his champagne. And froze.

Emily stood on the opposite side of the crowded room, flanked by her mother and her aunt Agatha. He stared at her in disbelief, then blinked just to make certain he wasn't imagining her presence. But no, there she stood, sipping a glass of punch, as if she hadn't nearly been strangled only hours.ago. His gaze swept over her, taking in the pearls woven through her shiny dark hair and the beguiling tendrils framing her face. Her aqua gown set off her creamy complexion, as did the triple-strand pearl choker encircling her neck that cleverly hid the red marks he knew marred her pale skin.

A combination of heated awareness and utter aggravation surged through him. Damn it, what was she doing here? She was supposed to be home resting, as she'd promised. Obviously, promises didn't mean much to her. Well, that was good to know—and actually quite a relief. He certainly wouldn't need to ever again ask himself that idiotic *Could I be in love with her?* question. He couldn't possibly love a woman who didn't keep her word. And he intended to let her know he'd caught her in a falsehood.

He was about to march across the room when he noticed a tall blond man approach her. Logan's jaw tightened. It was that same fop who'd practically drooled on her at Lord Teller's party. What the hell was his name? Oh, yes. Lord Kaster.

Some young viscount or earl or some such title. Yes, one of those damn noblemen with too much time and money on their hands and who seemed to have eight sets of eyeballs. And right now all eight sets of Kaster's eyeballs were once again ogling Emily as if she were a sugary confection from which he wanted to take a nice big bite.

Kaster leaned down, ostensibly to hear whatever it was Emily was saying, but Logan noted the bastard's overactive eyeballs delving into her bodice. His fingers tightened around his champagne glass, and he quickly set it down in the cloisonné planter before he snapped the stem in two. Then the ogling bastard leaned even closer to Emily and whispered in her ear. To Logan's disgust, she smiled at him—a full, bright smile—then nodded. He offered her his hand, and they made their way toward the dance floor.

Feeling as if he were nailed in place, he watched Kaster take her hand and place his palm on the curve at the small of her back then swing her onto the parquet floor in perfect time with the music. Watched her smile at Kaster. And watched Kaster's eight sets of wandering eyeballs practically undress her. A red haze seemed to cloud Logan's vision. The depth of the jealousy he felt shocked him. It was an emotion he hadn't felt in years. Why would he? It was a waste of time and effort, and besides which, he had everything. What was there to be jealous of? Nothing.

Until he saw the woman who tempted him beyond all reason talking to, smiling at, and dancing with another man. And not just any dance. No, it was a waltz—the very dance Logan had invited her to share with him. But now instead she shared it with that blond fop who was regarding her with the same glittery-eyed zeal a rodent would bestow upon a hunk of cheese. And he didn't like it. Not one bit.

"That's *my* damn hunk of cheese, you bastard," he muttered.

Kaster's hand slid lower on her back to pull her closer, and he gritted his teeth so hard it was a miracle they didn't grind down to stubs.

"That's it," he said aloud to the palm fronds. Eyes riveted on the swirling couple, he made his way to the dance floor. When they circled around again, he stepped directly into their path. Kaster pulled them to an abrupt halt to avoid a collision and shot Logan a scowl.

"I say, Benson, what do you think you're doing?" the viscount or earl or whatever the hell he was asked in a testy voice.

"Jennsen," he corrected in a silky tone layered with ice. "I'm cutting in. Lady Emily promised this dance to me. Isn't that right, Lady Emily?" He shifted his gaze to Emily, who didn't look any happier to see him than Kaster did, a fact that annoyed—and damn it, hurt—him.

Emily licked her lips, a gesture that called forth unwanted erotic thoughts and did nothing to improve Logan's rapidly deteriorating mood. Clearly she sensed he wasn't going to take no for an answer, because after several seconds she offered Kaster an apologetic smile, "I'm sorry, my lord. I did promise this dance to Mr. Jennsen, but when he didn't show himself, I assumed he'd forgotten."

"You assumed wrong." Without another word he stepped between her and Kaster and whirled her into the throng of swirling couples.

"What on earth are you doing?" she asked in a low hiss as he circled her around the floor. If looks could have chopped off heads, Logan would have been decapitated.

"I should think that's obvious. I'm claiming my dance. However, I believe the more pertinent question is what the hell are you doing here?" *And what the hell are you doing with that eight-set-of-eyeballs, ogling, arrogant fop?*

She lifted her chin. "I should think that's obvious. I'm dancing with you. And in case you're interested, you just trod upon my toe."

"I suppose Lord Kaster didn't tread upon your toe."

"As a matter of fact, he didn't. Nor did he scowl at me as if I'd committed some heinous crime. Would you care to tell me why you're so . . ."

"Annoyed?" he supplied helpfully when she paused. "Irritated? Damn angry?"

"Since I haven't a clue, that might be nice."

"Haven't a clue," he muttered, shaking his head. "Unbelievable." Fixing her with a cold glare he asked, "Do you happen to recall the last thing you said to me before I departed your town house this afternoon?"

"Of course. I said, 'Good-bye.' "

His patience clung on by the slimmest of tethers. "Before that," he said through gritted teeth."

She pursed her lips and considered. "'Safe journey?' "

"No. You said, and I quote," he cleared his throat and adopted a high falsetto voice, "'I promise I shall retire to my bedchamber and rest this evening.' " He narrowed his eyes. "Yet here you are. In a place that is obviously not your bedchamber. Dancing—an activity which no matter how you dissect it is in no way synonymous with resting. Do you know what that makes you?"

"I'm certain you're about to tell me."

"Damn right I am. It makes you a *promise breaker.*"

She narrowed her eyes right back at him. "Are you finished?"

"For the moment."

"Excellent. First of all, I do not *sound like this,*" she said, imitating his falsetto. "Second, I didn't break my promise as I *did* rest in my bedchamber. For the entire remainder of the afternoon into early evening. I awoke two hours ago, and after a light meal I felt greatly refreshed and well enough to attend the party. If my mother doesn't object to me being here, I cannot see why you would. And third—I never promised not to come to the party."

"I assumed that was understood."

"Well, to coin your phrase, you assumed wrong. And you just trod on my toe again."

"Sorry." He barely managed the word through his clenched jaw. Damn it, he knew he wasn't the world's best dancer, but he normally wasn't so clumsy. Obviously his irritation with her was throwing off his sense of rhythm.

"Really? You don't look sorry. Nor do you sound sorry. You look and sound angry. Which is not only ridiculous but unreasonable, as you have no cause to be."

Damn it, she was right, which only made him more unreasonably angry. At her, for not resting more after the ordeal she'd suffered today. At that fop Kaster for ogling her with his eight pairs of eyeballs. Bastard probably had eight pairs of hands to go with them. But angry mostly at himself for not being able to shove aside his unwanted jealousy.

"If you're so annoyed with me," she continued, her voice low and fuming, "I wonder why you bothered to cut in on my dance."

He muttered under his breath, and confusion clouded her eyes. "What's that about a hunk of cheese?" she asked.

He shook his head and gave himself a mental slap. "Nothing." He pulled in a calming breath then looked into her eyes. The pastel hue of her dress coaxed the aquamarine undertones to shine through the sparkling emerald, and he felt his anger evaporating like water in a desert, replaced by a wave of raw need and profound want so intense it stunned him.

He curled his fingers tighter around hers and pulled her a bit closer. "I bothered to cut in because you'd promised me a waltz."

"Actually, I didn't. You asked me to save you one, but I never promised to do so."

"Ah. Well, I'm certain you meant to."

She arched a single brow. "And why is that?"

"Because who else but an uncouth American could you get to tread upon your toes? Surely you don't think any of these English dandies could provide you with such a treat."

"Obviously our definitions of *treat* differ greatly."

His lips twitched. He simply couldn't remain angry with her. Not when it felt so damn good to be holding her. "You may tread upon my toes if you wish," he offered.

"Very well." An instant later, her foot came upon his and he sucked in a breath, more from surprise than pain. She batted her eyelashes at him in an exaggerated fashion. "Sorry."

"How did you do that without losing your step?" he asked with grudging admiration. "When I step on you, I feel as if I'm going to fall over."

"Lots of practice with my clumsy brothers. Kenneth and William aren't bad, but Percy is a dreadful dancer. You're much better than him."

"How delightful to know I'm better than *dreadful*. How are your brothers?"

"Fine, thank you. Arthur asked about you today."

"What did he ask?"

A wash of color suffused her cheeks. "He wondered

when he and Tiny might see you again. You made quite an impression."

"As did they. What did you tell him?"

Her blush deepened. "I said I didn't know, that you were a very busy man. That perhaps we'd happen upon you in the park again someday."

"I see." His eyes drank her in, and he felt himself falling into the familiar abyss where the need to pull her closer, touch her, kiss her overwhelmed him. "I'd be delighted to make firmer plans to visit with him. Perhaps you'd both like to join me for an outing to Gunter's tomorrow? The rest of your family is welcome as well."

There was no missing her surprise. "That's very kind—"

"Your obvious shock wounds me, madam."

A sheepish look ghosted over her face. "At this point, I'm really no longer surprised you'd make a kind gesture—"

"My wounded pride thanks you."

"But surely you have other things to do. Business matters to attend to."

"I do. But even soulless businessmen such as myself take pleasure in Gunter's ices. I enjoyed your family's company." He should have stopped there, but as if of their own volition his suddenly runaway lips kept flapping, and he added softly, "I enjoy *your* company."

It required all his will not to erase the proper distance between them and brush his lips over the twin scarlet flags on her cheeks, a blush that made his heart thump in the most ridiculous way with the hope that she might echo the sentiment.

"Logan, I—"

Whatever she was about to say was interrupted when the music ended. He reluctantly released her and joined the other couples in applauding the musicians. He escorted her from the dance floor, but before he could resume their conversation, he felt a tap on his shoulder. He turned and to his surprise found himself facing Gideon.

After greeting him and Emily, Gideon said to him in an undertone, "I need to speak with you." He inclined his head toward the foyer.

Logan nodded. Clearly Gideon had news regarding the

man Atwater had killed. Anxious to find out what he'd discovered, Logan escorted Emily back to her aunt and mother.

"Nice to see you again, Mr. Jennsen," Lady Agatha shouted.

"And you as well, Lady Agatha. How are you?"

A look of confusion passed over her wrinkled face. "I'm right here," she shouted, waving her hand in front of his face.

He realized she thought he'd asked *where* are you. Leaning closer to her, he yelled, "*How* are you?"

Her expression cleared. "Very well, thank you, but there's no need to shout, dear boy. I'm not deaf, you know."

He smiled and lifted her proffered hand to his lips, a gesture that brought a delighted blush to her cheeks. He then turned to Emily's mother and offered her a formal bow.

"Good evening, Lady Fenstraw."

"Mr. Jennsen. I thought you might be here this evening." Her gaze bounced between him and Emily, and then she gifted him with a smile that to him looked ripe with . . . something. Speculation? Suspicion? Calculation? He wasn't certain, but it made him wonder if she suspected he'd shared more than a waltz with her daughter.

After exchanging brief pleasantries about the weather, he excused himself and made his way toward the foyer. He was determined to continue his conversation with Emily, but right now he needed to find out what information had brought Gideon here.

"Let's go outside," Gideon said without preamble as soon as Logan stepped into the marble-tiled vestibule. They exited the house and were greeted by a blast of icy air. "I want to walk the mansion's perimeter while we talk," Gideon said in an undertone.

"Any particular reason?" Logan asked just as quietly, his eyes scanning the area as they moved.

"Just a precaution. I've learned that the man who attacked Emily was one Ralph Ashton."

Logan frowned. "That name is not familiar to me."

"I'm not surprised, as it appears he isn't the person trying to harm you and Emily but rather was hired to do so."

Logan's every muscle tightened. "How do you know this?"

"My investigations yielded the fact that Ashton was heard

bragging in an alehouse in St. Giles last night about how he'd been hired for a great wad of blunt to get rid of a 'problem.' "

"Any clue as to who hired him?"

"Not yet. When asked what the problem was, Ashton laughed and replied the man who'd hired him said it was some woman who was making a pest of herself and wouldn't go away on her own. So she was going to have to be made to go away. Clearly Ashton didn't think anyone with Emily would be armed or prepared to kill to protect her."

Logan's hands clenched into fists. "And it also means that this isn't over. That whoever hired Ashton is still out there. Which means Emily is still in danger."

"And you as well," Gideon said. "Which is why we're performing this security check."

But Logan barely heard him. His instincts were telling him to find Emily. Now. "You keep on. I'm going back inside to find Emily. She needs to know to be on her guard. And I want to make certain she's safe."

Gideon nodded. "I left word for Atwater to meet us here, but I'm not sure when he'll arrive."

Without another word, Logan turned around and started making his way back toward the front of the mansion, cursing that Farmington's home and property were so large. Why couldn't they live in a town house like so many of the *ton*? He'd just turned the corner when he halted at the sight of a figure moving silently toward him along the shadows close to the house. He instantly crouched down and slipped his knife from his boot.

The figure continued toward him, halting just outside the pool of light cast onto the terrace from the drawing room windows. Ready to pounce, he watched the figure uncork a small glass vial and sprinkle something onto the flagstones, then step into the yellow circle of light. Grim determination and satisfaction filled him at the sight of the black hooded cloak. *You're mine, you bastard.*

The figure reached up and pushed back the hood, and Logan watched, stunned, as pale blond curls appeared. A black mask obscured the figure's face. Just then, what appeared to be a pair of bright white fangs flashed.

What the hell—?

His thought was cut off by a piercing scream that came from just beyond the French windows leading to the drawing room. "The vampire," cried a high-pitched feminine voice from inside the house. "The vampiress is on the terrace!"

"Yes, there she is!" cried another voice followed quickly by several others.

Logan looked through the windows. A large woman with one hand held to her ample bosom was pointing toward the terrace. She went down in a swoon, and four men leapt forward to keep her from hitting the floor. Several other people were pointing as well, and a crowd was quickly gathering.

Logan looked back toward the figure and muttered a curse. In the few seconds he'd been distracted, the vampire—or whatever the hell it was—had melted back into the shadows and was swiftly moving away from him. Knife in hand, he quickly followed, determined that tonight would be the hooded figure's last night of freedom.

⬦⬦⬦

Heart pounding with exhilaration, Emily raced through the shadows, keeping close to the house. The vampire had been seen! And by numerous people. By this time tomorrow, the news would have spread all over the city. And hopefully a few days after that, success would be hers.

And all this after thinking not once but twice that she might have to cancel her performance. First when she'd seen Logan. Her heart had simultaneously tripped over itself and sank to her feet when he'd appeared on the dance floor. Botheration, she hadn't expected him to be at the party, especially after she'd led him to believe she wasn't going to attend. But there he was, looking beautiful and masculine and fiercely annoyed. She'd hoped not to have his very observant self about for her masquerade.

But then she'd seen Gideon. Good heavens, what was *he* doing here? The last thing she needed was a Bow Street Runner snooping about. But to her vast relief, Logan and Gideon had headed toward the foyer. She'd quickly followed and after watching in relief as they left the party, she'd known it was time for the vampire to appear. And look how perfectly it had gone! She'd even spilled the vial of chicken blood.

Almost giddy with excitement, she halted outside the windows leading to the library. After a quick check to make certain she wasn't observed, she entered the dark room, then turned around to pull the windows closed.

And found herself face-to-face with Logan.

Before she could even pull in a gasp, he grabbed her wrists and yanked her arms behind her back. Anchoring both her hands there with one of his, he stepped into the library, then closed and locked the windows. Her muscles turned to liquid when she felt the cold blade of a knife rested against her throat.

"Well, what have we here?" he asked, his voice a dangerous purr. He stepped forward, forcing her to stumble backward. "The female vampire who's been terrorizing the fair citizens of London? Or perhaps my very own personal little arsonist. Let's take a look."

They'd reached the hearth, where the low-burning fire cast them in a golden glow. She'd turned her head to the side in an attempt to hide her face, but with a single flick of his knife, he cut through her mask. It fluttered to the floor, a fat blond curl landing on her shoe.

"What the hell . . . ? Look at me," he demanded.

When she didn't instantly comply, he pressed the knife tighter under her chin. "Or I can slit your throat, if you'd prefer."

Icy fear shivered through her. Based on his tone, she didn't doubt he would carry out his threat. Knowing there was no escaping his iron grip and feeling as if she'd turned to stone, she slowly turned her head then lifted her gaze. For several seconds he simply stared at her. Confusion clouded his gaze for a single heartbeat. Then his eyes filled with rage.

Without taking his gaze from her, he lowered the knife. She heard a slight whoosh—the sound of him sheathing the blade in his boot. Then he picked up her mask. After studying it for several tense seconds he tossed it into the fire. If she'd been capable of speech, she might have protested, but her throat was bone-dry and tight with misery, anger, and dread.

The sudden flare in the hearth illuminated his expression, which appeared hewn from granite. He then untied the hooded cape she'd made and tossed it, along with the empty vial in the pocket, into the fire as well. His gaze raked over her from head to foot before returning to her face.

"I knew you were up to something," he said in a soft voice at complete odds with the fury burning in his eyes, "but never in my wildest dreams, no, make that my most horrific nightmares, had I imagined something like this. I'm seeing this, yet I'm still having trouble believing it. What the hell is going on?"

Determined to see this through to the end, she lifted her chin. "I don't know what you mean." Her words sounded odd, as it was difficult to speak with her fangs in.

"Really?" His tone was drier than a desert. He reached out and plucked the fangs from her mouth. After giving them a long look, he shook his head then tucked them into his waistcoat pocket. "You're obviously involved in some scheme. Or am I to believe you're actually a vampire and plan to suck my blood?"

"I don't owe you any explanations."

A look she could describe as downright dangerous glittered in his eyes. "I disagree, but regardless, you'll give me one just the same."

Emily raised her chin. "I'll do no such thing." She yanked on her hands and was surprised when he let her go. She took two steps back, putting some distance between them, and allowed her own anger and frustration to bubble to the surface. "This is none of your concern. I only hope you haven't ruined everything." She held out her hand. "Give me back my fangs."

"Now there's a sentence I never imagined hearing from a woman."

Her hands fisted. "Give them back."

"Not until you tell me what the hell this is all about."

"As you've obviously guessed, I am the vampiress. There's nothing more to tell."

He heaved a heavy sigh. "Fine. Then we'll just call for the magistrate, and you can explain this masquerade to him."

"There's nothing to explain. You burned the evidence." Ha. So there.

"For your own protection." He patted his waistcoat pocket. "And I didn't burn all of it."

Damnation. A knot cinched Emily's stomach. "Summoning the magistrate is not necessary."

"Again we disagree. Your choice is me or the magistrate."

"And if I refuse?"

"Then I'll turn you in."

Emily narrowed her eyes. "You wouldn't!"

"Yes, I would."

"That's blackmail."

"Yes, it is."

"And you'd resort to such a thing to get what you want?"

"Without hesitation."

A chill ran down her spine at the icy calm in his voice. She could see he meant it. Not willing to let him see how much he'd unnerved her, she shot him her most disapproving glare. "Do you know what that makes you?"

"Yes. Determined."

"No. A blackmailer."

"I've been called worse. Now, what are you up to?"

"You're extremely annoying."

A humorless sound escaped him. "That's akin to the ocean calling the lake wet."

"And you're very demanding."

"And you're a trial on my patience. Tell me, Emily. Now."

She could tell by the rigid line of his shoulders and clenched hands that his patience was about to end. Seeing no way to escape or salvage the situation without complying, she drew a bracing breath and told him of her vampire plan. She left nothing out, ending with, "After tonight's sighting, interest in female vampires will increase dramatically. I'll sell my story and will hopefully earn a substantial sum very quickly, thus solving my family's financial problems."

"Without having to marry to do so."

"Correct."

He nodded slowly, his unreadable gaze never leaving hers. Finally he said, "On the one hand, I have to admit I'm amazed. And impressed. It's a very bold and innovative scheme. Quite brilliant, actually. Indeed, it's something I might have done myself."

Emily couldn't contain her surprise. "Th . . . thank you."

"You're welcome. On the other hand, I have one question."

"What is that?"

He reached out and clasped her shoulders and gave her a

slight shake. "Have you taken leave of your senses? Do you not realize the danger you put yourself in?"

"That's *two* questions. And I'll have you know I was doing extremely well and all was going according to plan until *you* ruined it."

He looked as if flames were about to shoot from the top of his head. "Until *I* ruined it?" he repeated in an incredulous voice. "Good God, Emily, you should give thanks it was me who discovered you. Had it been someone else, you'd be embroiled in a scandal that would utterly ruin you."

She knew it was true; still, it rankled to hear him say it. "I'm aware of that. I took every precaution not to be caught."

"Yet you were. You took an insane risk."

She shook her head. "No. Nothing bad happened, and after word of tonight's sighting spreads, my plan will work. It *has* to work."

"Something very bad *could* have happened. You've nearly been killed twice—"

"By a man who is now dead. The danger is over."

"No. That's why Gideon came here tonight. To tell me he learned that the man Atwater killed was merely hired by someone else. And that person is still out there."

Emily felt the blood drain from her head at the news. Before she could speak, his fingers tightened around her shoulders, and he stepped closer, erasing the distance between them. Heat that had nothing to do with the fire burning in the hearth raced through her, made all the hotter by the intensity of his gaze.

"You could have been hurt or worse tonight," he said in a low, ragged voice that sounded scraped from his throat. "And then what would I have done?" A shudder ran through him, and he briefly closed his eyes. When they opened again, her heart stuttered at the naked emotion in his gaze. "My God, what would I have done if something had happened to you?"

He gave her no opportunity to answer. His mouth came down on hers in a hard, hot, demanding kiss that tasted of pent-up need and raw want. He clasped her to him as if he'd never let her go, and she melted against him, wrapping her arms around his neck and rising up on her toes to press herself tighter to him. His tongue danced with hers, and she opened her mouth wider, wanting more, needing more. He kissed her as if he craved her, as if he wanted to devour her, one hand holding her head captive, the other running restlessly down her back to cup her bottom and press her more firmly against the hardness pressing into her belly.

She twined her fingers in his thick hair, tugging him closer, squirming against him, lost to everything except him and the inferno racing through her veins. She could feel her pulse beating through her body, setting up an insistent throb between her legs. He rubbed himself against her, his tongue sinking deeper into her mouth, the clean, masculine scent of him, the hard feel of him saturating her senses, until her entire world was reduced to a place where only one thing existed. Him. Logan. His kiss. His hands. His taste. And the incredible way he made her feel.

Lost in a thick haze of passion, she groaned in protest when he suddenly lifted his head. Dazed, she opened her heavy eyes and noted his tight expression. And the fact that he was staring at a place over her shoulder. Frowning, she turned her head. And froze in horror.

Her mother stood not three feet away, staring at them with a combination of shock and something else Emily couldn't decipher. But regardless of what it was, there was no doubt that she'd witnessed her daughter's passionate exchange with Logan.

Emily's insides seemed to curdle. Burning with mortification, she pulled herself from Logan's embrace and turned to fully face her mother. She noted Logan move to stand by her side. She opened her mouth to speak, but her mother silenced her with a severe frown and raised hand. Her mother then focused her attention on Logan.

"You realize what this means, Mr. Jennsen," her mother said in a tone that brooked no arguments.

From the corner of her eye, Emily saw him give a tight nod. "Yes, I do."

"Good. I think it's best if it's taken care of as soon as possible." She narrowed her eyes at him. "I trust you have no objections?"

He shook his head. "It will be as you wish. I'll arrange for the special license tomorrow. The wedding can take place the day after."

Emily snapped her head toward him. His rigid profile appeared carved from stone, except for the muscle ticking in his tight jaw.

"That is acceptable," her mother said.

Emily had to brace her knees to keep from slithering to the floor. "Special license?" she repeated weakly. "*Wedding?* The day after tomorrow?" When Logan didn't look at her, she shifted her gaze to her mother. "Acceptable? Mother, what are you talking about?"

Her mother pulled her gaze from Logan to look at her, and Emily cringed. Never could Emily recall seeing such a resolute expression in her normally good-natured mother's eyes. "Yes, Emily, wedding. Clearly you gave no thought to the consequences of your actions when you decided to embark upon this tryst with Mr. Jennsen."

Panic suffused her, and she shook her head. "It was merely a kiss—"

"What I witnessed was far more involved than a mere kiss, further proven by yours and Mr. Jennsen's extreme state of dishevelment."

Emily suppressed the urge to tug on her bodice and push away the wayward curl tickling her cheek. "We were only momentarily carried away. And since no one knows of it except you, surely a wedding isn't necessary."

Her mother fixed a steely-eyed glare on her that Emily wouldn't have believed her capable of. "Under the circumstances, a wedding is most certainly necessary, and I demand it to salvage your reputation, as will your father when I tell him what occurred here this evening. Mr. Jennsen realizes it, and I suggest you do the same."

She had to fight the overwhelming urge to fist her hands in her hair and scream. Time. She needed time. To think. To breathe. To plan.

"But why must we marry so quickly?" she asked in a rush. "Why can we not just announce a betrothal, post the banns, and plan a wedding to take place three or four months from now? A spring wedding would be lovely." Yes, and that would give her time to plan. Time to sell her story. Surely she'd have solved her family's financial problems by then. And a betrothal could always be broken . . .

"I'm more concerned about your safety than a few raised eyebrows over a hasty wedding," Logan said in a terse voice. Although he was speaking to her, he scowled at the floor. "I can better protect you as your husband; therefore, the wedding will take place the day after tomorrow."

"I agree," said her mother in a firm voice that left Emily feeling battered and betrayed.

Still, she had to argue. "But—"

"No buts, Emily," her mother said in a fierce hiss. "The day after tomorrow. That is *final*." She turned to Logan. "I suggest you attempt to put your appearance back to rights and return to the party now, Mr. Jennsen. We'll follow in a few minutes, then depart for home. I'll expect you to call tomorrow afternoon so we can go over the wedding arrangements."

Logan, standing unyielding as a statue beside her, jerked his head in a tight nod then said in a stiff voice, "I will see you tomorrow."

Emily listened, heard the words, but somehow none of it seemed real. This couldn't be happening. It was happening to someone else. She felt . . . numb.

As if from far away she watched Logan comb his fingers through his rumpled hair, tug his clothing into place, then make her mother a formal bow. He then turned toward her and did the same. Their eyes met for several seconds, and Emily could only stare at the flat expression in his dark eyes. Where only moments ago fire had burned, now a layer of ice resided.

He walked toward the door, his gait heavy and stiff, as if he were making his way to the gallows. Dear God, he looked so . . . stoic, so resigned to his fate.

So humiliatingly unenthusiastic.

Without a backward glance, he quit the room.

She turned toward her mother, who was regarding her with an expression Emily simply couldn't decipher. Mother looked . . . pleased? Surely not, but she couldn't figure it out now. Because now all she could think of was the fact that she was getting married. To a man who didn't love her. Who was doing so only because he had to. She'd risked everything so she could marry for love. So she could have everything she'd dreamed of.

And now she had nothing.

Chapter 20

There were times I would catch him staring into space, and I knew, just knew, he was missing his mortal existence. Yearning for his friends and his work and being able to walk in the sunshine. And even though guilt consumed me for taking his life, I selfishly knew I'd do the same thing, make the same choices, all over again.

The Vampire Lady's Kiss *by Anonymous*

Gideon stared at Logan over the edge of his coffee cup. "Married?"

"Married?" echoed Matthew.

"Tomorrow?" Daniel's voice sounded as if he were choking.

"Yes, married. Tomorrow," Logan confirmed testily. He'd requested that the three men he considered his closest friends—at least until this moment—join him for breakfast. Things had gone well until he'd announced that he and Emily were to marry the next day. Now all of them were looking at him as if a third eyeball had appeared in the center of his forehead. "All of you are married, yet you're acting as if you've never heard the word before."

His three soon to be former friends exchanged a look, then returned their attention to Logan. The corners of Gideon's lips twitched. "Thought so."

A grin split Matthew's face. "Told you so."

Daniel shot him a speculative look. "Tomorrow . . . makes one wonder what you were caught doing."

Logan glared. "'Twas a kiss, nothing more." Which was true. Sort of.

Matthew's brows rose, and he forked up a bite of egg. "Must have been one bloody hell of a kiss."

Which was true. Definitely.

"For the sake of Emily's reputation, I hope it was her mother or aunt who discovered you rather than some gossiping biddy," Daniel said.

"Her mother," Logan confirmed stiffly, "but beyond that, I've no intention of discussing it further, other than to say that as a wedding was necessary, the expeditious timing of the ceremony is more a practical matter than anything." He quickly brought Daniel and Matthew up-to-date on the recent events, concluding with, "Until this man is caught, I'm not taking any chances with Emily's safety. The sooner we are married, the sooner I can keep a close watch over her and protect her round the clock. Atwater is guarding her home today, and he'll continue doing so at my house after the wedding until this bastard is stopped."

Several beats of silence followed his words, then Matthew said quietly, "If there's anything I can do to help, do not hesitate to ask."

"Me as well," said Daniel.

Logan nodded. "Thank you."

"Now—back to your wedding," Daniel said, stirring sugar into his coffee. "You owe me two hundred pounds."

Logan frowned. "I don't see why."

"You're getting married. To a society diamond as you call the ladies of the ton. Since you wagered you'd never marry such a woman, you lost. I won."

Logan carefully set down his fork and touched his napkin to his mouth. Then he levered a look at Daniel meant to nail him to his chair. "Our wager was regarding me *falling in love* with a society chit. Nothing was mentioned about marriage."

Daniel lowered his own fork and leaned forward. "Are you saying you're not in love with her?"

The word *yes* rose in his throat, but for some reason, he couldn't seem to spit it out, which was utterly ridiculous. Hadn't he already decided that the insane whirlwind of emotions she inspired was merely a potent combination of desire, lust, and infatuation? Yes, he had. He coughed twice and managed to dislodge his answer. "Yes."

Silence greeted his reply. Matthew, Gideon, and Daniel exchanged another glance. Then all three burst into raucous laughter.

"What the hell is so funny?" Logan asked, thoroughly irritated.

"You," Daniel said with another whoop of laughter. He wiped the corner of his eye with the back of his hand. "Bloody hell, I haven't laughed so hard in weeks. Thank you for that."

"Always delighted to provide humor," he said through clenched teeth, "although I cannot imagine what is so amusing."

Still grinning, Matthew shook his head. "Who's going to tell him?"

"I will," Gideon volunteered. He fixed his dark gaze on Logan's. "You're an intelligent man, Logan. I like and respect you, so please know I'm saying this with the utmost manly affection. You, my friend, are a bird-witted idiot."

"A complete nincompoop," added Matthew.

"An absolute arse," came Daniel's contribution.

Logan's eyes narrowed to slits. "Yes, I'm sensing all the manly affection. So what is it you're trying to tell me?"

Gideon looked toward the ceiling. "That you love her, you dolt."

"Completely," agreed Matthew.

"Arse over backward," confirmed Daniel, nodding.

Everything inside Logan stilled—except his heart, which gave a queer sideways lurch. "You're all daft."

"No, we're *experienced*," corrected Daniel. "We've all recently been exactly where you are now."

"Right," said Matthew, nodding. "In love, but too stupid to realize it or admit it. Don't worry, you'll eventually figure it out."

"I am not stupid," Logan managed through his clenched jaw.

"Neither are we—under normal circumstances," said Gideon cheerfully, spreading butter on a muffin. "But there's nothing normal about women. Something about them makes even the smartest of men act like—"

"Nincompoops," finished Matthew.

"And daft arses," added Daniel. He grinned. "You do owe me two hundred pounds, my friend. But I can wait until you're ready to pay."

Logan wanted to inform him that he'd be waiting a damn long time, but he couldn't seem to force the words from his throat. *Maybe because they're not true?* his inner voice asked smugly.

Damn stupid inner voice.

"I'm delighted you're so entertained," he said sourly. "When precisely did you all become such pains in the arse?"

"We're not," Matthew said with a sunny smile. "You just think we are because you're ill-tempered about this love situation."

"Which is my point," Logan said, pouncing in triumph. "You three are all in love, correct?"

After they'd each agreed, he continued, "And you're all happy, correct?"

"Extremely," said Gideon.

"Completely," said Matthew.

"Deliriously," agreed Daniel.

"See? Not an ill-tempered one in the bunch. Therefore, if I *were* in love, I, too, would be happy and not ill-tempered. Therefore, I am not in love."

Daniel shook his head. "No, the problem is that you *are* in love, but due to any number of reasons—and there are many—you are refusing to accept it."

"Exactly," chimed in Matthew, breaking off a piece of bacon. "As soon as you realize you're in love and accept your fate, you'll no longer be ill-tempered." He popped the bacon in his mouth.

"And you'll be happy, just like us," Gideon concluded.

Logan lifted his coffee cup and stared into the dark contents. Could it really be as simple as that? He sincerely doubted it. Because while his three friends were undeniably happy, a big part of their contentment hinged on the fact that they were loved in return. If he were to decide that what he felt for Emily was indeed love, that would only bring more misery rather than happiness, because his feelings would be unrequited.

The image of her horrified, bereft expression when she'd heard a wedding would take place and so quickly had burned a scar on his heart. He'd heard the panic in her voice, the desperation when she'd suggested a betrothal followed by a spring wedding. He didn't doubt she'd have spent the intervening months planning a way to break their engagement, a fact that had filled him with a hollow sensation he couldn't name. She would marry him tomorrow—because she had to. Because their actions left her no other choice. Not because she wanted to. Not because she loved him.

Her earlier words about her wedding night echoed through his mind . . . that it would someday occur with a man she was madly, passionately in love with. *I have no intention of marrying for any reason other than love. Certainly not because I was kissed.*

Yet now she was trapped into doing the very thing she most desired not to. And he was forced to marry a society diamond, a fact that should have upset him but surprisingly did not. Indeed, if he had to marry anyone, he was at least relieved it was someone he desired so deeply. If nothing else, he certainly looked forward to bedding her. And he was committed to protecting her—a much easier prospect if they were living under the same roof.

He also recalled how she'd disparaged his proposal when he'd asked her to marry him. Good God, if she'd thought *that* proposal was unromantic, then last night's debacle—when he hadn't even proposed, had instead merely agreed to marry her—must have severely disappointed her. Which he couldn't deny was understandable. Like many women, she'd no doubt always dreamed of a romantic proposal and fancy wedding. Well, the least he could do was try to remedy that. And he had every intention of doing so. She might not love him, but he was determined to try to make her happy. For, if nothing else, he'd owe her something because he'd no longer be alone.

"Now that that's settled," Logan said—even though nothing had been settled—"I do need some help."

"With what?" Daniel asked.

"Seeing as how I'm getting married tomorrow, it would appear I need to procure a special license."

∽

Sarah stared at Emily over the edge of her teacup. "Married?"

"Married?" echoed Carolyn.

"*Married?*" Julianne's voice rose in a squeal.

"Yes, married," Emily confirmed, her cheeks flaming as if she'd set a match to them. She'd asked her friends to gather at Sarah's house to tell them her news since her very pregnant friend could barely waddle about, let alone ride in a carriage. She hadn't been certain Carolyn would come but was delighted she was feeling up to it. Her coloring was better, and she looked much more rested. Carolyn happily accepted tearful congratulations from her sister and Julianne when she told them of her pregnancy. But soon the moment had arrived for Emily to impart her news. And now her three friends were looking at her with glowing, happy expressions that did nothing to alleviate the knot cramping her stomach. Just two days ago she'd been thinking that the results of her vampire masquerade would determine her future. Well, it certainly had, but not in any way she would have anticipated.

"And who is it you're going to marry?" Sarah asked, a knowing look gleaming behind her spectacles.

"Oh, yes, don't keep us in suspense," said Julianne, practically bouncing on her seat, her eyes shining.

"I can't *imagine* who the groom might be," murmured Carolyn, whose acting skills had not improved one iota since yesterday.

"I'm marrying Logan Jennsen."

A trio of beaming smiles greeted her.

"Tomorrow."

Those three beaming smiles melted into varying degrees of confusion, shock, and concern.

"*Tomorrow?*" repeated Carolyn. "Why on earth tomorrow?"

An embarrassed flush suffused Emily. Before she could

explain, Sarah pushed up her glasses and said, "Oh, for goodness' sake, Carolyn, you know as well as I do that there's only one possible reason." Her eyes were troubled as she looked at Emily. "Obviously you were discovered in a compromising position. I hope for your sake there wasn't a terrible scene."

Burning with mortification, Emily shook her head. "Mother discovered us kissing—after Logan discovered me in my vampire regalia." Gasps greeted her revelation, and she quickly told her wide-eyed friends what had transpired. She ended her tale with, "In spite of my objections, Mother demanded a wedding. Logan clearly wasn't any happier about the situation than I was, but there wasn't anything he could do. He said he would arrange for a special license and the wedding would take place tomorrow."

Carolyn was the first to break the heavy silence. Clasping Emily's hand she said, "I'm certain he was just stunned. I cannot believe he wouldn't want to marry you."

"Of course he wants to marry you," Julianne concurred. "What man wouldn't want to?"

A humorless sound escaped Emily. "The one who is being forced to do so."

Sarah shook her head. "If he wasn't anxious to marry you as soon as possible, why go to the trouble and expense of a special license?"

"There's nothing romantic about it, I assure you." She hesitated, then told them about the attack on her the day before. "He believes I am in danger—"

"Clearly you are," broke in Julianne, her face pale with concern.

"He doesn't want any harm to come to me. He believes that as long as we have to marry anyway, if we do so sooner, he'll be better able to protect me."

"And you think this man doesn't care about you?" Carolyn asked softly. "From everything you've told us, it is patently obvious that he does. Deeply."

"I never said he doesn't care *at all*," Emily said, her heart heavy. "I'm sure he does, a little. Enough that he wouldn't want any harm to befall me. But that's not the same thing as loving me." She lowered her gaze to the floor and plucked at her gown. "You know how much I wanted a love match, how much I risked to have it."

"Do you not think you could love him?" Sarah asked. "'Tis clear you desire him and at the very least like him."

"Yes, but he is so . . . maddening. And confusing. One minute he makes me laugh and in the next minute I want to cosh him and in the next I want to kiss him."

To her surprise—and irritation—rather than hearing the sympathetic noises she'd expected, her words were greeted with hoots of laughter.

"Well, we no longer need to wonder if she could love him," Sarah said, chuckling.

"Clearly she already does," agreed Julianne.

Emily sent them the darkest scowl she could manage over the flush suffusing her. "I don't know what you mean."

Carolyn took her hand and offered her a warm smile. "She means that that's exactly how she feels about Matthew. And how I feel about Daniel."

"And how I feel about Gideon," Julianne chimed in. "But just wait until you're expecting a child, and he thinks you'll break if you so much as walk from one room to another."

"Oh, yes. Then you'll want to cosh him much more frequently," Sarah agreed, resting her hands on her swollen midsection.

Emily lifted her teacup to her lips to hide her confusion over her friends' assessment. And the mere thought of carrying Logan's child . . . dear God, that stole her breath. Could her friends possibly be right? She then asked herself the question she'd until now steadfastly refused to consider for fear of the answer.

Did she love Logan?

The moment she allowed the words to enter her mind, the answer was clear: *yes*. Yes, she loved him. Completely. Irrevocably.

She wasn't certain how it had happened, or when precisely, but she knew, her heart knew, that she did.

But instead of the elation she'd always thought she'd feel at the discovery of being in love, all she felt was dismay. Because a true love match required *two* people in love. And she knew the only reason he was marrying her was because he had to—not because he wanted to.

"Logan will make a wonderful husband." Carolyn's quiet words broke into her thoughts. "And you'll be a wonderful wife for him. He may not realize it yet, but you are precisely what he needs."

"A woman he has to marry?" Emily asked glumly.

"No, a woman who will make him laugh," Sarah said, all hints of amusement gone from her eyes. "And challenge him. Make him see that there's more to life than business."

"You'll bring a spark to his life that he needs," Julianne added. "You'll erase that loneliness we've long sensed about him."

Carolyn squeezed her hand. "And once you do, he'll realize what is already obvious to me: that he loves you."

Her heart leapt with hope at Carolyn's words. Could it possibly happen that way? She didn't know, but she suddenly felt better than she had since last night.

A smile trembled on her lips. "I hope you're right."

"Of course she is," Sarah said. "And now that that's settled, onto more important matters. Where is the wedding to take place?"

"What are you going to wear?" asked Julianne.

Carolyn smiled at her. "And how can we help?"

❧

Early that afternoon Emily stood on a dais in her bedchamber and slowly turned in a circle. When she completed the turn, nine pairs of eyes stared at her.

"It's perfect," said Mother, her green eyes bright with tears as she looked at the gown Emily wore. She turned to Madame Renee, London's most exclusive dressmaker, and breathed a rapturous sigh. "Madame, you've done a wonderful job."

"Of course I have," Madame said with a dismissive wave of her hand. "But zee alterations, they were not extensive, and as zee dress is one of my own magnificent creations, it was a pleasure to work on it again."

"It was very generous of Carolyn to loan me her wedding gown," Emily said, brushing her fingers over the beautiful pastel blue muslin embroidered with delicate cream flowers.

"You look like a princess," Mary said, her voice filled with adolescent feminine envy.

"Like an angel," corrected Arthur.

"You look lovely, dear," Aunt Agatha yelled.

Tiny, Ophelia, Romeo, and Juliet panted enthusiastically, making the verdict unanimous.

"Zee groom, he ees a very lucky man," Madame decreed.

Emily prayed the groom shared that sentiment.

Her mother shooed everyone from the room but remained behind and closed the door. "I'll help you with your dress."

Emily nodded, feeling the need to say something but not knowing what. Mother assisted her in removing the beautiful wedding gown, and after she was once again garbed in her soft yellow day gown, her mother clasped her hands and smiled.

"You're going to be a beautiful bride, Emily."

Tears swam into Emily's eyes, and her mother's expression grew tender. "My darling girl," she murmured, gently pushing back a stray curl from Emily's cheek. "I know you think I was harsh insisting on this hasty wedding, but you must know I only want your happiness."

"Then why did you insist?"

Her mother's gaze searched hers. "Do you really not know? Can you truly not see what is so plainly obvious to me? Darling, I knew the moment I saw you and Mr. Jennsen together in the park the other day."

"Knew what?"

"Why, that you belong together! The sparks that bounced between you . . ." Mother heaved a gushy sigh. "It was exactly that way between your father and me. Oh, of course we didn't realize it at first, but that is often the case. That is why I was so delighted when Tiny soiled Lady Hombly's pelisse." Mother leaned forward and confided in a conspiratorial tone, "It was the perfect excuse to get that awful, clinging woman away from Mr. Jennsen. I was considering tossing mud on her myself."

Emily blinked. "You mean you—"

"Hustled her out of there with all deliberate haste? Of course. And it's why I followed you into the library last night—after allowing you and Mr. Jennsen sufficient time to get into a compromising position."

Emily stared at her angelically smiling mother. "But . . . how did you know we'd get into a compromising position?"

"Darling, the man cannot keep his eyes off you! And the way he looks at you!" She waved her hand in front of her face. "It is enough to melt bricks. When a man has that look in his eyes for a woman, his hands and lips will soon follow." She shot Emily a grin that could only be described as naughty. "Believe me, I know. And you look at him as if he is the only man in the room."

"So you *meant* to discover us." It was a stunned statement rather than a question.

"Of course." Her expression turned serious. "But only because I could see that you love him. And that he loves you."

"You're wrong." Seeing her mother was about to argue, she amended hastily, "That is to say you're correct about *my* feelings, but not about Logan's."

Mother shook her head. "I'm not. I'd wager my grandmother's tiara on it."

"You hate that tiara," Emily reminded her.

"That doesn't mean it isn't worth a great deal. If Mr. Jennsen hasn't told you his feelings, then he simply hasn't realized them yet, which I'm afraid is quite typical. Men tend to be much slower than women in these matters." She gently squeezed Emily's hands. "I just wanted you to know I wouldn't have done anything to jeopardize your happiness, and although you may not thank me now for insisting upon this hasty wedding, you will eventually."

Her mother leaned forward and kissed her cheek. "Take a few minutes to think about what I've said. Mr. Jennsen should be here soon. I'll be in the drawing room with your father awaiting his arrival. Join us when you're ready."

With that, her mother quit the room, closing the door quietly behind her.

Emily stared at the closed door and pulled in a slow, careful breath. She knew her mother possessed a mischievous streak; Emily had inherited it from her. But she hadn't known about this apparent penchant for subterfuge. Her mother had certainly correctly read her feelings regarding Logan. Was it not then possible she'd correctly read Logan's for her? She'd seen the desire, but Emily could see that for herself. Was love blooming in Logan's heart as well? She didn't know, but her mother's words, combined with those of Carolyn, Sarah, and Julianne, filled her with undeniable hope.

She exited her bedchamber, intent upon joining her parents in the drawing room to await Logan's arrival. She was halfway down the stairs when she heard his deep voice in the foyer. Her heart skipped a beat, and she had to suppress the urge to dash down the steps.

"Lord and Lady Fenstraw are expecting me," Logan's voice drifted toward her as he spoke to Rupert, "but I was wondering if before I saw them I might speak to Lady Emily."

"I'll see if she's in, sir," Rupert said.

"I'm in," she said, gripping the banister due to her suddenly unsteady knees.

Logan looked up. Their eyes met, and she felt as if Cupid shot an arrow straight through her heart. Her gaze dipped to the bouquet of flowers he held, and her arrow-shot heart turned over at the sight of puffy pink blooms. Peonies. Her favorite flower.

God help her, she truly loved him. She wanted to marry him. To be his wife. If only her mother and friends were right, and it all meant more to him than fulfilling a duty and a responsibility to protect her. But at least it was a start, enough to hope that he might someday share her feelings. Until then, she'd do her best to encourage him.

Determination lifted her chin. Yes, she would encourage him. Damnation, she'd *make* him fall in love with her. She'd read enough books to know the power of seduction. She'd simply seduce him with her feminine wiles. Well, as soon as she figured out precisely which wiles she might possess. But once she did, she'd absolutely make good use of them. *Prepare yourself, Logan. This is a battle and I intend to win.*

Looking at him now, she realized *she* was the one who needed to be prepared. Good heavens, what this man could do to her with a mere look was simply ridiculous! The pounding heart, the moist palms, the shortness of breath, the weak knees . . . by God, he practically made her forget her own name. Yet he appeared completely unruffled. How incredibly vexing. Still, she wanted nothing more than to launch herself at him, wrap her arms around his neck, and kiss him until neither one of them could catch their breath.

Dressed in a Devonshire brown jacket, cream waistcoat, buff breeches, and gleaming Hessians, he looked big and strong and masculine and utterly beautiful. And very, very serious.

His gaze skimmed over her while he waited for her to descend the remaining steps, shooting a tingle down to her toes at the unmistakable and gratifying heat that flared in his eyes. When she stood in front of him, he said, "You look lovely."

"Thank you. So do you. In a very manly way, of course."

A whiff of humor entered his eyes. "Thank you." He handed her the flowers. "For you."

She buried her face in the fragrant blooms and breathed deeply. "I love peonies."

"I know. Which is why I wanted you to have them. Your parents are expecting me, but may we speak privately for a moment first?"

She didn't see why not. The damage was already done and the wedding already planned. She raised a brow. "Will the library do?"

He nodded solemnly. "It always seems to."

She turned her laugh into a cough and handed the bouquet to Rupert with a request that they be set in the foyer. She then led Logan down the corridor.

She crossed the threshold first, and her heart performed a somersault when she heard him close the door, ensconcing them in privacy. She moved to the center of the room, where weak ribbons of sunshine streaked through the windows to land on the blue and gold Axminster rug. She turned and was surprised to find him standing a mere arm's length away.

Clearly her surprise showed, because his lips twitched and he asked, "Did I startle you?"

"You do have a habit of sneaking up on me."

He raised his brows but appeared amused. "Perhaps your hearing is not all it should be."

"My hearing is fine. The problem is you move like a ghost." She eyed the spot where his snowy white cravat lay neatly tied. "I think perhaps I shall have to hang a cowbell around your neck."

"Perhaps I shall hang one about yours as well, so I'll know when you're sneaking off to don fangs and terrorize the citizens of our fair city."

She narrowed her eyes. "Is that why you wished to see me? To aggravate me?"

"No, but that is an extra bonus. Your skin turns the most fascinating color when you're annoyed." He reached out and brushed a single fingertip over her cheek, a gesture that halted her already jagged breathing. "It's as if an invisible watercolor brush laden with the softest red has washed color over the palest cream."

She wanted to reply, but the combination of his featherlight touch, the intense way he was looking at her, and the intimate timbre of his voice all conspired to render her mute. He lowered his hand, and it required all her will not to snatch it up and place it back against her face.

"Despite evidence to the contrary, I wish not to aggravate but to please you. At least I hope to do so." He reached into his waistcoat pocket and withdrew a small silver box. Emily stared at the *Rundell and Bridge* engraved on the top. The city's most fashionable and exclusive jeweler.

"I received a rather harsh—but upon reflection welldeserved—critique of my last proposal attempt," he said. "Although I've had no practice in the meantime, I'm hoping this one goes better." To her amazement he dropped to one knee before her and opened the box. Nestled inside a bed of white satin was a glittering oval-cut emerald, surrounded by a dozen twinkling aquamarines, set in a delicate gold filigree band.

A gasp escaped her at the magnificent ring, but before she could catch her breath, he removed it from the box and lifted her left hand. Sliding the band onto her finger, he said, "Emily, will you do me the honor of marrying me?"

She pulled her mesmerized gaze from the ring to look at him. A ribbon of sunlight streamed over his dark hair. His ebony eyes were intent, searching hers with an expression that suggested she had a choice and might say no. It was completely unnecessary and superfluous that he ask, that he give her this on-bended-knee romantic proposal, complete with the most incredible ring she'd ever seen.

She swallowed to dislodge the lump of emotion clogging her throat and lifted her hand so that the sunlight caught the facets of the jewels. "This is the most beautiful ring I've ever seen."

"I'm glad you like it. I thought of you the instant I saw it. It reminds me of your eyes."

She returned her gaze to his. "This is very thoughtful of you."

"Is that a yes?"

Because they both knew the only answer she could give was yes, a devil inside her made her ask, "What if I said no?"

Something flickered in his dark eyes. "Then I'd just have to convince you to change your mind."

"Oh? And how would you do that?"

Her breath caught at the fire that flared in his eyes. Gaze steady on hers, he slowly rose. Wrapping one strong arm around her waist, he cupped her cheek in his large hand, and leaned forward.

His lips brushed over hers in a whisper of a kiss that instantly made her crave more. Her arms encircled his neck, and she rose on her toes, but instead of obliging her with the hard demanding kiss she wanted, he continued to lightly tease her, circling her mouth with his, brushing his tongue over her bottom lip, then peppering light kisses along her jaw to her ear. He lightly scraped his teeth over her sensitive lobe, rippling a shudder of pleasure through her.

"Logan . . ." she whispered, arching her neck to give him better access.

He dragged his tongue down her neck then returned to her lips. Impatience had her tunneling her fingers into his hair and tugging his head lower. She traced the tip of her tongue over his upper lip, and with a groan he finally covered her mouth with his in a slow, deep, heart-stopping kiss that made her feel as if she'd been drugged. Need clawed at her, pooling between her thighs, and she pressed herself against his hard ridge of flesh rising between them.

Even though she knew it was unwise, she wanted to ignite him, to shatter his frustratingly ironclad control. To turn him into the man whose hands impatiently roamed her body, leaving trails of fire in their wake. But instead he ended the kiss, as slowly as he'd started it, and she had to cling to his lapels to keep from melting into a wisp of steam at his feet.

"If you say yes rather than no," he whispered against her mouth, "we can do that as often as you like."

"Yes." The word rushed from her lips with embarrassing speed, but she simply couldn't contain it.

She felt him smile against her mouth. After pressing a quick kiss to her forehead, he stepped back and released her. Her hands reluctantly slipped from his jacket, and she braced her not-yet-steady knees. Disappointment rippled through her at his perfectly composed demeanor. Botheration, he wasn't even breathing hard. Indeed, if it weren't for the evidence of his arousal outlined by his snug breeches, she might have believed him completely unaffected by their kiss. A kiss that had left her reeling.

"I've seen to the special license," he said.

She nodded, feeling as if she were coming out of a trance. "Sarah has offered to have the wedding at her home. I hope you don't mind; if it isn't there, I'm afraid she wouldn't be able to attend."

"Then it should certainly take place at her home. It was nice of her to offer."

"She suggested the drawing room, but I told her we'd prefer the library."

He smiled. "An excellent choice. Indeed, I'm thinking of converting a number of rooms in my house—or rather *our* house—into extra libraries."

She returned his smile. "How many libraries does one house need?"

"In our case, I was thinking six. Perhaps seven." His gaze skimmed over her, lingering on her lips. "Eight might very well be necessary."

"Oh . . . my. That certainly sounds . . . promising."

He reached out and took her hands. "I'm glad you think so."

"I do. Especially since . . ." Her words trailed off and she bit her lip.

"Especially since what?"

Embarrassment flooded her, but she pressed on. "Since the way you just kissed me was so, um, *soft*. And of such a, er, *short* duration."

Confusion flickered in his eyes, then understanding dawned in his gaze. "And you're wondering if my soft, short kiss indicates a waning of my enthusiasm for you."

Yes. "No. At least not exactly." She attempted a lighthearted laugh, and pride filled her when she succeeded. "It's just that it doesn't bode particularly well if your interest is fading before the wedding even takes place."

"Interest fading?" He briefly squeezed his eyes shut. When he opened them, the fire burning in his gaze singed her. In a heartbeat he yanked her against him and rolled his hips. She gasped at his erection rubbing at the juncture of her thighs.

"I assure you there is nothing faded about my interest." He grabbed her hand and pressed her palm against the hard bulge. She felt him jerk, and her fingers curled around his length. He sucked in a hissing breath. With his eyes all but breathing smoke, he said in a low, ragged voice, "*This*"—he thrust into her hand—"is what you do to me every time you touch me. Hell, every time you so much as look at me. Every time I think of you. It feels as if I'm hard *all the time*."

Another thrust against her hand. "I kept that kiss soft and short for your sake. Trust me when I say that it is requiring a Herculean effort on my part not to rip off your clothes with my damn teeth then sink into you so deeply you can't tell where you start and I end. If I didn't have to meet with your parents only moments from now, I would have you naked and coming until you screamed for mercy. If it weren't for the fact that you'll be my wife in less than twenty-four hours, I'd do it anyway." He drew in a ragged-sounding breath then slowly eased away from her until he held her at arm's length. "*That's* how much my interest has faded. Any questions?"

Good heavens. She felt as if steam emitted from her every pore. She cleared her throat to find her voice. "No. I understand."

"I'm not certain you do, but you will. Tomorrow."

Tomorrow. God help her, she couldn't wait.

He slowly released her shoulders and opened his mouth as if to speak but then closed it. His expression turned troubled, and it was clear he had something else to say. When the silence continued to stretch, she prompted, "Is there something else you wished to tell me?"

He hesitated, then nodded. "Something to tell you, and a request."

"I'm listening."

He exhaled a long breath. "I want you to know that I met

with my solicitor and bankers this morning to set up a trust for you. You'll have your own money, and should anything happen to me, you'll be well provided for."

She blinked. "I . . . thank you."

"I also set up accounts to provide for your siblings' education and grand tour allowances. If they choose not to travel, they may use the funds in any manner they wish."

Before she could even think up a reply to the news of that extraordinary generosity, he continued, "I also settled your father's debts, including forgiving the monies he owed me."

For several seconds, Emily could only stare in stunned amazement. A tremor ran through her, and she realized she was trembling. She'd spent months trying to conceive of then execute a plan to save her family, and within hours he'd accomplished it. She supposed she should feel some sort of annoyance or dismay about that, but all she felt was heartfelt gratitude that no scandal or hardship would befall the people she loved.

"Why . . . ?" It was the only word she could manage.

His gaze searched hers but gave nothing away. "Because you're going to be my wife. Your family will be my family. I know how important they are to you, and that makes them important to me."

To her mortification, tears filled her eyes. "It's too much. That's an enormous amount of money—"

He touched his fingers to her lips. "I want to do it. For you. For them. I consider it a good investment." He cupped her face in his palm, brushed his thumb over her lips, and gave a fleeting smile. "I've never had anyone to spend my money on besides myself." His gaze flicked to her ring. "I like it."

"I don't know what to say. How to thank you."

He considered, then said, "A kiss would suffice."

A huff of laughter escaped her. "I'm afraid it would require a great many kisses."

"Very well. If you insist." He heaved a put-upon sigh. "I'll try to take it like a man."

She reached up and framed his face between her unsteady hands. A wave of love washed through her, and the words rushed onto her tongue, begging to be said. "Logan, I—" She stopped, afraid that if she said them now, he would think it was only out of gratitude for what he'd done. Or worse, that he'd feel compelled to repeat the sentiment without really meaning it. Or even worse, reject her feelings.

But she had to say something, something to convey her thanks without revealing the true depth of her feelings. She cleared her throat. "Thank you. For being so . . . wonderful. For giving me this beautiful ring. For taking care of the people I love. For being . . . you." She rose on her toes and touched her lips to his. Then she settled back down on her heels and lowered her hands.

He touched his finger to his own lips, as if feeling her mouth there. "You're welcome. But by your own words you still owe me a great many more kisses."

"I shall do my best to settle my debt."

"Excellent. And now, about my request . . ."

When he hesitated, she said, "Surely after all you've done for me and my family, you cannot think I would deny you. Whatever it is, consider it done."

He cocked a questioning brow. "You say that without knowing what it is?"

She looked into his beautiful ebony eyes and knew she could deny him nothing it was in her power to give. This man who had so unexpectedly stolen her heart. "Yes," she whispered.

"I hope you don't live to regret that vow. I would like to read your story."

Emily stared, nonplussed. She didn't know what she'd expected him to say, but it certainly hadn't been that. "My vampire story?"

"Yes. Why? Have you written others?"

"No. Why do you want to read it?"

"I'm curious. I admire initiative, and I'm impressed by yours in both coming up with such an intriguing idea and then having the talent to execute it. I'd very much like to see the finished product."

When she hesitated, he said quietly, "If you'd rather not show me, I'll release you from your offer."

She shook her head. "A promise is a promise. I'm just surprised you'd be interested."

He lifted her hand and pressed a kiss against the backs of her fingers. "I think I've already proven how deeply I'm interested. But believe it or not, I'm interested in more than—"

"Ripping my clothes off with your teeth?"

His grin flashed. "Yes, although that is on the top of my list. Still, I'm interested in *everything* that has to do with my bride."

A blush heated her cheeks. "Very well. As I've penned several extra copies, I'll give you one before you leave."

"Thank you. Emily . . . I do have one more request."

She hiked up a brow. "I see a pattern developing here, sir."

He stepped closer and drew her into his arms. "Yes. One I could grow very fond of: me asking you to do something, you promising to say yes." He lightly palmed her breast, stalling her breath. Leaning forward, he brushed his lips over the sensitive skin just behind her ear. "I can think of several dozen requests that I believe we'd both find very . . . pleasurable."

She closed her eyes and breathed in his heavenly scent, that delicious combination of clean linen and warm skin and sandalwood that made her head spin. "Several *dozen*?" she asked breathlessly.

"Without even trying." He gently nibbled on her earlobe, and her eyes slid closed, absorbing the tingle rippling through her. "Imagine what I might come up with if I gave it some effort."

"Yes . . . imagine," she murmured.

He straightened, and she struggled to open her eyes. "What is it you want, Logan?" she asked, hoping, praying, it involved taking her somewhere private, then a demonstration of how clothing could be removed using teeth.

"So many things," he said softly. "So many things, as you tempt me beyond all reason. But for now, just one. And it's something we discussed yesterday. I'd like to take you and your family on an outing to Gunter's. It would give us an opportunity to become better acquainted, and I think they'd enjoy it. Especially Mary and Arthur."

Another swell of love hit her, and it occurred to her that if he continued being so wonderful, it was going to be very difficult to keep her feelings hidden for long. She just hoped that when he realized what he'd come to mean to her that he might return a fraction of her feelings. Otherwise she would suffer a badly broken heart. At her husband's hands.

Chapter 21

There are very few ways to kill a vampire, none of them easy, all of them messy. Therefore I wasn't expecting to die the way I did. Because it never occurred to me that a vampire could die of a broken heart.

The Vampire Lady's Kiss *by Anonymous*

Logan stood in his appointed spot near the marble fireplace in Matthew and Sarah's library and tried his damnedest to relax but utterly failed. Bright sunlight flooded the room from the tall windows, bathing the room with golden warmth. His gaze shifted to the mantel. Five minutes to ten. Five minutes until the ceremony that would change his life began.

A hand landed on his shoulder, and he nearly jumped out of his skin. He turned and found himself facing Matthew, who was flanked by Daniel and Gideon. All three men looked more than a little amused.

"Bloody hell, you're a wreck," said Matthew.

Daniel leaned forward and squinted at Logan's face. "You look . . . green?"

Gideon held out a snifter filled with enough brandy to intoxicate five men. "Here. Drink this."

Logan couldn't help but laugh. "If I drink that, I'll be unconscious for two days. I'm not a wreck. I'm . . ." *Ridiculously impatient. Anxious to begin, so I can call her my wife. Make her my wife.* " . . . just nervous about mucking it up and saying the wrong thing at the wrong time."

"Don't be," Matthew said. "It's very easy. Just keep saying, 'I do.'"

"Even after the ceremony, just keep saying that," Daniel advised.

"Right," concurred Gideon. "And if you ever don't feel like saying it, kiss her instead."

Matthew nodded. "Kissing forestalls a lot of potential disagreements."

Logan managed a weak smile. "So that's the secret to a happy marriage? Kissing?"

"It's working well for me," Gideon said.

"Me, too," Daniel agreed.

"And me," said Matthew. "We're all happy, and soon to be fathers."

Logan raised a brow. "So then clearly there's more than mere kissing involved in this happy marriage formula."

Daniel clapped him on the back. "As often as possible. But you're an intelligent bloke. Usually. You'll figure it out."

Armed with that wisdom, Logan kept glancing at the clock. The next five minutes felt like five decades. When Emily finally entered the library holding her father's arm, the sight of her knocked the breath from his lungs. Her pale blue gown fell in a soft column from the scooped bodice to her feet, the material marked with delicate vines of embroidered flowers. Her dark hair was upswept and dotted with aquamarine pins. The same triple-strand choker of pearls she'd worn last night encircled her neck, a gut-tightening reminder that the red marks marring her skin from the attack still lingered. He was touched to see she carried the bouquet of pink peonies he'd brought her yesterday, their stems wrapped in a cream satin ribbon. Her ring sparkled in the sunlight, the facets bouncing sparkles around the room. His gaze found hers, and the warmth in her eyes reached deep inside him, as if she'd grabbed hold of his heart.

Her father escorted her to him, then kissed her cheek and sat next to her mother in the seats that had been arranged in the room for the intimate ceremony. He turned to look at her and for several seconds couldn't speak around his suddenly constricted throat. He swallowed then whispered, "You look beautiful."

Her smile made him feel as if he stood in a warm ray of sunshine. "So do you. In a very manly way, of course," she said, repeating her words from the day before.

The ceremony began and went by in a blur. Looking into her gorgeous sea goddess eyes, he recited the vows that would bind him to her for the rest of his life. He'd halfway expected panic to seize him at some point, but the moment he'd seen her enter the library, a sense of quiet calm had come over him. His heart pounded throughout the ceremony, but not because of any sort of nerves. No, the rapid beating was due to an excitement he normally only felt when in the midst of complicated business negotiations. Yet it was more than that . . . something he hadn't felt in so long he barely recognized it. It was pure, undiluted joy. And he couldn't ever recall feeling it to this extent.

When the brief ceremony ended, he stood beside his *wife* and accepted congratulations from her family—*their* family—and friends. When it came Arthur's turn, the boy wrapped his arms around Logan's waist in a hug that brought a lump to his throat. "We're brothers now," the lad said, looking up at Logan with worshipful eyes.

"I'm delighted to be a brother," Logan said solemnly, offering up a prayer that he'd be a good one. "You'll have to teach me how, as I've never been one before."

"It's easy," said Percy with a smile, shaking Logan's hand. "All you have to do is let your brothers win at every game you play."

"Yes, and allow them to borrow your exceptionally fine carriage," added William.

"And introduce them to all the attractive women you know," said Kenneth with a grin.

"I don't want to meet any women," said Arthur in a horrified voice. "I want to catch frogs and worms."

"You'll find having a sister much more enjoyable than brothers," Mary informed him. "*I* like tea parties and playing with my dolls."

"Boys don't play with dolls," Arthur informed her with an impressive amount of masculine disdain for a seven-year-old.

"But I enjoy tea parties," Logan told Mary, then shot her a conspiratorial wink, which she cheekily returned.

A wedding breakfast followed. He sat at one end of the long cherrywood table, while Emily sat at the other. Throughout the meal his gaze wandered to her. He watched her laugh and smile, conversing so easily with everyone around her. That smile of hers, combined with that whiff of mischief in her eyes, was nothing short of magic. There was an enthusiasm about her that drew him like metal to a magnet. She filled him with a sense of energy, one that made him feel as if a grin constantly lurked at the corners of his mouth.

His wife—damn, a pleasurable tingle ran through him just thinking those words—was a fascinating combination of innocence and allure, and if he hadn't been so damn impatient to get her alone and all to himself, he could have happily sat and simply watched her for hours. But all to himself is where he wanted her. With a desperation it was growing increasingly difficult to ignore. There were so many things he wanted to say to her. And damn it, do to her. As much as he was enjoying the meal, he couldn't wait for it to end. Every time their gazes met, she blushed, and he would shift in his seat, overwhelmed with the urge to stride down to the other end of the table, scoop her up, carry her out, get her home, and give her something to really blush about.

Finally, finally, the meal was finished. He held back his impatience while they said their good-byes, Emily's taking considerably longer than his. Had it been up to him, he would have just given an all-encompassing wave to the gathered group, yelled good-bye, and they'd have been on their way.

Finally, finally, they climbed into his carriage, and after another barrage of waving and kiss blowing and promises to see each other soon, Paul put the horses in motion, and they were off.

"Anyone would think we were embarking upon a yearlong journey to the other side of the world rather than a mere few miles to Berkeley Square," he teased.

"I know," she said, settling herself in the seat across from him now that they'd rounded the corner and were out of sight. "But I've never lived apart from them before."

"Once this man is caught and this situation resolved, I'll take you on a wedding trip."

Interest sparkled in her eyes. "Where?"

"Anywhere you'd like to go."

"There is somewhere. I'd like to visit the estate you recently purchased. I love the country, and it would give us an opportunity to explore the area and see how Mrs. Whitaker and Lara are getting on."

A combination of tenderness and pride suffused him that she hadn't asked for an elaborate trip to the Continent but rather the opportunity to visit with the widow and her daughter. "We'll go as soon as we can. In the meanwhile, I think you'll find our house in Berkeley Square very comfortable."

She smiled at him, and he had to grip his hands together to keep from snatching her against him. "Thank you for calling it *our* house, although from what I've heard, *house* is not the right word to apply to such a magnificent residence. I'm certain I shall be perfectly comfortable." She opened her reticule and withdrew a small package. "This is for you."

Surprised and pleased, he took the package. "What is it?"

"If you open it, you'll find out."

He carefully untied the bow. "It's been a very long time since anyone's given me a present." He set aside the wrapping and stared at the oval enamel box. Emily's image was painted on the top.

"Open it," she said.

He did and smiled at the small mound of cinnamon-and-sugar-coated nuts inside. They instantly brought to mind erotic images of the night she'd given him one of the delicious treats. Of his mouth on her. Her hands on him . . .

He pulled in an unsteady breath. Good God, it was hot in here.

"It's from my collection of enamel boxes. I thought you might like it. And that it would come in handy, should you forget what I look like."

He would have laughed if he'd been able to around the lump of emotion clogging his throat. His wife . . . his beautiful, thoughtful, desirable wife was bringing him to his knees.

He brushed his finger over the beautiful likeness, imagining he was touching her soft skin. "There's not much chance of me forgetting. And I do like it. Very much. Thank you." Slipping the treasure into his pocket, he said, "I didn't know you collected enamel boxes."

"I think there are lots of things we don't know about each other."

God knows there were things about him she didn't know. Things he knew he should tell her, wanted to tell her, yet wasn't certain he could. He cleared his throat. "We have plenty of time to learn."

And that, he realized, was the extent of his conversational prowess at the moment. Unless he cared to blurt out, *I want you so badly I can hardly sit still.* Damn it, he felt as if he required a leather strap to bite down on to ease the pain of the aching need clawing at him. Silence stretched between them, and he desperately searched his brain for something to say, but no, try as he might, the only thing he could think of was, *I want you so badly I can hardly sit still.*

After a moment, her smile faded. "Are you all right, Logan?"

No. Because I want you so badly I can hardly sit still. He swallowed then nodded. "Fine." The single word sounded hoarse and ragged.

Her frown deepened. "Are you certain? You look . . . flushed." She pulled off her glove and leaned toward him to touch her fingers to his forehead. He sucked in a breath and slammed his eyes shut.

"Dear God, you're burning up," she said, her voice laced with concern.

You have no idea. He opened his eyes. Clearly his intense desire for her showed, because the instant their gazes met, her eyes widened and she stilled.

"Oh," she whispered. "You have that look about you again."

He could actually feel his good intentions crumbling to dust. Unable to stop himself, he captured her hand. Brought it to his mouth. Inhaled. God, she smelled so damn good. "What look is that?"

"The same one you had before you lowered me to the floor

in the library at my parents' house. The same one you had yesterday when you told me you wanted to rip off my clothes. With your teeth."

He pressed a kiss to the center of her palm and swallowed a groan. God, she felt so damn good. "I see. Is that a . . . problem?"

"No." Her gaze dipped to where his mouth pressed against her hand. "Actually, I find it . . ." Her voice trailed off when he touched his tongue to her palm. God, she tasted so damn good.

"Find it what?"

Her eyes met his. "Exciting."

His pulse sped up. "How exciting?"

She shifted in her seat. His gaze dipped to her breasts. Her hard nipples pressed against the demure muslin of her dress, giving her the look of a wanton, sinful angel. "Unbearably so."

His erection jerked against his snug breeches at her husky admission. Good God, at this rate, he wouldn't survive the carriage ride. "I read your story," he murmured against her hand.

Cautious interest kindled in her eyes. "Oh?"

When she said nothing more, he asked, "Don't you want to know what I thought of it?"

"If you wish to tell me."

"You want the truth?"

"Of course."

"Very well. I found it . . . shocking."

A combination of hurt and annoyance flashed in her eyes, and she hiked up one brow. "Why? You thought I didn't know how to take pen to paper?"

"No, the writing was excellent. It was the content I found shocking. And extremely . . . arousing. When I read the scene where the female vampire seduced her mate, my eyes actually glazed over." Yes, and his body had hardened like a brick. As far as he could tell, he'd been hard ever since. "How is it you know of such things?"

"You may thank the Ladies Literary Society of London."

He lightly bit the end of her index finger. "I intend to."

It appeared as if *her* eyes glazed over. "Of course, I've never actually experienced most of the things my lady vampire did."

"I can assure you we'll fix that."

Bright color suffused her cheeks. "Good. But I've imagined doing them." She wet her lips. "With you."

He clenched his jaw against the building ache in his groin. He looked outside and saw that they had at least another ten minutes before they arrived. He wasn't going to last another ten seconds.

"No time like the present," he murmured. Reaching out, he flicked the curtains closed, plucked her off her seat as if she were a daisy in a field, and settled her across his lap.

"Can't wait to touch you," he whispered against her lush mouth. "Can't wait."

His mouth covered hers in a kiss he'd surely meant to be brief, just a quick exchange to take the edge off his ardor. And he might have succeeded if she'd remained docile in his arms. But instead, his wife wrapped her arms around his neck, parted her lips, and ran her tongue over his bottom lip.

He might as well have been a keg of gunpowder onto which a match had been tossed. His control exploded, and with a deep growl he kissed her with all the pent-up longing and want and need pounding through him, his tongue exploring the delicious warmth of her mouth. He teased her hard nipple through the soft muslin of her gown while his other hand slipped beneath her hem to run up the smooth curves of her calf and thigh.

"Spread your legs." The words were a rough rasp against her throat. Her breaths coming in uneven pants, she complied, then gasped when his fingers glided over her folds. He dampened two fingers with her juices then slipped them inside her. "You are so beautifully wet."

She moaned and spread her legs wider. "It feels as if I am all the time. I have only to think of you and . . ." Her voice trailed off into a low groan as he withdrew his fingers to lightly tease her sensitive nub of flesh.

"And you grow wet?"

"Y . . . yes. And hot. Like I'm standing in the midst of a fire, and my skin is too tight. And . . . oh, my. That feels so—" She gasped and strained against his hand. "Incredibly good."

He rolled his hips, pressing his erection tighter against her hip. He kissed her deeply, his tongue thrusting against hers. The fragrance of sugar and flowers rose from her warm skin, mixing with the scent of her arousal, making him feel as if his damn head were spinning.

His fingers continued their relentless stroking, delving, circling, teasing. He felt her body tighten, then she arched her back and ground against his hand. He swallowed her groans as her slick sheath pulsed around his fingers. When her tremors subsided, he raised his head and looked down into her flushed face. Her eyes opened partway. She resembled a sleepy-eyed, sated temptress.

"You made me feel *that way* again," she whispered.

He leaned down to nuzzle her soft neck with his lips. "I'm afraid it's my duty as your husband. I hope you don't mind."

"Not at all. In fact, I fear I might become rather demanding and insist on feeling that way frequently. I hope *you* don't mind."

He heaved a put-upon sigh. "A chore, to be certain, but I'll try not to complain overmuch."

"Good. Because do you know what that would make you?"

"What?"

"A complainer. And do you know who likes a complainer?"

"Who?"

"No one." She sifted her fingers through his hair, the simple touch shuddering inordinate pleasure through him. "But there is a problem."

"What's that?"

"I want to make you feel that way, too."

"Believe me, that is not going to be a problem."

"You've brought me a great deal of pleasure, and I haven't brought you any. That's hardly fair."

Something inside him seemed to shift, and he turned his head to kiss the soft skin of her inner wrist. "You have brought me more pleasure than you know. I cannot tell you how much it pleases me to touch you."

"I'm glad. But I want to touch you as well." She slid her hand down his torso, her intent clear. With a quick laugh he grabbed her fingers and placed them against his chest.

"I want that, too." More than he wanted to take his next breath. "But if you touch me now, I'll be . . . lost." A sheepish smile tugged at his lips. "And wetter than you."

Her gaze searched his. "Would that be so terrible?"

"Not terrible, I suppose, but a bit awkward in this instance, as my entire household staff will be lined up to greet us upon our arrival." He raised her hand to his lips. "Besides, I'd much rather be inside you when I feel *that way*," he murmured against her palm.

Her moist lips parted, dragging another groan from him, and he prayed he'd actually have the strength to make it that long. He felt one heartbeat away from exploding.

The carriage slowed, and he pulled aside the curtain and saw to his vast relief that they'd nearly arrived. He dropped a quick kiss to her lips then resettled her on the seat opposite him.

"Hopefully, I don't look as wanton as I feel," she said, her hands fluttering over her pelisse.

"You look . . ." His gaze took in her heightened color, glittering eyes, and kiss-swollen lips. "Spectacular."

The carriage rocked to a halt, and he helped her alight. As they walked up the flagstone walkway, he found himself unexpectedly nervous, hoping she would like the house. In spite of the grandeur and opulence and dozens of rooms, he found it comfortable and wanted her to as well. However, when they entered the marble-tiled foyer, it wasn't the huge crystal chandelier or the bronze statuary or the antique tapestries adorning the walls or the magnificent curving staircase that delighted her. No, the thing that captured her attention was the enormous crystal vase on the round lanterloo table filled with dozens of peonies in every shade of pink from the palest blush to the deepest rose.

A delighted smile lit her face. "Logan, they're beautiful."

He smiled in return. "I'm glad you like them." Damn, a few days ago he hadn't even known what the hell a peony was, and now they filled his house, scenting the air with her subtle fragrance, a fact he found profoundly satisfying. He'd purchased every flower to be had in anticipation of her arrival—quite a task, considering that the blooms weren't native to England and were only grown in hothouses. Indeed, he'd be surprised if there was a single peony bloom left in the entire country.

He introduced her to Eversham, who in turn introduced her to the staff. Pride filled him as he watched his beautiful wife charm each and every footman and maid. He noticed Adam wasn't present, and when the introductions were finished, he questioned Eversham as to the whereabouts of his factotum.

"He sent round a note saying he was ill, sir," the butler informed him in his usual monotone, "and would have to remain at home today. Wrote he was very sorry and would do his best to return to work tomorrow."

"Did he say what was wrong?"

"Mentioned a stomach ailment, sir, the sort that usually passes after suffering through a bad day."

Logan's stomach tightened with sympathy. He'd suffered such a malady before and knew Adam was in for a miserable day. He then said in an undertone, "I trust the arrangements I requested have been made?"

"Everything is precisely as you ordered, sir."

"Excellent. And there is a Runner keeping watch outside?"

"Yes, sir. Said he'd be here until Mr. Atwater relieves him this evening."

Satisfied all was well, Logan nodded and was about to turn away when the butler cleared his throat. "Was there something else, Eversham?"

Eversham's gaze flicked to Emily, who was chatting with his housekeeper. "Congratulations, sir. I wish you and your bride every happiness."

Logan raised his brows then grinned. "Why, Eversham, I do believe you're thawing a bit."

"Don't grow accustomed to it, sir."

He chuckled then joined Emily at the base of the curving staircase, and together they climbed the steps then made their way down the corridor.

"Here we are," he said, stopping at the last door. He turned the knob, then before she could move, he bent his knees, scooped her up into his arms, and carried her across the threshold.

"I think you are perhaps more romantic than I'd originally thought," she said in a teasing voice.

"I think perhaps you inspire me."

He pushed the door closed with his foot then gently set her down. Standing behind her, he watched her slowly turn in a full circle, taking in the pale green silk walls, gilt-framed landscapes, delicate antique escritoire, cherrywood wardrobe, flowered enamel dressing screen, chintz-covered recamier chaise, the large bed with its green velvet counterpane, and the ceramic vase of peonies on the night table.

"You may redecorate in any manner you wish," he said, when she continued to look around without speaking. "Your clothing and personal items that arrived yesterday have been unpacked. I believe you'll find everything in order."

"Everything is perfect, Logan." She completed her circle and looked at him through shining eyes. "It's a beautiful chamber."

Relief filled him. "I'm glad you like it."

"Where is *your* bedchamber?"

"Through there," he said nodding toward the door set in the far wall.

"May I see it?"

"Of course." He took her hand and led her through the doorway.

Her attention riveted on the bed, covered with a royal blue, gold, and maroon striped counterpane. "Heavens, I don't think I've ever seen such an enormous bed. You must get lost in it."

No, but he'd certainly suffered more lonely nights in it than he cared to remember. "I like space."

Her gaze took in the bookcases, the carved wardrobe, the overstuffed sofa set in front of the dancing fire. She nodded at the door in the corner. "Where does that lead?"

"To the bathing chamber."

"A separate room for a bathtub?" she asked in surprise.

"Yes, but it's a bit more involved than that. It's an innovation I added immediately after I purchased the house. An Italian count I met during my travels described such a room in his villa, and I knew I had to have one for myself. Come, I'll show you."

Again he took her hand, loving the way her slim fingers felt entwined with his. When he opened the door, they were greeted by a waft of steam. He drew her inside, then quickly closed the door so none of the moist heat escaped.

Her eyes widened at the sight of the sunken tub, which could easily accommodate two people. Steamy tendrils rose lazily from the water, and from the large grate set in the corner.

"I've never seen such a big tub," she said, "or one set in the floor. It must take hours to fill."

He shook his head and pointed to a door in the wall next to the tub. "That leads directly down to the kitchen. With a series of ropes and pulleys, buckets of water are continuously fed into this room."

"That's ingenious!"

"I agree. The count told me it was like having a private Roman bath in his home."

"I can see why you'd want one. And what is that?" she asked, nodding toward the grate.

"The count also had one of those. The grate is filled with porous stones, which are heated for hours in the fireplace. Water is then poured on them to produce the steam." He lifted a kettle next to the grate and trickled a slow stream of water over the rocks. A hissing sound echoed in the room, and clouds of moist steam filled the air. "It is very relaxing, and according to the count, excellent for both the lungs and the complexion."

His gaze followed hers to the upholstered chaise in the corner. "I enjoy resting in the steam after I bathe."

"I see." She looked back at the steaming bathwater. "It looks very inviting."

"I'm delighted you think so."

"It's also very, um, warm in here."

His lips twitched, and he moved to stand in front of her. "Perhaps I can assist you in cooling off." He lowered himself to one knee in front of her. When he reached for her foot, she held on to his shoulder. He removed her satin embroidered shoe, then set her foot on his upraised knee and slipped his hands beneath her gown. With his gaze on hers, he unfastened her garter then slowly rolled her white silk stocking down her leg. After removing her other shoe and stocking, he stood.

"Better?" he asked, brushing his fingertips over her plush mouth.

"Actually, no."

"Ah. I see I shall have to continue then." He again reached out, this time slipping her gown from her shoulders, forcing himself to go slowly, even though his body strongly opposed the wait, pulling the material down to her waist then releasing it to pool at her feet.

"Cooler?" he asked.

She swallowed and shook her head. "I'm afraid not."

He slipped off her petticoat, then moved behind her to unlace her stays, leaving her clad only in her thin chemise. After setting the stays aside, he unfastened her pearl choker then slowly slipped the pins from her hair, letting loose a curtain of shiny curls that unfurled down her back to release the subtle scent of peonies. Brushing aside the curls, he leaned forward to press his lips to her soft nape. She pulled in a quick breath, and a tremor ran through her.

"Cooler yet?"

"No. Indeed, it seems that the less clothing I have on, the hotter I become."

"Interesting." He moved to stand in front of her once again, dragging his fingertips along her collarbone. "Perhaps it is this last bit of a garment that keeps you so warm." He slipped the fine linen down her arms, his avid gaze devouring every inch of soft, creamy skin as it was revealed. When he released the chemise, it joined the pile of material surrounding her feet.

Logan stepped back and drew in an unsteady breath at the vision she made. His gaze skimmed over her full breasts, topped with taut coral nipples, the indent of her waist that flared to the curve of her hips, the triangle of dark curls nestled between her shapely thighs. He helped her step out of the mound of her clothing then simply stared. Standing naked before him, surrounded by steam, her luxuriant spirals of hair brushing her hips, she looked like a . . .

"Sea goddess," he murmured. "A beautiful sea goddess." He lifted his hands and cupped her soft breasts, stroking his thumbs over her nipples.

She sucked in a breath, and her eyes slid closed. "Logan . . . this is not helping to cool me off." She arched into his touch. "At all."

He dragged one hand down her torso to brush his fingers over that alluring triangle of curls. "Nor me."

She opened her eyes to reveal dilated pupils. "You are hot as well?"

Only so much that he felt as if he were about to ignite. "Now that you mention it, yes, I am."

She lifted her hands to his lapels and started to push his jacket from his shoulders. "Then perhaps I can help cool *you* off."

He would have laughed if he could. Other than covering him in ice, there wasn't a damn thing she could do that would achieve that end, and he doubted even the ice would work. "Perhaps," he conceded. He helped her remove his jacket then tossed the garment aside.

"Better?" she asked, mimicking his earlier question to her, her eyes filled with a fascinating combination of arousal and mischief.

"I'm afraid not."

"Then I fear I shall have to continue."

"As I've been informed how no one likes a complainer, I shall endeavor to bear it as a Brit would—with a stiff upper lip." Certainly *stiff* wouldn't present a problem.

With a grin lurking around the corners of her mouth, she set about unbuttoning his waistcoat. When it joined the pile of discarded clothing, she cocked a brow at him. "Well?"

"Didn't help. Sorry."

She heaved an exaggerated sigh then set about untying his cravat, an exercise in torture for him as he waited in an agony of impatience for her to undo the complicated knot. Simple knots . . . he'd have nothing but simple knots from now on.

When she finished, he yanked his shirttails from his breeches then helped her lift the garment over his head. Her avid gaze roamed over him, halting on the scabbed-over skin on his upper arm.

"What happened here?" she asked, brushing a fingertip below the injury.

Logan inwardly grimaced. Damn. He'd forgotten about that. As there was no way not to tell her, he quickly related the shooting incident in Hyde Park. When he finished, she crossed her arms over her chest and glared at him.

"You're telling me you were *shot* three days ago and didn't bother to tell me."

"I wasn't *shot*, I was *shot at*. I couldn't tell you at the time, and after that, well, the injury was so minor, I all but forgot about it. And besides, I'm telling you now."

"Only because you had to. Because we're . . ."

"Getting naked. Yes. I know." And he dearly wanted to continue. He could see the fury brewing in her eyes, and he cupped her face between his hands. "I'm fine. It's barely a scratch. I swear."

"But you could have been killed!"

"But I wasn't."

"You should have told me."

"You're right. I should have. I'm sorry."

She pursed her lips. "It's very difficult to argue with you when you're so conciliatory."

He kissed the corners of her mouth. "Good. I don't want to argue."

"Neither do I, but—"

He halted her words with a kiss. "No more secrets. I promise." He leaned back and made himself say it again, hoping the vow wouldn't come back to haunt him. "I promise." He took her hands and pressed them against his chest. "Forgive me?"

For several seconds she didn't move, then she splayed her fingers over his skin. "I suppose." She skimmed her hands across his shoulders. "I can see it's going to be very difficult to ever say no to you."

"That is very good news indeed." Grateful the storm had passed so quickly, he leaned into her touch. "That feels so good."

She dragged her palms slowly downward. "Cooler?" she whispered.

His muscles jumped, and a groan escaped him as she ran her hands over him. Damn, as much as he was enjoying this, he wasn't sure how much more he could take. "I'm afraid not."

Her gaze flicked down to his breeches and boots. "That leaves little choice as to what's next."

With a nod, he moved with jerky steps to the chaise and sat. He may have removed his boots and breeches faster in his life, but he couldn't recall the circumstances. Certainly he'd never wanted them off more than he did now. When he finished, he walked slowly toward her, loving the way her gaze roamed over him then riveted on his erection, but knowing that if he allowed her eager hands to explore the rest of him as she had his chest, he'd be done.

"Not cooler," he said. Without pausing, he scooped her up in his arms and headed toward the tub. He walked down the two steps then gently lowered her into the warm water. After settling his back against the smooth tiles, he spread his legs then pulled her toward him until she sat in the vee of his thighs, facing away from him.

"Comfortable?" he asked against her neck, slipping his arms around her waist and cupping her breasts.

"This is"—she ran her hands slowly over his thighs—"delightful."

He teased her hard nipples between his fingers and lightly sucked on the tender skin behind her ear. "Delightful," he agreed. "Relax."

She rested her head against his shoulder. "I'll try, but you're making it exceedingly difficult."

He chuckled lightly and reached for the square of soap resting in a ceramic dish next to the tub. After working up a frothy lather, he slowly worked his soapy hands down one of her slim arms, lightly massaging. When he reached her hands, he caressed each finger then gave her other arm the same treatment.

"By the time it is my turn to do this to you, I'll be too limp with bliss to return the favor," she murmured.

"Rendering you limp with bliss is my job as a husband," he said, lathering his hands again, this time running them down her chest and over her breasts.

A long *ooooh* escaped her, and she arched her back. "You seem to have many jobs as my husband, but I've yet to hear any jobs I may have as a wife."

His hands slid lower, over her abdomen, then between her legs. "You're doing your most important job right now."

"Spreading my legs so you can touch me more easily?" she asked, doing just that.

"No, although that is, of course, much appreciated." He ran one finger down the seam of her sex before easing it inside her. "I think the most important job we each have is to try to make the other happy. And right now, you're making me very happy."

"And right now you're driving me mad."

He withdrew his finger and lazily circled it over her clitoris. "Just another one of my husbandly duties."

"Logan . . ." With a moan she grabbed his wrist then twisted herself around until she kneeled between his splayed thighs. "When I feel *that way* again, I want you inside me."

God knows that's where he wanted to be. He braced his hands on the bottom of the tub, preparing to push himself up to stand, but she stilled him by reaching out and stroking his erection. He sucked in a hissing breath and slammed his eyes shut.

"Am I making you happy?" she asked, slowly swirling her fingers around the engorged head.

Helpless to stop himself, he rolled his hips, seeking more. "Happy, yes," he managed, then groaned when her fingers encircled him and lightly squeezed. "Insane, yes." He lifted his hands and filled them with her breasts. "God, Emily, you have no idea how incredible that feels."

"Says a man who can make me feel *that way* with almost ridiculous ease."

She squeezed him again, and he slowly thrust upward. He opened his eyes and through heavy lids watched her fingers stroke and tease him, gritting his teeth against the intense pleasure, letting her continue until he couldn't take it any longer.

Teetering on the brink of spilling, he grabbed her hands and abruptly stood, scooping her up as he did. "Can't take any more," he said in a hoarse rasp. Heedless of the water sluicing off them, he stalked to the chaise where he deposited her with a gentle bounce then followed her down, settling himself between her wet, splayed thighs. Bracing his weight on his forearms, he looked down into her beautiful flushed face. He wanted to say something, to reassure her that he wouldn't hurt her, but speaking was beyond him. He rubbed the head of his erection along her sex then slowly entered her. When he reached the barrier of her maidenhead he paused, then, with his eyes on hers, he gave a hard thrust and sank to the hilt in her tight heat. Her eyes widened, and she gasped.

"I'm sorry," he said, forcing himself to remain still. "I didn't mean to hurt you."

She shook her head. "You didn't. I was merely surprised."
She ran her hands over his chest. "I feel . . . deliciously full.
Of you. I like it very much."

His powers of speech were vanishing at a rapid rate. "Wrap
your legs around me."

After she complied, he withdrew nearly all the way, then
slowly glided deep once again.

"Oh, my," she whispered, closing her eyes. "Do that
again."

He made another slow withdrawal then sank deep again,
then again, gritting his teeth against the hot, slick friction.
His thrusts grew faster, more intense, each one pushing him
closer to the climax roaring up his spine. Her fingers bit into
his shoulders, then with a gasp, she arched beneath him. Her
tight sheath convulsed around him, and with an agonized
groan he drove into her and found the release he felt he'd been
waiting for forever.

When the shudders racking him finally subsided, he rested
his forehead against hers and fought to catch his breath. When
he could finally pull in a deep lungful, he raised his head. And
found her looking at him through half-closed, glazed eyes, a
smile playing around the corners of her kiss-swollen lips.

A sensation unlike anything he'd ever experienced before
washed through him. It was contentment, but more. Fulfill-
ment, but different. Satisfaction, but better. A combination of
all three, yet even that didn't fully describe the warm feeling
of well-being suffusing him. It was a profound sense of calm
and . . . *rightness*. As if he'd arrived safely home after a bitter, grueling battle. Looking down into her face, he knew he'd
never seen anything as beautiful as her. As his wife.

Not wanting to squash his beautiful wife who'd just given
him more pleasure than he'd ever before experienced, he
made to slide off her, but she wrapped her arms and legs more
tightly around him and shook her head.

"Don't leave," she murmured. "I love the feel of you on top
of me. Inside of me."

He brushed his lips over hers. "I'm delighted to hear it, as I
can honestly say it's my favorite place to be."

She heaved a soft sigh. "Now I understand."

"Understand what?"

"What all the fuss is about. In spite of all the reading I've done, I now realize I didn't have the slightest comprehension of the wonders of making love." She reached up and brushed his hair from his brow. "The intimacy of your body in mine is breathtaking. I'd imagined it would be magical, but even in my wildest dreams I'd never envisioned it could be like that."

"I'm glad you're pleased."

"I am." Uncertainty clouded her eyes. "Are you?"

A bark of incredulous laughter escaped him. "I'm amazed you'd need to ask, but since you have, allow me assure you that I am *beyond* pleased."

In spite of his words, the uncertainty lingered. "I'm sure I'm not the only woman you've done this with—"

He cut off her words with a gentle kiss then raised his head to look into her eyes. And felt himself drowning. "Emily. No one has ever pleased me as you just did. Ever."

"How many women have you entertained in this room?"

"None," he answered without hesitation. He laid one hand against her soft cheek. "Only you."

Her gaze cleared. "I'm glad. But I find myself suddenly jealous of every woman who has ever touched you. Ever shared this with you."

"You have no reason to be jealous." And she didn't—because what he'd just shared with her made his every past sexual encounter pale into insignificance. And he realized it was because that's all they'd been, sexual encounters, while with Emily, he'd made love. The realization struck him like a blow to the head. And the heart. He'd just made love—for the first time in his life.

And he was suddenly able to put a name to the unfamiliar sensation that now filled him. It was . . .

Love.

He loved her. By damn, he'd fallen in love. With his wife.

This time neither his heart nor his mind even attempted to reject the realization. The words *I love you*, words he'd never spoken to another person, rushed into his throat, demanding to be said, but he clamped his lips shut to contain them. Something warned him this was not the time to tell her. It was too soon. His emotions were too raw. She might think he'd just spouted the sentiment in the aftermath of passion.

And what might she say in return? Would she feel obligated to return the sentiment, no matter if she meant it or not, in order to spare his feelings? Or even worse, not say anything? His insides cringed at both possibilities, and self-preservation had him clamping his lips even tighter together.

Damn, why did falling in love have to be so complicated? So fraught with uncertainty?

"Logan, are you all right?"

Her question yanked him from his thoughts. "Yes," he replied, although he wasn't convinced it was the truth.

"Good. Because, well, I was hoping we might . . ." her voice trailed off and a rose blush suffused her cheeks.

"Might what?"

"Well, do it again." She lowered her gaze to where their bodies were still joined then looked up at him with a demure expression. "If you don't mind overly much."

He heaved a heavy sigh. "Not *overly* much, I suppose." He shot her his fiercest glare. "I can see where you're going to be very demanding."

She raised her brows. "You will recall what I told you about complainers."

"Oh, I'm not complaining. In fact, demanding, wet, and naked are my three favorite qualities in a wife."

She shot him a saucy smile. "How fortunate that I am all three."

He rolled them over until she sat astride him, and he smiled into her beautiful eyes. "Yes, I am indeed very fortunate."

And as soon as the bastard who was trying to hurt them was caught and out of their lives, everything would be perfect.

Chapter 22

Being immortal meant that eventually, with the passage of enough time, my past would fade away. But to my horror I learned that the past could sometimes find you, no matter how far in the distance it might have seemed.

The Vampire Lady's Kiss *by Anonymous*

Emily rose from Logan's enormous bed and slipped her arms into her satin robe, tightening the sash around her waist. She crossed the room to the water pitcher, her feet sinking into the thick carpet, and poured herself a glass, which she drank quickly. A smile curved her lips as she poured herself another. Making love all day and evening certainly made one thirsty. She pressed her thighs together, and her smile deepened. And tender—in the most delightful way.

Sipping her second glass, she turned to stare at the man she'd married that morning. The man who, for the past—she glanced at the mantel clock and saw it was just past midnight—fourteen hours had made her feel things she'd never imagined possible. Who had made her laugh and had treated her as if she were the most precious thing in the world to him. Who had made exquisite love to her three more times and explored every centimeter of her body with his hands and lips and tongue, and who'd encouraged her to take the same liberties with him.

He now lay stretched out on his back, his strong arms raised over his head, his head cushioned by a mammoth pillow and his loosely linked fingers. Her gaze ran over him, touching on his profile, rendered imperfect yet perfectly masculine by the bump on his nose. His breathing was even and deep, his features relaxed in repose.

Her gaze continued its downward journey, memorizing the slope of his wide chest, which looked so hard yet provided such a comfortable pillow for her head, one which allowed her to listen to the steady thump of his heart; over his ridged abdomen, bisected by that fascinating ribbon of dark hair that wandered down in a silky trail she knew spread to cradle his impressive manhood, the view of which was currently thwarted by the sheet resting low on his hips.

Looking at him now, her heart overflowing with love, it seemed impossible to believe there'd been a time when she'd disliked him. How had she misjudged him so completely? Part of her animosity had sprung from loyalty to her father and the fact that Logan was one of his many creditors. But after considering the matter, she concluded that the rest of her enmity was due to the fact that she had, in spite of her wish to have it otherwise, been strongly attracted to him. In a way that had confused and irritated her, as she'd never experienced such a powerful reaction to a man before. She hadn't recognized the attraction for what it was as he wasn't the sort of man she would have ever expected to find appealing. She always thought her affections would be won by a British peer. Certainly not an uncouth American.

But he wasn't uncouth. Not at all. He was . . . bold. Thrillingly so. Exciting. And kind. And wonderful. Witty, intelligent, and amusing. And she loved him more with each passing moment.

Yet there were things about him she still didn't know, that she wanted to know. Indeed, she wanted to know everything about him. Unwilling to be away from him any longer, she quickly finished her drink then went back to the bed and settled herself on her side so she could continue watching him sleep.

"I missed you."

His soft voice startled her. "How is it that even when you're sleeping you still manage to sneak up on me?" she asked.

He rolled onto his side and propped his head in his hand. The low glow from the fire cast his face in intriguing shadows, highlighted by the dusky day's growth of beard darkening his square jaw. "I didn't sneak up on you. But I did miss you."

"I was only gone for a moment."

"Two minutes and fourteen seconds. Not that I was counting."

"I would have offered you a drink, but I thought you were asleep."

"I'm not thirsty." He reached out and idly twirled a lock of her hair around his finger. "You were watching me for a long time."

An embarrassed flush crept up her neck. "Yes. I couldn't seem to help myself. I hope you don't mind."

"Not at all." He brushed the pad of his thumb over her flaming cheek. "What were you thinking?"

"What makes you believe I was thinking anything? Perhaps I was just admiring."

One corner of his lips cinched upward. "Thank you, but I could practically hear the wheels in your head turning."

"I was just wondering. About you. Your life." A self-conscious sound escaped her. "I find myself insatiably curious and wanting to know everything."

All traces of amusement faded from his eyes, replaced by a guarded expression. "What do you want to know?"

"Well, where are you from?"

"New York."

When he didn't elaborate, she hesitated, then said, "I was wondering why you left America."

His gaze dropped to where his fingers played with her dark spiral curl. A long silence filled the air until he finally raised his gaze to hers. The haunted look in his eyes tied a knot in her stomach and had her saying quietly, "You don't have to tell me, Logan."

He frowned and shook his head. "No, I want to. I promised you there'd be no more secrets between us, and I don't want to lie to you." He heaved out a long breath. "But I fear you may be sorry you asked."

Whatever his reason for leaving, it clearly had affected him profoundly and still did. And based on his expression and warning that she might be sorry, she suspected it would be difficult for him to tell her and equally as difficult for her to hear. She reached out and clasped his hand, entwining their fingers. "Whatever it is, Logan, I'll understand."

His gaze searched hers. "I know you think that now, but—"

"No buts. I've done things I'm not proud of. Things I regret. Will you cast me aside when you learn of those?"

"No, but—"

"No buts," she repeated firmly. "I won't cast you aside, Logan. No matter what you tell me."

He remained silent for so long she thought he'd changed his mind and wasn't going to tell her. He sat up, raked his hands through his hair, then rose and donned his robe. She watched him cross to the crystal decanters and pour a finger of brandy, which he tossed back in a single gulp. He grimaced as he swallowed the potent liquor, then set down the snifter and returned to the bed where he sat on the edge of the mattress. He silently held out his hand to her, and without a word she placed her hand in his and moved to sit beside him.

Finally he turned toward her and said, "The day we walked in Hyde Park, I mentioned a man named Martin Becknell."

"The man who took you in when you were thirteen and taught you everything you know about business. You said you owe him everything."

"Yes. And I do. God only knows what I would have become if not for him. Martin taught me well, and I had a definite knack for numbers and making deals. By the time I was twenty, I'd already kept all the accounting records for his vast shipping interests for several years. That's around the time that Martin began a new venture with a new partner, a man named Thomas Heller. I took an instant dislike to Heller. He was rude and arrogant, but many wealthy men are, so I shrugged it off. But as time went on, I grew suspicious of him. Nothing I could pinpoint or prove, just my instincts warning me.

"Another month went by, during which time I made it my business to watch Heller. I knew something was wrong but couldn't figure out what. Finally it came to light through a series of cleverly forged receipts. I dug deeper and realized Heller was running an elaborate scam and had already managed to steal a small fortune from Martin. I was furious with myself for not realizing it sooner, but now that I had the proof I needed, I went to Martin and told him everything."

He paused to take a slow breath, then continued, "Martin was naturally furious with Heller and very generously grateful to me rather than upset that it had taken me so long to discern the theft. Indeed, he praised me for my good work and assured me he'd take care of the situation. I assumed that meant he'd go to the authorities, but apparently instead he went to Heller. That evening as I was leaving my office I heard them arguing in Martin's office. I was concerned, so I knocked and opened the door. The evidence I'd given Martin was spread out on his desk. Before I could say anything, he told me everything was fine and I should go home."

A muscle ticked in his jaw. "But I couldn't. I decided to stay and went back to my office. For the next half hour I could hear the murmur of their voices, then everything grew quiet. I waited for about a quarter of an hour, but when I heard nothing else, I went back to Martin's office. The door was ajar and the lamp still lit. I entered and found him. Dead. He'd been stabbed."

Emily gasped and squeezed his hand. He dragged his free hand through his hair. "The evidence was gone, and so was Heller. There was no doubt in my mind that the bastard had killed Martin. Or that Martin's death was my fault. If only I'd gone to the authorities myself. If only I'd stayed with Martin that night. If only I hadn't waited fifteen minutes before going back to his office."

She squeezed his fingers, her heart hurting for the raw guilt so evident in his voice. "Logan, it wasn't your fault."

But he shook his head then continued, his words coming faster now, pouring out of him in a low, tense voice. "I notified the authorities, told them the entire story, and looked forward to Heller being hanged for what he'd done. Heller admitted he'd had a meeting with Martin but lied about the time, swearing they'd met an hour earlier than they actually had and that Martin was alive when he'd left. Then the bastard suggested that I was the culprit. It was a case of my word against his, and the next thing I knew, the authorities were looking at me as a suspect. Just when I thought matters couldn't get worse, they did. First, Martin's will was read and I learned he'd left me an enormous amount of money and a fleet of ships or, in other words, a huge motive for me to kill him."

The bleak look in his eyes tore at her soul. "I didn't know. I had no idea he'd made such provisions."

"He obviously loved you like a son."

He jerked his head in a nod. "Even worse, half a dozen witnesses came forward and swore they'd been with Heller that night at a time and location far enough away that it would have been impossible for him to have killed Martin. Obviously they were lying, no doubt paid handsomely to do so. At that point I knew he was going to get away with murder, and that I might well hang for his crime."

He pulled his gaze from hers and looked down at their joined hands. "I followed him that night, waited until I got him alone, then confronted him. Told him I knew what he'd done and I wanted him to turn himself in. He just laughed. Said I'd never be able to prove it and how he was going to enjoy watching me swing by the neck for a crime he knew I hadn't committed. But I could tell he was afraid of me. I was bigger and stronger, and he was worried about what I might do. I guess that's why he pulled the knife from his boot." He turned toward her. His dark eyes were flat as stones. "Turns out I was faster, too. Before he had a chance to put his knife in me, I got mine in him."

Silence engulfed them, broken only by his rapid, shallow breaths. The sympathy rushing through Emily nearly drowned her. She wanted to enfold him in her arms and comfort him, but he sat so rigid and tense she wasn't certain if he would accept the gesture. Instead, she said quietly, "If you hadn't, he would have killed you."

He nodded slowly. "Yes, I'm sure he would have."

"You can't be blamed for defending yourself."

A bitter sound escaped him, and he again stared at the floor. "At that point I wasn't certain anyone would believe I'd been defending myself. And it was a risk I wasn't willing to take. I dragged his body into the woods and buried it in a deep grave. I'm not sure if I was more horrified that I'd killed a man, or by the fact that I didn't feel any remorse having done so. When Heller was reported missing and no sign of him turned up, it was assumed that he had indeed been guilty and had run away to escape prosecution for the crime.

"Although I'm certain some people harbored lingering suspicions of me, no accusations were ever made, and I didn't stay around long enough to see if that would change. So even though I didn't deserve it, I collected the windfall Martin left me and left. Never looked back."

"Where did you go?" Emily asked.

"I spent the first nine years traveling extensively through Europe, growing my enterprises. About a year ago I found myself growing weary of all the moving, of not having a place to call home. As London was the best location for my businesses, I chose to settle here. I used what Martin bequeathed me to build what I have today."

He briefly squeezed his eyes shut, and she could tell he was dreading looking at her, was afraid of what he'd see in her eyes. She willed him to turn toward her, to see all the sympathy and concern and sadness but most of all the acceptance and love rushing through her. His story had nearly broken her heart, but it was clear it had broken his long ago, and that only made her love him more. For all the years he'd suffered, blaming himself for the death of the man he considered a father.

"Now you know," he whispered.

"Yes, now I know."

Finally he turned to face her. His gaze searched hers, and he appeared confused, as if he couldn't believe he wasn't seeing condemnation in her eyes. "I've never told anyone before."

The area surrounding her heart went hollow then filled to overflowing. "Thank you for telling me. For trusting me. You have my word that I'll never tell another soul."

"I can only imagine what you're thinking. That you've married a man who is capable of—"

"Defending himself. Of righting a horrible wrong. Of enduring years of guilt over something that wasn't his fault." She lifted his hand and pressed a fervent kiss against his fingers. "I'm thinking I married a wonderful, brave, honorable man who I am proud to call my husband. A man who has suffered a great deal for all he has, and who has my deepest respect and admiration for all he has accomplished."

Myriad emotions flickered across his face: confusion, surprise, disbelief, then gratitude and finally something that looked like awe. He rested his palm against her cheek, and she felt the unsteadiness in his hand, the tremor that shook his body.

"Thank you. You have no idea what that means to me. What *you* mean to me." His eyes softened with a look so filled with tenderness her breath caught. "Emily, I want you to know that I—"

A noise sounded from the balcony, cutting off his words. He whipped his head around and peered toward the window, and Emily followed his gaze. Nothing but unrelenting black showed through the panes.

"Do you suppose that's Gideon?" she whispered, knowing he was patrolling the grounds. "Or perhaps the wind?"

"I don't know. Stay here." He reached for the knife he'd set on the night table next to the bed then moved cautiously toward the French windows leading to the balcony. He peered outside, then looked at her over his shoulder and said, "I don't see anything, but I'm going outside to check."

He opened the window, and a cold blast of air swirled into the room. Logan stepped outside and was swallowed by the darkness. An uneasy feeling slithered through Emily, and she stood. Just then she heard Logan say, "You! What the— how the hell can you—" A loud thump and grunt sounded, followed by a dull thud, then silence. Before she could even move or think, a man entered the room from the balcony. A man wearing a hooded cape. The pistol he held was trained directly at her.

"If you make a sound, you'll die," he said in a low rasp.

She opened her mouth to scream anyway, instinctively knowing it was her only chance, but she'd barely managed to utter a cry when he grabbed her with rough hands and stuffed a foul-tasting rag in her mouth. Terrified, she grunted and moaned as loud as she could, fighting with all her might, but he quickly overpowered her, securing her hands behind her back with a coarse rope then binding her ankles together with another piece. She struggled frantically, her gaze riveted on the darkened balcony. Clearly this man had injured Logan—or worse—or else he'd be in here. *Dear God, please let him be all right.*

Her abductor slung her over his shoulder. She continued to grunt and squirm, but the massive arm he clamped around her thighs thwarted her movements. He grabbed something from the night table, and she twisted around to see what. The oil lamp.

He set it on the bed, yanked off the glass globe, and turned the lamp over, spraying the flammable oil all over the counterpane, rug, and curtains. Then to her horror he lit a match and tossed it onto the bed. Flames caught and immediately spread. Terror and rage ripped through her, and she redoubled her struggles but to no avail. He hurried toward the balcony and stepped outside.

"Say good-bye to your dead husband," her abductor said in a low growl. "It's the last you'll ever see of him."

Emily looked, and her heart stalled. Logan lay facedown on the balcony. With the growing glow from the rapidly spreading fire in the bedchamber, she could see the dark pool of wet blood surrounding his head. A scream rose in her throat, one that came out as nothing more than a hoarse, muffled moan. Her abductor swung himself over the railing and nimbly climbed down the ladder leaning against the balcony. When they reached the ground, he tossed the ladder in the bushes. To her horror she saw another figure prone on the ground. Her eyes widened, and she again struggled and tried to scream, but it appeared Gideon had met the same fate as Logan. She pulled in a breath and froze at the smell of smoke . . . smoke that was too thick and close to be from the fire her abductor had just set upstairs.

She swiveled around, and her blood ran cold. Flames licked up the walls of the house from the ground floor. This monster had set fire to the entire house.

She tried again to scream, but the air left her lungs in a painful burst when she bounced against his beefy shoulder as he ran through the garden toward the mews. Dear God, no one would know what happened to her, to even look for her. They'd assume she died in the fire. She had to do something . . . but what?

She struggled against the ropes binding her hands, but they were so tight they cut into her wrists. Her ring bit into her finger.

Her ring. Focusing all her concentration, she wriggled the jewel, moving it bit by bit until she was able to work it off her finger. It fell to the dirt, and she prayed someone would find it and know she was alive. At least for now.

She lifted her head and saw the smoke and flames rising all around the house. Tears poured from her eyes, blurring the horrifying image of Logan lying facedown in that pool of blood. A pain so intense she couldn't breathe gripped her. He was gone. She'd never told him how much she loved him, and now she'd never have the chance. The pain in her chest was surely her heart shattering.

An instant later they entered the mews, and she was roughly shoved into a carriage. The door shut, and the vehicle took off at a brisk pace.

Chapter 23

❧

*As a vampire I possessed extraordinary healing capabili-
ties. Cuts and bruises healed almost instantly, and since
I had no blood, I couldn't bleed. But unfortunately, that
didn't mean I couldn't hurt or feel broken, although how
my heart could break when I didn't physically have one
remains a mystery.*

The Vampire Lady's Kiss *by Anonymous*

Logan came awake slowly. Bit by bit he became aware of the
fact that he was cold. Extremely cold. And damn, why was a
battalion of hammer-wielding demons pounding on his skull?
From far off he heard a groan and realized it came from his
own throat, which felt as if he'd swallowed broken glass.
He tried to push himself up, but the blinding pain vibrating
through his head left him dizzy and nauseated. He made it
to his knees then snapped his eyes shut and pulled in slow,
deep breaths. He raised one unsteady hand to his head and felt
warm wetness, an odd contrast to the cold air.

He sucked in another breath and recognized the metallic
scent of blood mixed with the acrid smell of smoke. He forced
his eyes open and realized he was outside, on the balcony

of his bedchamber. A wave of confusion and pain washed through him. What the hell?

He turned toward the bedchamber, and his blood froze at the sight of the flames licking up the walls and curtains. Memory returned in flashing pieces. A noise on the balcony. Going outside. Seeing, impossibly seeing Thomas Heller. He'd killed the bastard, buried his body, yet there he'd stood. Then everything went black. Emily . . .

Emily.

With a feral growl he pushed himself to his feet and staggered into the bedchamber. Heat shoved him back several paces, and thick smoke burned his eyes.

"Emily!" he yelled, his frantic gaze searching the room, terror grabbing him by the throat at the sight of the bed where he'd last seen her consumed in flames. Fighting dizziness, he dashed across the room and looked into the bathing chamber. Empty. Panic clawed at him, and he snatched a hand towel, held it over his mouth and nose, then ran back into the bedchamber, searching through the thickening smoke and blistering heat, his horror growing with each passing second. Was she here? Had Heller left her here to die in the fire? Or had the bastard taken her with him? He made his way across the room, squinting through the smoke, coughing, shouting her name. He'd just determined she wasn't in the room when the door from the corridor burst open. The rush of air made the flames leap higher.

"Logan!" A soot-streaked Gideon raced toward him. "We have to get out of here. The entire house is aflame."

Logan shook his head. "Emily," he gasped. "Have to find Emily." He reached out to pull open the door leading to the adjoining bedchamber, but Gideon grabbed his shoulders and swung him around.

"She's not in there. I've looked through as much of the house as I can and couldn't find her. I thought everyone was out until I heard you calling for her."

"Damn it, I can't leave without her. I won't leave without her."

"I'm telling you she's not in that room or any of the others I checked," Gideon yelled above the loud snapping of the hungry flames. "The bastard who set this fire undoubtedly has her, and if we die in here, we'll never get her back. We have to get out *now*, or it will be too late."

Torn and panicked, Logan still didn't move, his gaze sweeping the room one more time. How could he leave if there was a chance she was in here? But how could he stay if she was out there with Heller and in need of rescuing? Even though it tore at his heart, he'd have to trust that Gideon's search was thorough. Holding the towel to his face, he yelled, "Let's go."

They dashed through the doorway and down the corridor. Suffocating heat singed him, scorching the bottoms of his bare feet, the smoke dragging hot tears from his stinging eyes. He held his breath as best he could, and they raced down the curved staircase, jumping over burning fallen beams. As they ran through the double oak doors leading outside, Logan heard the crystal chandelier shatter on the floor behind them, the crash shaking the smoldering floor.

When they were a safe distance from the crackling flames, Logan stopped and bent over, set his hands on his knees, and pulled in great gulps of cold air. His servants stood about twenty feet away, huddled together, staring at the fire, several of them crying, all of them looking stunned. According to Gideon, no one remained in the house, for which he could only thank God.

Ignoring his watering eyes, scorched lungs, and blistered feet, he turned to Gideon. Black soot streaked his friend's face and clothing, and he was breathing heavily.

"What the hell happened?" Logan asked, the raspy words interspersed with hacking coughs.

"I was patrolling the grounds when the bastard managed to catch me unawares and knock me cold. When I regained my wits, the ground floor of the house was in flames, and the fire was spreading fast. I ran to the front. Eversham and several footmen were working on getting the servants out. I ran upstairs to your bedchamber. The room was on fire but empty, so I continued to search the other rooms upstairs. When I couldn't find you or Emily, I knew you'd either gotten outside or the arsonist had somehow taken you. By that time the smoke and flames were so thick, I knew I had to get out. I was leaving when I heard you calling for Emily. Where the bloody hell were you?"

"The balcony." He quickly told Gideon what had transpired, ending with, "I saw the man; I know him. His name is Thomas Heller. I thought he was dead, but somehow he's not. He has reasons to want revenge against me that I don't have time to tell you right now. Not when it appears he has Emily." He squeezed his burning eyes shut. As much as he hated to hope for that, he had to pray it was true, as it gave him hope she was alive and not trapped in the fire.

He couldn't think of that. Couldn't. "Heller's got her," he said grimly. "And we've got to get her back." *And then I'll kill you again, you bastard. And this time I'll make certain you stay dead.* "But where in God's name do we start to look?"

"With the people right here," Gideon said. "Come on."

Logan followed him toward the group of servants, trying to gather his addled wits and think calmly, logically, about how to go about finding Emily. Now. Because every second counted.

"Your mistress is missing," Gideon hollered to the assembled servants to be heard above the roar of the fire. "We have reason to believe she was abducted by the man who started the fire. Did any of you see or hear anything?"

Shocked eyes looked his way, followed by concerned murmurs and shaking heads.

An idea occurred to Logan, and he called out, "The man was on the balcony of my bedchamber, therefore he probably escaped through the garden then into the mews. My wife is a very intelligent and resourceful woman who wouldn't allow herself to be dragged off without a fight. She may have tried to leave behind a clue."

"Wot sort of clue?" shouted John, one of his footmen.

"Maybe a slipper. A torn piece from her robe. Something. I don't know." Christ, had she even been wearing slippers? He didn't know. But he knew if she was able, she'd leave something behind to help him find her. "I want you all to spread out and scour the grounds," he yelled. "There's a substantial reward for anyone who finds something that could aid in the rescue of my wife."

The huddled group immediately broke up, hurrying toward

the gardens, giving the burning house a wide berth. He turned to Gideon. "He must have escaped that way. Did you see a ladder?"

"No, but he could have tossed it in the bushes."

"Let's go," Logan urged. Every second they delayed could mean the end of Emily's life at that bastard Heller's hands.

Before he could move, however, his footman John approached him. "Noticed ye haven't any shoes, sir," John said. "Or, um, breeches or a shirt. Just yer robe. Ye'll need some proper clothes to fetch the mistress back from the bastard wot took her." He held out a pair of black breeches, a shirt, and a pair of shoes. "Take mine."

Gideon noticed the young man wore a coat. "And what will you wear?"

"I've got me coat, me smalls, and a heavy pair of wool socks, sir. 'Tis enough. And now if ye'll excuse me, I'll be searchin' for that clue ye think the mistress might have left. I pray ye're right, sir." He turned to go.

"Thank you, John. I won't forget this kindness."

"'Tis my pleasure, sir." He hurried off, and Logan quickly donned the clothing. He was shoving his blistered feet into the shoes when an unfamiliar man approached him from out of the darkness. He immediately reached for his knife, only to realize he was unarmed. Gideon, however, had his knife unsheathed in a heartbeat.

"Who are you?" Logan asked, eyeing him. He was short and wore an ill-fitting, ragged coat. The flames illuminated features that reminded Logan of a rodent: sharp, beady eyes, thin face, pointed chin.

"Ye can call me Jonesy. I heard wot ye said to yer fancy servants about a reward to git yer lady back. Well, just so happens I know where she is. And for the right price, I might decide to tell ye."

Logan's hand lashed out like a whip. He grabbed the man by the collar, lifted him off his feet, dragging him up until they stood nose to nose. "If you know where she is—"

"I do know where she is," Jonesy said in a strangled voice. "But I ain't talkin' till ye put me down."

Logan was more inclined to shake him like a terrier with a bone, but he dropped him to his feet. "Talk," he demanded.

"You have precisely ten seconds to give me a reason not to toss you into that inferno behind me."

"I drove the carriage for the bloke what stole her," Jonesy said hastily. "Waited in the mews behind yer fine mansion, just like he told me. Didn't know what he was about, but then he came runnin' back with the lady trussed up like a game bird and tossed her inside the carriage and told me to move out quick. He'd already paid me five quid, but I got to thinkin' he coulda paid me more. A lot more. When we arrived, I told him I wanted more to forget what I'd seen, and he just laughed, then gave me a cosh on me head for me trouble." He reached up and rubbed the back of his skull. "I don't owe 'im no loyalty, and I figured a rich bloke like you might pay handsome to know where yer lady is."

Logan's heart pounded with a painful combination of hope and fear: hope that he might find her and paralyzing fear he might be too late. "How much?"

Jonesy's beady eyes glittered. "A hundred pounds."

He would have paid a hundred times that. A thousand times that. Any amount. Anything. And if he hadn't had enough, he would have stolen the rest. "Done. Where did you take them?"

"Not so fast. How do I know ye won't stiff me like that other bloke?"

Logan's hand shot out again, and this time he shook the weasel before dragging him up so they were eye to eye. "I give you my word. I also give you my word that if you don't tell me what I want to know *right now*, this will be your last night on this earth."

Jonesy swallowed then said in a choked voice, "To Wickam Street. Number six."

Logan turned to Gideon. "How far is that?"

"Ten minutes if we run."

Logan jerked Jonesy closer. "I want your knife."

"Wot makes ye think I've got one?"

"Fifty pounds makes me think so."

Jonesy's eyes glittered with avarice, then he nodded. Logan released him then held out his hand. Jonesy unsheathed a lethal blade from his boot but before handing it over said, "That's one hundred fifty pounds ye owe me."

"Yes. Unless you've lied to me. In which case there won't be enough money in the kingdom to keep me from hunting you down and using your own knife to gut you."

Jonesy's thin lips pressed together, and he slapped the knife's handle into Logan's waiting palm. "I ain't lyin'. And ye'll be the sorry one if I don't get my blunt."

Logan wanted to shove the tip of the knife against Jonesy's throat and tell him it wasn't wise to threaten the very desperate man who was going to pay him more money than he'd ever seen in his entire life, but he didn't want to waste another second. With the knife secure in his hand, he turned to Gideon.

"Lead the way."

He followed Gideon as they ran swiftly through the streets, his lungs still burning from the smoke, his rapid breaths forming puffs of vapor in the cold air. His head throbbed, and his blistered feet screamed at him, but he pushed aside the pain and focused on the one thing, the only thing that mattered: Emily.

Finding Emily alive. And unharmed. He couldn't consider any outcome other than that, or he wouldn't be able to breathe at all. He concentrated on the image of her branded in his mind—of that expression in her beautiful eyes after he'd told her the worst of himself, the truth he'd never told anyone. The truth that had led to this damnable situation in which they now found themselves. Another sea of guilt for him to drown in, for he'd brought this danger directly to her door. If anything happened to her—

He cut off the impossible thought and refocused on the way she'd looked at him after he'd told her. The caring and concern, the sympathy and acceptance in her eyes had touched a place inside him he hadn't even known existed until she'd unlocked the spot where it had hidden sleeping, as if just waiting for her to arrive and awaken it.

I married a wonderful, brave, honorable man who I am proud to call my husband. A man who has suffered a great deal for all he has, and who has my deepest respect and admiration for all he has accomplished.

He'd known—in spite of her assertion that she wouldn't cast him aside, no matter what he told her—that with his revelation he risked erecting a wall between them. One that could cast a shadow on the remainder of their lives. But he'd had to tell her. Wanted to tell her. He'd promised her no more secrets. He knew how secrets could eat at the soul, how his had eaten at him, and he didn't want that between them. He wanted her to know him in a way no one else ever had. And he prayed that once he'd revealed the sordid details of his past, she still could find a way to care for him. And hopefully to someday love him.

Love . . . God, he'd been about to tell her he loved her. The way she'd looked at him, held and kissed his hand, the caring and compassionate words she'd spoken had all filled him with such overwhelming emotion, he'd had to tell her. But the noise on the balcony had interrupted him, and now he was running through the streets of London, not knowing if she was dead or alive, praying he'd have the chance to tell her how much he loved her. And to show her. Every day. To prove he was worthy of her. In every way. Of that look in her eyes that had proclaimed him a hero.

Gideon slowed his pace then signaled a halt. "That's it," he whispered, nodding toward a shabby two-story brick building just ahead. "Looks like a typical boardinghouse, which means only one door leading in. Probably not more than two rooms: a bedchamber and some sort of sitting area." He squinted at the numbers on the doors. "Number six is on the first floor, left corner, which means he could escape out a window."

Logan narrowed his eyes. "He's not going to escape. You go in through the front. Break down the door. While you're making a huge commotion, I'll enter through the side window and get Emily to safety."

"Element of surprise," Gideon agreed.

"Yes, and he'll be trapped between us with no way out."

Gideon nodded and, keeping to the shadows, they approached the house. Logan moved to the window and cautiously peered inside. A combination of fear and relief roared through him. Emily lay on the narrow bed, her hands and feet bound. Because she faced away from him, he couldn't tell if she was alive. But he'd found her. Which meant she had to be alive. Had to be. *Had* to be.

Heller crouched before the fireplace, his back to Logan. He'd believed he hated Heller years ago, but that was a mere iota of the loathing consuming him now. His gaze shifted to the door through which Gideon would burst, and he pressed his lips into a grim line. With every nerve tingling, every muscle poised to pounce, he waited. Seconds later, the door crashed open, and Gideon ran into the room with a feral scream that could have woken the dead. Logan rammed the French windows open with his shoulder, shattering glass, and ran straight for Emily. A quick glance over his shoulder assured him Gideon had indeed surprised Heller and had the situation well in hand.

He dropped to his knees beside the bed, and with trembling hands he rolled Emily onto her back. And was greeted by the incredible sight of her wide eyes blinking up at him.

By God he'd never swooned in his life, but the relief that walloped him at the sight of her, alive, rendered him light-headed.

"Emily." It was the only word he could choke out. He pulled the gag from her mouth.

"Logan." That single word, spoken in that hoarse croak was the single sweetest sound he'd ever heard.

"I'm here, sweetheart. You're safe." He quickly sliced through the rough ropes binding her wrists and ankles then gathered her into his arms. With a sob she wrapped her arms around his neck.

"Dear God, I thought you were dead," she cried against his neck. "You were on the balcony, there was so much blood . . . the fire . . ." A shudder ran through her, and he gathered her closer, pressing his lips against her temple. He squeezed his eyes shut, and with his heart pounding hard enough to break his ribs, he offered up a heartfelt prayer of thanks.

He leaned back and ran gentle hands over her. "Are you hurt?"

"No. A few bumps and bruises from being carried over his shoulder, but nothing else. How did you—?"

He stopped her question and the barrage of others he knew would follow with a gentle kiss to her lips. "I'll explain later. For now, stay right here." He picked up the ropes he'd cut from her and crossed to Gideon, who held Heller subdued on the floor. They quickly tied him, then Logan dragged Heller to his feet. And stared into the eyes of the man he'd killed.

"By God, I *thought* I saw you several days ago in the park, watching me. But I knew it couldn't be you. Yet here you are. How is it you're still alive?" he asked the bastard who, by taking Emily, had nearly succeeded in destroying his entire world.

"How is it *you're* still alive?" Heller countered with a sneer, his eyes glittering with hatred. "You should be dead. *Dead*. Just the way you killed Zachary."

Logan's eyes narrowed. "What the hell are you talking about? I killed you, yet somehow you're standing right in front of me."

"You didn't kill *me*, you bastard," Heller spat out, "you killed my brother, Zachary. My twin brother." His eyes seemed to spew venom. "We had the perfect system. No one knew there were two of us. It allowed us great freedom to run our scams. The scheme with Martin Becknell was to be our greatest coup and set us up for life."

Understanding hit Logan like a punch. "That's why all those people swore you were with them at the time Martin was killed. It wasn't you. It was your brother they were with."

A sly gleam lit Thomas's eyes. "It worked perfectly." Fierce hatred replaced the gleam. "Until you ruined everything. Zachary had warned me about you and your suspicions, and about the evidence you'd found. Both you and Martin had to be eliminated. And what better way than to kill Martin and see you punished for it? But you were equally determined to see Zachary hang. When he disappeared, I knew you'd murdered him. I wanted to kill you then and there, but I decided to bide my time. You thought I was dead, so I let you go on thinking that while I plotted my revenge to take everything that mattered to you and ruin you, just as you'd taken everything from me and ruined my life." Fury mixed with the loathing in his eyes, and, Logan realized, madness. "But before I could carry out my plan, I was arrested." A harsh, bitter sound escaped him. "For a crime I didn't even commit."

"You'd committed plenty of others. You deserved to be punished."

"You killed my brother, and you were never punished. Instead, you collected a fortune and lived in luxury, while my brother rotted wherever you disposed of him and I rotted in a hellhole of a prison." He pulled in a harsh breath. "But I finally escaped. And I finally found out where you were. And when I got here, I found out what mattered to you." His gaze shifted to Emily. Logan jerked on Heller's collar, then moved to block the bastard's view of her.

He looked at Logan with insanity and hate simmering in his eyes. "You killed the wrong man, Jennsen. And I've made you pay for it. Not as much as I wanted to, since you and your wife are still alive, but your ship and your fine house are gone, and that's enough, at least for now."

Logan's hands burned with the desire to wrap themselves around Heller's neck and squeeze until he gasped his last breath. But there were better ways to see him punished. "When you burned my ship, you killed two fine men. As for the cargo and my house, they are easily replaced. The damage you have wrought isn't enough 'for now.' It's the end. You will never have another opportunity to hurt me or anyone else ever again."

He yanked Heller close and spoke in a voice only he could hear. "You'll never see the outside of a jail cell again—except for that instant before they lower the hangman's noose around your neck. I'm sure you'll think of me at that moment, you bastard, but I won't be thinking of you. I'll be enjoying my life with the family you tried to take from me. While you burn in hell."

He pushed Heller away and looked at Gideon. "You'll take him to the magistrate?"

"With pleasure." Gideon grabbed Heller by the back of the collar and headed toward the broken door. "Where can I reach you?"

Logan turned to Emily. She'd done as he'd asked and stayed put, but the instant their gazes met, she rose and hurried across to him. He wrapped an arm around her and pulled her close.

"I think we should go back to the house, to see what we can do to resettle the servants," she said. "After that we can spend what's left of the night at my parents' town house."

Logan nodded, not in the least surprised that she'd be worried about the servants and knowing her parents would be relieved to know she was well. "I'll let you know after that," he told Gideon.

"Thank you for your part in rescuing me, Gideon," Emily said. "I owe you a great deal."

Logan nodded. "We both do."

Gideon inclined his head. "You're welcome." Armed with his knife and holding Heller by the collar, he led the man through the broken door, his prisoner's steps slow due to the ropes shackling his ankles.

Logan immediately scooped her into his arms and headed toward the window he'd crashed through. "Let's get out of here."

"I can walk," she said even as she wrapped her arms around his neck.

"Of course you can, but there's glass all around, and you're not wearing shoes."

He strode outside into the cold air and walked briskly to the corner. Luck must have been shining upon him, because a hack stood under the pale yellow circle of light cast by the gas lamp. Logan gave a sharp whistle, and the driver put the horses in motion, heading toward them.

After giving the driver his direction in Berkeley Square, he handed Emily into the carriage then climbed in. As soon as he shut the door and sat, he pulled her onto his lap and held her as close as he could.

"Emily," he whispered. Her name felt like a prayer. He brushed back her tangled hair and stared into her beautiful eyes. "I've never been so frightened in my life as when I woke up on that terrace and couldn't find you."

"And I was never so frightened in my life as when I saw you lying on that terrace." She grabbed his hand and pressed a kiss against his palm. "I never, ever want to feel that way again."

"Neither do I." And then words he'd almost not had the chance to tell her rushed into his throat. "Emily, I love you." He pulled in a shuddering breath. "God, I love you. So much. And I was so afraid I wouldn't have the chance to tell you. I was about to when I heard the noise on the balcony, and then . . ." Another tremor ran through him. "It doesn't matter if you love me back, but I'm giving you fair warning; I'm going to do my damnedest to see to it that you eventually do. I haven't been able to think of anyone but you since the moment you kissed me in Sarah and Matthew's library three months ago. I was drawn to you before that, but that kiss . . . you've owned me since that day."

"Logan . . ." Moisture glistened in her eyes, but his breath stalled at the flare of emotion shining through the tears. "I love you so much I . . . ache with it. I've always dreamed of marrying for love and you, my brave, bold, wonderful husband who risked everything to save me, you have made all my dreams come true. You haven't been out of my thoughts since long before I kissed you that day." A trembling smile curved her lips. "And now I'll get to steal kisses from you every day for the rest of my life."

"Emily . . ." He covered her lips with his and kissed her with all the joy and love and passion pounding through him. And he made a mental note to pay his two-hundred-pound debt to Daniel.

When he finally raised his head, she murmured, "Yes, kisses just like that."

He nuzzled the soft skin behind her ear. "Do you know what makes you?"

"What's that?"

"A kiss stealer. My most favorite type of thief."

She framed his face between her hands and shook her head. "No. It makes me the luckiest woman in the world."

And he, now the bearer of the title Luckiest Man in the World, sealed that decree with another stolen kiss.

Epilogue

Although my vampire lover and I had to live in darkness, our existence was filled with the golden glow of love and white-hot beams of passion. Every night was a new adventure, and I knew I would love him for all eternity.

The Vampire Lady's Kiss *by Anonymous*

Two Years Later

Seated in one of the eight libraries in her and Logan's rebuilt mansion in Berkeley Square, Emily lifted her champagne glass and smiled. Her emerald and aquamarine ring, which their footman John had found and restored to her, caught a ray of sunshine and splashed glittering reflections around the room. "Here's to the Ladies Literary Society of London."

Carolyn, Sarah, and Julianne all raised their glasses, and the tinkle of delicate crystal rang in the room.

"And here's to the publication of Emily's second vampire story," Carolyn added.

"May it be as successful as the first story," Julianne said with a smile.

A pleased blush suffused Emily's cheeks. "Thank you. I cannot wait to begin on the third installment."

"We can't wait, either," said Carolyn with a grin. "I want to know what that naughty lady vampire will be up to next."

"We also have to decide what our next reading selection will be," Sarah said, pushing up her glasses. "I have several suggestions—"

Her words were cut off when the door burst open, and a gaggle of giggling toddlers made their way toward them, followed by a quartet of smiling men. First across the room was Sarah's two-year-old daughter Daphne, who threw herself against Sarah's knees and grinned up at her. Julianne and Carolyn's daughters, Frances and Beatrice, headed for their mothers' open arms, where they were received with smiles and kisses. Last came Amanda, who resembled Logan so much that the mere sight of her brought a lump of love to Emily's throat. Amanda's pudgy little hand clung to Logan's index finger, her sturdy legs toddling unsteadily, and she favored Emily with a drooling smile and a heart-melting "Mama."

Emily's gaze met Logan's, and again her heart melted, just as it did every time she looked at him. A warm, intimate look passed between them, then he nodded toward the four toddlers and said to Matthew, Daniel, and Gideon, "You realize what we have here. It's the next generation of the Ladies Literary Society."

Daniel gave an exaggerated shudder. "Heaven help us. I'm predicting mayhem in Mayfair for years to come."

Logan scooped up Amanda, who cooed with delight then promptly filled her fingers with his hair and yanked. "Have you gentlemen noticed that we are hugely outnumbered?"

"God, yes," said Matthew. "Nothing but females everywhere I look."

"And here they sit, picking out another book to read." Gideon made a tsking sound. "And you know what that means."

The four men exchanged a look and nodded. "Trouble," they all said in unison.

"But sometimes trouble is good," Gideon pointed out.

"Sometimes *very* good," Matthew said.

"Sometimes *extremely* good," Logan said. "Which is why the four of us have decided to form our own club."

Emily hiked up her brows. "What sort of club?"

"Since you've refused to allow us to join your Ladies Literary Society, we've decided to form the Gentlemen's Takeover Society."

Emily and her friends exchanged amused glances. "Oh? And what is the purpose of this club?" she asked.

"It is to encourage our wives to read their scandalous tomes faster."

"And to then share the licentious details with their husbands," Daniel said in a very serious voice.

"Every last detail," Gideon added, while Matthew nodded.

"And if we refuse to meet these heinous demands?" Emily asked.

"Then we shall be forced to live up to the name of our club and take over. Spirit each of you away to a private destination until you're ready to give in and cooperate."

"I can see I'm going to need to do that right away," said Daniel. His eyes gleaming with love and the promise of passion, he held out his hand to Carolyn. She shot her friends a mock-dismayed look, and Emily suppressed a chuckle. Carolyn was still a horrid actress.

"It appears I'm leaving," she said, slipping her hand into Daniel's and rising. Daniel swung his daughter into his arms, and with a wave they quit the room.

"I don't know why you're laughing," Matthew said with an exaggerated frown at Sarah—one that turned into an equally exaggerated leer. "You're next."

Sarah stood, settled Daphne on her hip, then lifted her nose in the air. "Well, if you insist." Like a ship under full sail, they exited the room.

Julianne rose, picked up Frances, then looked at Gideon. "I suppose you think I'm just going to go quietly along with this plan of yours to spirit me off to do heaven knows what with me."

"I suppose I do."

"And what if I'm not quiet about it?"

Gideon grinned. "Fine by me. I like it when you moan and—"

"Let's go!" she said, grabbing his hand, her face turning bright red. They quit the room, closing the door behind them.

"Alone at last," Logan said with a slow smile.

She rose and watched him walk toward her, Amanda's dark, curly head resting against his broad shoulder, her eyelids drooping.

He stopped in front of Emily and pulled her flush against him with his free arm. Their lips met in a warm, lush kiss that left her breathless. When he lifted his head, heat rushed through her at the desire burning in his eyes.

"I suppose you have plans for me as well?" she asked.

"I do. Is that a . . . problem?"

"No, but I know that look in your eyes. Which means I know your plans will result in me ending up flat on my back."

He leaned in to nuzzle her neck with his warm lips. "Again I must ask . . . is that a problem?"

"Not a bit. Indeed, I'm curious as to what you have in mind."

"Hmmm . . . I like that you're curious."

"I like that you're bold. And adventurous."

He smiled down at her, his eyes filled with so much love and happiness and passion, she thought she would burst from it.

"Emily, sweetheart, the adventure has just begun."

Chapter 1

Balmoral Castle, July 1885

The moment he set eyes on her, Alex knew that this woman was
going to be trouble. Though she was pretty enough and trim
enough to catch the eye of any red-blooded male, that was not
the kind of trouble he had in mind. He was thinking about the
case he was working on, wondering if she could be the one.

It was the blond hair that made her stand out. In this corner
of the Highlands of Deeside, the natives were mostly dark-
haired Celts like himself. This young woman had the look of
an English rose. He was sure that her eyes would be blue.

She turned her head quickly, as though she realized that
someone was studying her, and their eyes brushed and held. In
the split second before she tore her gaze from his, he felt it: a ripple of recognition, like a tiny electric current passing through his
brain. Strange, when he knew that he had never met the woman.

Watch her, Hepburn, he told himself.

After watching her wander among the assembled guests as
though she were looking for a friend, Alex dismissed her from
his mind. She seemed harmless enough. Besides, it wasn't a
woman he was looking for but a man. *Ca bheil sibh, Mac an
diaboil?* Where are you, son of the devil?

A voice at his elbow said softly, "Her Majesty is about to make her entrance. What happens now?" The speaker was Alex's brother, Gavin. Though the resemblance between them was striking, Gavin's manner and expression revealed a charm that was entirely lacking in Alex.

"Now we wait," Alex responded.

His gaze traveled the crush of guests in the castle's ballroom, noting that the cream of Scotland's Highland society had come to pay its respects to Her Majesty, Queen Victoria. There would be no dancing at this reception. Since her husband's death, the queen had retired into semi-obscurity. Frivolity was now frowned upon.

A silence fell as the doors to the queen's gallery opened and Her Majesty entered, flanked by her kilted guard of honor. Alex had positioned himself to watch the guests. He was scanning faces, seeking out anything and everything that struck him as odd. He hoped that his counterpart on the other side was not as vigilant, because he'd soon deduce that this trumped-up drama was a lie, a carefully choreographed trap to ensnare a traitor.

The "queen" was not the queen but only someone who resembled her; the "footmen" in their dark green coats and tartan sashes were not footmen but police officers. Alex was not part of the official operation but worked alone and reported only to his section chief, Commander Durward, and in his absence, as now, to Dickens, the local man in charge of security.

Gavin had no part in the operation. He was one of the guests, but he'd known that something was up when his elder brother had arrived at the family's fishing and hunting lodge the week before. They expected trouble at the queen's reception, Alex had told him. He'd also told Gavin to keep his mouth shut and his eyes open, and that was the only part Alex would allow him to play. At the moment, Gavin was weaving in and out of the guests, doing much the same as Alex was.

As the queen and her escort began to process slowly down the aisle that her aides had cleared for her, every head was lowered. The ladies' skirts rustled as they made their curtsies. Alex's bow was perfunctory. When he looked up, he saw the blond-haired woman moving quickly toward him. The thought had hardly registered when she raised a revolver that had been concealed in the folds of her skirts and pulled the trigger. He heard the deafening report of the gun going off, felt the whiz of the bullet as it missed him by a hair, heard the groan of someone behind him who had been hit, then he braced himself as the crush of screaming guests surged and ebbed like waves on an angry sea. It was a relief to see that the queen's guard had closed ranks around "Her Majesty" and were hustling the look-alike up the gallery stairs and out of the reception area. When a second shot rang out, however, and hit the chandelier overhead, making it teeter alarmingly, the panicked crowd rushed for the set of French doors giving onto the gardens. The "footmen" could do nothing to hold them back.

Alex scanned the pulsating wave of people forcing their way out. There was nary a sign of the woman with blond hair.

"Gavin," he shouted above the din, "look for a woman with blond hair. Don't let her get away." He gestured to the exit he thought she would have made for.

Gavin nodded and pushed his way through the crowd.

Muttering a furious curse, Alex went down on bended knee to tend to the wounded man. He was younger than Gavin by a year or two, and his face was vivid with color. "Did you see that?" the young man demanded. "Someone tried to murder me!"

The bullet had lodged in his arm, just below the elbow, and though the wound was bleeding profusely, he did not appear to be in any danger. After fishing in his pocket for his handkerchief, Alex folded it into a pad and told the young man to use it to stem the flow of blood.

He was beside himself with fury. He'd misjudged the scheming bitch. He'd been confident that, even if she were the assassin—and it didn't seem likely that a woman would be up to the job—she wasn't in a position to get off a clear shot at the queen. It had never occurred to him that he would be her target. And he had no doubt that it was he and not the man whom she'd accidentally shot. With him out of the way, she'd have a clear shot at her real target. That bullet had missed him by a hair. It was a miracle he was still breathing.

A moment or two later, breathless from his exertions, Gavin returned. In his hand, he held a blond wig. "I found this on the terrace," he said. "It's possible that she's one of the guests the footmen are rounding up for questioning, or she may be panicked and making for the river."

"She won't be." She was too cool and too clever not to have a well thought out escape route in place. He got up, helped the wounded man to rise and, taking the wig from Gavin, stuffed it into his pocket. "Get this gentleman—what is your name, by the way?"

"Ramsey." The young man grimaced in pain. "Ronald Ramsey."

"Get Mr. Ramsey medical attention, then meet me in the courtyard."

"Lean on my arm, Mr. Ramsey," said Gavin soothingly. "I don't believe we've met. I'm Gavin Hepburn, and the gentleman you just met—he of few words, and all of them orders—is my brother, Alex. We are the Hepburns of Feughside. Are you visiting in the area? I ask because I don't recognize your face."

As Gavin led Ramsey away, Alex strode for the exit. He admired his brother's tactics. Gavin might appear to be engaged in a casual conversation, but he was, in effect, getting the man's statement. There would be many statements taken tonight, and many frayed tempers before these exalted guests could get to their beds.

On the terrace, he cleared his mind and took a moment to study the lie of the land. In the Highlands, the sun set early. Off to his left, he could see the sun's rosy rim as it disappeared behind the peaks of the Cairngorms. In front of him was the path to the river. A forest of trees obscured the view as did the forest of guests who were now being herded back into the castle.

He closed his eyes and shut off the active part of his brain.

All his senses were humming, but the one sense that might be of use to him, his sixth sense, had obviously dozed off.

His sixth sense. It wasn't a joke. It was a legacy from his granny, the celebrated Witch of Drumore, as the superstitious country folk called her. Much good it had done him. He couldn't read minds or hear voices. The best he could say about it was that it sometimes pointed him in the right direction. But when he needed it most, such as now, it would desert him like a fickle woman.

Where was the wench? How did she know that he was the one to take down before trying for the queen? He was supposed to be a secret service agent, for God's sake. He was supposed to blend in with the crowd. But more important than any of that was, where was the woman now?

He dug in his coat pocket, produced the blond wig, and crushed it between his fingers. He felt it again, a ripple of recognition, like a tiny electric current, passing through his brain. He rubbed it against his cheek, and the current became stronger, more compelling.

His dark brows snapped together as he tried to recall every small detail of the woman who had bested him at his own game.

Average height. Delicately sculpted features. A slender figure set off by a gown that wasn't showy but was suitable for the occasion, a gray blue silk, as he remembered. Her eyes were blue . . . no, not blue, but gray, as gray and clear as the waters of the River Dee on a fine day. She baffled him and intrigued him. Why had he singled her out? Was it his training as an agent? Was it his sixth sense? Or was it something else? And why hadn't he acted on his first impression, that this woman was going to be trouble?

He put the wig to his face and inhaled.

A picture formed in his mind. He saw a young man, a boy really, in tartan trews and bonnet, kneeling beside a spring of crystal-clear water. The boy scooped some water into his cupped hands and drank greedily. Behind him rose the peaks of the Cairngorms.

That was better. His sixth sense was working just as it should. He couldn't read minds or get premonitions from his dreams as others with his gift were able to do. His gift was most potent when he touched objects that belonged to his quarry. And that was what the blond woman was now: his quarry. The boy in his vision was surely her accomplice.

"So there you are." Gavin's voice came to him as though from a great distance. "Didn't you hear me calling you?"

The picture in Alex's mind instantly dissolved. He thrust the wig into his pocket. "I was lost in thought. Did you find anything out from Mr. Ramsey?"

"Damn little. He says that he didn't see anything. He's quite shaken up. Well, he would be, wouldn't he? All he wants is to go home and forget the whole thing."

"He must have seen the woman with the gun."

"He insists that he didn't see anything. One moment he was looking at the queen, and the next, a bullet slammed into his arm." Gavin propped one elbow on the parapet and peered up at Alex. "Are you sure it was a woman?" When Alex turned his head and gave his brother a straight look, Gavin shrugged. "Sorry I asked. Of course, you're sure. It's just that it seems criminal to me to involve a woman in this kind of dirty work."

"Gavin," Alex's voice was pleasantly modulated, "they *are* criminals, traitors, in fact, and the woman must be one of their prime operators. She is bold, brave, and resourceful. I'll tell you something else. She meant to kill me, not Mr. Ramsey. With me out of the way, she'd have had a clear shot at the queen."

Gavin stood stock-still. Finally, he said irritably, "What's going on, Alex? You've told me very little. I'm picking things up in dribs and drabs."

"I've told you as much as you need to know and only because you're my brother and I trust you implicitly."

"You're not acting as though you trust me."

Their eyes met, one seer of Grampian to another. Gavin's gift was to put ideas into his subjects' minds. Alex knew that if he wasn't careful, he would be blabbing like a baby, telling Gavin all his secrets.

Smiling a little, Alex replied, "I'm up to all your tricks, brother, so don't even think of meddling with my mind. I trust you more than I trust anyone. Let that suffice."

"Don't you trust your colleagues?"

"Up to a point." He was becoming irritable, and when Gavin opened his mouth to say more, Alex cut him off. "Look, I shouldn't be telling you anything. You're not in the game. All I'll say is that someone took a potshot at me tonight, and I mean to find her."

These somber words were followed by a long, reflective silence. At length, Gavin said, "I don't suppose that erratic muse of yours can show us which way she went?"

"That depends." Alex looked toward the peaks. "Tell me, Gavin, where are we most likely to find a spring of ice-cold water?"

"In the mountains." Gavin took one look at Alex's expression and said slowly, "Where did that idea come from? Your muse?"

"Where else would I get a damn fool idea like that? We'd best get a move on."

"Are you joking? It will soon be as black as pitch out there, and it gets damn cold in these mountains. Why can't we wait till morning?"

"And give her a head start? Not on your life."

A slow grin creased Gavin's face.

"What?" Alex demanded.

"In spite of your words, brother, I think I've just been invited into the game."

Alex grunted.

A little later, Gavin observed, "The castle is locked up like a prison. They're not likely to give us horses. We're supposed to be guests, remember? They'll want to question us."

"They'll give us horses," said Alex, "or Her Majesty will want to know the reason why." He held up his hand. "Watch me, little brother, and see how it's done."

"The last time you said that to me," replied Gavin moodily, "I broke my arm when I fell out of our tree house."

Alex's only response was a grin, but it soon faded. As they struck out toward the stable, he was thinking of the woman, remembering another time and place, when another pretty woman, a blond, no less, had led him and three of his agents into a deadly trap.

Chapter 2

Mahri ran like a hare, weaving in and out of the trees as though the hounds were snapping at her heels. Though she'd chosen the route that gave her the best chance of escaping detection, she did not count on it. There was always one agent sharper than the others, one who would put two and two together and realize that she'd outwitted them. While agents had followed the guests who swarmed onto the lawn, she had stayed close to the castle walls and disappeared round the corner and into the shadows.

It was the dark-haired man who worried her most. A flicker of recognition had crossed his face. She hoped he wasn't an agent. An agent with a good memory for faces was more trouble than she could handle right now.

The odd thing was, she had no memory of him, and he was the kind of man a woman would remember, not because he was tall, dark, and handsome, but because he seemed . . . remote . . . untouchable. A challenge, in fact. But not for her. She'd had enough challenges in the last little while to last her a lifetime.

If she didn't get a move on, her lifetime would be numbered in hours. She couldn't turn back the clock, nor did she want to. She had foiled the plot to assassinate the queen. Now she'd have two sets of killers after her: Her Majesty's Secret Service and the members of her own cell.

Up, up she went until she reached the dry stone dike that marked the boundary of the old estate. Here she paused to drag air into her lungs and look back the way she had come. It was darker in the valley than it was on the slopes, and lights were winking in and out of the trees that surrounded the castle. She assumed that groundsmen were beating the bushes to flush her out. If her ruse worked, they would find the blond wig and think she was making for the river. If . . . if . . . if . . .

She lifted her head as she listened for sounds of pursuit. There was nothing, only the sound of the wind playing a restless game with the leaves of nearby trees.

Her revolver was still clutched in her hand. She set it on top of the dike and pulled on one of the stones until it fell with a soft thud to the ground. In the gap left by the stone, she found a satchel that she'd hidden there the night before. It took her only a few minutes to strip out of her own things and dress in the boy's clothes she'd packed in the satchel. Having replaced the satchel and stone, she took a step back and examined her handiwork. Perfect.

"I'll be back for you," she promised her satchel. She was

almost tempted to take the dress with her, but caution prevailed. If she were captured, it would give her away.

She picked up her pistol and was off and running again.

There were great cairns of stones dotted around the estate, monuments to the queen's joys and sorrows during her long reign. One of those cairns was close to the tree line. She hauled herself up to the top of the incline and slumped against the hard granite face. Her arms and legs ached, and her lungs burned. She could hear her breath whistling painfully between her parted lips. At one time, she'd been a courier and was used to pushing herself to the limit, but those days were over. She could no longer race up and down hills like a fleet-footed athlete. Nor could she sustain the role of a boy except in exceptional circumstances and only when the light was dim. Nature had done its work, softening her hard edges, adding curves. But when her life was in the balance, it was amazing how she slipped into her old skin.

Having ascertained that she was in the clear, she put two fingers to her mouth and emitted a shrill whistle. A moment later, a rider emerged from the trees leading a pony. Dugald was a deerstalker in the hunting season and a man of all trades in the summer. He was also her staunchest ally, and she had sore need of an ally after tonight's work. He'd known her since she was a babe in swaddling clothes, when he was gamekeeper on her grandfather's estate near Gairnshiel on the other side of the river. Their relationship was not that of master and mistress. Dugald was not only her mentor but also her closest friend.

"Did ye stop the bastard?" he asked. His voice was as gravelly as the rest of him. Craggy features and grizzled hair completed the picture.

"I didna kill him if that's what ye mean." Though Mahri spoke the cultured English of the educated Scot, she was just as comfortable in broad Scots or Gaelic. "I'm no' a murderer."

Dugald held the reins till she mounted up. "Lassie," he said, "ye dinna have to tell me that. Did ye save the queen is a' I meant."

"Aye. She was well-guarded, but I wasna taking any chances. Ramsey is a fanatic. He doesn't care if he lives or dies. He thinks God is on his side." She gave a brilliant smile.

"I put a hole in his arm. It will be a long time before he uses that murderous hand to hold a gun."

"Possibly." Dugald's tone was dry. "But I'm thinking it would have been better if ye had shot the knave dead."

She made a face. "Dugald, you know I couldna. I just don't have the instinct to kill."

Dugald nodded. "Well, ye can't change yer nature, but if ye went to the authorities and told them all that ye know—"

"No!" She'd had that debate with herself for a long time now, and there was no easy solution. Fearing that she'd hurt Dugald's feelings, she said gently, "I can't betray my comrades. This was the best I could do."

"But if it's you or them?"

"I don't know. I just don't know."

"Whisht! What was that?"

Mahri's hands tightened on the reins, and her head came up as she listened.

Dugald held up two fingers.

She nodded. There were two riders coming their way. Dugald made another signal. He wanted them to split up. She felt a shiver of alarm, not for herself but for Dugald. He didn't know what he was getting into. He wouldn't know friend from foe. She knew what he hoped to do. He was going to draw off their pursuers and give her a chance to get away.

Perhaps it was for the best, because if they found Dugald with her, they might well shoot him on sight. As for herself, she did not expect either side to treat her with kid gloves. They'd want to know how much she knew, and when she refused to tell them, they would turn nasty.

Dugald was gesturing to her to get going. She dug in her heels, and her pony tensed every muscle, then sprang forward.

⤬

She kept to the plan. There was a room under the name of Thomas Gordon waiting for her at the Inver Arms in Braemar. She'd arrived a few days before and told the proprietor that she had come from Aberdeen for a little visit in hopes that the mountain air would help her breathe more easily. It was a credible tale, for it was common knowledge, at least among Highlanders, that the air in the mountains was superior to all others.

The plan had gone awry, but it wasn't lost altogether. She had shaken off the rider who was following her. Dugald, she hoped, would do the same, and when he turned up, all would be well. He was going to guide her over the hills to Perth, and once she reached Perth, she would take the train south, and Miss Mahri Scot would sink into obscurity.

There was a train at Ballater going to Aberdeen, but Ballater was too close to the castle for comfort. That was how they would expect her to make her escape, on the train from Ballater. Dugald was her best bet.

Meantime, she had a part to play.

In the privacy of her small room under the eaves, she pulled her leather hand grip from beneath the bed. The first thing she did after she stripped was to bind her breasts with a linen towel, then she wriggled into a set of clean clothes. The sight of herself in tight tartan trews made her grimace. This would never do. She'd flattened her breasts, but her hips and posterior were too curvaceous to fool anyone. When she unbuttoned her deerskin jacket, she was better pleased with the result. At least her rounded bottom was less noticeable. Her dark hair was too long for a boy's, so she stuffed it under her tartan tam. The final touch was to slip her dirk into her right boot. She dithered about her gun but decided to leave it behind. It was too obvious, too hard to conceal in her boy's getup. At the reception, she'd kept it in her reticule until the last moment.

After taking a step back, she made an elegant bow to the reflection in the mirror. "Thomas Gordon," she said, "at your service."

As she continued to stare at her reflection, her expression turned wistful. She was looking at the Cairngorm brooch pinned to her tam. It brought back memories of happier days when they had all been together, her mother and father and brother, Bruce. Now those happy days had turned into a nightmare.

She turned from her reflection, muttering a Gaelic curse. More irritation. She must remember that she was passing herself off as a lowlander, and lowlanders had allowed the ancient tongue to die out centuries before. Only Highlanders kept to the old ways.

That last thought was reinforced when she entered the tap-room. Oil lamps gave out the only light. It would be a long time before electricity came to the Highlands. No electricity, no telephones, and damn few trains—so much the better for Thomas Gordon.

She found a place for herself at a table in the darkest corner, ordered a wee dram of whiskey, and took a moment to study the other patrons. They were a far cry from the guests at the queen's reception. They were all males, of course, except for the two women who waited on tables. She made a thorough inventory: estate workers, local businessmen, and perhaps the odd doctor or solicitor. In spite of it being an older crowd, they were a lively lot. But the one thing that impressed her was that word of the attack at Balmoral had not yet reached them.

The woman who waited on her was Mrs. Cluny, the proprietor's wife. "Been out walking the hills, Tam?" she asked conversationally.

"Riding," replied Mahri. "I don't know when I was last on a horse." That was a lie. Her father kept a fine stable at his house in Edinburgh.

Mrs. Cluny clicked her tongue. "I dinna know how folks can abide living in towns. Now get that down ye, shepherd's pie, made to my ain secret recipe. Ye could do with a little more padding on ye, laddie."

There was no menu at these isolated inns and no restaurants to be had. Visitors accepted what was offered at the place where they were staying, or they went hungry. Mahri tucked into the shepherd's pie, savoring each bite. She thought that Mr. and Mrs. Cluny were the most fortunate of people. The whole family was involved in some aspect of running the inn. They were not rich, but they had what money could not buy. They were a close-knit family; they were warmhearted and content with their lot. She envied them.

She toyed with the glass of whiskey and occasionally put it to her lips. She'd asked for it because she thought it made her look more manly. It also made her hoarse so that she frequently had to clear her throat, which was all to the good for someone who was supposed to be prone to lung infections.

She kept her eye on the door while she ate her dinner. People came and went, but there was no sign of Dugald. Her anxiety increased tenfold, however, when a gentleman, a cut above the other patrons, pushed into the taproom and paused just inside the door.

The light wasn't bright enough to see his face clearly, and he had yet to move away from the door. He had that quiet air of assurance that marked him as someone who was used to taking charge. She hoped he was a butler from one of the grand houses in the area, but she couldn't quite see him in that role. Too grand for an ordinary policeman. Ramsey's partner? Someone to take over if the plot misfired? She'd never met a member of Her Majesty's Secret Service, but she thought that he might fit that bill, too.

When he stepped up to the bar counter, she had a clear view of his face. She didn't suck in a breath; she simply stopped breathing altogether. This was the man who, she thought, had recognized her when they waited at Balmoral for the queen to make her entrance. Tall, dark, and handsome and infinitely dangerous, the man who had a good memory for faces.

She had no doubts now. It made no difference whether he was Ramsey's partner or a secret service agent. He was no friend to her.

It was time to get out of there.

She took a healthy swig of whiskey with the desired result. She started to cough, not harshly but controlled so as not to draw undue attention to herself. The fit of coughing gave her an excuse to produce her white linen handkerchief and cover the lower half of her face. Perfect camouflage, she hoped.

The stranger had ordered a tankard of ale or beer. As he turned to survey the inn's customers, she averted her eyes. She felt exposed, sitting by herself with nothing to do. She'd eaten her dinner, she'd finished her whiskey, but she couldn't smoke, not only because she didn't know how, but because it would arouse suspicion. A lad with weak lungs would be loath to put a foul-smelling pipe in his mouth. Whiskey was different. Every Scot knew that *uisque beatha* was medicinal.

She chanced a quick look at the stranger. He was propped against the bar counter, looking very much at ease as he surveyed the taproom and its patrons. She understood only too well what he was doing. He was making a mental note of all the exits and summing up each person as she had done when she'd entered the taproom. Agents were trained to notice anything that was out of place.

He was coming her way!

She'd been in worse fixes, she reminded herself. She'd crossed swords with the best of them. She had to forget that she was Mahri Scot and think herself into the part of Thomas Gordon.

He stopped at her table and smiled down at her. It softened his features but did not warm his eyes. "I'm Hepburn," he said, "Alex Hepburn. May I join you?" He was already seating himself before she opened her mouth.

"Thomas Gordon," she replied and stifled a yawn. "I was just leaving."

She made to rise, but Hepburn pushed on the table with both hands, pinning her in place. "Make it easy on yourself, Thomas," he said. "I don't want you. I want your mistress. Take me to her, and I'll let you go."

Mahri's mind was frozen. "My mistress?"

Hepburn slapped a blond wig on the table between them. "She left her calling card at the queen's reception earlier this evening. I don't think you're involved in that, but you're her guide, aren't you? Tonight, you led her over the hills to wherever she wanted to go. Take me to her hideout, and I'll let you go."

Mahri's mind was now buzzing. "It wasna me. I'm here for my health." She rubbed her chest. "Ask the Clunies."

"Yes, so they told me, but today you went out riding after breakfast and did not return until late. You like to ride in the hills, don't you?" His smile would have done credit to a shark. "You're small fry, Thomas. It's the woman I want."

The thought of sharks and small fry made her shudder. "I go riding in the hills," she said, "because it's good for my lungs." When he raised a skeptical brow, she added, "There were other lads there. What makes you think I'm the lad you want?"

Hepburn took a swig of beer, made a smacking sound with his lips, then smiled slowly to himself. "If I told you," he said, studying his tankard, "you wouldn't believe me." He looked up. "What is it to be, then? Do I hand you over to the authorities, or do you take me to the woman?"

Only an agent would hand her over to the authorities. Ramsey and his cohorts would want a secure cellar or dungeon where they could terrorize her in private. However, they were hardly likely to tell her that.

She was still no better off. "If I take you to the woman," she said, "do you promise not to hurt her?"

"Ah. Now we're getting somewhere. Give me her name."

She watched him warily as he pocketed the blond wig she had worn earlier. "Martha McGregor," she said, giving him one of her own aliases. "She seemed like a nice lady."

Something moved in his eyes, something hard and unforgiving.

Without thinking, Mahri edged closer to him. "Why do you hate her? What has she done?"

He scraped back his chair and got up. "First things first. When I have the woman, we'll sit down and have a long chat, you and I. There's a lot you haven't told me, but that can wait."

She thought a show of defiance might be in order, just enough to convince him that she really was small fry. "We're not going out right now, in the dark?"

"Move," he ordered. "I know she can't be far from here. You've only been back an hour or so. And don't try any foolish tricks. It will be the worse for you if you do."

Mahri believed him. The trouble was, it would be even worse for her if she didn't try to trick him. The thought stayed with her as she shuffled out of the taproom.

Also Available From *USA Today*
Bestselling Author

Jacquie D'Alessandro

Seduced at Midnight

*The Ladies Literary Society of London gathers
again for a ghost story…*

Lady Julianne Bradley has always longed to indulge in a wild adventure. Unfortunately, the man with whom she wishes to share her fervor can never be hers. Tormented by her desire, she's preparing for a suitable marriage when she witnesses ghostly occurrences straight out of her latest read. To protect Julianne, her father hires the very man her heart cries out for